The SECRET LIFE OF
LASZLO,
COUNT
DRACULA

The SECRET LIFE of
LASZLO, COUNT DRACULA

Roderick Anscombe

BLOOMSBURY

First published in Great Britain 1994

This paperback edition published 1995

Copyright © 1994 by Roderick Anscombe

The moral right of the author has been asserted

Bloomsbury Publishing Plc, 2 Soho Square, London W1V 6HB

A CIP catalogue record for this book is available from the
British Library

ISBN 0 7475 2198 0

10 9 8 7 6 5 4 3 2

Typeset by Hewer Text Composition Services, Edinburgh.
Printed in England by Cox and Wyman Ltd, Reading, Berkshire.

MAY 18, 1866

There should be a preface, I know. Some setting of the stage or manifesto of purpose. But I can't wait. Paris is everything I had hoped for – more grand and inspiring than even my childish dreams – and one day this week I shall describe my impressions. But now I must put down on paper the extraordinary scene I have just witnessed.

As instructed in the letter accepting my application, I reported to the Salpêtrière Hospital yesterday and spent the whole day waiting for the registrar to assign me cases. None came my way. Indeed, Dr Ducasse seemed unaware of my existence, and gruffly told me to wait when I approached him. Friday, of course, is the Master's day, and this morning I went early to the amphitheater to catch my first glimpse of Professor Charcot. Few of the other physicians had yet arrived for his demonstration, and I was able to secure an excellent place in the second row.

Behind and above me, people soon took their places in the banked rows of seats, and a buzz of conversation filled the lecture chamber. I turned and looked about – not that I expected to see anyone I recognized in this elegant throng. Nevertheless, I scanned the crowd for a friendly face with whom I might strike up a conversation, because, to tell the truth, I have been a little lonely since I arrived in this city, especially since I have received no response from Aunt Sophie. The man beside me was engrossed in a monograph on hysteria, and I hesitated to disturb him. About me, men posed in foppish attitudes and drawled in the most affected way, or called to each other from one corner of the room to the other, but in spite of their gregariousness, I thought their gestures seemed calculated for effect, as if each wanted to be noticed by the rest. I missed the simple boisterousness with which we students awaited lectures in Budapest. In Paris, I suppose such lack of reserve would be considered hopelessly provincial.

I must have appeared gauche as I peered about, at the huge domed ceiling, through the window at the formal gardens outside, at the lectern on the raised platform before us and the stretcher draped by a sheet to one side. The fellow beside me glanced up from his book and jerked his head at the crowd behind us.

'Damn circus,' he said dismissively.

Having come so far for this occasion, I was a little put out by his irreverent attitude. 'It's the anticipation, I expect,' I said. 'Everyone's hoping to hear the very latest from Charcot.'

'Half of these people aren't even doctors,' he replied.

I looked around again. While there were several interns in the long white apron reaching from waist to ankle, at the back were people wearing artists' caps, and others were attired in fashionably cut morning coats and wore their top hats at a jaunty angle.

'Poets, journalists, philosophy professors, men about town – *tout Paris*,' he said.

'All students of the mind, surely?' I put in.

'Members of the leisured classes,' he snorted. 'They'd faint clean away if they saw blood.'

Our attention was drawn to a woman who had come into the room through the door behind the lectern. Her entrance had the same effect as that of the conductor of an orchestra on a theater audience: The level of noise lessened, but the crowd did not fall silent. Rather, the conversations took on a more intense, sibilant quality, as an air of expectancy filled the room. For my part, I felt my chest constrict in eager anticipation of the moment when the man who knew more of the hidden realm of the soul than anyone else on earth would lay before me the secrets of the abyss which lies within the human mind.

The woman strode purposefully and took her position behind the chair which stood on one side of the platform. She was about fifty years old and her iron-gray hair was pulled back and tied in a tight bun. Even allowing for the plainness of the nurse's uniform there was something stern and austere in her appearance and in her cool indifference to the hundred faces that watched her every move. A silver chain hung low from her belt and a varied bunch of keys, some of which appeared quite ancient, swayed as she walked and signified her importance within the institution.

'Madame Verdun. Charcot has her tend the subject,' my companion told me in a low voice. 'She's immune,' he added, and I fancied I detected a shade of respect even in his jaded commentary.

'Is the case one of infection?' I asked.

He looked at me strangely, as if to wonder how anyone could be so green. 'Hysterical contagion,' he pronounced impatiently. 'The nurse stands directly behind the chair. She must be subjected to the same influence which Charcot directs upon the patient. Madame Verdun resists all trances.'

The professor's assistants filed in and took their places in the empty row in front of me, Ducasse among them. They were serious, intent men who carried themselves like deacons in a church. We waited.

Then Charcot entered. He paused with a hand resting on the door behind him and stilled the vast auditorium with one brief, imperious glance. It was as if a giant puppet master had pulled a hundred strings and taken up all the slackness in the room.

He is a small man and somewhat stout, and so they call him the 'Napoleon of the Neuroses.' He is dressed entirely in black with a velvet frock coat. His hands and face are unnaturally pale. He is not given to gesture and holds his hands at chest height; they are restless all the while as he talks, as if he is selecting from a stream of words which run through his fingers like small fish. He is close to forty and his hair, which is long and swept back from his large forehead, is already flecked with gray. So far, the professor may not seem a remarkable personage, but that is because I have not described his eyes. They are utterly penetrating. They are set deep, and are rimmed darkly as if he does not sleep, so they glare out like fire burning far within a cave.

Charcot scanned the audience, and I fancied that his gaze rested on me for a split second, an unfamiliar face at the front of the crowd. During that moment of scrutiny, I felt caught beneath a lens, helpless to retain my innermost secrets if he should have demanded them of me. His eyes moved on and took in the audience in general before he turned his back and strode to the lectern.

He wished to show us, he announced, something new: a division in consciousness. After some introductory remarks, he nodded almost imperceptibly to Madame Verdun and she strode to the door and beckoned to assistants in the gloom who were not visible to us. A pale wraith approached the doorway, and Madame took the figure by the arm and led her to the chair that awaited her.

Charcot inclined his head to this person. 'We are indebted to you, Mademoiselle Stacia,' he said.

In the light, Stacia was a fetching young woman with fair hair. She was dressed simply, without adornments, in a skirt and blouse held about her shoulders by a drawstring. She looked over the gentlemen of the audience with some alarm. When Charcot addressed her, she turned to him as if distracted. She seemed to be making an effort to compose herself, and I had the impression of someone who must balance herself on a point of courage. She turned to Charcot.

'I am ready, Professor,' she told him.

'Very well,' he said with the same air of gravity.

For a long moment they considered each other as if the

4

rest of us did not exist. Charcot made some passes with his hands, all the while holding her in his gaze. He spoke to her gently, so softly that I could not make out the words. It was a soothing sound, like a mother lulling a child, except that it had the appearance of a spell cast on her, for all at once Stacia appeared to lose consciousness. That is, her eyes remained open and fixed on the Master's face as before, but the volitional force had gone from her body, and she seemed entirely bent to him, her inner thoughts even, within his power.

I heard him murmur, 'Sleep,' and her eyelids slid down infinitely slowly, with a terminal flutter, like the death throes of a small animal, and her body quivered at the moment of their closing. Madame Verdun stood watchful and unmoved behind the chair.

Charcot turned to us as if he had never interrupted his lecture. 'I wish to demonstrate a phenomenon which I believe is unfamiliar to you. To my knowledge it has not been described before in the scientific literature. The phenomenon shares features with the suggestibility of hysteria, with traumatic amnesia, and with psychogenic paralysis, and yet it surpasses all these to an extraordinary degree.'

The men around me leaned forward with even greater attentiveness. Stacia slept beautifully. There was an expression of infinite calm upon her features, her brow clear and untroubled.

'To be conscious is to know what one knows,' Charcot declared. 'To be unconscious is to know nothing. To register nothing. To remember nothing. Our understanding recoils from the possibility of some middle ground, between consciousness and unconsciousness, which is not mere confusion or delirium.' He turned to glance at Stacia and appeared to lose himself in thought. 'And yet . . . Well, we will see.' He collected himself from his reverie. 'And see you must,' he declared. 'I believe that mere description would be insufficient to compel belief. Only a demonstration could be plausible.'

5

He stood to one side so that we could see every move. 'Stacia,' he called gently.

'Sir,' came her soft reply. She seemed to breathe the word, and yet in the chamber's hush no one missed the sound.

'In a moment I will give you a simple instruction.' With her eyes still closed she turned her head as if, alone in a darkened room, she was seeking the source of speech which came from another world. 'When I rouse you from your state of waking sleep, you will regain possession of yourself, but' – his voice deepened and resonated with emphasis – 'you will remember nothing of what has occurred while you have slept.'

'I understand.'

'Open, then.'

Stacia's eyes, blue as cornflowers, stared unwaveringly ahead as she waited in perfect patience for her instruction. She had a remarkable pale beauty, and I suppose that I was not alone in experiencing the enchantment wrought by the trusting stillness of her features; the abandon of her flaxen hair, unbraided and free to follow its lustrous affinity for the sunlight from the window; the vulnerability of her bared shoulders.

'To your right you will see the lectern.' Her head turned like that of a mechanical toy. 'And on it is a carafe of water and a glass. When you receive the signal you will get up, pour yourself a glass of water from the carafe, and drink it down. Immediately, mind. No matter what the circumstances.'

Charcot paused and his eyes passed over the faces ranged before him and came to rest on mine!

'Your name?' he asked me.

I told him and heard the familiar syllables fill the amphitheater as if they were a strange sound made by another person.

'At some opportune time during this lecture, you will raise your hand to ask a question.'

I nodded my agreement, hardly trusting my voice.

'Dracula,' he said reflectively and drew out the sound of each vowel so that it sounded like a short sentence in another language. I watched his face for any expression which would indicate a familiarity with my father's memory, but I suppose a Hungarian patriot, however celebrated in his own country, would be considered obscure within the greatness of Paris, and I fancy that it was nothing more that the musical quality of our family name which amused him.

'Very well,' he said, and I felt myself immediately lost to his attention and consigned again to insignificance. 'When the doctor raises his hand, that is your sign, Mademoiselle Stacia. You will go to the lectern to carry out my instruction. And you will do this without recognizing what has induced you to do it.'

He turned to the audience once again as if to goad us to disbelief. There was something of the music hall conjurer in this small stout man in the black velvet frock coat.

'Close your eyes,' he told Stacia. 'When I count to three, you will awake. You will feel calm, refreshed, and you will have no memory for the events which have just occurred. One. Two. And three!'

He snapped his fingers, and life seemed to reinvest the young woman. Breath filled her body and she stretched as if awakening on a Sunday morning in the country. She looked about her, bewildered at first, and then her shyness before the assembled doctors returned. She turned inquiringly to Madame Verdun, but found no support or confirmation there.

Charcot had returned to his place behind the lectern and was sorting through his notes, but all eyes were on Stacia. I am not sure what we expected of her. She seemed herself unaware of what her purpose was to be, and sat with her hands in her lap and her eyes lowered demurely.

The professor summoned our attention once again by resuming the lecture on the topics he had introduced before the demonstration. I waited for my moment. I was aware that people glanced at me from time to time, but needless

7

to say, I received no hint of what I was to do from Charcot himself. After choosing me on a whim, he appeared utterly unaware of my existence. It was my impression that he had no intention of being interrupted in the full flow of his lecture, and so I waited, in some turmoil.

At last, he concluded his lecture and announced, 'I will now take questions.'

I was in the midst of catching up in my notebook with the final words of his summary, but I looked up at that moment. An expectant hush filled the room, but I did nothing. Still Charcot did not look at me. In the front row, Babinski, the professor's first assistant, cleared his throat.

'Would you elaborate, Professor, on the differences between normal forgetting and the unavailability of knowledge gained during the somnambulistic state?'

'Indeed,' said Charcot.

Once again I was writing furiously, trying not to lose one precious word of his answer, when I became aware that the Master had stopped speaking. But this time I did not interrupt what I was about. I continued scribbling, and the tiny sounds of the steel nib against paper resounded in the auditorium like squeaking shoes in a cathedral. In that palpable silence, I felt one hundred and one pairs of eyes assiduously avoiding me, one hundred and one wills urging me to my task. Instead, I wrote another word while I savored the teetering, gleeful, itching excitement in the pit of my stomach. With a flourish, I finished my task and to the accompaniment of several people shifting in relief, raised my hand.

'You propose that the subject does not know that she knows,' I began. Charcot nodded for me to continue my question, even though he must have been aware that behind him Stacia had risen from her chair. She looked about her uncertainly.

'That is correct,' Charcot nodded encouragingly. He had removed himself from the lectern and stood in front me.

8

No one listened to my question or to Charcot's reply. Stacia had caught sight of the carafe of water on the lectern. She took one hesitant step toward it and glanced at Charcot. But he was engaged in an uncharacteristically circuitous response to the question I had asked and seemed oblivious to her. Stacia turned to Madame Verdun to seek permission. But Madame Verdun was preoccupied with a small blemish on the back of her hand that she was attempting to remove with a thumbnail. Stacia bit her lower lip in indecision. All her social instincts forbade her to touch what was reserved for a man far above her station. For some of my colleagues, desperately suppressing grins, the scene had an aspect of a practical joke. But for myself, the girl's distress was so real, her scruples so evident, that the scene was touched with pathos.

Her mind made up at last, Stacia walked toward the lectern. Charcot caught sight of her and appeared taken aback.

'Mademoiselle?' he inquired sharply.

She turned, almost at her goal, her hand reaching to take the glass from the top of the carafe, and my heart went out to her when I saw the stricken look upon her face.

'Be so good as to return to your seat until the lecture is finished.' This was the professor at his most imperious. I could not have withstood him.

Stacia was torn, but she held her ground. 'Excuse me, sir, but I am very thirsty,' she said.

Charcot looked to Madame Verdun for an explanation; she made a polite gesture of incomprehension. 'In a few minutes you will return to the ward and there you can drink all the water you desire,' Charcot told Stacia.

Stacia made a slight bow of gratitude, but she seemed troubled and vaguely dissatisfied as she made her way back to her chair. Charcot resumed his discussion, but Stacia fidgeted and looked this way and that. Abruptly, she got up and walked purposefully to the lectern. The conflict was resolved, the scruples quelled. She was forceful as she grasped the carafe and paid no heed to the gurgle and splash of the water she poured. She filled the glass to the brim. Defiantly she drained it, and with the act completed seemed abruptly to be without volition.

Charcot intercepted her as she passed back to her seat. 'And was it good, Mademoiselle?' he asked.

There was a humorous glint in his eye. Like the arrival of rain relieving the tension of a thunderstorm, laughter and then applause filled the room. They were clapping for the Master, for his *coup de théâtre*, his *coup de science*, for the way in which he had brought the conviction of the theater to bear on that most elusive object of science, the human mind. But my applause was for Stacia.

There was a new informality in the room. That, at least, was the impression the Master permitted us to assume, as he lounged with one elbow on the lectern and held the glass musingly in his fingertips, a small, rotund Hamlet with Yorick's skull.

'We are scientists, Stacia. You must humor us,' he said, inviting her to join him at the lectern. She smiled sweetly. 'Just as other scientists would study the structure of a flower, we would know the composition of a thought.'

'I'll answer your questions as best I can, I'm sure.'

I wondered at the disappearance of the forceful woman who had drunk the water. This docile girl with the fatherly arm of the professor about her shoulders could have been another person.

'I believe you can help us understand something we are curious about.' His tone was casual, as if he needed only to clear up a loose detail to be done for the day and go home to eat lunch with his wife and family. 'We are curious – only curious, mind – to know what made you get up and drink from the carafe over there.'

She seemed at a loss. 'It was just a feeling came over me, sir, and I saw the water.'

'Did anyone here tell you to do it?'

It was obvious she was struggling to be helpful; she wanted to give him what he wanted, but she couldn't see what that was.

'Take a good look, Stacia. Take a good look at these doctors and tell me if any of them told you to do it.'

She was bashful at first, but then she looked with greater confidence and even with curiosity surveyed the whole gathering. I sat immediately in front of her. As her eyes came to me, passed over me, and on to the fellow who sat at my side, I felt again that pricking, teeming excitement which had suffused me when I had delayed asking my question. Now I remember why it was familiar. One winter afternoon, just before the light failed, I had been hunting on our estate. I was waiting in a thicket when a doe came into the clearing. She sniffed the air and looked about, but she could not smell me. And yet she would not graze. She sensed danger close by. I watched as she scanned across the spot where I crouched. And now Stacia's eyes passed over me unseeing.

MAY 21, 1866

Today Ducasse, who until Charcot's lecture has had no time for me, made a point of seeking me out.

'We must find some cases for you to work up,' he told me.

Finally, I am to be permitted to be part of things at the Salpêtrière. The hospital is unlike any other I have seen. It is more like a small town than a hospital, with roads that cross its grounds, one of the oldest churches in Paris, a laundry, a hall in which dances are held for the patients on Saturday evenings, and extensive gardens. The whole is surrounded by a wall, so that the community is self-contained. For centuries it has been the poorhouse for elderly women, beggars, prostitutes, and the insane. It is not clear whether Charcot was sent to serve in the Salpêtrière as a punishment, or whether he himself chose the assignment as an opportunity, but he has drawn in physicians from throughout Europe who come to learn his techniques.

I am glad to be assigned to the Central Building, because that is where Charcot has a special ward for selected patients, like Stacia, who demonstrate extraordinary symptoms and are capable of unusual feats of somnambulism, which is now the main focus of the Master's researches. The special ward is on the first floor, but I am to work on the second, sifting through the symptoms of the old women who have never been thoroughly examined. Even though I have been here only a few days, it is clear to me that the women of the special ward compose a caste apart. Most of them are young, and so it would not be unusual to find some among them who are attractive in a forward, gaudy kind of way. The somnambulistic ladies are pampered beings and know it. They are allowed to wear their own clothes and can move about the grounds of the hospital as they wish. They have no need to provide for the basic necessities of life and Charcot gives them all sorts of special privileges. I see them as I come and go, since they hang about the staircase and appraise those who pass through their throng. I think time is heavy on their hands, and they fill it, judging from the whispers and snatches of conversation I have heard, with gossip and spiteful feuds.

It is late, but at least I can retire to bed with a permanent roof over my head. My neighbor in the amphitheater, whom at first I had taken to be surly and indifferent, introduced himself after the lecture as Roland Vernier. He is indeed a jaded and cynical fellow. He moves slowly, almost reluctantly, and with his round face, full lips, and hooded eyes he appears congested and phlegmatic, but this would be a mistaken impression, since his mind is quick and agile, and at times he allows a twinkle in his eye to indicate that one is not to take everything he says too seriously.

I told Roland that I had come only that week from Budapest and was staying in a hotel near the Gare d'Austerlitz; he said he knew of a situation which might prove advantageous to me. My first concern has been to find less expensive accommodation. I walked from one district to another inquiring about lodgings and was amazed at the prices landlords ask for the dingiest set of rooms. Often they expect the prospective renter to share the only servant with the half dozen tenants who live in the building as well as making his own arrangements for the washing of his linen. In one place I was able to get no further than the concierge, who after suspicious looks and several insolent questions informed me that they did not rent to foreigners!

I must budget carefully, for my brother, George, has emphasized that no more money will be forthcoming from the family account to pay for my expenses here. In fact, he made it starkly clear that the funds he has given me for this period of study have been taken from moneys which would otherwise have been used to repair the roof of the east wing of the castle. Neither did my brother miss an opportunity to lecture me on my expectations, or lack of them. After wages and repairs, the estate does little more than break even, apparently, and that only by selling bit by bit the timber which is the birthright handed down by each count to his successor. As a consequence, I must make my own way in the world. I will do my best, even though I cannot help wondering whether the family finances would be so straitened were it not for the sums George loses at cards. There is nothing I can do about it, other than to improve his card playing, and that would be a futile labor, for George plays like the cavalryman he is, taking pride in his willingness to charge ahead in the face of horrible losses. George is the elder. He is the count, not I.

Roland, hearing of my situation, told me that rooms had become vacant in the building where he himself lives, in the Val de Grâce quarter, convenient to the hospital.

'Recently become available,' he repeated with a lingering look which hinted that I should ask him more.

'How so?' I obliged and saw him smile wickedly.

'Let's say the previous occupant vacated more than just his rooms.'

'I see,' I said, more or less truthfully.

'But it means you can hold the landlord to a good price.' Clearly it requires the most morbid matters to tickle the sense of humor of this moody and world-weary man.

And so I sit at midnight in the rooms of a suicide. The lodging is little more than a garret at the top of the house, but I have a view over rooftops, and in the evening I can see to the north the glow of the city's lights. A fine rain is falling and it has released a warm, moist fragrance from the roof tiles and the smell of earth from the spaces between the cobbles in the streets below. It is the scent of the great city, and yet it reminds me of the pungent smell of our pine forests at home.

2

MAY 23, 1866

This diary will be the place where I discover the unknown depths of my character. It will be the mirror I hold up to myself, a trick of thought by which I will catch hold of what I cannot see.

I look into the mirror now, the one I have propped on the desk before me. I see a man who looks slightly older than his twenty-three years, although that impression may be due to my wish to appear more experienced than I truly am. I am told I am handsome, though I fancy my looks appear foreign, exotic even, here in Paris. I wear my black hair long, so that I have a bohemian appearance. My mustache is neatly trimmed, yet I have allowed it a certain debonair sweep, a swagger even, which I like to think is roguish.

The most striking feature of the face that peers back at me is the eyes. There is an unmistakable hint in those eyes of my forefathers, the horsemen of the steppes. I can see a residue of those dark barbarians in my eyebrows: They are thick and black and slant upwards at the outer edges in a way which could be slightly devilish. How strange it is that this trace of Genghis's horsemen, the destroyers of civilization, should be displayed in the face of this man who is intent on becoming the epitome of culture!

It is fitting that I begin this diary, which was my mother's last birthday present to me, in the land of her birth. Her stories of Paris and the garrison towns where she grew up have made this a fantasy land for me, filled with elegant gentlemen and their gorgeous ladies who mix witty repartee with deep discourses on art and philosophy as they stroll along a springtime boulevard. I know this place existed nowhere but in the nostalgic imagination of a lonely widow turning to her two young boys for companionship in her exile in a drafty castle.

Paris is the city of light which I had hoped to spy – a seven-year-old with no sense of the world's immensity – from a wind-swept turret in Transylvania. It is the glimmering drawing room of worldly sophistication where, in the imagination of a brooding adolescent trapped in the forests of a distant province during endless school vacations, I made my triumphal entry into the world's spotlight. Paris is the embodiment of all the unformed, uninformed striving of the university student; it is the place for lectures and assignations, the occasion of revelations and denouements, an opportunity for the insight of understanding or the blindness of passion, a realm where the possibilities of knowledge, ideas, love, or sin might be grasped.

And Paris was and is the city of Nichole.

This afternoon, I put on my best coat and took a cab to my aunt's house off the Rue Faubourg Saint Honoré. My mother had told me she had married well, but I was not prepared for the huge edifice that I saw when the cab came to a halt. At first I thought the driver had stopped because of some problem with the horse, but he assured me that this was the correct house. With some misgivings, I dismissed him. The building is made of a pale stone with extensive decoration and allegorical statues on the facade in the Renaissance style. It is entirely magnificent and proclaims the wealth of its inhabitants without the slightest reserve. I felt quite apprehensive mounting the steps to the imposing doors.

A liveried footman, a man of about my own age, answered the door and showed no inclination to allow me admittance. There was a skeptical look on his face when I told him that I was a member of the family recently come to Paris.

'Madame is not at home,' he said.

Of course, I realized, she would be paying her calls, and Nichole would accompany her.

'Which is Madame Berthier's day?' I inquired.

He smiled faintly as if to suggest that if I was sufficiently familiar with the lady as to claim to be a member of the family, then I should already be aware of the day on which Madame received visitors.

'I will leave my card,' I said quickly, though on reflection I was not at all sure that I wanted Nichole to know the specific location of her cousin's humble lodgings.

The footman allowed me to enter the hallway. I was determined not to give him the satisfaction of seeing me act the country cousin by gawking about, although I could not help being taken with the glittering chandelier, a thousand facets of crystal, that was suspended above the well of the stairway which curved gracefully to the reception rooms above.

I took a card from my case and turned down one corner, as is the custom here to indicate that one has called in person and found the person not at home. I hesitated and then decided to write my address on the back of the card, since there was no other way for my aunt to contact me. The footman reluctantly motioned me to a table whose top was a slab of malachite quartered so that the veins of the stone made a symmetric pattern not unlike the rings of a tree. On this warm spring day, the surface imparted the chill of death to the palm of my hand.

I am disappointed that my aunt has taken no steps to reach out to me. I had written to them before I left Hungary. Could they not have left word with the servants, knowing that I would call sooner or later, to treat me with the respect due a member of the family?

I remember Aunt Sophie only from the visit she and Nichole made to us shortly before my mother's death, but my memories are overwhelmingly of Nichole. We were both thirteen years old, but in many ways she was more advanced than I. Nichole was a girl who was already part woman, whereas I was mostly boy – a wistful, dreamy boy whose emotions were far too intense for him to know what to do with them.

Nichole was pretty in a precise, symmetrical, wondrous way that I had never known before. Her eyes were long-lashed like a fawn's, and she had a mannerism of turning slightly to one side as if to give thought to some matter and blinking abstractedly, which I found hopelessly endearing. She was well aware of her effect on me. She teased me with herself, giving small tokens of affection and just as inexplicably subtracting, with a cool word or silence, from the sum of my happiness for that day. All this she did with no acknowledgment that any feeling lay between us other than the grudging camaraderie of cousins forced by circumstance to get along for a summer.

I have kept one memory of Nichole close to my heart. It is so precious that I rarely recall it in case I damage its delicate texture, fearing that bit by bit I will reinvent the incident to fill in gaps where the truth has worn away.

It was after lunch, and the adults had taken themselves off for naps or private activities in their own rooms. I was writing a poem to Nichole. Staring through the open French windows of the library into the garden, lost in contemplation with the end of the pen between my teeth, I should have become aware earlier of a stealthy approach. With a sinking feeling, I assumed the worst, that it was George who had crept up on me. Nothing so damning, so sissy, as a poem to love could ever be allowed to fall into his hands.

But it was Nichole who, with a peal of laughter, reached over my shoulder and snatched up the paper. I was slow to follow her through the windows into the garden, and as I came to the threshold I saw that she had paused on the lawn to see what it was that she had taken from me.

'My, but what airs Laszlo is putting on – poetry, no less!' her laughter said. And then the laughter was cut off – an instant of ecstasy which catches at me like a sob – because she had begun to read the words and knew that the poem was for her. Her forced, mocking laughter began again, but I had achieved my effect, and I emerged full tilt through the library windows in the pursuit she expected.

She stopped in the middle of the lawn to read another couplet. I was afraid she would read aloud and that George, attracted by the disturbance, would hear, and so I ran in earnest to retrieve the poem. I sprang and made a grab at the paper, but with surprising adroitness she sidestepped my charge and took off in the direction of the formal garden. This brought us a safe distance from the castle, and I felt that I could safely postpone the recapture of my work until she had absorbed every word. She had hidden behind the gazebo. I approached around one side of its circular wooden walls, and as I had expected, she ran from this shelter down a pathway. And as she ran, she pressed my poem with one hand to her heart.

I expended myself in energetic but ingeniously ineffective maneuvers along the paths which outlined the flower beds, and she gained yet another respite in which to read on, teasing me with one of my own turns of phrase across geraniums and miniature hedges of box which I could easily have jumped if I had wished to play a different game. Eventually, I felt I could feign breathlessness, and I walked toward her as she read the last lines aloud in a kind of nervous, titillated glee whose underlying emotion set a glow in my heart. She had read aloud the poem to the end, but now she returned to the beginning to read silently to herself, hungrily drinking in the adoring words.

'You have read it all,' I said tragically. 'You know everything of any importance about me. Now at least return my poem to me so that I shall have a keepsake.'

'Never,' she replied. There was a tone of mischief in her defiance. I would have preferred that the playfulness had given way to a more serious, heroic mood.

She ran away again, and I followed more slowly. But in allowing her time to chose the setting for our unknown finale, I had lost track of her. For several urgent minutes I searched overgrown paths where weeds and old cultivars had been allowed to grow to fantastic heights, and then I heard a slight cry to my right. She had attempted to enter the rose bower, which, after many years of neglect, resembled a green cave with thorny tendrils entirely enclosing the wooden frame. By design or accident, the loose fabric which formed the bodice and sleeves of her dress was caught. She held herself in an unnatural posture, yet perfectly still.

'Oh, oh. Please,' she said, and I realized that somewhere a thorn was piercing her skin.

The frond was entangled at her shoulder and curved around her arm. I came behind her and leaned to peer over her shoulder. Our heads came close, and I looked down at the outline of her budding breasts rising and falling, and I breathed in the musky, unperfumed scent of a young girl on a warm, summer afternoon.

'Do something!' she demanded.

I looked down to find the source of her pain. The rose branch was thick and woody, with fierce, dark thorns. But when I tried to move it away from her arm, I heard fabric tear.

'No, no!' she cried angrily and stamped her foot. She had dropped my poem, and it lay forgotten on the dank flagstones.

Carefully, I detached the thorns which held her dress at the shoulder. I had to angle the branch to free the last thorn. The wood was stiff, but it had become bowed by her attempts to disentangle herself, and when I released one end, it snapped straight suddenly. Nichole gasped. A large thorn was driven into the soft skin on the back of her arm above the elbow, and a dark, red pearl was forming about its shaft.

She looked at me with eyes made large with fear. 'Take it out. Please,' she said. She spoke as if I might not let her go.

I pulled the thorn from her arm and would have stopped

the blood, but she broke free and ran from me. When I emerged from the bower into the sunlight again, she was already halfway across the lawn and did not look back.

Shortly after, Aunt Sophie and Nichole left to return to France, Mother died, and I was sent away to school.

MAY 24, 1866

This morning Madame Thébauld, the concierge, knocked on my door. I have never known her to leave her post at the entranceway to the little courtyard of our building before, and certainly not on an errand concerning one of the tenants. We are a dissolute lot, her disapproving sniff gives each one of us to understand as we pass by her station, and her eternal vigilance is required to keep us from damnation.

'A messenger,' she announced.

I could see someone standing behind her, but in the dimness of the corridor could not make out who it was. Madame drew back and the footman from my aunt's house squeezed by and came into my sitting room. He carried an envelope in his hand, but his mission did not prevent him from looking about himself in an appraising way before presenting me with what he had brought. From the doorway, Madame Thébauld craned her head in blatant curiosity.

I opened the envelope and withdrew the thick card. On it was printed: 'Madame Berthier is at home on Thursdays from three to five.' And underneath, written in a small neat hand, I read, 'Do come. We should love to see you. Your aunt, Sophie.'

The servant waited, pointedly bored, for my response.

'I shall be delighted. Please thank Madame Berthier. I shall be delighted to attend.'

He received this intelligence as if the outcome had never been in doubt, gave me a barely perceptible bow, and left.

Madame Thébauld was dissatisfied. It was one of those rare occasions when something was happening in her building and she did not know what it was.

'A pretty invitation,' she began, and would have stayed to tempt me further into conversation had I not blocked the threshold. She remained so inquisitive that I closed the door almost in her face.

Alone at last, I can give vent to my delight. I have taken the card to the window to examine it closer for clues as to how I shall be received. My aunt's handwriting reveals nothing about the motivation of the writer. It is a controlled hand with no flourishes or idiosyncrasies of penmanship that would disclose anything of her feelings. The message itself is precisely centered at the bottom of the card – not written in haste or as an afterthought, at least, although I must admit I have some slight misgivings at the timing of the invitation. It is, after all, more than a week after I arrived in the city. But perhaps that is how it is done here. People are reserved, as if good humor were gauche or friendliness naive. I must affect languid disdain if I am to move successfully in Society though it goes against my true nature. As for the words of my aunt's note, I have read them over so many times in search of warmer nuances of affection that they have eventually lost all meaning and I can make no further progress.

There are no clues as to what I should expect. Time has changed our standings. The Berthiers have become grand while my own depleted family has stagnated in a rural backwater in an obscure province of the Austro–Hungarian empire. And I am anxious to confront the girl of my memory with the reality of Nichole the woman.

AFTERNOON

I have rushed through my work at the hospital so that I shall not be late for Aunt Sophie's 'at home,' and now

I find that I am early with time to kill. I would appear inexperienced and overeager if I were to turn up at the beginning of the reception. I have been thinking of Nichole all day, but of course I do not really know who I am thinking of. Nichole is an abstraction. I don't even know if she will remember me after these ten years. But that is ridiculous. There was something there, something unspoken and all the more mysterious and enduring for that.

Nichole has been a touchstone and a standard for me. I never again felt the same delight in another person's existence. I suppose that shows how inexperienced I really am. But the truth is that no one since Nichole has had the capacity to send me into raptures with merely a kind word or a gentle smile. I sensed that she felt the same way, but being a woman, and a Frenchwoman, and a woman of some sophistication, she hid her true feelings beneath a playful and sometimes teasing manner. Only sometimes I would catch her looking thoughtfully at me as I engaged in a task or conversed with another person, and the look on her face was one of such tenderness that my heart beat gladly in response.

George allowed me to bring Father's best frock coat. I have no recollections of my father, and yet the coat fits me well. It seems odd that the coat should bear the memory of his body and I do not remember him. I felt that I was standing in his body. Even the sleeves were of the correct length. The lapels and the skirts at the back, however, were decidedly unfashionable, even in Budapest, and I had to have them altered. The coat will pass, at least.

Still, it is too early. I have ordered a cab and must keep going back and forth from the table where I am writing to the window to see if it has arrived.

At the Salpêtrière this morning, Dr. Ducasse assigned me more patients to investigate. He seems quite pleased with my work. At least, he was made no criticisms. The patients are all old women, many in the third stage of syphilis, a condition of great interest to Charcot since he is making a study of abnormalities of the joints which accompany the nervous degeneration of the disease.

Today I encountered Stacia on the stairs. She was coming down as I ascended on my way to the ward, although I cannot imagine what business she had on the second floor, since apart from the regular wards there is only a dissecting room, doctors offices, and a small study room. I was hurrying up the stairs, but stopped when I saw her coming, as if out of breath, in order to conduct a small experiment. I paused against the banister as she passed, so that she would have an opportunity to see my face full on. Not a flicker of recognition did she show. She regarded me boldly, which is the style of Charcot's special patients, giving me an appraising look from head to toe which I found somewhat overfamiliar, and passed on without a word. I had expected that I would detect a hesitation, a question forming on her lips, a narrowing of the eyes for a harder scrutiny, but she appeared to be seeing me for the first time. I paused as the stairway made its last turn, at the point where I should be lost to sight to her as she descended, but she did not look back.

EVENING

The Berthiers' home is even more astounding when one goes beyond the entrance hall. The room in which Aunt Sophie receives visitors is like the cabinet of a Renaissance prince. There are extensive drapes which hang from the ceiling and give the impression that one is entering a tent. Sumptuous rugs in rich reds and yellow ocher cover the floor and complement the wall hangings. Pictures are everywhere, of saints writhing in ecstasy or martyrdom, or women of the harem waiting in languid sensuality. I do not wish to imply that the impression created is in any way degenerate or eccentric, for I think that Aunt Sophie is of an artistic inclination. The effect of the lavish textures and deep, mellow colors is rather one of luxurious informality. The wealth, of course, is obvious.

The room was crowded, of which I was glad, because I wanted an opportunity to reacquaint myself with my aunt and cousin before I spoke with them. Most of the throng were women. Everyone seemed to know everyone else. Since I knew no one and had not been introduced, I made my way around the edges of the room unobtrusively. A maid handed me a plate, and since I had eaten only a roll and coffee at breakfast time and nothing else, I helped myself to petits fours and canapés while I surveyed the crowd.

Sophie was seated in the middle of the room and rose from time to time to shake the hand of a new arrival. She was thinner and her hair was gray, a handsome and imposing woman in a gown of dark blue silk. I noticed the respect with which the other well-dressed women greeted her. A gentleman of my own age bowed to kiss her hand and said something amusing, which caused her to laugh and snatch her hand away from him, cautioning him with a raised finger in mock severity. He had a sleek and elegant appearance and a self-confident air about him I envied. I saw him linger, even though there were ladies waiting behind him to be received, flirting, it seemed, with this lady twice his age until she dismissed him with a wave of her hand and one more compressed smile of reluctant complicity.

The charming devil moved off in the direction of the conservatory, and I made my way toward the sofa on which my aunt sat to wait for my chance to present myself. I was not able to catch her eye, because she seemed engaged in asking a young woman about the health of each one of an interminable list of relatives. I was ill at ease, close enough to be recognized but excluded from the conversation, and at that moment I spotted the other center of social activity in the room. Three young women sat surrounded by several men. It was clear that one of the young women was the center of attention of the group and that the other two ladies were her friends.

Too late, I realized that the lady had moved on and that Aunt Sophie had spoken to me.

'Am I not right?' she was asking. She smiled when I seemed at a loss and could not answer. 'I recognize your mother's features. And your father's coloring.'

'I am Laszlo,' I said, finding myself at last.

Her mouth smiled a welcome, but her eyes did not smile. They were watchful, assessing the effects of the years on the character of a boy she had seen a decade before. She raised her cheek cautiously for me to kiss.

'My nephew Laszlo,' she said by introduction to the lady sitting next to her, 'is a scientist of the mind and has come to study with Professor Charcot.'

'Oh?' the lady said in a puzzled way that invited more information.

'My sister married Laszlo's father, the Count.'

'Indeed?'

'But Laszlo's father died when . . . you were no more than a small child, surely?'

'I was four years old.' In my nervousness I was about to confide to them that I was at this very moment wearing his coat, that it fit me like a glove, but I restrained the impulse to say whatever came into my mind before I could make a fool of myself.

'The Count was a martyr for the cause of freedom,' Sophie informed the lady.

'A Hungarian patriot,' I added. 'He is remembered to this day.'

'A victim of '48,' Sophie said in a kind of aside to the lady who nodded her head in partial understanding.

'I didn't know you had a sister,' the lady said.

'She died shortly after our last visit to the castle.'

'How sad.'

'Of consumption. It was a long illness. A mercy really.'

'I'm so pleased to be able to see you again,' I burst out. I had taken her hand, but she managed to slip it underneath mine.

'Indeed. Indeed,' Sophie said, patting the back of my hand with her other hand as one does to calm a feverish patient.

The mention of my mother's last days had made me emotional. It was hard to put into words what I wanted to say to Sophie, the only living connection to my mother, especially in a crowded room in front of this stranger. I was aware that my aunt glanced over my shoulder at others who were waiting to pay their respects.

'You must come again,' she said. The audience had come to an end. 'In fact, you must promise to come often. You are family, you know. We must get better acquainted!' There was a twinkle in her eye, which was my signal to leave her.

The sofa on which Aunt Sophie sat was like a clearing in the forest where one basked in the sunlight of social consequence, and I slipped back into the anonymous shadows of the crowd to think how best I might approach Nichole. She was disconcertingly elegant, daunting, unattainable. The transition to womanhood had enhanced her. Her lustrous dark eyes, slightly prominent as I remembered them, seemed both larger and more veiled. She wore a summer dress, less formal than her mother's, and the design accentuated her slim neck and shoulders. She turned from one talker to another; they were vying, I guessed, for her favor, and a smile or light laugh was the prize. She was a queen holding court, and the two ladies were the ladies-in-waiting.

She cannot have noticed that I was staring at her, because she had not been looking in my direction, but in one of those incidents which make one wonder at the power of attraction between man and woman, she glanced at me. I want to emphasize that she did not look in my general direction, surveying the crowd in a moment of distraction. No, she looked up and away from the man who was in mid-sentence and her eyes fixed directly and precisely on my own. She had shown that almost telepathic awareness during her visit to the castle, an ability to sense that someone was looking at her or thinking intensely about her – or, more exactly, an ability to sense when *I* was looking at her or thinking of her.

I looked away. It was an instinctive reflex. I immediately hated myself for it, because when I looked back, her attention was taken once again by the group which surrounded her. The moment had been too intense, and I had flinched. There had come a moment of quicksilver magic, of instant recognition, but it had slipped through my, too late, clutching fingers.

I raised food to my lips, sipped wine from a glass, without awareness of my surroundings. When I looked again in Nichole's direction, I saw she rarely laughed, even though the young men tried their best to amuse her. I thought that she gave her laughter only rarely to make her suitors strive all the harder for the favor.

I was considering my best option when I heard a voice at my shoulder.

'I know men who'd rather face a charge of Prussian cavalry than run the gauntlet of Nichole's admirers,' a gentleman of about sixty told me. 'But if you're too afraid of making a damn fool of yourself, you won't make anything of yourself.' He chuckled to himself as he moved off into the crowd.

I decided on a frontal approach. I squared my shoulders, gathered my best smile, and, staring unwaveringly at Nichole the whole time, strode toward the couch where she sat. I wavered slightly when, only a few feet from her, she still showed no sign of noticing me. I came to a stop altogether when I arrived at a social fortress, a wall of well-tailored backs, within which I could hear the conversation in full swing. I managed to find a gap, but by then I had lost all my emotional momentum and simply waited for a lull when I could catch Nichole's attention.

Her hair was slightly darker than I remembered, but it still had the chestnut tones of before. She wore it gathered up behind with pretty ringlets hanging down on either side, framing her oval face. Her heavy-lidded eyes conveyed a mood of languor and sultriness, although in reality Nichole is intelligent and very much alert. She wore an expression of sleepiness that I knew well; it was a look which came over her face when she was aware that a man who found her attractive was gazing at her, a look which said that she was indifferent, that his admiration had no effect other than to bore her. But I remember her eyes, flashing and dark when she was angry with me, and from time to time now I saw the hidden sparkle which she kept veiled from her subjects. Nichole was in her element, and I wondered what it had been like for her to spend a summer in the depths of Hungary, far from the attentions of her fashionable friends.

One of the gentlemen made a humorous remark and her eyes passed across my face as she surveyed the audience's response – passed across me and returned – and as her glance fastened on me there was a slight, inquiring tilt to her eyebrows, a look which was not quite recognition. I smiled and bowed.

'We have a poet amongst us,' she announced, much to my embarrassment, since the episode in the castle garden was not something I wanted revealed before these strangers, and the Nichole I remembered was quite capable of torturing me with that threat. 'I would like to introduce my cousin, Laszlo, recently arrived from Hungary,' she said without more ado.

I stepped forward and stooped to kiss the hand she offered. Common in Budapest, the gesture must have appeared either old-fashioned or else unusually intimate for a social gathering. In either case, it established my family priority in the group. The others made space for me. One of the ladies-in-waiting offered to give up her seat so that I could be close to my beloved cousin, but I would have none of it.

'After so many years, to be reunited,' the young lady sighed in a wistful way I found overly sentimental.

'I have looked forward to this moment for ten years,' I said. I tried to chose words which could be taken to convey a cousin's affection or more than that, for I had the dilemma of seizing the opportunity to let Nichole know of my feelings without baring my heart before all these people whom I had never met before. 'I have thought of you often,' I said simply.

Nichole regarded me with an enigmatic smile. 'Then we must pick up exactly at the point where we left off.'

'You came all the way to Paris simply to see Nichole?' a man asked incredulously. He was the fellow I had seen talking with my aunt. The others laughed. He seemed to have the role of court jester. Or perhaps more than that, since he was able to make fun of Nichole with impunity, as if he alone was not in awe of her and did not have to take her entirely seriously.

'Never,' Nichole put in before I could think of a suitable reply. 'I am an incidental detail. Laszlo has come to study mental phenomena.'

'Ah, a scientist and a poet,' the smooth fellow said knowingly.

Nichole introduced him as Lothar von Pick, along with all the others. She has surrounded herself with fops and simpering girls, and several times I thought I saw her swallow her impatience with some vacuous remark.

Lothar, on the other hand, seems substantial. His French is slightly accented, and when I heard his name this confirmed my impression that he is a fellow countryman, or, at least, that since he is an Austrian we are both subjects of the Emperor Franz Josef. Lothar is on the short side and not especially handsome, but he attracts people to him with his irreverent humor. He is self-confident almost to the point of rudeness and appears entirely indifferent to what other people may think of him, with the result that they are eager to gain his approval. This he never gives. Nichole patronizes him and would have him appear her pet, but I think he is too independent for that role. He resembles an otter: His hair is dark brown and smoothed back from his forehead, which gives him a sleek air in spite of his somewhat full lips and cheeks, as if he had just that moment emerged from the water, wet and glistening, sniffing the air intently for the foibles of mankind. When he is not talking there is a sardonic smile on his lips.

'And how do you find the University?' Nichole asked me.

'I am not studying at the University.' I thought she would have known this from the letter I sent her mother before I left Hungary. 'I am here as a clinical assistant at the Salpêtrière.' I saw looks of distaste on the faces of a few people, others looked blank. 'With Professor Charcot,' I added to no avail.

'That dreadful place for old women,' Nichole shuddered. 'How can you stand it?'

'Don't turn up your nose, fair Nichole,' Lothar said in a soft, mocking voice. 'Who knows what could become of you if you don't find a husband? Then you might need Laszlo's good graces at the Salptrire to secure you a comfortable berth.'

I thought he had gone too far, but apparently this kind of jarring remark at Nichole's expense was something they had come to expect from him, and no one appeared put out.

Nichole gazed at him with a smile like the Sphinx. 'Wherever I end my days, I will have the satisfaction of knowing I have kept my honor unblemished,' she said. 'Can you say the same?'

'Virtue is its own reward, but fortunately for me, not the only reward Paris has to offer.'

'But I do not believe you are truly deserving of any reward, Lothar.'

'So far God has seen fit to save me from what I truly deserve.' He bowed in mock humility, his eyes hooded, the small smile which negated everything playing on his lips.

'Save a place at the Salptrire for Lothar, will you Laszlo? Can you do that? Will they accept the occasional man, someone broken down in early middle age by a dissolute life?'

'There are parts of the hospital I haven't yet seen,' I began uncertainly. I was not practiced in their bantering exchange and felt that I was responding in a stupid and backward way. 'Perhaps if he were an extremely interesting case we could make an exception.'

I was pleased when everyone laughed, although I felt that I had hit a target by accident.

'Then your future is assured,' Nichole told Lothar. 'He will make an excellent case. An extremely curious case. Lothar's mind is full of secret passages that have never seen the light of day.'

They were laughing again, and the pattern became clear to me: Lothar could say whatever outrageous thing came to mind, but Nichole must have the last word. I glanced over at him and was surprised to see him staring quite seriously at Nichole, the mask of cynical amusement having fallen from his face for the first time.

It seemed to be a good time to tell them about the Friday demonstration and of Stacia's extraordinary lapse of memory.

'A trick,' Nichole pronounced before I had a chance to finish the story. 'She faked the whole thing.'

'You are judging her by your own standards,' Lothar said, but Nichole ignored him.

'She hoodwinked a whole room full of brilliant scientists!' Nichole scoffed. 'A dramatic performance by a pretty face – she was pretty, wasn't she?' she shot at me like an accusation.

'Well, as a matter of fact, she was,' I admitted, although I don't know why Nichole should make me feel guilty.

'Of course she was.'

'But that has nothing to do with it,' I insisted. Nichole gave me a look of pity. 'You had to be there to see that she was sincere. It was terribly convincing.'

'Can anyone come to watch?' Lothar asked. He had followed my account with great attention, never interrupting

me once, although previously he had not shown himself
in the least constrained from jumping into the middle of
other peoples' sentences. All the same, I did not wish to be
made a fool of in front of Nichole by taking his question
seriously.

But Lothar seemed genuinely interested. I was surprised
when he touched my elbow.

'How about a cigar in the conservatory?' he suggested.

'Thanks, but I don't smoke,' I said, not wanting to leave
Nichole's company.

'She hides her pleasure at seeing you,' he muttered in
my ear so low that no one else could hear. I felt a shiver of
the uncanny run down my spine. It was as if he had read
my mind. How could he have known what I wanted so
vehemently to hear?

'She'll keep,' he said tugging at my sleeve, and I turned
and walked with him. He took my arm and we strolled
like old friends. 'She pretends indifference,' he said, as if
we were two doctors confiding our views on a difficult
case. 'It's all a pose. Everything in Paris is a pose. No one is
spontaneous. No one tells the truth. It's unfashionable. So
when I tell the truth they think I must be either an unholy
fool or a comedian of sublime subtlety. Consequently I
say whatever I like.'

'I'm amazed that you insult Nichole.' I was already
feeling some proprietary duty to protect her.

'But she's not insulted, is she?'

I had to admit that he was right. He opened the glass
door of the conservatory and I stepped into the warm,
humid atmosphere.

'On the contrary,' Lothar insisted. 'She is intrigued.
And even flattered. The truth cannot be believed.'

'I hardly think Nichole is likely to end up in the
Salptrire.'

'Of course not. Her dowry will be substantial. She can
take her pick of the field. That's what the gang of idiots
is all about; that's why they sit at her feet and hang on
her every word.' He was intent on clipping the end of a

cheroot. 'She despises them, of course,' he said, looking up suddenly. 'Nichole is stubborn, scheming, and shallow.' He ignored my protests. 'The girl may simply not be willing to submit to being some fellow's wife. That's how she could find herself on the shelf.'

The conservatory was a miniature jungle with clearings for tables and seats here and there beneath the arching palms. Fan-shaped fronds and the curling bows of huge ferns hid these spaces from each other, so that we turned a corner and came unexpectedly upon the older gentleman who had spoken to me earlier. He seemed lost in his own thoughts, contemplating the blue wraith of smoke which rose from the thick Havana he held between his thumb and middle finger.

Lothar didn't miss a beat. 'Ah, there you are, sir,' he proclaimed. 'We were discussing the chances of your daughter ending her days in the Salptrire.'

I cringed, but instead of springing to his feet in outrage, the old man chuckled.

'That would save me a pretty penny,' he said as if he were talking to himself.

Lothar gave me a look as if to say, 'Didn't I tell you so?' which I was afraid the man would notice.

Sophie and Nichole had come to visit us alone, so that I had never had an opportunity to meet my uncle Aristide. He was said to be very wealthy, a financier who took positions in a variety of enterprises which were forever changing, and I had the impression from what George had said – with heavy disapproval – that he was basically a speculator, although you would not have thought so to look at him.

When I introduced myself to him, he sprang up and warmly pumped my hand. 'I had no idea. My dear boy! Welcome. Welcome. Are they giving you everything you want?'

He was a small, wiry man with a long thin face accentuated by a pointed beard that was turning white. He had been pensive when we came upon him, but he was lively now and I thought that he had perhaps slipped away from the throng to hide among the ferns for a few minutes' relief from the manic conversations going on in the other rooms. He kept hold of my hand to look at my face.

'I see your dear mother's resemblance. She was a great beauty, you know,' he told Lothar. 'The two sisters,' he said wistfully, remembering some far-off day he did not reveal to us.

He asked about George and seemed particularly interested in the condition of the estate. 'Don't sell off any of that land.' He wagged his finger in front of my face like a schoolmaster giving a most important lesson. He had been warm without effusiveness, but now I saw the other side of him, the hard moneymaker. 'Not an acre. Do you know why?'

'Because it's been in our family for five hundred years,' I replied.

'No,' he said dismissively, as if the irrelevance of my answer had thrown him off course. 'Because they're going to build a railway through your area. And that means you'll get your grain and your vegetables and your cattle to markets your ancestors never even dreamed of.'

'What about these African trading companies?' Lothar asked. 'Are they a buy?'

'They're not for you.'

'I'm a man that can stand some risk.'

'They're for empire-builders and fools.' Aristide was growing impatient. 'These African companies are puffed up with nothing but hope and glory. The stocks are strictly for flag-toters and drum-bangers. They'll never make a profit for anyone but the issuers. Believe me, I know.'

I thought he winked at us as he turned to go, tossing his cigar into the lily pool where several goldfish rose to gape at it.

The crowd in the reception room was thinning when we returned, and many people were making their good-byes. Nichole took my hand briefly and murmured the conventional phrases of departure, but her mother had

35

more time for me now that the press of her obligations as hostess had lessened. She stared at me fondly and sadly as she took my hand, and I suppose she saw in me some embodiment of my mother and her lonely life far from home and family.

'Come again, my boy,' Aristide said, tapping me on the shoulder and nodding as if to assure me that he meant what he said. He turned to Lothar, who had become my shadow that afternoon. 'And if you must dabble, buy Occidental Traders. But stay out of Africa, for goodness' sake!'

We left together, and on the sidewalk I turned to shake Lothar's hand, but he offered me a ride. An open landau, its black lacquer so thick and lustrous that its surface reflected like a sinister mirror, waited curbside. The coachman waited respectfully with his hand on the open door, but the two gray geldings were restless in the traces and eager to be gone. I was embarrassed by the thought of Lothar in his magnificent equipage drawing up to my meager lodgings.

'No, really. I have business in town,' I said.

'Then let me drop you off there.'

I could hardly refuse, and invented an errand which would bring us to a spot which would not be far out of the way. I must admit I enjoyed the rush of air and the heads that turned to see us speed by on the Champs-Élysées, and I settled into the soft leather upholstery as if I had been accustomed to it from birth.

I got out soon after we crossed back over the river.

'We must meet again,' Lothar said.

'No doubt I will see you at the Berthiers',' I replied.

'No, before then. You must see my tailor.'

'I don't understand.'

'Then we'll have some fun.'

'But I don't want to see your tailor.'

'Yes, you do. Down there on the left. You can't miss it.' And with that he tapped his man on the shoulder and the grays took off. 'See you there tomorrow,' he called out over his shoulder. 'Four o'clock.'

Lothar is an impudent, presumptuous fellow I can't help liking. I do not think there is anything between him and Nichole. They amuse one another. There is no more to it than that. I would not like to think of him as a rival. He has so many of the practical things – like money and good prospects – which I do not possess and which matter to mothers and fathers of daughters. I am already thinking of a liaison with Nichole and I hardly know her! My mind is so full of romantic possibilities that I must remind myself constantly that none of this has anything to do with a real person. (Is she really superficial, as Lothar says, or is he misleading me for his own purposes?) Nichole is a dream. But I am starting to imagine a life in Paris with her!

George would not miss me. Elizabeth is a kind and decent person, but we have had little opportunity to get to know each other in the three years she has been married to my brother. Uncle Kalman will find another hunting companion – I have had precious little time for that lately, anyway. Gregory is immersed in the concerns of his parish, and lately I have perceived less and less of the dear friend who shared my school days and more of the severe priest who is gradually replacing him. There is little I would regret in Hungary, if I could have Paris.

3

MAY 26, 1866

I have sent a message that I cannot come to work today. My head feels as though it was split open last night. My mouth is dry, and my tongue discovers foul fragments in its folds. If I cannot fulfill my medical duties, at least I can write my journal and try to gain some perspective on the disturbing events of yesterday.

In the morning I went to the hospital. Ducasse is a stickler. He has assigned me a clutch of old women and has me cataloging them down to the minutest detail. I must measure and record the range of motion of each and every joint in their bodies so that Charcot will have data to support his theories on the progression of syphilitic symptoms. Consequently, I was engaged the whole morning with a single patient. She was extraordinarily talkative, and I had to interrupt her frequently in order to get her to cooperate with the examination.

I was impatient to finish my work early, for I had resolved to meet Lothar at the spot he had proposed. There is something mischievous about him which appeals to me. I do not think he is reckless, but I need leavening. I am becoming altogether too serious and preoccupied with the morbid phenomena I study, and I must allow time for recreation and restoration.

While I moved her fingers and wrists and knees, the old woman prattled on about her 'protector,' whom I am given to understand was a rich lover who maintained her like a lady of rank – that is, if she is to be believed. She was full of the finery and jewels and noble admirers of her heyday, and showed no awareness of the destitute position which is her lot at the Salptrire.

I arrived at the tailor's shop at four o'clock as agreed, but Lothar was nowhere to be seen, and I spent an uncomfortable twenty minutes pretending to examine the fabrics on display. It was one of those small, discreet, horribly expensive establishments where prices are never mentioned. The manager, a small man with beady eyes who fussed with the tape measure around his neck, measured me with his eyes as he advanced to greet me. I informed him I was not there on my own account but was meeting an acquaintance who had business with him. I wandered about feeling the fineness of this stuff or the softness of that. Whenever I looked up, I found his inquisitive eyes upon me, and he immediately summoned a smile to his face which he just as quickly dropped as soon as I turned my attention elsewhere. To test him, I scanned the bales of cloth on shelves on either side of his head so that he was forced to hold his obliging grin for several minutes until he found something to busy himself with in his account ledger.

Lothar arrived at last and was greeted obsequiously by the manager, whom he ignored. The man bowed, took his top hat and ebony cane and in turn handed them to an assistant. Lothar wore a black frock coat with satin facings and trim. He appeared the height of elegance, and I told him that he did not look like a man in need of a new suit of clothes.

'Not me, old chap. You.'

'I have all the coats I need,' I protested, laughing to show that I was taking it as a joke, but uncertainly, because I had my doubts about Father's frock coat.

'Listen to me,' Lothar said quietly, putting his arm around my shoulder in that familiar way he has and turning away from the manager, who hovered about him expectantly. 'The heirloom you wore yesterday may be all very well and good for the old ladies at the hospital, but it simply won't cut it at the Berthiers'. Let me speak to this fellow. He owes me a favor or two, and I'll get you a good price.'

Lothar was off down the length of the shop. He would indicate a bale, the manager would gesture with a sharp motion of his hand, and an assistant would spring forward, seize the bale, toss it onto the counter and unravel it with a sharp backward jerk for Lothar's inspection. Lothar wandered on without paying attention, apparently having lost interest already, his attention taken with a new shade or fabric. At one point I saw Lothar talking to the manager who listened most intently and from time to time cast glances in my direction. Eventually they returned to where I toyed with a display of cravats.

'Count!' the manager exclaimed.

I was somewhat taken aback and looked to Lothar for an explanation. He was holding some material up to catch the light on its surface and gave no sign of having heard.

'Forgive me, Count,' the fawning fellow insisted. 'I was uninformed until this moment. I had no idea!'

And without more ado, he set to measuring me, poking the end of his tape into all the intimate angles of my body before I could gather sufficient wit to protest.

An assistant advanced with four bales in his arms.

'I rather fancy this one,' Lothar suggested. 'It strikes the right tone for the clientele you'll be seeing in your practice. Those rich, asthenic ladies who never get better and keep on paying and paying,' he whispered conspiratorially as the manager and his assistant went in search of a coat in order to show the kind of lapels they had in mind for me.

'But I can't possibly afford it,' I said angrily, forced at last to confess my penury.

'Then don't pay,' Lothar said lightly.

'Then let's have done with this charade and be gone.'

'First the coat.'

The manager and assistant were returning along the aisle proudly bearing the frock coat.

'I thought we had already established that I won't pay.'

'Understood. But let us take the coat on credit.'

'I don't have any,' I replied tersely. 'I am unknown here. At least, I thought I was.'

'All you need is your good name and the most basic penmanship.'

The manager inquired anxiously, 'Count, would this be satisfactory, or would you prefer the lapel narrower still?'

It was a wonderful coat, and the one in the fabric I had selected would be even more striking. I was speechless.

'On Sunday I saw the Duc de Beaumont wearing something similar,' Lothar said. 'Nowadays, in fashionable circles, it's almost impossible to wear lapels which are too thin.'

'Quite so,' the manager agreed, delighted to have a connoisseur with whom to confer.

'Then the decision is made?' Lothar asked me in a public voice.

'That is . . . the gray or the black silk edging?' the manager put in.

'The gray,' I said, distracted by his inquiry, and then realizing that in answering his question, I was also committing myself to the suit.

'An excellent choice, if I may say so, Count,' the manager enthused.

'Sober, but with just the right touch of panache,' Lothar said. 'And also,' he added lowering his voice, 'very much to the taste of you know who.'

He was smiling, as if he had succeeded in luring me across an invisible line. I felt myself in new waters. I was faintly nauseated with anxiety, but at the same time I felt a devil-may-care excitement as if I were sneaking out of school for a delicious afternoon of truancy.

The manager proffered me a pen. He affected embarrassment. 'If you would be so good to sign here, Count. A mere formality, I assure you.'

He seemed nervous that I would take offense, and I was tempted to torture him further by insisting that my word

41

should be sufficient. There was also the problem of what name I was to use. Going alone with Lothar's game in order to gain some consideration from a tradesman was one thing; actually signing with a title I had no claim to was something else altogether. I compromised by concocting something, with much squeaking of the pen and flourishes of the elbow, which was both impressively grand and illegible.

The manager seemed more than satisfied. 'Your suit will be ready in a week,' he said.

'Monday,' Lothar corrected him in a matter-of-fact way.

'Of course, sir, Monday,' he said, bowing us out.

We had no sooner climbed into the landau when the driver whipped up the horses and we took off with such impetus that I almost fell back into my seat.

'You see,' Lothar said, making a roundabout motion of the silver knob of his cane as if he was holding forth at a lecture. 'The more you pile on the demands, the more they respect you for it. He says the suit will be ready in a week; I tell him to make it in three days. The result is that he pays no attention at all to that remarkable specimen of calligraphy you left with him.'

'Are you suggesting I can't make good on the bill?' I demanded rather heatedly. His insinuation that I would attempt to evade my obligations I thought ridiculous rather than insulting. It seemed to be his first assumption, pronounced so casually, that someone he scarcely knew would naturally be inclined to cheat a tradesman.

'I thought you told me yourself that you couldn't afford to pay for it?' he said, tapping me on the shoulder. There were no considerations of honor. It was all a big joke to Lothar. 'But I have the feeling that you'll soon come into some money.'

'I don't think that's very likely.'

'Enough, at least, to pay your tailor's bill.'

'How's that?' I asked.

'I put some money into Occidental Traders for you.'

'You shouldn't have.' I was annoyed at his presumption of my penury and angry that he had put me in his debt.

'Why not? It was simple enough. I bought a few shares for you and some for myself. You can pay me back out of the money you make, and then we're even.'

'And what if the stock goes down and you lose money?'

'We won't. It's Aristide's tip. He means you to profit from it. It's his gift. He wouldn't have mentioned it if you hadn't been there. You're family, after all.'

'The stock market's no different from betting on a horse race,' I said uneasily, thinking of George's losses.

'Precisely.'

'Most people lose most of the time. It's a statistical certainty.'

'And that's true most of the time. But in some races the outcome's known before the starter drops the flag.'

'You think this stock is rigged?'

'If Aristide Berthier has something to do with it, we can assume that the laws of chance are not what propels Occidental Traders's progress.'

'I want no part of it.'

'Tell that to your tailor.'

'It was you who told the man that I was a count.'

'Not "a count." *The* Count. Which you went along with quite happily, I noticed.'

'What do you mean, "the Count"?' I asked.

'I told him your name. It's close enough. If it weren't for your brother, George, it would be true.'

'But I've never mentioned my brother to you.'

'I looked it up.'

'Looked it up? You make it sound like something you can find in a railway timetable.' I kept my cool, but there is something disturbing about someone knowing a whole lot more about you than you have been inclined to tell him.

'Didn't you know? I'm an attaché at the embassy.'

I had never thought of him as involved in anything so mundane as work. Lothar seemed to float above all routines which were necessary to the existence of ordinary mortals.

Lothar was enjoying himself. He dangled his cane between finger and thumb, playing the affected diplomat: 'I simply rang the bell on my desk and told the clerk to fetch your file. A very thin file, it turned out to be. Nothing very juicy in it at all. Quite disappointing, really. Still, you've only been here a week or two. Let's see if we can't fatten it up.'

'I hadn't supposed I was so important.'

'You're not. It's just paperwork. The bureaucrats in Vienna like to keep track of our nobility abroad.'

'Is that what you do?'

'Good Lord, I don't "do" anything,' he said with distaste, and I thought for the first time that I might have offended him. 'It's a position my father got for me. It's his idea of keeping me out of trouble while I'm in Paris. He has this strange idea that I must make something of myself. The ambassador can't stand me, but he owes Father a favor, so he keeps an eye on me. Whatever I do, apparently, he'll keep advancing my career. Father must have some hook into him.' He smiled cheerfully. 'Does that offend you?'

I was hesitant to endorse his point of view. 'Where would we be without our families?' I managed with a worldly shrug.

'After all, for the nobility, doors open without they're having to push on them.'

'You should know. You're a "von."'

'My father bought it.'

'That's overstating it, surely.'

'He made his fortune selling the army its uniforms. Have you ever wondered who profited from the defeat at Solferino? Think about it! Think of all those dead soldiers. What a killing we made! You see, every time a soldier gets shot, they have to replace him with another one. And unless he's shot clean through the head, there's only one way a soldier can get himself killed: Something has to ruin

44

his uniform.' He found this thought inordinately funny, and my seriousness seemed to provoke him to even greater amusement. 'That's why my father is so rich. That's how you and I come to be riding in this carriage with these handsome horses on our way to the best restaurant in the city!'

We had left the busy thoroughfares of the city behind us and for some minutes had been riding through the welcome greenness of the Bois de Boulogne. In the center of the forest we came upon a restaurant in something of the style of a Greek temple, set amidst manicured gardens. Lothar jumped down as soon as the carriage came to a stop and held the door open for me to alight.

'I take it you accept my invitation?' he said.

Inside, the maître d'hôtel conducted us to a corner table. Gas lighting had not been brought to this part of the Bois, and so illumination came from candelabra placed on tables and sideboards at the edges of the dining rooms and from small candles placed on each table. The result was a dim background illumination and a further gloom from which waiters appeared with food and into which they receded with empty plates; and scattered here and there, it seemed at random, were the small, intimate circles of light which held the diners at each table and made their faces glow mysteriously. The walls and even the doors were mirrored, and these surfaces gave a disorienting perspective of shadows and receding duplications of figures bent toward each focus of candlelight. The dimensions of the room magically disappeared; I felt myself to be in a dreamlike space with no certainty as to my real location. All one could be sure of was the light of the candle on the table and the face opposite, which it illuminated.

It was a discreet and mysterious place, and I wondered what kind of evening entertainment Lothar had in mind. The other diners were mostly men of an older generation, and here and there at small tables gentlemen had as their guests young women of striking looks.

'Best food in Paris, but not the place they'd ever bring their wives to,' Lothar said, looking around to survey the clientele. 'Champagne!' he ordered of a passing waiter who immediately changed course to fetch what Lothar had demanded. 'What you see here are the most celebrated, the most expensive women in the world.'

'Kept women, I suppose.'

'These are the *grandes horizontales*. Too expensive for you, or for me.'

A waiter brought the champagne and nestled the bottle in a bucket of crushed ice. 'Is this a celebration?' I asked. Lothar waived the man away and popped the cork expertly.

'To a new friendship!' he proposed, and we drank.

I hadn't drank champagne since George married Elizabeth three years ago, and I don't remember it being so glacially cold and yet alive in the mouth. It was like swallowing freezing, fuming smoke.

'Good Lord, you were thirsty!' Lothar laughed.

I suppose I must have drained the glass. He refilled it, and I proposed the next toast. 'To Nichole,' I proclaimed.

'To sweet Nichole,' he repeated, all the while watching me stealthily over the rim of his glass. 'May she never come between us,' he added at the last moment as I began to drink. His words came exactly as I swallowed, and I had the same feeling as in the tailor's shop, that he had slipped something by my customary intelligence.

'Are you . . .' I couldn't think of an innocuous word for what I was determined would appear a causal inquiry.

'Interested?' Lothar suggested.

'Yes,' I said with an offhand gesture. He was grinning at me wolfishly in the candlelight. 'Are you interested in Nichole?' I asked.

'Are you?'

'I hardly know her, really.'

'What has that got to do with being . . . interested?'

'I knew her a long time ago. We were children.'

46

'But children are so intense. Such a purity of love and hate!'

'I suppose. You haven't answered my question.'

'Am I interested in Nichole?' He rolled the stem of the glass between finger and thumb in a contemplative sort of way and stared at me with a small, enigmatic smile. 'I find you much more interesting.'

I had been leaning forward to hear what he would say, and I must have started back in my chair. I wasn't sure what I had heard, but Lothar was already reaching to pour more wine, his demeanor smooth and unruffled as if nothing untoward had passed between us. Perhaps I had been mistaken about the whole thing. There is nothing effeminate about the man. He displays no mannerisms or gestures that would indicate a homosexual bent.

'She's unworthy of you,' he went on, and I had no desire to take him up on what he had said a moment previously. He leaned back in his chair and passed outside the candle's circle of intimacy; his face was in shadow and the nuances of his expression indistinct. He talked of her in a tired and jaded manner, with irritation just beneath the surface, and I wondered if Nichole had already rejected him.

Our food arrived at last. We were both hungry, the dishes indeed delicious, and we fell to eating without talking further for several minutes. It provided a welcome change of conversation. Lothar asked about my work at the Salptrire and was interested in Charcot's Friday lectures. He is particularly curious about the more extreme and bizarre forms of behavior, including sexual deviations. I told him that I had read about these syndromes but had not yet had occasion to study them in the flesh, as it were – an unintentional pun which he found amusing, which pleased me since I often have difficulty thinking up jokes in an opportune manner. I think the champagne was partly responsible and must have loosened up some part of my mind which is usually more constrained. The result was that I was quite amusing, and by the end of dinner Lothar (and

I, too) were roaring with laughter at almost everything I had to say.

'Now we must further our scientific researches,' he said.

I hadn't the faintest idea what he meant, but tumbled into the landau, which, as always, was waiting for us as if by magic at the door.

'Rue de Londres,' Lothar called out to his driver. 'You know where.' He leaned forward and clutched my knee to get my attention. 'You'll like this, I promise you. Much more fun than Nichole,' he said and collapsed into laughter. I suppose we were both quite drunk even at that stage of the evening.

The house we stopped in front of looked perfectly respectable. Lothar jumped down, but I stayed in the carriage. Unaccustomed to drink, I mistrusted my ability to balance on my own legs.

'What is this place?' I asked uneasily.

The coachman, who could have been made of stone for all the notice he took of us beyond the instructions Lothar gave him, now peered round with a smirk on his face as he looked to his master.

'It's the best of its kind,' Lothar said. 'It's whatever you want it to be.'

'It's a brothel,' I said flatly.

'Oh, no, that's far too mundane a term for this place.'

'I think you might have told me before you brought me here.'

He leaned with his arms resting on the landau's door and looked up at me curiously. 'It's not a case of scruples, is it?'

'Don't be ridiculous!' I protested.

'Surely, you owe it to yourself to take a look at least. You're a student of behavior. You can't get it all from books. This is the real thing. There's real human nature inside. Where do you think the professors get their case studies to write about? They're on the other side of that door, waiting to meet you. Why don't you just

48

imagine that it's one of your Professor Charcot's Friday demonstrations? I promise you won't be disappointed.'

Never having been inside a brothel, I was curious, I'll admit. George, visiting Budapest on a furlough from some godforsaken garrison town, would try to get me to accompany him to some house of ill-repute favored by cavalrymen, but I would never go. I couldn't imagine the act in such a place as anything but sordid and dispiriting. I have held out like some romantic monk who has taken a vow of chastity for the sake of love. It was the image of the girl Nichole, my talisman all these years, that sustained me. And now that image was hard to reconcile with the flesh and blood woman I knew. The dream, like a cut flower, was fading.

'You don't have to actually do anything, you know,' Lothar said, half coaxing, half supporting me as I climbed down to the pavement. He took my arm and whispered hoarsely in my ear. 'You can watch, if you want!'

'You mean, other people doing it?'

'Absolutely! It's great fun.'

'Do they know?'

'Hmm, I'm not sure. That's what makes it interesting. It's so much more sincere if they don't know.'

Lothar rapped loudly with the brass knocker, and after a minute a spy hole slid open. We were regarded for several seconds. Evidently Lothar was known, because the person behind the door swung it open without a word being exchanged. A woman of uncertain age, not uncultured in appearance, and wearing a sober black dress which covered her from wrist to neck, bid us enter.

'Madame,' Lothar said, taking her hand and bowing. 'I have the honor of presenting . . .' and he introduced me again as "the Count." 'He is to be my guest tonight.'

She led us from the hallway toward receiving rooms from which came the sound of a piano. Lothar was about to follow but I held him back.

'I'm just here to observe,' I insisted.

He shrugged. 'Do as you wish.'

'Just as long as that's understood.'

'I understand. Your interest is purely scientific.'

I looked for the ironically raised eyebrow by which Lothar silently conveyed his amusement at the self-deceptions of lesser mortals, but I could see no sign of mockery.

We passed the main room where I glimpsed a young lady playing the melody of a music hall song which seems to be on every-one's lips these days. Madame took us instead to a small parlor which appeared to serve as her office. She poured us each a glass of wine. We drank her health. Then she sat silently, looking at us expectantly.

'Perhaps,' she began, looking at me, 'if you could give me some idea . . .'

'My friend is modest,' Lothar said for me.

'Ah,' said Madame, apparently enlightened. She looked at me with a fresh, professional interest and nodded her head thoughtfully.

When she took my hand as if to reassure me, I almost jumped.

'Come now, Count,' she said soothingly. 'You mustn't be shy. I shan't bite you, you know.'

With that she took my hand between her own and held it in her motherly lap while she considered me. I had a feeling of impending panic in which I would be forced to run from the place. Madame stroked my hand while she went through various possibilities in her mind, and I felt the intense emotion quelled to the point that it resembled the pricking thrill of the moment in which I had sat before Stacia in the auditorium and her eyes had passed over me without recognition.

'I would like to meet the . . .'

'Ladies,' Madame put in. 'But of course. That is the best way to begin.' I took back my hand and was glad when she turned her attention to Lothar. 'And you, sir. You have always known exactly what you wanted.'

She rose and bade me follow her. 'Let me introduce you to the ladies,' she said. We passed the main staircase, and I was aware of muffled, distant sounds, which I could not identify, coming from the floor above. Madame glanced upwards and gave me a look with an ambiguously raised eyebrow.

Lothar remained in the parlor and we were alone in the hall when she stopped as if arrested by a sudden thought. 'If you prefer, Count, we do have boys.'

I shook my head.

'They're very accommodating.'

'Thank you, no,' I said, feeling foolishly polite, as if I were declining a second piece of cake at a tea party.

'One never knows. Since you are a friend of Herr von Pick,' she added with a smile, watching the reaction in my face for one alert moment before she turned to resume our tour. 'He is a man of such varied interests,' she murmured.

She ushered me into a room which could almost have been the drawing room in the home of a well-off family. The young lady playing the piano was named Lola. She could have been a school-teacher. Lola asked me if there was a piece of music I wished to hear; I said I should enjoy some Strauss, and she launched into a waltz which she played with great gusto. A gentleman in the corner whom I had not previously noticed awoke and lurched from the room in search of a dancing partner.

I heard a man's guffaw and the titter of several women coming from the adjoining room and went to investigate. I found a fifty-year-old man reclining on a couch supported by three young women in their underclothes who were draped around him in various poses. With his florid, rotund features and face surrounded by a white beard he looked like a Bacchus from a mythological painting. At some point that night he had been in evening dress, but his jacket and shirt were missing and all that remained on his upper body were his cuffs and collar.

'Take whichever one you want,' he called out to me. 'Don't let me hold you back, old chap. I'm spent. Entirely spent.'

The girls laughed and teased him, tweaking his beard and running their hands over his belly.

'Mercy!' he cried.

'Please don't let me disturb you,' I said, but his attention had already been distracted, and I passed on without pausing further.

The next room might have been a café or the bar in a gentlemen's club. A waiter stood attentively to one side, and several gentlemen sat with women of the house at tables. There was a relaxed air in which the men felt it permissible to remove their jackets and drink wine in their suspenders. Everyone felt free in this atmosphere of easy fellowship to address remarks to someone sitting at another table, whoever he might be. I found Lothar in an intent conversation with Madame, but she got up and left him when she saw me approach.

'Have you been upstairs yet?' he asked. I told him I had not. 'Then you need more champagne,' he said.

Apparently it was the only drink they served. I was thirsty and drank deeply. I had kept my eyes lowered because I did not want to give offense by appearing curious, but my attention was drawn to four ladies who sat by themselves at a table to one side. Lola sauntered in and joined them. She smiled and waved to me, but I was careful not to encourage her.

'Who are you looking at?' Lothar asked.

'Lola, the piano player. I met her in the other room.'

'I didn't mean her. The other one you can't keep your eyes off.'

Lothar has an uncanny ability to detect attraction, or interest, or any emotion which rises above the ordinary in the person he is with. He is like a gun dog scenting game and then pointing to the object of desire. In fact, I had noticed one of the women sitting at the table, but I was not able to see her clearly because she was partly turned away from us, and that was why my eyes came back to her several times.

'The girly one!' Lothar declared triumphantly. 'Am I right?'

'I was looking at the one with blond hair,' I said mildly, but I was unnerved that he had spotted my interest so precisely. 'But I haven't been able to get a good look at her.' Nevertheless, there was something even then which was familiar about her hair.

Before I could stop him, Lothar waved over Madame.

'Ah, Suzanne,' she said. 'Yes, an excellent choice.'

She went directly to the table where the girl sat, and inwardly I writhed in an agony of embarrassment and excitement to have my secret desire so nakedly revealed. Madame leaned over the girl and whispered instructions in her ear. Suzanne turned to see the man who had requested her. When she looked in our direction I saw her face in full view for the first time, and the world lurched. My mind refused to work, to give her a name, but my heart thudded with sudden recognition.

'You look as if you've seen a ghost,' Lothar said.

It was the woman I knew as Stacia who walked toward me.

I turned to look at Lothar as if he could confirm that the experience I was undergoing was not a dream, and I regret that I allowed him the opportunity to see my expression during that moment of shock.

'You don't know her, do you?' he asked. He was looking at me closely, and I felt him reading my face like a page in a book.

It was too late to tell Madame that I had changed my mind, that she was not the one I wanted at all. Stacia wore her hair down and tied simply behind. She was indeed dressed like a girl and came forward with a sprightly, insouciant step, brushing her dress with her hands as a girl does who is unused to the outline of adult clothes, as if to suggest youth and innocence. It was play-acting, whorehouse make-believe which would deceive nobody, but I hoped that if she recognized me she would be able to cover her knowledge with the pantomime. Or better yet, I prayed the state of amnesia which Charcot had induced would hold. After all, she had more to lose by being recognized in such a place than I.

I told Lothar, 'For a moment she reminded me of someone I knew in Hungary, that's all.' I shrugged to suggest the absurdity of my overreaction. I managed a rueful smile, a wistful look. 'It was all a long time ago, but it ended quite badly.'

Stacia – Suzanne – sat down at our table. She smiled at me in the professional manner, and I gave silent thanks that she showed no sign of recognition.

'She's rather nice,' he said to me, talking about her in her presence quite openly and looking directly at Suzanne as if he were appraising a picture.

'Thank you,' she told him calmly, and turned her attention to me.

I had passed her on the stairs at the Salpêtrière, but I had not allowed myself more than a glance at her, because I did not want to attract her attention and so jeopardize the hypnotic suggestion which Charcot had placed within her subconscious. Now I saw that Stacia was somewhat older – I would put her at something approaching thirty – than she had appeared when I had first set eyes upon her during the demonstration. Her face was painted, and the colors and shades which had appeared confluent and natural across the room, decomposed as they do when one views an oil painting close to, so that she appeared bizarre and toylike. For a moment, I wondered whether I had been mistaken, that perhaps this was indeed another woman, that perhaps she was even Stacia's elder sister.

'You were the one who chose me?' she asked.

'Yes,' I confessed. It was not going to be as difficult as I had feared. Somehow the meeting seemed easier now.

'I like to be chosen,' Stacia said almost shyly. It could have been sincere. It didn't matter, any more than the flatness of stage scenery detracts from the drama which unfolds before it. She portrayed for me a good facsimile of coy attraction. I felt that I needed no more as I looked at her docile, downcast eyes which fluttered now under my gaze.

'You may take my hand, if you wish,' she said.

I did. 'So soft,' I murmured. I was falling into her idiom and already beginning to feel like a rustic swain wooing his tender shepherdess.

Lothar sat with his chin resting on his hand, observing our encounter with sardonic interest.

'Very nicely done!' he said. I wondered if he was jealous beneath his disengaged pose. He had taken the role of audience and critic, as if we were a play put on for his benefit. And in retrospect, that may have been close to the truth.

He refilled the glasses so casually, so apparently absentmindedly, that I hardly noticed mine was never empty, and so I never knew how much I drank.

'Shall I join you?' Lothar asked me in a matter-of-fact kind of way. It wasn't clear to me what he meant. He leaned across the table toward me with a drunken leer. 'After all, it can get lonely the first time.'

'A virgin!' Stacia said. She touched my cheek reverently with her fingertips. I had seen that gaze on the face of medical students who encounter a patient with a rare but celebrated disease.

'We could share her,' Lothar breathed. His languid pose had fallen away and his face was flushed with excitement.

I was speechless with revulsion and turned to Stacia for confirmation of what I suspected Lothar was proposing. But far from the outrage I expected from her, she seemed unconcerned.

'It'll cost you triple,' she told him.

'That is the most loathsome . . . degenerate . . .' I began, but I could see my words had no effect on him, and it was pointless to continue.

'Oh, come on! Don't be such a prude! I can give you some tips. Hints from an old hand.' He moved his fingers in a pliant and suggestive manner; the import of the gesture was lost to me though its purpose was unmistakably obscene. 'Back you up if you find yourself in a tight spot,' he said, thrusting in his chair and almost falling out of it. He found himself inordinately funny.

'I need no assistance from you!' I burst out. I recollected myself just in time. Lothar was provoking me, and I was giving him exactly the entertainment he was looking for. 'Perhaps I am not so inexperienced as you assume.'

My air of mystery merely drew him on. 'Oh,' he said in mock appreciation. 'Uh-huh?' he murmured, nodding his head slowly and staring at me all the while with that devilish, mischievous glint in his eyes.

'Yes, indeed,' I replied calmly. I was determined to lie in his teeth if he called my bluff. I gave Stacia's hand a reassuring squeeze and was gratified when she took it in both of hers.

'This experience being more in the line of observation than practical in nature?'

'Certainly. As a doctor, I've had certain dealings with women's bodies. When it comes to love, there are precious few mysteries for me in the physical department, I can tell you.'

'I was thinking more along the lines' – Lothar had made the sign of a keyhole between forefinger and thumb and held it to his eye like a monocle, turning about in his chair to survey different aspects of the room while he was speaking and coming to rest on me – 'of the peeking department.'

I had a nasty feeling about the direction the conversation was taking. 'The observations of a doctor are scientific and clinical. It's quite different from the lewd kind of voyeurism you go in for.'

Stacia was bored by our talk and now put my hand in her lap. That would have been unobjectionable, except that she opened her thighs and herded my fingers between them.

'I'm surprised you bring it up,' Lothar persisted.

'I didn't. You did.'

'The voyeurism, I mean.'

'I distinctly recall you mentioning that it was one of the specialties of the house.' I wondered where all this was leading, but felt on safe ground. I sipped wine in a relaxed fashion. What Lothar said next astounded me.

'I was thinking of the specialty of your house. Wasn't there some kind of optical contraption?' he asked.

I scoffed as if to say his bluff was called and he'd been caught grasping at straws. 'I haven't the faintest idea what you're talking about.' Although of course I did, but I saw he wasn't going to push it any further.

There is something exciting, erotically so, in almost being found out. Stacia had put my hand between her thighs, and I felt this was sufficient permission to advance it upwards, which I did slowly, feeling the swell of her inner thigh beneath the thin muslin of her frock. All the while I was staring Lothar in the eye, daring him to advance his thesis. I was working my hand upward with meticulous caution, almost at the portals of Venus, when I encountered another hand covering the object of my quest. Stacia's other hand was placed over mine, permitting and encouraging my secret exploration. I caressed the coy fingers which barred my way, as if to persuade them with the softness of my touch to allow passage. Stacia turned to me and smiled encouragement. She raised the flute of champagne to her lips and drank in obvious pleasure, while my emotions collapsed like a house of playing cards as I realized that the fingers even now entwining mine in that intimate place could not possibly be hers.

I recoiled in disgust and would have jumped up to confront Lothar, except that I had no desire to add to his amusement by revealing my state of arousal.

'Everything's a joke to you!' I exclaimed.

'More or less,' he agreed easily.

'You're depraved!'

'Aren't we all? Is there really such a difference between you and me? I'm more honest with myself, that's all.'

'Have you no shame?'

'It fades with practice. Doesn't it, Suzanne?'

I grasped Stacia's hand and sprang up, bringing her to her feet with me. My balance had not been tested when I was sitting down, and I now found that I was a lot less stable in the upright posture than I had expected. Stacia looped her arm through mine to steady me, and before I knew what was happening, we were climbing the staircase.

A diary should record the momentous events of one's life. This was my first night of love. Love! I have cocooned myself in a romantic myth. When I crossed the threshold of that room, when Stacia closed the door behind us, I lost all my gallant notions, all the observing capacity of the scientist or the transmuting spells of the poet or the tender feelings of the lover. I was a beast.

4

MORNING, MAY 28, 1866

With some trepidation, I return to the hospital today. It is impossible to delay it any longer. The day before yesterday, Roland knocked on my door to find out how I was. It was he who brought my note saying that I was unwell to Dr Ducasse.

'Just a hangover,' I told Roland. 'I'll be back on Monday.'

'Guard your liver,' he advised. 'It is the only organ of the body a man can't do without.'

The hangover was sufficiently cruel for me to look the part, although the excuse was only partly true. So much for the widely touted aphorism that the more one pays for the wine the night before, the less one pays in the morning. More to the point is a complete funk at coming face-to-face with Stacia. I have had carnal relations with a patient! I am not afraid that she will report me to Madame Verdun, since to do so she would have to reveal her nighttime employment. At bottom is the fear that I will see in her face the loathing which I feel for myself. I was like an animal, thrusting and sucking at every part of her body. I am revolted. I shudder when a detail comes unbidden to my mind. I do not know how she stood it. And then again, perhaps my behavior was no worse than that of the other clients such women must endure in their line of work. I cannot allow that consideration to excuse myself.

And Nichole? I have betrayed her. I had kept myself pure, if not for her then for someone, so far unknown, to whom I would eventually give my love. What am I now? Just another fast-and-loose, penniless man about town.

Lothar, on the surface so sleek, so urbane, is revealed as a degenerate. He is a perverse, corrupting influence. I will see him no more. Lothar parades his cynicism openly so that people are inclined to believe it is a pose to hide a sensitive, secretive nature. No one takes him at his word. He is without shame. He says so openly, but no one will believe him. He really does not appear to experience the normal constraints of society. Conscience, scruple, ideals, decency – these concepts are alien to his mind. This in itself is a phenomenon worthy of study. But I cannot pursue this relationship, even though the man interests me from the scientific point of view. In addition, he is without doubt sexually ambiguous.

I seem to remember Lothar making some oblique allusion to an 'optical contraption.' At the time I thought he was referring to an incident in my own life. Now that supposition seems rather farfetched. It was a lucky hit. Lothar sprinkles his conversation with all sorts of hints and double meanings. They are like hooks he baits to catch one of your secrets. Nothing delights him more than extracting a guilty secret. However, there is no way that he could have known that the phrase had any relevance to myself. It was a fishing expedition, no more than that. Nevertheless, this morning I have resolved to be starkly honest in this journal – harsh, even, if need be. It is the only antidote to my recent actions.

My father had a keen though amateur interest in science and had amassed a collection of optical instruments which passed to me on his death, since George would have no use for them. Among them was a telescope of unusual power. How embarrassing to record this! I had all but forgotten the incident. Or, at least, I had wanted to forget it.

Plumbing at the castle was – and is – of the most primitive kind. It consists of little more than downspouts which empty into the remains of the medieval moat on the north side. Taking a bath, consequently, is not a simple matter, but involves a relay of servants carrying hot water from the kitchens. This in turn requires some organization and supervision if the bath is to be filled before the water cools. Taking a bath, therefore, is a major, disruptive event in the household that requires advance notice, people entering and leaving the cavernous bath room, opening or closing windows depending on the season, and so on.

When Aunt Sophie and Nichole arrived for their visit, I was experimenting with my father's optical equipment, particularly the telescope in combination with a fine mirror. By positioning the mirror at a precise angle I found that I could see around corners. The system required a great deal of fiddling, since a small change in the angle of the mirror left me looking at a crack in the ceiling rather than the doorknob I wished to focus on. Moreover, once I had mastered the principle, there was nothing very interesting on which I could test my newfound skill.

Sophie and Nichole were used to bathing frequently. This was the custom in Paris, my mother told me. I suppose we must have appeared unwashed to them. On the side of the courtyard opposite the bath room were the old battlements, a place one would avoid walking when someone was taking a bath, and so the servants would throw open the room's windows in summer to let in any cooling breeze. I could not see directly into the bath room from my bedroom, but with careful adjustment of the inconspicuously placed mirror I could command a view of a small segment of the room. It required endless trips back and forth, up and down the winding stairs of the castle to focus the mirror on the bath, but by halfway through their stay I had perfected the technique. Some sense of propriety prevented me from using my telescope on my aunt. She was my mother's sister. Anyway, that wasn't the reason. The fact was that she did not interest me.

But I sweated and strained through that summer to catch a glimpse of Nichole. The vision as I eventually achieved it was blurred, something in the line of a sketch. But I remember how, with a shock that made my mouth dry and my knees feel weak so that I could hardly stand, I brought her into focus for the first time. She had the slimness of a girl with the rounding of her hips and buttocks hinting at future voluptuousness. Her breasts were buds, but she seemed most interested in this part of her body, holding them up and looking at herself from one angle and then another in the larger mirror beside the bath. I was intoxicated by the tiny triangle of dark hair beneath her belly and tried without success to bring this mystery into sharper focus.

Whenever Nichole's bath was ready, I found some reason to slip away. It was already accepted that solitary study was part of my nature. Over the weeks, I brought my telescope to bear less on the individual body parts and more on Nichole and her secret life when she thought herself alone, and I adjusted my mirror accordingly. I watched her as she danced in some imagined embrace, or stared at her image critically as she practiced a growing repertoire of facial expressions and gestures of a femme fatale, or as she lovingly followed the curving surfaces of her developing body. I should have felt guilty, but I didn't. I loved her. Then I might see her at tea later in the afternoon and our ordinary talk would have a deeper meaning because of my secret relationship with her secret self.

'Optical contraption.' Lothar shot an arrow blindly into the air and it landed on the target's bull's-eye. Nichole herself never knew I watched her.

While I am in the mood for confession, I must write to Gregory. I cannot tell him everything, because he has grown doctrinaire since the seminary and has little leeway in his opinions. But he will read between the lines. And if I write to Gregory, I must first send a letter to George and Elizabeth, since Gregory will take the first opportunity to call on them at the castle with my news. A letter from Elizabeth arrived yesterday care of the hospital, telling me I have been remiss in not writing to them. They are much preoccupied with Germany's belligerence toward the Empire and fear there will be war – at least, Elizabeth fears this; George, I am sure, relishes the prospect of charging into battle. I had not even been aware that a crisis existed, which shows how oblivious to worldly affairs I have become. Elizabeth writes: 'I say, "Phooey to Bismarck and his Prussian grenadiers!"' How simple life would be if women ran the world. She is modest and good – too good for George, since I believe he does not appreciate what a fine wife he has.

But these letters must wait until later. I can delay no longer. I must go now to the hospital and face whatever Stacia has in store for me.

EVENING

The sun was shining boldly, and I hurried because I was late, so that I was sweating and I'll admit somewhat flustered by the time I arrived at the Salpêtrière. I chose to enter through the west gate, which approaches the main building through the formal gardens. There is a watchman on the main gate at night, but the other entrances are close to frequented spots in the hospital, and I fancied that it would be the west gate through which Stacia would come and go, slipping around the edge of the garden in the shadows of the trees.

The gate was let into an arch in the ancient walls. It was a heavy, studded structure of old wood, but it opened without much effort and I passed into an avenue of pleached lime trees which formed one of the borders of the garden. The gate would be locked at night, so Stacia must have a key, or has negotiated some arrangement with the watchman.

I walked through the shade of the trees rather than in the intense sunlight of the garden, so that I was not readily noticeable to the old ladies sitting on benches by the flower beds or the occasional lunatic who roamed along the paths. In the distance I caught sight of two young women strolling arm in arm, and I stopped behind a tree to observe them as they came nearer in case one of them might be her. It was, indeed, Stacia, together with another of Charcot's 'specials' from the ward overseen by Madame Verdun. They were moving in a direction away from the building where I was headed, but I saw that if I walked quickly I would converge on them at the point where their path intersected one of the diagonals.

I hurried initially so that I could appear to be walking at my ease when I encountered them. Stacia appeared in animated conversation with her companion. They huddled in easy intimacy within the shade of the parasol they shared, and their laughter carried across the beds of geraniums, Stacia's voice rising musically above the other. I am ashamed to say that my heart raced in common lust and my eyes involuntarily sought out the curves and contours of her limbs beneath the simple gray dress she wore. I reminded myself that I was a doctor within the confines of a hospital, that I had a role there which was close to sacred. Stacia was without adornment or artifice, her manner natural and unaffected; there was nothing of the actress's sophisticated simplicity of the night before, no provoking gesture or enticing glance. This was a far different creature from the one with whom I had debased myself. Still I desired her with an animal passion I could not stem.

Her companion appeared to notice my presence first. I wondered what they had been talking about, because she cautioned Stacia that they might be overheard, and their demeanor became immediately more restrained. Stacia's companion was known to me by sight, as I must have been to her, and she primped and gave sidelong glances in my direction as single women do at the approach of an eligible man. Stacia paid no attention, even when the convergence of the paths we had chosen brought us almost together.

I stopped to let them pass and lifted my hat. Their comportment was formal and unexceptionably respectful as they curtsied in acknowledgment. And that was all, except that I believe I discerned in Stacia's companion the hint of a coquettish moue. Stacia herself gave no hint of recognition either in friendliness or revulsion.

They passed on, and I stood alone, nonplussed, bareheaded in the blinding sun. I asked myself if perhaps her extraordinary hypnotic capacity was at work here. Could she have blanked out the events of the previous evening so that her actions – and, mercifully, mine – were no longer available to her conscious mind? Charcot had described in a lecture rare cases in which a person has led parallel lives, with two personae, each unaware of the doings of the other, and I wondered whether this could be true of Stacia: a demure and modest subject by day and a whore by night.

As I entered the building which housed my ward and the special ward for Charcot's women, I remembered the laughter of Stacia and her companion, which they had cut short as I approached, and it occurred to me that their conversation could have concerned myself. These women had nothing to do all day and were notorious gossips and flirts. I have caught snatches, which obviously the woman intended for me to overhear as I climbed the staircase to the ward above, of their discussions dissecting some imagined interest shown them by a doctor, or their bitter complaints over some minor slight or preference shown to another. My doings of two nights ago might now be common knowledge. I braced myself, therefore, for a sudden silence as I passed through their midst, and waited, my nerves on edge, for the sudden titter as I turned at the top of the stairs. Instead, I encountered their studied indifference as they continued their conversations apparently oblivious to my presence.

With a sense of relief, I hung up my jacket in the writing room and took a white starched apron from the locker. I was in the act of tying the strings before me as I hurried onto the ward, head down, hoping Dr Ducasse would not notice my lateness, but he turned from the patient whose arm he was examining as I passed.

'I trust you are feeling better, Doctor,' he called to me.

'Thank you, yes,' I replied. 'A touch of the grippe. Nothing serious.'

He turned away with a look which I think was disapproving. I feel he has put me down as a slacker with a private income, who has turned to medicine as a form of entertainment. Nothing could be further from the truth. He misunderstands my enthusiasm. Perhaps he takes it for idle curiosity. Once again he assigned me the dullest group of patients. They suffer from various palsies, which I am to catalog and determine whether they are associated with other symptoms.

He called me back. 'The lady with the arthropathies whom you clerked on Friday?'

'Yes?' This was the grand courtesan who in her old age had fallen on hard times. I was afraid he had found something important that I had missed.

'She has developed further symptoms, apparently. Would you be so good as to examine her again?'

'Of course.'

I had expected my work at the Salptrire to open fresh vistas, but it was becoming increasingly dreary. I did not wish to be a mason of science, laying one stone – one fact – upon another, day after day, slowly working on a corner of an edifice whose completion I might never see. When I left Budapest I had in mind the role of architect. I suppose that was naive, and even vain.

The woman was waiting for me in pleasurable expectation. She had the bearing of a lady and carried herself well even in her old age. Time had not been kind, and yet she retained some faded residue of what had once been beauty. I thought I detected spots of rouge on her cheeks, and as I bent over her, I caught the distinct scent of perfume. It struck me as odd, although I was hardly going to complain, since any change from the customary uriniferous miasma which hung about these women was a welcome relief.

'Dr Ducasse informed me that you have reported a new symptom,' I began.

'That I have,' she replied, and I thought I detected a glint in her eye of suppressed excitement. She cast a sidelong glance at the nurse who accompanied me. 'It's something of a personal nature. If you take my meaning,' she simpered.

I nodded for the nurse to bring the screens which offered some sparse privacy on the barracklike ward.

'Very well, then,' I said when the screens were in place around her bed.

'It's a matter of the heart,' she murmured delicately. 'I feel a flutter of my heart.'

The nurse helped her undo the bodice of her dress while I turned away to consult my notebook to refresh my memory of my previous finding in the case. With one hand she held up the material of her dress to cover her ancient breasts and offered the other to me so that I might feel her pulse while I pressed my ear against the back of her chest to perform the auscultation. At first I could not make out the sounds of her heart beneath the rattling of her breathing, but as I focused on the pulse at my fingertips I discerned the faint drumming within and marveled once more at the organ whose blind, fragile persistence sustained life within this dried-up old woman.

'I can hear nothing untoward,' I started to say when I became aware that she had taken away the wrist whose pulse I had been palpating and now took my hand in hers. There was something between our two palms. On an impulse, I directed the nurse to hand her a cup of water which stood on the table beside the bed, and while the nurse's head was turned, the object was transferred from her hand to mine.

'Very well. You can get dressed now,' I said. With my notebook under one arm, and keeping both hands behind me, I maneuvered backwards between the screens into the ward.

Now that I was free to manipulate it, I could feel that the object was a piece of paper folded into a tight wad. I was making my way swiftly along the aisle between the rows of beds, heading for a quiet spot in the library where I could peruse this mysterious message, when Ducasse called me.

'Come and tell me what you think of this.'

He had Roland and the other assistants gathered around a seated patient. I hesitated, not knowing what to do with the object clenched in my fist. I did not want the sharp–eyed Ducasse to see me stuff something as intriguing as a note obtained from one of his patients into my jacket pocket, nor could I surreptitiously, with a casual gesture, slip it into one of the pockets of my trousers. The truth of the matter is that my trousers are ancient, and both pockets have such large holes in them that I cannot even trust them to retain a handkerchief.

'Come and take a look at this woman's neck,' he commanded. I think Ducasse means well. His gruff manner may be suited to hectoring medical students, but it is extremely irritating to colleagues. I kept my hands behind my back and scrutinized the woman's scrawny neck.

'Well?' Ducasse asked impatiently. The others, I could see from their smug expressions, were already appraised of the secret. It would be something obscure, but obvious once one recognized what it was. Unfortunately, I could see no abnormality. I was about to tell Ducasse this.

'Well, come on, man, you can't make a diagnosis with your hands behind your back. Examine the patient!'

I moved behind the woman to the position to palpate her neck. Now that I was on the other side of the patient, facing Ducasse and the others, I felt I could drop the wad of paper and take the risk of recovering it later. I handed my notebook to Roland to hold, shuffling my feet as I did so in order to cover the sound of the paper falling to the floor.

The patient's neck was so thin, so devoid of subcutaneous fat, that the major anatomical landmarks were as sharply defined to my probing fingers as if she had been dissected. I located the strap muscles and moved forward to the pulsating cords of her carotid arteries. I asked the nurse to give her water so that I might feel the thyroid gland as she swallowed. Again I felt nothing that should not be there and everything which should be there. Ducasse stroked his beard as he watched my face for signs of discovery or the gradual fluster of a fruitless search. I gave him nothing. I allowed my eyes to wander as one does when one is concentrating on one's fingertips, but none of the others were willing to give me a clue. My hands dropped down to the woman's shoulders and almost absentmindedly my thumbs traced the groove between the clavicles and the edge of the trapezius muscle. On the left side, my thumb stumbled over a nodule, hard as a pebble, halfway along the bone. I stiffened at the contact with this palpable manifestation of death.

Ducasse saw that I had found it, the little seed tucked so innocently behind the clavicle, cast off from that malignant flower which bloomed deep within her body.

'I thought that you would be interested in a sign whose significance was discovered by one of your countrymen,' he said.

'Professor Virchow is German,' I corrected him. 'I am Hungarian.'

The distinction did not interest Ducasse. He shrugged, as if to say, 'I do not care to understand these distant politics.' He was not to be deflected from his quest. 'But you are aware of the condition associated with Virchow's node?' he persisted.

The woman was looking from one of us to the other, no doubt both awed and terrified by the close interest of these gentlemen. She reminded me of a small bird which has flown into a room and now, panicked, cannot find its way out and flies against the glass of the window panes.

'I hesitate to say.'

'Do you know?'

'Yes, I do.'

'Then say it, if you know. Otherwise let someone else take the question.'

'Cancer of the stomach.' I breathed the words rather than spoke them aloud, but she heard them clear enough and her hands went in horror to cover her mouth. The nurse stepped forward to comfort her, and the simple act of kindness so disarmed her that she let out a sob.

Having done his damage, Dr Ducasse now patted the poor woman's shoulder to no avail. I risked a quick glance at the floor behind me, but I did not see the note. The others were discreetly leaving the scene as the cries of the poor woman gathered force.

'Come, it's not a death sentence,' Ducasse lied without much conviction, bringing forth moans and a flood of tears from the patient.

Other nurses were putting screens in place and during this distraction I had felt able to change my position and cast about more openly for the message. It was nowhere to be found.

Dr Ducasse beckoned me away. 'Let's leave this to the nurses,' he said.

In a manner I was afraid would appear dangerously contrived, I let drop a sheet of paper from my notebook and stooped to pick it up. From my squatting position I could survey the floor for several meters on either side of me. There could be no doubt: The message had disappeared. I could delay no longer and followed Ducasse through the screens the nurses had placed.

'Did you see it?' he asked me.

'No,' I replied in some consternation, wondering how he could have been aware of what I had done from his point of view on the other side of the patient.

He looked at me shrewdly. 'Be honest,' he coaxed. 'Someone tipped you off, didn't they?'

It took me a moment to realize he was talking about the lymph node, not the note. It was hard to hide the emotional relief which flooded me and must have been evident to so acute an observer as Ducasse. I hoped to pass it off as the embarrassment of modesty. 'No, I just happened upon it,' I said. 'Good luck, more or less.'

'Perhaps.' Dr Ducasse turned to go, then said in grudging praise, 'But no one else found it.'

Why had I been so furtive about the message before Ducasse, and why now was I thrown into turmoil at its disappearance, if I did not already have some intimation, some guilty hope, of what its contents might be? Why did I fear that it would incriminate me if another found it? Why did I so intensely lament its loss? The answer, in short, is that I knew – I longed – for the message to be from Stacia.

Someone picked it up. Doctors being what they are – believing in their God-given right to nose into anyone's business – that person has read it by now. I can only hope that it will not identify me.

I found Roland in the library, and after a great deal of inward argument finally decided to ask him quietly if he had noticed a piece of paper I dropped when I examined the patient.

'You handed me your notebook,' he said abstractedly without looking up from the monograph which absorbed him. I hesitated to ask him to reconsider in case I should turn what I wanted to appear as a minor inconvenience into a significant event. Above all, I wanted to avoid arousing his curiosity. I must have hovered over him a moment too long, for he looked up. 'Sorry,' he said. 'Was it important?'

'No,' I averred a trifle hastily. 'Some observations I jotted down while I was examining a patient. Rough notes. It's just that I'd hate to have to repeat the exam.'

'In your notebook, surely?'

'I'm sure it will turn up sooner or later. I must have put it down somewhere without thinking.'

'Lucky for you you hit on that node. I thought you'd never find it.'

'Yes, I was lucky.'

'There's no reason for false modesty, you know.' I thought there was a sour tone to his voice. 'Spotting a supraclavicular node may rank as a coup in Budapest, or Warsaw, or wherever, but in Paris we take that kind of thing for granted.'

'Anyone could have found it. I just happened to be the one, that's all.'

'That's what I'm trying to tell you. You shouldn't assume that because Charcot happens to pick you entirely at random in a lecture that you stand out in any fashion.' He chuckled in a way which seemed forced, as if intent on proving that the matter was really of no importance to him. 'Everybody found it, you know,' he said, already immersed again in his book. I was sorry to see his jealousy, because I had thought we might become friends in spite of the difference in our backgrounds.

The environment at the Salptrire is an intensely competitive one; few permanent positions become available, and the assistantships in which Roland and myself are employed carry meager stipends. The intention is for a doctor to fill the position temporarily, gain training in the specialty of neurology, and return from whence he comes. Except that everyone, once they arrive at this medical Mecca, scrambles to remain here, with the consequence that mature men, of some distinction, and family men, labor in humble roles and vie with one another when there occurs one of those sparse opportunities in which they can demonstrate ability to their superiors. Advancement depends on recognition, but how to be recognized? I suppose the node was such an occasion.

I have no reason to know for sure, since we have never established an intimacy in which such matters could be discussed, but I think Roland has even slimmer means than my own, and his family is not able to help him. Perhaps he saw that the opportunity which was so crucial to his own hopes of distinguishing himself did not matter to me. That bounty of chance was squandered on this

72

aristocratic dilettante. No doubt the irony engages his republican sentiments. I would rather have the note.

In the afternoon there was something of a stir which can only have inflamed Roland's prejudices about me. The Berthiers' footman arrived on the ward with several flunkies who accompanied him ostensibly to help him find his way but in reality to satisfy their own curiosity. The hospital has any number of these older men and women who do not seem to have any clear function other than to spy and gossip and, I suspect, to collect bribes for various petty favors.

I heard the commotion from behind the screens which had been placed around the bed of the patient I was examining and paid no attention, until I heard my name. I emerged to find the same young man who on previous occasions had ventured close to insolence in his manner toward me. Now I was gratified to see how extremely uncomfortable he was after an hour or so of wandering lost in a lunatic asylum, disoriented and sweating in the hot sun, and no doubt afraid to ask directions from any of the patients he encountered in case he should set them off. In fact, his demeanor showed both relief and a fulsome attempt to convey the respect in which he had been remiss, sensing that his journey back to the sane world might well depend on my good graces.

How marvelous of Nichole to have sent him on this errand! For the card he delivered to my hand was from her, with apologies for the impromptu nature of the invitation, but suggesting that, as a poet myself, I would allow the muse some forbearance. Tonight there is to be a reception for a poet (it was not a name I recognized) who has consented to read some of his latest work.

On the back of my card I scribbled, 'I shall be delighted!' and gave it to the man. The intrusion had collected quite an audience. The patients stared openly, nurses interrupted their tasks, and even a few of the other doctors found reasons to busy themselves in the vicinity. I directed an overseer to show the footman the way back to the main gate. When I returned to the patient behind the screens, I could hear the sudden buzz of speculation. When later that afternoon I left the ward early, they nudged one another or drew the attention of someone nearby. The people about me pay attention to my comings and goings, and I think I am developing a reputation as a man of mystery and intrigue, a man with friends in high places.

I had to leave early to be at the tailor shop before it closed. I was going to put off my final fitting because I cannot possibly afford the suit, although the manager assured me this morning that it would be ready. Lothar's breezy talk of a gentleman's right to credit was all very well for a man of his means. While I had been with him I had somehow slipped into his way of thinking – a devil-damn-the-consequences attitude – which had seemed so liberating after my cautious and constraining upbringing. In retrospect, I think I must have been under his spell. It had evaporated the next day, and ever since I have been awaiting the day of reckoning in which the steely-eyed manager leads a posse of bailiffs to my door.

Now, quite simply, I needed the suit. I did not want to appear again as the poor relation amid the splendor and opulence of the Berthiers' home dressed, as Lothar put it, in my heirloom. Who knew what people might be saying behind my back? Most importantly, I do not want Nichole to feel ashamed of me. I cannot bear that she would think of me as the country cousin from the backwoods of Transylvania. Rather, I want her to consider me a rising young scientist-doctor, a man of the future, a man who mingles naturally with *tout le monde*.

I have tried on the suit once. I dashed in this morning when I should have been on my way to the hospital, claiming to be in a terrible hurry, with the implication that I could stand still long enough for the fitter to chalk a line here or let out a seam there, but that I had no time to waste on business matters. Even at that first fitting it was a marvel of elegance, and I longed to possess it. I dreamed of distinguished heads turning in appreciation as I strode forward to be received by Madame Berthier with Nichole smiling admiringly at her side, of women turning to one another to whisper, Who is he?

This afternoon the manager fussed about me. I think he was relieved that I had actually come to take possession of the suit. The fit is perfect. The trousers show my figure to advantage without hindering movement, and the coat contrives exactly the right balance between fashionable panache and sober substantiality.

I turned about before the three mirrors to see the splendid thing from all sides. How odd to catch sight of the back of one's head, or to study oneself from the side studying oneself! Change the point of view, and everything is different. It was a strange sensation to be unfamiliar to myself.

'I'll wear it,' I announced.

'And these?' the manager inquired. He gestured indecisively in the direction of the suit I had removed.

'I'm sure you know a worthy cause,' I responded grandly. I felt it was expected of me.

I then made my exit. I was gracious, noble, debonair, appreciative, and swift. The manager, with some exertion on his part, kept up with me, and I couldn't outpace him along the shop's aisle without revealing, with the inevitable collapse of credit, my hurry. I wasn't sure whether, being of short stature, he was merely struggling to keep up with me or whether he was trying to overtake me before I could reach the door. To avoid any unseemliness I stopped before some hats.

He cleared his throat several times but seemed unable to find the correct form of address for collecting money from a count. Having guillotined their aristocracy, the French are now the biggest snobs in Europe. A fitting penance.

I mimed coming to a decision. 'Perhaps another time,' I said, indicating the hats, and began to move toward the door.

'There is the matter of the bill, Count,' he began with a sickly smile.

'By all means,' I replied. I had taken to imagining Lothar's presence, and the trick brought out in me an insouciance I didn't know I had. 'Put it on my account, why don't you?'

'Of course,' he said unhappily. 'But I was wondering . . .'

'Yes?'

'Whether you would care to . . .'

'To demonstrate my good faith? Of course.'

'No!' He was aghast at his indiscretion.

'But, of course.'

'No, please, Count!'

'But I'm a complete stranger, and I can quite understand . . .'

'Count, please accept that I would never question – never!'

I watched his anguish and I felt some new potential awaken inside me. I sighed benevolently. He felt forgiven. 'Whatever arrangements you think fit,' I told him as he ushered me through the door.

Power does not reside in laws alone. I have been surrounded by rules and regulations, from Uncle Kalman and the Jesuits at St Sebastian's to the pedants at the University. Now I am here in Paris to discover new ones, the laws of nature as they apply to the mind. I have kept to the paths of life and I have not strayed. Now I am beginning to wonder: Is there really anyone who enforces the 'Keep off the grass' rule written on the signs along the pathways? And if there is, is he paying any attention to me? I had no money, and yet the tailor had made me a beautiful new suit.

I walked the short distance down the side street into the fine afternoon sunlight on the Rue de Rivoli and paused at the curb before crossing to the Tuileries Gardens. I wanted to savor the moment. The street was crowded at that hour; some people were hurrying about their business, others promenaded at their leisure. They passed about me, but I was distinct. I was a butterfly emerging from the cocoon; I stretched my limbs to feel the fit of the splendid, fresh covering and I felt myself fill and take possession of this new embodiment.

I was full of excitement at seeing Nichole again. The invitation was a special one; she had taken the time to write on it herself, and I doubted that this was a favor which she extended to many other people. And she had alluded to the poem I had written her. She could not know the pangs of humiliation I had suffered from having revealed myself to her in such a demeaning way. All poetry seemed to me mincing and effete. Tenderness was weakness. I had destroyed my work by tearing the poem into tiny flakes which I scattered from the height of the castle's tower, and they floated down, turning and spreading in the air, to land in the moat where they floated on the surface amongst the bloated sewage. I almost followed them.

My visit to the tailor had taken longer than I had expected, and I was late arriving at the Berthiers' house. On entering the reception rooms, I was surprised to see so many people there at such short notice. Apparently the poet Stanislowski is a follower of Baudelaire and quite the coming thing. The man was dressed in the most extraordinary get-up, part Montmartre *apache*, part Gypsy prince. He had long black hair swept back from his pallid forehead, with lugubrious, elongated features and doleful eyes. He looked most woebegone and unhealthy, which of course contributed to his air of fashionable spirituality. He accentuated this with a stance full of pathos, suggesting suffering too profound for words. He is stooped with the massive burden of creativity upon his narrow shoulders.

I saw him as little more than a circus turn, although I was told that it was something of a coup for Aunt Sophie to have lured him to her salon, since he rarely consents to give readings beyond the circle of his devotees who gather about him in the back room of an obscure café. Many clustered about him in the hope that Sophie would introduce them to this celebrity. He was mostly listening to what people were telling him (lavish praise, no doubt), and I gather the main purpose of this preliminary was to allow himself to be looked at from close quarters, much as one might peruse an animal at the zoo: This subversive, this decadent, this disciple of evil could be viewed in a comfortable reception room just as one might stare with impunity into the eyes of the tiger through the bars of his cage. How thrilling for the assembled company to have in their midst this man whose reputation springs from his cry to overthrow the very values and institutions upon which their comfort is based! Stanislowski was like the magician who is paid to perform at a children's party: His job is to frighten and shock, but only up to a precisely regulated degree.

Aristide Berthier received me most warmly. I have the impression that he feels himself to be an outsider at these gatherings. It is Aunt Sophie and Nichole who are the moving force behind the family's social ambitions, and Aristide wanders around the outskirts of the occasion nodding abstractedly at people whom he ought to greet while he cooks up fresh financial schemes in his head. For some reason, he has taken a shine to me. I have a feeling that this derives from some fondness he felt for my mother.

'Here he is!' he exclaimed on catching sight of me.

I was surprised and looked around to see whom else he might be addressing, but he advanced to take my hand and put his other hand on my shoulder in a fatherly gesture.

'My boy, this is a night when we have special need of your services.'

As is often the case, I didn't recognize that his intention was humorous and expected to see some commotion where a lady had fainted from an overzealous maid lacing her corsets too tightly.

'Did you ever see such hysteria?' he asked, indicating the flurry of activity around the poet.

'The fellow's something of a poseur, I'd say.'

'But he pleases the ladies,' Aristide sighed.

'And that's what counts,' Lothar put in, appearing suddenly at my elbow. 'Good evening, sir,' he said, shaking hands in a most proper and respectful manner which I knew to be entirely foreign to his nature. 'Never seen such a turnout to hear poetry.'

'He's the sensation of the season, they say. Everyone's here to be seen.'

Lothar turned as if to survey the crowd, but leaned close to Aristide. 'Many thanks, by the way, for your advice on Occidental Traders,' he murmured.

Aristide beamed. 'Are you having a good ride?'

'A damned good gallop!'

They both laughed.

'Very good,' Aristide said. 'Easy to mount. Easy to ride. The trick is knowing when to get off. You're on your own there,' he said as he moved on.

'You caused something of a sensation yourself,' Lothar drawled in the same conspiratorial aside with which he had thanked Aristide.

'I prefer to forget the whole thing.'

'A man never forgets his first time.'

'It's not something I feel particularly proud of.'

'But you should, old chap. Caused quite a stir with the ladies, I can tell you. An astonishing debut.'

'I have my reputation to think of.'

'Your reputation is made.'

'I do wish you'd shut up.'

'Next time it's on you. You can use your ill-gotten gains from Occidental Traders which Uncle Aristide so kindly dropped into our laps.'

'What you do with your money is of no concern of mine. I know that I will never again enter that depraved place.'

'Now is that entirely fair? Is it the place itself that's depraved? Surely not. Is it the ladies? They're just trying to oblige. Or is it the clientele? What would you say? Hmm?'

'I think I'd rather listen to poetry,' I said and began to walk away.

'The coat is absolutely right,' I heard him say.

I made straight for Nichole. Her smile opened a passage

for me through the crowd. I took her hand and thought I detected a welcoming pressure in her fingertips, a fondness within the public courtesies, and most uplifting of all, a hesitation, a hint of confusion and shyness in my presence.

'Mama,' she said, turning to my aunt. 'Don't you think we should begin the program? Everyone is here.'

'Very well, my dear.' She looked around for her husband and beckoned him with her fan. 'Aristide, let us lead the way.'

Nichole turned to me and I took her cue without a moment's hesitation. 'May I escort you?' I asked.

'Of course,' she replied and took my arm.

I felt that she wanted to convey by her tone that although it was for me to request, she had already decided that I was to escort her before I had made up my mind to ask.

'And do you still compose?' she asked innocently as we walked to the front of the rows of seats which the servants had arranged before the piano.

'You read my last work,' I replied. I felt a sadness I had not expected.

'And was it your best work?'

I was reluctant to make myself vulnerable to her again, since I sensed that what was for myself a memory of treasured poignancy was for Nichole merely a pretext for play. Nevertheless, I said, 'It was the best thing I ever wrote.'

'It was kind of dreamy,' she said with a wistful sigh. 'I still have it, you know, in one of my boxes of treasures, somewhere. Every so often I come across it and take it out and read it and think of those times.' She turned to me suddenly with a frank and earnest stare. 'Do you think me hopelessly sentimental?'

'No,' I replied helplessly.

'But I am. I'm a slave to emotion.'

'I would never have guessed.'

'No?' she asked me with a curiosity which seemed more genuine than ingenuous.

'Honestly. I think of you as being so self-possessed.'

'So you do think of me from time to time?'

'Every waking moment,' I blurted out. Even though it wasn't strictly true, there are so few opportunities for us to converse privately that I felt the exaggeration was fair.

'Now you're the sentimental one,' she said in a deep and mysterious voice as I leaned over her to move the chair in place behind her.

On Nichole's left sat her father. Lothar had somehow managed to insinuate himself into the seat on my right by escorting Nichole's friend Amie. While we waited for Stanislowski to take his place beside the piano, Lothar was constantly leaning across me to whisper some inconsequential remark to Nichole. The two of them seemed to enjoy a facet of humor which was imperceptible to me. Lothar snickered, and Nichole mimed disapproval with pursed lips while the rest of her face warmed with an expression of indulgent complicity. Amie was recruited with a quick aside from Lothar and responded with a suppressed giggle which sounded like a hiccup. I sat in the middle of these exchanges, yet alienated, sensing an undercurrent, convinced that Lothar's real purpose was to allude to a secret familiarity with Nichole. Then, as if to indicate that he included me within the charmed circle, he had the habit of placing his hand on my knee in a manner which made me decidedly uncomfortable. And I was confused by Nichole's affectionate overtures when at the same time she could be so mistaken about something as important to me as the poem.

Finally, Stanislowski shuffled on. Chatter petered out and a silence fell upon the room. He stood with one hand on the piano and the other clutching a sheaf of papers behind his back; his head was bowed. At first I thought he was talking to himself, mumbling indistinctly without any sign that he was addressing his audience, but apparently this was part of the appeal of his delivery. Gradually, his voice gathered volume, although I was still hard put to make sense of the staccato phrases he tossed in our general direction. But Nichole squeezed my arm in excitement, and I turned to see her expression of intense sensitivity, her lips parted and moist, a hectic color over her cheekbones, her very being tuned to the meaning which moved beneath the sound of his words. He had talent, that waiflike man, I will not deny it. When I settled and allowed his words to enter my mind without the intervention of the critical gatekeeper, they cast a melancholy, luxurious spell upon me, and I ventured to take Nichole's hand during one such affecting moment and felt the urgent pressure of her response.

I had forgotten the magical power of words. It was illusion, nothing more, and yet the enchantment which bound Nichole and myself in one common consciousness was real enough. I cannot let it go. I will not repudiate it. The poet spoke of decay which lies at the center of life, the worm within the bud, the sensuousness of blown roses, open and loose and so far beyond ripeness that a touch will destroy them, the petals fluttering to the ground to reveal the naked stem, the seed to be. I do not know how he did it, layering phrases one upon the other, or why the audience tolerated his decadent, perverse skill. We were his subjects, just as Charcot manipulates the emotions of his hysterics. I felt a quiver run through me as I gave myself up to the flow of impressions the poet evoked, and I saw tears of longing in Nichole's eyes which she did not attempt to hide from me. I would satisfy that passion if I could. If I could make her find me worthy.

5

MAY 31, 1866

When I was with Nichole, I forgot about Stacia. Apparently there is not room in a man's heart for the sacred and the profane at the same time. I am a miserable wretch to have allowed her to slip from my thoughts so easily. She is in dire straights, I know it. There was a hush when I entered the ward building of the Salpêtrière this morning. The usual vivacious chatter of Charcot's special patients about the stairwell was stilled. Few were in evidence, and those who draped themselves about the banister and the railings appeared listless and depressed.

I registered none of this until later, being preoccupied with my happy prospects with Nichole. Upstairs, the ward was unusually quiet. One bed in a corner had been screened off, a conspicuous break with the day's routine which usually signified that one of the old women was in the process of dying. Even more untoward, Madame Verdun, who generally had little to do with the upper ward, emerged full of bustling efficiency from behind the screened area and strode past me as if I had been invisible. Junior doctors as a rule were a species for which she had little regard and she ignored us whenever possible, so I did not take her behavior personally. It was said she had been let down by a doctor who led her on with vague promises of marriage.

One becomes oblivious to the niceties of normal life after one has spent some time in a charity hospital. It seems that dignity, individuality, and privacy are things one relinquishes along with worldly goods on passing through the main gate. Their loss is part of the loss of poverty. And so, being curious, I did not hesitate to step inside the screened area. It never occurred to me that I required due cause or even permission to enter there.

Stacia, pallid as the gray sheets on which she lay, turned her head from me. I took one step toward her and then noticed the bandages which swathed her wrists.

'Go!' she hissed. She would not look at me. In anger? In shame? Only her fierce, cornered defiance was clear.

Madame Verdun, her approach so silent that I was unaware of her presence until she brushed past me into the screened enclave, turned to face me at the foot of the bed.

'Doctor?' she inquired coldly.

'I had thought . . . one of my patients,' I mumbled.

'Evidently not.'

I lingered under her dispassionate gaze. I did not want to leave without saying something to Stacia, but Madame Verdun made that impossible. I dithered, if the truth be told. 'My apologies,' I said, retreating.

Composing myself on the other side of the screen, I went in search of someone who could tell me what had happened. Stacia was a celebrity within the confines of the Salpêtrière, in part for her looks, in part for her virtuosity as a hypnotic subject. When it came to Charcot's Friday demonstrations she was a star; within the small world of the hospital, she was accorded some of the admiration and acclaim bestowed on a famous actress in the world outside. Anyone who had spent more than an hour in the Salpêtrière that morning would know the story. Rather than ask one of my colleagues, I chose a nurse who was folding linen in the pantry.

'What's up with Stacia?' I inquired in a sidelong, conspiratorial whisper.

She was flattered by the opportunity to gossip with a doctor and paused only to look right and left to make sure that Madame Verdun did not catch her slacking. 'Dr Ducasse sewed her up himself,' she said significantly.

It was a mark of Stacia's status within the institution. 'She slashed her arms to bits. With a scalpel,' she added with melodramatic emphasis.

My eyes closed involuntarily and I shuddered.

'Fifty-four stitches!'

I tried not to imagine the gaping flesh.

'She could have bled to death,' the girl persisted. She was delighted with the effect her intelligence had upon me.

I tried to deflect her from details which were beginning to unnerve me. 'And did she do it here in the hospital?' I asked stupidly.

She gave me a look of curiosity, and I saw that I had clumsily released a new possibility for her to consider. 'Why, of course,' she answered. 'Where else could she have done it?'

'It's too bad. Altogether too bad,' I blustered. 'Do we have any idea why she did this terrible thing?'

The girl was coy. 'What are the reasons for a young woman to attempt her own life?'

I cast about and would not say. Pregnancy was the first thing that came to mind.

'What could it be but a matter of the heart?' she whispered. She rocked her shoulders and tilted her head in a flirtatious manner.

I drew back in astonishment. It was my own turn to be coy. 'But here?' I pressed her. 'How could such circumstances arise here within the hospital?'

In answer she only continued her knowing look.

EVENING

Throughout the long day, I have expected a tap on the shoulder, a quiet word in my ear, indicating that the note had been found and that I had been summoned to account for myself. At any moment, I expected to be packed off to Budapest in disgrace. Yet I do not know for sure whether the message implicates me. Perhaps it is the stirring of an uneasy conscience, and I have nothing in reality to fear.

This evening, the servant woman brought up to my room a bowl of the stew they call ragout, but I have no appetite. Madame Thébauld, the concierge, hovering with a vulture's scent for misfortune, ascended the stairs to ask if I am sick. I heard her footstep approach along the passage, and then she waited outside my door for several minutes, listening I suppose, as if I might talk to myself, rave, cry out, or harangue hallucinations. She knows I have no visitors whose conversation she can listen in on. Growing impatient eventually, she knocked on the door.

'Are you not well, Doctor?' she inquired, peering about my room.

'Madame, I do not know what could have given you that idea.'

'Why, you did not eat any supper! How are you to keep up your strength?'

I was at a loss to chose among the diverse lies which presented themselves to my mind. 'A minor bout of indigestion. Please do not concern yourself.'

'Are you sure?'

'Absolutely. But I thank you for your inquiry.' It does not pay to get on the wrong side of this woman.

'Very well,' she conceded doubtfully.

Before she left she passed me an envelope, almost as an after-thought. It is the tailor's bill, a fantastic amount which I cannot possibly pay. I know that I cannot ask George for money. I do not know where to turn. I have never been in debt before. What will they do if I cannot pay it? I imagine myself being hauled off to prison in the middle of the night, but I think this has more to do with my guilty feelings over what has happened to Stacia.

I have examined my face in the mirror to see if there has been any perceptible change. It is pale and drawn, and there is a feverish animation to my eyes. I am thinking of Stacia's pallor and of the deep gashes in her arms. What does it take to inflict that upon oneself? Is it desperation? Or a perverse courage? Or is it some wild abandon (whatever the opposite may be of the self-possession we modern men so value) which alone permits full vent to fury, to cut and slash and strike blood? My mind flinches from the thought. I cannot get my imagined fingers to pick up the razor, to bare my arm. And yet she did it. Stacia laid open her soft white skin and watched the hot blood well up and overflow the wound. The salty tang is in my mouth, as if, with a kiss, I could seal the lips of those cut edges. I must not torment myself with these thoughts.

I have wondered how much of my decision to become a doctor was to prove to George that I would not shrink from blood and gore. After he was commissioned into the hussars, George was full of tales of frightful gashes from the saber, of limbs torn from men's bodies by whistling cannon balls, or, and this intrigued the philosopher in me, the physical disappearance of an entire company of infantry who charged a battery just at the moment that the guns discharged a load of grapeshot. These tales were of a kind with the stories of hunting mishaps with which he had frightened me when we were boys.

In the event, I proved him wrong, but by then the point no longer mattered. Blood did perturb me, but for reasons quite opposite to those I had feared. I remember the first operation I witnessed. A child, a boy I think, was held down in order to drain an empyema within the right lung. We students gathered in a circle around the bench as the professor, seemingly oblivious to the child's terrified screams, prepared to insert the trocar into his chest. He looked up to ensure that we marked how he had determined the precise point of penetration. We were all restless, eyes averted as much as was possible, not wanting to look, but knowing that we had to appear to be paying attention. I did not shrink from it. I found myself transfixed by the sight of it, eyes staring at the helpless boy, heart palpitating, rooted to the spot.

I suppose a neurologist would refer to my sympathy with the suffering patient as a fascination. I felt a potent mixture of horror and furtive, tingling excitement. Women in childbirth were the cases which most affected me. And of course at the teaching hospital, it was the disasters of Mother Nature which we saw most often. I remember one young woman in particular. She had given birth the day before but was hemorrhaging still from the retained afterbirth. She seemed to possess an otherworldly beauty. Perhaps it was the blood loss, but she seemed to me as pale as an angel. There was a sheen of perspiration on her face which glistened as she rolled her head this way and that on the stretcher; she was possessed by that restless apprehension which comes upon patients who have lost a significant proportion of their blood, as if the body recognizes the closeness of death. But the sheet which covered her body from toes to chin was a pristine white.

The midwife came then to clean her and I saw that her thighs were smeared with blood and great clots filled the space between her legs. I had never seen a woman's sex before, except for the cadaver. I stood gazing at her and a shiver went through me. At that moment, the midwife who sat between her legs must have sensed my presence; she looked over her shoulder and told me in a pointed way that she would call me when she had the patient ready. I tore my eyes away. My interest was not prurient. I was caught up in the spiritual dimension of the scene, by the conjunction of the girl's angelic beauty and the earthliness of her bloodied body. For the rest of that night I experienced a heavy, lingering melancholy which was close to joy. It was profound and fitting. Part of that feeling, indeed mingled essentially within it, was a vague sense of guilt like a fragrance which is familiar but whose full identity eludes one's conscious grasp.

I have revisited that scene in my imagination. Many times. I have made it my own. I have allowed the horror of it to enter my mind and I have enveloped it like an oyster coating a piece of grit. In my imagination, it is I who gently dab away with a towel dripping from the bowl of warm water the dried blood from her golden hair.

I worked constantly to remind myself that blood was connected with suffering, wounding, death. But it continued to be a miraculous substance. I saw it when I pulled down the conjunctiva to check for anemia, or more gaudily splashed on the aprons and forearms of the surgeons. I studied the large glistening clots which formed on the scrubbed wood of the operating tables and the mingling and the curling of the vermilion within the clear water with which it had been sluiced across the tiles toward the drain in the floor. But this was dead blood. It had lost it vital magic, its sensuous power, as soon as it left the body.

It was madness to taste it. It was a foolish whim. I suppose I wanted to test myself, to prove to a George I still felt to be at my shoulder that I had hardened myself. On one occasion, I turned from the bedside of the patient I had finished bleeding as if to consider a clinical point and thoughtfully placed the reddened finger to my lips to secretly taste the deep, deep flavor of a stolen drop. The risk of taint did not deter me. On the contrary, the possibility of infection was part of the test. And when I did not fall sick, I was free to assume that I had been granted the gift of life, that I was charmed.

I write this as I would examine my face in the mirror: to objectify it and to make it observable. I am inclined to laugh at myself, and yet I cannot entirely shake the irrational interest. It is a foolish whim, and I must not take it seriously, otherwise I shall be no better than the peasants working our estates who wear garlic to ward off vampires. Yet I share their origins, and the root of superstition is planted deep within my nature.

I had hoped to get further with this line of thought, but I am tired and cannot concentrate with the infernal racket coming from next door. Roland, evidently, has returned quite drunk. He keeps up a tirade, damning the human race, but I cannot make out the subject of his anger since his words are thankfully muffled by the wall between us. His speechifying is interrupted from time to time when he falls over furniture and curses, and if I am not mistaken, sobs. I don't think I will sleep if I cannot help him settle.

NIGHT

I am under sentence of death. Worse. My stupid musings about blood – and all the time I have been tainted. Charmed! I thought I was charmed!

I had left my room to help Roland get to bed. His door stood ajar; I knocked, but he was too caught up in his drunken rambling to notice, so I entered and closed the door behind me so that he wouldn't wake the rest of the house. When he saw me at last he gave me the most ridiculous pastiche of a bow and promptly over-balanced backward into a chair.

'Oh, Count!' He shook his head in incoherent grief.

'Why do you call me that?' I asked.

'Isn't that what you call yourself? Huh?' He laughed bitterly. 'I don't mean around the hospital. You couldn't get away with that crap for five minutes. I mean just when you're preying on the vulnerable. The gullible. The easily impressed.'

'I don't know what you're talking about,' I said uneasily.

'What did you do . . . hypnotize her?' He was digging in a pocket, then another one, and finally fished out a crumpled piece of paper. 'Here, take it!' he snarled, throwing the note at my feet.

It was the message the old woman had pressed into my palm two days before, though it was much read and refolded. I opened it and smoothed out the creases.

Count – I am in mortal danger. I do not know where to turn. Only you, who knows both sides of my life, can save me. I am desperate! Otherwise I would not have

*presumed to call upon your good graces. Can I trust to
your compassion, to your noble efforts to right injustice?
I can! I must believe I can! I beseech you. Come, if you
harbor any regard for me at all, this evening to the address
above after nine. I surrender my destiny to you. I place
myself, helpless, in your hands, again.*

It was signed simply, 'S.'

The street she named is not far from these lodgings,
in the Latin Quarter. She had called me to her (for what
urgent purpose?), but I had been listening to poetry,
oblivious to the demands of the real world.

When I looked up, Roland was watching my face
closely. Perhaps he wasn't as drunk as he seemed.

'Don't worry,' he sneered. 'I'm not going to turn you
in. You've got enough to worry about.'

'What makes you think this has anything to do with
me?'

It was a feeble attempt at evasion. Lothar would have
thought of something far more elusive.

'You dropped it when Ducasse called you over to
examine the patient. I saw you.'

'Then if you knew the note was addressed to me, why
didn't you return it to me?'

'Because I knew she'd written it.'

'And what makes that your business?'

He laughed without joy or humor. 'I wish I knew. But
I have made it my business. And Stacia has no one else
she can count on.'

He was staring at me as if to discern whether I understood the deeper import of what he said.

'Do you know her at all?' he asked. 'Do you have any
idea who she is?' He held up his hand, although I had not
been about to speak. 'Oh, I know about that. I got her
to tell me. It means nothing. Sex could just as well be a
matter of thermodynamics. It's of no importance to her.
You should know that. It doesn't matter to me either.'

I was beginning to get the gist of what he was about.

He must have seen my awakening understanding. And I had thought he was jealous that I had found the node! The poor, deluded fool was in love with her!

'Love is her weakness. She craves affection as an apoplectic craves oxygen!' He was becoming increasingly intense in his passionate defense of her, and not at all drunk. The more he spoke, the less he seemed aware of me, and the more he appeared to be repeating the substance of some drawn-out debate he had had with himself.

'I have no intention of renewing what has been nothing more than a fleeting acquaintance, I can assure you,' I said, but he paid no attention. He gave the impression that nothing I could possibly tell him would add to the sum of his knowledge on this subject.

'She is promiscuous, I tell you! Hopelessly so!' he insisted savagely, although I had made no attempt to disagree with him. He got up and began pacing about the room, lurching from one piece of furniture to another. 'Do you understand that in Stacia's case, promiscuity is a disease? Are you such a green doctor that you do not understand that? So naive that you can find the node, but you can't see the motive?'

I resented this attack, especially since I had offered to withdraw from the liaison in deference to the depth of his feelings for the woman. Wasn't it, after all, myself and not Roland whose assistance Stacia had called upon in the note? I have been generous, I thought, and now I must endure this surliness?

What a difference an hour makes! What a self-satisfied fool the author of that thought was! How judicious, how gentle, was Roland in his rebuttal!

'I am like a brother to her,' he went on.

An infatuated drunk will not be contradicted, and so I hid my skepticism on this last point behind a look of tolerant interest.

'Can't you see that she can't help herself? I try to save her from herself, to save others from her, but she gives herself to anyone who shows a spark of kindness, an ounce of attention. And afterwards she is filled with remorse, self-disgust – you've seen the results for yourself today.'

I found this description impossible to reconcile with the entirely adept shepherdess who had pleasured me at the house Lothar had induced me to enter. The picture Roland was painting of Stacia as compliant victim and myself as callous seducer was a grotesque reversal of the facts.

'I had thought her more experienced. Perhaps I was wrong.' I had put my disagreement out in the open, but deftly, as a man of the world.

Roland waved it away. 'She is not concerned about herself. She bears you no ill will. In fact, it is you she is concerned about.'

'But her note says that it is she who is in danger.'

'To get your attention. She wanted you to come to her. She'll say anything for attention, for what she calls love.'

He was silent for the first time, but it was not the silence of a man who has finished speaking. He was looking at me wonderingly, as if I might arrive at the conclusion on my own. Some faint inkling of impending disaster, like the slightest draft which had played on the back of one's neck for several minutes, but which one only now notices, sent a shiver down my spine.

'Do you know why the fellow who lived in your rooms blew his brains out?' he asked.

'As a matter of fact, I never thought to ask,' I said with false bravado.

'His name was Guy Desmoulins. He was an admirer of Stacia's, like you.'

'Look, I've been trying to tell you, that's over and done with.'

'He was an ardent admirer,' Roland persisted with a peculiar emphasis on 'ardent.'

'I really think I can look after myself.' There was something I was missing, but I couldn't see what it was.

'Guy killed himself when he found out he had syphilis. He made the diagnosis himself.'

EARLY MORNING, JUNE 1, 1866

Already there is a glow in the sky from the coming dawn. The silhouette of the city, at first no more than a faint shadow in the greater darkness, is now a clear outline and any moment will assume dimension and substance. From the window, I hear sounds of people stirring and beginning to go about their business. A cook is banging pans as she washes them in a trough in a courtyard nearby. Below, a dog barks at someone passing on foot. Nothing brings home to me the shortness of life so much as the dawn of a new day. It is its very ordinariness which makes it so precious.

Time is flying by. Each second is beyond value. I feel and see with an acuteness my senses have never had before. I hunger for sensation. I strive to possess each moment. I want to slow the process in my body, to stall the loathsome parasite that swims in my blood. I exist for him now. I am his home. Slowly, he will take possession of me. In ten years – fifteen at the most – I will be dead, or mad. And in between I can expect any one of a hundred manifestations of this protean disease, each one humbling, humiliating, disabling. Thank God I am not called upon to father heirs. I have seen such offspring: half-wits with flattened noses on their faces like badges of their fathers' sins.

I examined myself as soon as I left Roland. I searched my privates for the painless chancre, but found none. I have made myself sore by palpating for lymph nodes in my groin. One on the left side is slightly enlarged, but so slightly that I cannot be sure that it is abnormal. It is still too soon for the parasite to show himself. Give him time. I will wait, but I cannot afford the indulgence of hope. There is no cure for syphilis, and I will not delude myself on that score, nor will I submit to mountebanks or go from one quack to another until they have stripped me of all my money and my dignity.

I will kill myself when the time comes. Not now. Until that time – will I know it? – I am a new man. Each day is a bounty. While I have my faculties, I will live each moment, fanning each sensation to its ultimate intensity, following each impulse along its tortuous course within my nature. I am afraid I will cling too strongly to life and leave it too late.

Will I know when?

Yes!

How?

6

AFTERNOON, JUNE 1, 1866

It has been a dreamlike day. I went to work as if nothing had happened, as if I were the same person I was yesterday. All the while, I am aware of having been transformed. So many considerations that loomed large now seem petty. Time – the present – is the essence of my existence. I do not mind the lack of sleep. It fits with my otherworldly mood. I am fatigued almost beyond endurance, and yet I feel strangely alert and composed. There is a new equilibrium within.

I had forgotten that today was the Friday on which I had agreed to escort Lothar to Professor Charcot's demonstration. I happened to be standing at the window, lost in a half-conscious reverie as I gazed at the roses in the flower bed below, when I saw his black landau roll along the main avenue of the hospital.

I went out the back entrance of the building, took a shortcut through the laundry, and arrived at the main door to the amphitheater just at the moment he was handing Nichole down from the carriage.

'I thought you might say "no" if I asked,' she said. 'So here I am unannounced.'

'I tried to put her off,' Lothar said. 'But the more I told her of the disgusting clinical details she could expect to hear, the more she wanted to come.'

'Will it be too, too animalistic?' she asked eagerly.

She was glorious in a severe black silk gown and a tiny bonnet perched atop her hair. Her eyes were glistening and ardent with excitement. She gazed at me for a duration, and I at her, as if my life were suspended.

'You are pale and drawn, Laszlo. I do not think you are looking after yourself properly.'

She reached out and brushed my cheek with the back of her fingers. It was a tender gesture of concern, but I recoiled as if her fingertip had poked a weeping sore.

'I'm working too hard, I expect,' I said quickly, and managed a tight smile. 'I'm a bit on edge, as you see.' But my excuse did not remove the hurt I saw on her face. I am ashamed to say that I felt a tiny spark of gratification that I had the power to cause her pain.

I ushered her forward, and we began to climb the steps of the building. Lothar detained me momentarily with a hand on my arm; he was grinning wickedly.

'You will deplete yourself with these amorous exertions, you fiend,' he murmured, hiding his mouth with the back of his hand as he spoke. Then, catching up with Nichole with a bound, he said openly, 'For God's sake, save something of yourself for posterity.'

'Are you to be famous, Laszlo?' Nichole asked. She seemed to think it was something one simply decided upon, like getting married.

Others, colleagues and competitors, were walking in our vicinity as we entered the amphitheater, and I was at a loss as to how to frame a reply which would open her to the possibility that I might some day be worthy of her admiration, without boasting before my rivals. Only my work as a doctor now offers any hope that the life remaining to me can be of any worth.

'Of course he is,' Lothar cut in. 'It's simply a question of what he's going to be famous for.'

'But do you expect to make something of yourself, Laszlo? Do you strive to be held in esteem by society?'

I thought that Nichole was teasing and had not expected that her line of questioning had a serious side. She was, I realize now, asking me about my prospects in life, whether I aspired to the same status as she herself did.

'This is my vocation,' I said. 'I intend to pursue it with all my energies.' Lothar was clapping his hands silently, ironically, behind Nichole, but I ignored him. 'This is a time when our discoveries can have an enormous potential for good. If we can understand the hysteric today, we can decipher the madman tomorrow. Then we will restore their peace of mind, their sanity, even. I hope to witness this in my lifetime.'

'Bravo,' said Lothar.

'It seems to me a most noble endeavor,' Nichole told him in rebuke.

'Not only noble, but self-sacrificing,' Lothar replied. 'A career in which one's income is based upon a clientele of lunatics – I'd call that saintly.'

Fortunately, I did not have to respond to him, since we next took our seats and this involved us easing in single file along one of the curved benches of the amphitheater. I considered Lothar's reply heavy-handed, without the usual touch which was so deft that it could be taken for indifference, and I thought that he might be jealous. It seems Lothar enjoys the counterbalancing possibilities of relations *trois* – I think the stability of friendship or love bores him – as long as he controls the movement. But the growing rapport between Nichole and myself takes the initiative from him so that there are fewer opportunities for his mischief.

The auditorium was especially full today, but we had managed to secure places near the front. I turned to see who else was present, as did Nichole and Lothar and everyone else, for it seems that the Master's demonstrations are becoming something of a Society event at which one must be seen and exchange greetings. Nichole, as one of the few women present, and the only one of striking beauty, occasioned much whispered comment, which she pretended not to hear. I noticed Roland sitting but two rows directly behind me. We have not spoken since his revelation. I could not meet his eyes although he looked at me pointedly.

Professor Charcot was in grand form. He lectured first on memory and amnesia. Next he discussed intermediate states of consciousness, especially the clouding of consciousness, or the twilight states of Knapf. As ever, he was eloquent and incisive, although I am not sure what Nichole and Lothar made of it. Whenever I ventured to steal a glance at her, I was surprised by Nichole's attentive expression, since I had been led by her behavior with her coterie to think of her as frivolous. I now believe that Lothar's characterization of her as superficial was a deliberate attempt to mislead me.

When the time came for the Master's demonstration, I was not prepared when the impassive Madame Verdun brought Stacia forward from the door behind the lectern. Stacia was a different woman from the self-confident demimondaine with whom I had spent a fateful night. We have both paid the price. She wore a simple white cotton dress without adornment. It hung upon her like a drab husk. But I have seen her walking in the hospital gardens: She filled a dress and moved it to the rhythm of her walk so that it became an expression of her mood as much as the gestures of her hands. Today she had nothing to express. Her eyes were dull, sightless it seemed, as Madame Verdun led her by the hand to the seat placed so painfully alone before us. Her golden hair lay loose about her shoulders like a girl's. She did not care. The life had gone from her. She sat slumped forward with her hands braced upon her knees and her head bowed. It was not shame or despair which she displayed so much as a hopelessness that lay at an extreme beyond them both.

My heart bled for her. I was filled with a vicious self-hatred for having brought her so low. It was not necessary for me to turn to see if Roland's eyes bore into the back of my head, for I sensed them. In an impulse of madness I felt impelled to stand before the assembled world and confess my prurient acts. But I did not do so. Instead, I consoled myself with the thought (how the moral order of this new man is turned upside down!) that my just executioner was even now insinuating himself into the nether tissues of my body.

Next to me, Nichole sat totally absorbed by the events before us. Her mouth was slightly open and her breathing was rapid. I was surprised that she should feel so intense a sympathy for the young woman whose life was so very different from her own. I wondered whether she was responding merely to a scene in a wonderful new form of drama, or whether Nichole had some understanding of what it was to be Stacia. But how could she possibly appreciate the full, squalid reality of the situation? I cringed at the thought of her gaining so much as an inkling of the truth.

There could be no doubt in Lothar's mind now as to the identity of the woman before us. Out of the corner of my eye I could see him lean forward to catch my attention. I ignored him. To return his gaze was to acknowledge my complicity in concealing Stacia's identity at the house. If I did so, who knew what other suspicions, fabrications of Lothar's perverse imagination, I would implicitly confirm? But he persisted in staring in my direction, and at last, exasperated, I gave in and glanced toward him. He grinned and tapped the side of his nose knowingly with his cane, as if to say, 'You sly devil, Laszlo.' He approved thoroughly, though what he thought I was up to I dread to think. He sniffs the subtle odor of intrigue, and I am afraid that the situation is far too interesting for him to leave it alone.

I turned pointedly back to the demonstration. Professor Charcot came from behind the lectern and stood slightly behind Stacia. He addressed his remarks to the floor, as if he and Stacia were disembodied spirits with no physical location, as if he were musing aloud in the hope of being overheard. 'Stacia,' he said softly.

Slowly, as if the movement required great effort, Stacia lifted her head. I feared – I hoped – as her eyes became visible, that she would fix them upon me, and that I would be picked out by the silent accusation of her gaze. But we did not exist for her. She was a medium who communed with a spirit which was elsewhere.

'Yes,' she sighed, and with the sound gathered substance and concentration.

'Would you tell what you have been engaged in these last three days?'

'I occupy my time with needlework and knitting. I walk in the gardens. I answer the questions of the doctors.'

'And that is all . . . nothing unusual, no unusual events you could tell us about?'

'I've been in bed on account of my arms.'

'And what has happened to your arms?'

'I don't know.' She spoke listlessly, as if entirely indifferent to her existence. She was still so pale from loss of blood that she could have been talking from beyond the grave.

'Nothing . . . violent?' asked Charcot, tossing the word out.

'Violent?' she repeated. At least he had her attention. He waited for her to consider the possibility. 'No,' she said, shaking her head sadly.

'But you have wounds on your arms.'

'If you say so.'

'Do you know how they came to be there?'

'No.'

'Your arms have deep lacerations, but you do not know how this happened?'

She stared dully at her arms which were covered by the long sleeves of her dress. 'No,' she said finally.

'Are you not curious, at least?'

'It must have happened while I was asleep.'

'Have you not seen the wounds?'

'I saw them when they were being dressed.'

'Are they the kind of cuts a person could have slept through?' Stacia seemed to be considering a point far, far away. 'Very well,' Charcot said. He nodded to Madame Verdun, who came forward and gingerly began to roll up one sleeve of Stacia's dress and then the other.

The arms were not a pretty sight. I felt Nichole wince, but she did not look away. For myself, I was aghast at the extent of the damage Stacia had inflicted upon herself. She had slashed at her forearms with the scalpel and they were bruised and mottled with a half dozen long cuts running diagonally across them. We were close enough to make out the neat black silk sutures along each wound. It must have taken Ducasse hours to close them. Charcot was right: It was the violence of the act which stood out, even three days later, with the damage repaired and the blood cleaned up.

I was so lost to these thoughts that I did not realize at first that it was Nichole's hand which stole beneath the desk and closed about my own. I did not know she had the strength to squeeze so tightly, and yet her face revealed nothing. She was fixated upon Stacia's bared arm. The lacerations spoke of an insane, savage rage which showed not the slightest regard for flesh, for the body as an abode of the soul, for the humanity of perpetrator and victim. Had I been the cause of this act? Nichole's hand held mine with a fierceness that would not let me draw into myself.

'How many days ago did this happen, Stacia?' Charcot was asking.

'I've lost my count.'

I am sure she said that. Not, 'I've lost count,' but 'I've lost *my* count.' I half expected Lothar to turn and leer in my direction. I listened for the sound of Roland coming to his feet behind me. But no one seemed to notice.

'It's been three days,' the professor told her. Stacia shrugged. 'It doesn't seem to matter to you.'

'That's because I don't count.'

'Surely you do.' Charcot seemed uncomfortable with the direction the conversation was taking, and a hint of irritation crept into his tone. He tried to bring it back to the topic of memory and away from these expressions of sentiment which did not fit into his scheme of things. 'If I told you that you inflicted these wounds upon yourself, could you think of a reason why you would have done it?'

Stacia raised her face to the ceiling. Her eyes were closed and a sinister, beatific smile made me shudder. 'Because I can't count on the Count,' she said.

It was gibberish to all the assembled doctors and representatives of fashionable Paris, save three. The Master himself was undecided as to whether his star subject was pulling his leg or had finally become totally unbalanced.

In the moment of his hesitation, Stacia stood and held her hands at an angle from her so that the bared forearms faced us.

'Oh, will you not help me?' she entreated the silent crowd. She looked at no one, yet her simple plea spoke to every heart. I hung my head in shame.

There were tears in Nichole's eyes, but she could not tear her gaze from Stacia to hide them. The pathos of Stacia's appeal had cast such a spell over the room that it would have seemed a violent act to break the silence. The Master was not accustomed to dramatic eclipse by subjects whose role was to illustrate the points of his theories, but even he seemed loath to speak. He nodded his head slowly in sympathy.

'We will do what we can,' he said quietly.

His words released the audience from Stacia's spell. People who a minute before could not move a muscle now shifted positions with a sense of relief. The room filled with the low hum of muttered comments and asides. We accepted that some unperceived, unthought action that would redress her state lay behind his words, just as one accepts that the Treasury's hoard of gold backs the flimsy piece of paper which is a banknote for a thousand francs.

Professor Charcot did his best to guide Stacia back through a number of mundane recollections to the day of her self-mutilation in order to show the patchy nature of what she could recall. 'Islands of memory in a sea of unconsciousness' was the phrase he used. He concluded the demonstration with further proofs of her profound capacity for amnesia. Stacia, whose Ophelia-like presence was proving to be a continuing distraction to the audience, was then ushered from the room, and Charcot ended with a marvelous summation.

Afterwards I sent word to the ward that I would not be in attendance during the afternoon, so that I could join Nichole and Lothar for lunch. Apparently he had planned to turn the visit to the Salpêtrière into a social excursion and had arranged a picnic for us in a secluded corner of the Bois. When we arrived, servants had already laid rugs and cushions for us to recline upon Roman style, and as we took our places beneath the shade of a great oak tree, they brought chilled spritzers of wine to refresh us. There followed cold chicken, quenelles of venison, jellied tongue, and an elaborate steak pie whose pastry crust could have been designed by an architect; these the servants left before us and retired to a distance so that we could lounge informally and talk without the constraint of their presence.

Nichole had been thoughtful and unusually silent through much of our drive from the hospital. She had clearly been affected by the demonstration. While we picnicked she merely toyed with her food.

'That poor woman!' she burst out finally. There were tears in her eyes.

Lothar looked to me to respond. He lay on a Turkish rug with his head propped on one hand and drew lazily on one of his cheroots while he savored the irony of my predicament.

'She is such a pitiable creature,' she said, turning to me for confirmation that her sympathies were not misplaced. 'I do believe she feels most acutely, although she says little. Her face is so sad. She is eloquent in her own way. She speaks with her posture; she is cast down but will not let herself be defeated. Everything about her conveys the impression that she is the victim of an unhappy love affair. Is that so? We know these things. We women have a sense about such things.'

I wondered if she spoke from experience. Had her heart been broken? When? By whom? And if so, had she regained the capacity to love again? Foolish questions by a man whose heart ignored the knowledge in his head.

She mistook my inability to find a suitably evasive answer for professional delicacy. 'But perhaps you cannot say?' she offered. 'I understand implicitly. But I can speculate, can I not, based upon my woman's intuition? You would not deny me that?'

'No, of course not.'

'She is not mad,' Nichole began, looking at me intently to see whether my expression offered some hint as to whether she was on the right track. 'Although there are some, doctors included, who think she is.' A slight shrug on my part conceded that this might be so. 'But she is a person of strong emotion – overruling emotion. She is a person whose emotions overrule her reason.' Nichole reached into some intuitive recess in her mind. She was far more knowledgeable about human nature than I had given her credit for. 'And because she is not clear to herself – she is like a chameleon, taking on the character of her surroundings – it is easy for her to lose herself. And then she appears emptied, as she did this morning. But she is far from empty. Her emotions are intense, and she loves too easily and too strongly.'

She seized my hand impulsively. Her eyes blazed with a passionate sincerity. 'Oh Laszlo,' she cried. 'I think it is so noble of you to give yourself to these people.'

'I don't think we know half the good deeds Laszlo performs,' Lothar said laconically.

She ignored him. Nichole has shown signs that she has grown tired of Lothar's cynical wit.

'I believe,' she went on, 'this is a woman who loved too much. She is not naive. I expect that she knew what she was doing when she surrendered her virtue. But she didn't expect to fall in love with her protector. Now he has cast her off, and she finds she cannot live without him.'

'What do you say, Laszlo?' Lothar asked. 'You must give us some indication if we are close to the truth.'

I was amazed at Nichole's astuteness. If this was who she was, why did she surround herself with giggling girls and fawning layabouts?

'I don't know if she's really in love,' I began cautiously. 'I rather think she believes herself to be, but it's the drama, the excitement, the adventure which sucks her in. She's playing a part.'

Nichole was listening with a rapturous, admiring expression, drinking in my every, stumbling word. 'But if she's playing a part, it's with everything she has. With nothing held back!'

Stacia fascinated Nichole. When the conversation drifted on to other topics, Nichole did not join in but sat musing on her own thoughts. When we tried to draw her, she gave distracted answers to our questions and eventually we left her to her own devices. I was pleased that Nichole showed such a strong enthusiasm for my work, but I thought her interest in Stacia unhealthy and overwrought.

The afternoon was balmy, and there was little traffic to impede us as we drove back to town. The speed of the landau was a pleasant counterpoint to the indolence of the day, and it created a delicious breeze across our heads and shoulders. Lulled by the rhythmic motion of the carriage and the steady pattern of the horses' hooves, I forgot entirely how my life was foreshortened.

Suddenly, Nichole said, 'I know what I shall do!'

'Of course!' Lothar chimed in. He is like a hound, ready to chase after any enthusiasm. But he has so few of his own.

'I would like to help Stacia.'

'We are doing everything we can,' I said.

'No, I would like to do something to help her.'

'But Nichole, she's a patient . . . she needs the care of those who are trained to deal with her moods – more than you can possibly give her.'

'But she's not mad; isn't that right?'

'Well, "mad" isn't really a term we use – '

'Let's not quibble about words. She's not dangerous?'

'Not to others. But you've seen . . . obviously she is to herself.'

She considered this for a quarter of a mile, but I could see she wasn't going to let the matter go.

'Mama has said I can have another dresser.'

I didn't like the direction her thoughts were tending.

'Surely,' I began, 'you can't be considering having her in your employ?'

'When she is recovered,' Nichole said brightly.

'I think it's a magnificent gesture,' Lothar offered. He had been silent until then, and I thought that he had had the good grace to forgo his meddling, but now I saw that he had simply been waiting for an opportune moment. I flashed him a warning look of utmost menace, but he continued. 'A good home. With the correct supervision, it would be a second chance.'

'I have so little scope to do any good – to do anything which has any real effect on anything. And now here is this opportunity which chance has put in my way. I have a feeling about it I can't ignore.'

I was horrified as the possibilities began to unravel in my imagination. I envisioned the reaction of my uncle and aunt when they discovered that I had allowed a syphilitic whore to enter their home, that I had recommended this chancred creature to wait upon their only child. But is it any different from my own presence there? What would they say if they knew that their daughter found one pretext after another throughout the afternoon to squeeze the hand, skin to skin, of this infected wastrel?

'Not now,' she cooed. She was reassuring me, coaxing me, easing me toward her conclusion in a seductive manner I did not want her to stop. 'When you tell me she's well.' She laid her hand on mine to seal the covenant.

When we arrived at the home of Nichole's parents, I walked with her up the front steps and, when the footman answered the door, slipped inside after her. In implicit understanding, we waited as the click of the man's heels on the marble receded along the hallway, until we could be alone for the first time that day. I had never before seen Nichole bashful. If she had wanted, she could have said her good-byes and left this fraught encounter. Yet she stayed.

'I'm glad I saw the demonstration,' she said. It was a lame statement, but the tension of the moment and her embarrassment told me that she meant to tell me something by it without revealing too much of the true state of her feelings. I had not realized until then how shy she is. In Lothar's presence she assumes a boldness which I saw now was not part of her true nature.

'Now you know how I waste my time.'

'I don't think you waste your time,' she said. Her words were a secret code which transmitted a tenderness that could not yet be acknowledged. We stood together in the hallway, without looking at one another, and as the silence lengthened an intimacy of unspoken thoughts intensified until it reached a pitch which was almost unbearable.

'I hope we shall see you when we receive on Thursday,' Nichole said at last. The sound of her voice was a precious thing. The unstated message of her affection filled me like a physical sensation. At that moment, I would have traded one of her trite words for all of Stacia's caresses.

'I shall think of nothing else until I see you again,' I told her as I took my leave.

Lothar looked at me speculatively when I returned to the landau. 'You took your time,' he said, but did not get a rise out of me.

For several minutes we traveled in silence. The traffic was thick at this time of day, and we made slow headway. Lothar was deep in contemplation with his chin resting on his hands, which were in turn supported by his cane. He swayed slightly when the vehicle stopped or started again, but seemed to incorporate this absent-mindedly into some inner rhythm. When he came back to the present, his eyes fixed on me. Humor or irony were such a constant feature of his communication, either in the expression of his face or the tone of his voice, that their absence now made me uneasy.

'Stacia,' he said by way of announcing the topic for discussion. 'You should go to her.'

I was annoyed as much by the peremptory tone in which this judgment was delivered as by his interference in my private affairs. 'Don't be ridiculous!' I protested.

'For God's sake, man, the poor girl almost killed herself!'

'What does this have to do with me?'

'Because you're the Count.'

I did not want him to take my angry silence as a sign that I conceded his point. 'This is an intolerable intrusion,' I blustered. But I knew he had an ally within. He pressed precisely on a sore spot of conscience which I had been trying to hide from my own scrutiny.

'You don't have to be an alienist to decipher what she was saying,' he persisted.

'She must have had hundreds of men.'

'Apparently not.'

'What would you know of her history?'

'That she was new to the house. Not a regular. Not a whore.'

The news stripped another layer of justification from me, and I felt the slow seep of shame enter my soul. Stacia had not been an innocent, that had been obvious enough. But had I used an honest woman for my debauch, someone who for the first time that evening had given herself for money? My course of action was becoming painfully clear. Yet if this was so, how did she come by her infection? 'I tell you I'm not involved,' I insisted stubbornly.

'It's the only decent thing you can now do.'

'I hardly expected to receive a lecture on morality from someone of your qualifications.'

'Nevertheless, you know it's true.'

'I know nothing of the kind!'

'Any man of the world will tell you so.'

'I am not a man of the world, I'm proud to say.'

'You don't even have the experience to know you have to clear up your own mess,' he flared. Then he shrugged off this moment of anger and went on in a lighter tone, as if he were wondering aloud. 'I could help, you know. I don't mind. I'm sure she doesn't spend all her time in the hospital. Does she? Perhaps a place of her own, some help with the rent, would make her life a little easier.' He paused to see if I would volunteer information, but I mistrusted his motives and said nothing. 'But perhaps she already has a pied-à-terre,' he suggested. 'Do you happen to know?'

'Let me give you some advice: Stay away from her. If you go to that brothel, chose someone else.'

'She's never been back, much to my disappointment!'

'Stay away from her!'

'You want her all for yourself?'

'That's not the issue.'

'It doesn't do to go soft on a whore.'

'I have my reasons.'

'Of course. Everybody has reasons.'

'These are good reasons. Trust me.'

'Trust you? Why? Good Lord, Laszlo, don't you know sincerity's the oldest trick in the book? You didn't level with me, you know. Not that I blame you. She's delightful. Rather like one of those heroines of a poem by the Decadents. You knew her at the house that night, but you didn't say a word. You've known her all along and you've been keeping her to yourself, you cad!'

He prodded me playfully with the end of his cane. I was in no mood for levity.

'She's not mad is she?' Lothar inquired in a matter-of-fact sort of way.

'Of course not!'

'That would be a twist. Not that it matters – I'm quite partial to a pinch of spice, as you know.'

'You saw for yourself.'

'But she's not entirely normal, though, is she? Something of a strange beast. A unicorn. Someone with unusual abilities. Proclivities. Vulnerabilities.'

He dangled his cane between finger and thumb, controlling its pendular movement so that it moved in a precise arc over the tip of his shoe. I watched as if hypnotized. I do not understand why this trivial mannerism should have assumed such an aspect of obscure obscenity, but I know that only Lothar could have endowed it with this sinister quality.

EVENING

Alone in my room, I threw myself on my bed. Immediately I felt the need for sleep steal over me, and it would have carried me off if I had not jumped up and paced up and down on the worn piece of carpet in the middle of that small space. I feel feverish, deranged almost, on account of the lack of sleep and the flurry of events which had buffeted me through the day. In less than twenty hours I have been faced with the prospect of madness and death; Stacia, whom I have cruelly seduced with another man's money, has tried to kill herself and has called to me for help in a public gathering; and Nichole, the object of my romantic longing since I have been capable of such sentiment, has given me unmistakable signs of encouragement.

I have been rummaging in the debris on the other side of the desk for the piece of paper which contains Stacia's address. It is the place where I throw all business I do not wish to deal with, including the outrageous bill from the tailor. (How things which once loomed large now fade into insignificance! When I returned this evening, Madame Thébauld informed me, addressing me as 'Count' in the most obsequious manner, that a man had called to see me. No doubt he is the tailor's man and will report to his master that their new client lives in circumstances which do not bode well for collecting on his debt.) In the same pile I discovered a letter of Elizabeth's from the day before which I had not even bothered to open. George has been called to the colors and they fear war is imminent. It seems so far away, in another world. I should feel more, but I lack concern for everything except what involves me here and now.

I must have crammed Stacia's note into a ball and thrown it from me with some force, for it had rolled into the farthest corner. It was there also that I discovered that the removal of the room's previous tenant had been incomplete. Down at knee level were splotches on the wall which could only be of dried blood, and lower still was a gory memento, a yellow and shriveled fragment which I took to be a spicule of bone with brain tissue adherent. From the direction of the blast, the man had sat on this very chair at this desk where I sit now, looking through this window at the last moment of his life. Perhaps I have been unfair in characterizing Madame Thébauld's nosiness. I wonder now if her curiosity is not more protective in nature, prompted by a concern that I do not repeat the sad fate of the room's previous tenant. But I intend to make the most of the life which remains to me. Do we not all live under sentence of death?

I am tempted to sleep, to let fatigue drug me so that I am incapable of doing my duty. If I lie down, if I so much as close my eyes, I shall sleep until tomorrow and then it will be too late for me to visit Stacia. For that is what I have determined to do. I must make restitution. She has done me wrong in infecting me with this foul disease. (I have found no chancre yet, but give it time. I am alert to crush out any spark of hope which arises in me, for otherwise I will eventually delude myself and live within a fool's paradise.) Stacia could have warned me. She could have withdrawn herself from that place where she knew it was inevitable that she would pass on the disease.

But some demon possessed her to sell herself that night. Though I hate to admit it, Lothar is correct in this moral point: I must go to her. As the Master himself said: 'We will do what we can.'

EARLY MORNING, JUNE 2, 1866

I have read the last page, written before I left to find Stacia. What noble thoughts! Who was the man who wrote those words? I do not recognize him. Who was this fool who espoused these ideals of courage, fortitude, and self-denial; who set out to save Stacia from her despair, from the demon which possessed her – this man who did not recognize that the demon lay curled within himself?

For the occasion, I put on my magnificent new suit. Surely such vanity should have jarred some awareness as to the true nature of my mission? Not in the least. Rather than admit that I wanted to dazzle her, to play the Count, I reasoned that it would be better if I presented myself not in my doctorly garb but as a private citizen, as it were. I waited until nine o'clock, which was the time she had previously asked me to come in her note, since I expected she had some arrangement with the night watchman at the hospital and would not be able to leave until late. I walked through the streets buoyed by lofty intentions, warmed with a rare, altruistic glow. Hypocrite!

The address she had given me was not far from my lodgings, but what a distance in social station even from my modest neighborhood! Neglected, ragged children looked up from their scavenging in the gutters and refuse heaps when they heard my approach and, seeing the manner of my dress, begged for coins with an insistence which was positively feral. Offal rotted amid raw feces in stagnant pools where the road's disrepair prevented runoff. Several times I had to step off the narrow pavement into the street so that drunkards could stagger past me. Prostitutes of the meanest kind hissed and gestured at me from darkened doorways.

Fortunately, I found the place without having to ask any of the denizens for directions. It was a tall, dilapidated building like the rest, with no concierge on duty. I passed into the courtyard and climbed the stairs past the all too intimate noises of couples and families. Doors cracked open just after I passed by, and I felt eyes in my back appraising me. I climbed to the top, to the single door in the garret where the staircase, which had narrowed to little more than a ladder, ended.

No light showed beneath the door. I knocked, feeling that my journey had been in vain. I was about to leave, wondering who might be lying in wait to rob me on my descent, when I heard a bolt withdrawn, then another, and finally the door opened an inch. I wondered if she would be able to recognize me in the dim light.

'It is I,' I said stupidly, not knowing by which mode of address I should identify myself.

'Count!' she exclaimed. I flinched at the word. Stacia flung back the door. 'I knew you would come! I knew it!'

I had not expected to find her so happy to see me. She was overjoyed. She was exultant, as if by this one action I had restored her faith in humankind. To my point of view, her happiness confirmed that my decision to come here had been the right one.

She brought me in and closed the door behind me. I had advanced into the room, expecting her to come forward, but she lingered at the door, and when I turned to look for her I found her staring at me with a disconcerting intensity which was akin to hunger. She had forgot herself; so absorbed was she by my presence in her room that she seemed to lose sight of the fact that I was an autonomous being with impulses and motions of my own. By turning to her, it was as if I had awakened her from a reverie.

She came forward with a dancer's grace, extending her hand in a slow pirouette to indicate the small space. She wore a simple white dress of muslin with long sleeves, and her hair was pulled back and gathered at the back of her head so that her golden locks fell down about her shoulders. She looked fresh and quite revived in spirit. Where was the ghostly, tormented soul who had called to me this morning at the demonstration? I was confused by her ability to change aspects and felt strangely disoriented, as if this was a person whom I had never before encountered.

'I call this my lair,' Stacia said. She seemed confident and unaffected. 'I hope you will feel able to share my secret?' She looked to me for an answer.

'Yes, of course,' I said somewhat late. 'I shan't breathe a word.'

'They wouldn't understand at the hospital. But I knew you would.'

'I don't see any reason why you shouldn't have a place of your own.'

'There are rules.'

'But rules must be made to fit the individual case.'

'I couldn't exist without my own place to come to.'

I looked about me. A single taper burned on a table next to a book she had been reading. In contrast to the squalor of the neighborhood, the room was clean and contained touches – curtains about the small window, some daisies in a vase on the table, a shelf of books – which suggested that the person who lived here had been used to better circumstances. The furniture was simple in the small space, just a table with two chairs, a chest, a bookcase with ornaments on some of the shelves, and a stool by the hearth. The bed was the most substantial object in the room.

'Where are my manners?' Stacia exclaimed. 'Won't you sit down?'

We sat in somewhat awkward intimacy across from one another on opposite sides of the small table. The taper cast a soft glow upon her face, giving her a spiritual allure. It seemed natural to lean inward, toward each other, to stay within the illumination of the flame, and so we found ourselves talking in whispers. There was so much unsaid.

'I hope you won't judge me by my present circumstances,' she began. 'I come from a good family.'

'That was what I had thought.'

'You did?'

'I would also venture that you have had instruction in dance and perhaps other of the arts,' I said, feeling rather pleased with myself because her expression of delight proved that my surmises were correct.

'I was a governess before my illness.'

'I was so sorry to hear what . . . happened,' I mumbled, half in apology, half in regret, wholly cowardly in my avoidance of specifics. 'I felt so awful for you!' Gone was all possibility of maintaining a doctorly distance. I had taken her hand in a gesture of sympathy, or at least I remember her hand being within mine, but not how it got there. Immediately, her other hand lay on the back of mine, and then she had clasped my hand tightly between both her own, and she had fallen on her knees before me, her head bowed upon my lap, sobbing uncontrollably.

'I have wronged you!' she cried and dissolved into heart-wrenching sobs.

I was afraid she would debase herself and took her by the shoulders to try to get her to stand, but she clasped me even more tightly in her gesture of fierce contrition, and my attempts left me holding her in a kind of embrace. I was greatly moved by her humility.

'How can you forgive me?' she moaned within my arms.

I was close to tears myself. 'No, it is I who have wronged you,' I insisted.

If I had had more presence of mind, I should have asked

her what she meant. But the scene had already played itself out too far. How was one to keep one's head with an ardent woman intent on making amends burrowing into one's lap? I shifted position to find a more stable posture, and in that moment she seemed to fall between my legs and had to reach her arm about my waist in order to steady herself. Her other hand was curled about my thigh. I held her head between my hands, wet with her tears. There were many adjustments amid the protestations of guilt which offered opportunities for subtle pressure here, a touch there, which would have been a caress had the movement not been accidental. I kissed her face to prove my forgiveness. She would not accept it, so I must do it over and over again. She could not be satisfied. Our mouths met, lips parted, tongues gliding together and snaking about each other in a passion of moral fervor.

How long may lust live within a disguise of high ethical purpose? Forever! And the more saintly and implausible the motivation, the more breathtaking, the more self-annihilating, the more shuddering is the excruciating ecstasy of its satisfaction.

I will not pretend to be an authority on the subject, but I have noticed in my own case that there is within the orgasm, slightly after the peak, an instant of icy clarity. It was during this moment, during this sudden dissipation of passion, that I became fully aware of what I had done. If, by some undeserved intervention of the Divine, I had escaped infection before, I have now established the disease in my body beyond a clinical doubt. If I had once wished to disentangle myself from Stacia in an honorable way, I have now cemented myself to her. Where I had tried to elevate our relation to the professional plane where I can be of most help to her, I am now compromised beyond relief, without hope of extricating myself.

I am the lover of a patient from a lunatic asylum. When I disappoint her, she slashes at her wrists with a scalpel. She seduced me with malice aforethought, I have no doubt. But I found my way to her. I brought myself to her.

And all the time, I managed not to notice where I was going, what was my true destination. Like a blind man tapping his way along the street, feeling his way with his white stick, I have followed my throbbing member. Yet my fault is worse than self-deception, or foolishness, or even the damnation of syphilis: It is that I do not fully regret what I have done. There is part of me which exults in my destruction.

7

JUNE 5, 1866

Today I have a letter from Gregory. Much of his life is lived on the inside, so there is little news. In fact, he is so deeply involved in his spiritual quest that it is difficult for him to communicate even the outlines of his life. The material world, he says, is becoming a pale shadow. I suspect that some of these sentiments are produced by prolonged fasting. He would like his body to disappear altogether. When he first entered the seminary, he was given a long linen shirt which reached past his knees. 'For bathing,' he was told. Apparently the authorities are concerned that even the sight of his own body could provoke untoward arousal in the novitiate. He jokes about it now, as if this temptation were something he no longer has to contend with. I cannot really believe that the sexual urge withers and dies, however much it is suppressed.

As I read the words he has written to me, I am taken with the fear that I shall never see him again. The person who was his friend no longer exists. I feel myself rolling down a moral incline, gathering speed. Why does sin feel so natural, so inherent, so instinctual?

When I encounter her in the hospital, Stacia is the picture of decorum. She either ignores me, or if an encounter is unavoidable (and I admit that I have maneuvered this on more than one occasion) she will acknowledge me with the merest hint of a courtesy. I see a tightness about her lips when we come face-to-face, as if she resents the intrusion of one of her worlds into the other.

Then, at nine o'clock, in her room at the top of the stairs

of that dilapidated tenement, she is a different woman. She is abandoned, a voluptuary. There is nothing she will not venture. I had not even imagined that such things were possible. I have never known such consuming delight. I can scarcely wait until nine. Lately I have taken to leaving my lodgings early so that I have been forced to wander aimlessly about the mean streets of her neighborhood. I am an addict for her body. I think of nothing but her sex, her breasts, her mouth. When I am not with her, I live only for the time of our next meeting.

I am a pig routing deeper into the muck for that tantalizing morsel which just eludes me. I am an enthusiast of degradation. I have a nose for it, as a connoisseur has a nose for fine wine. I am a slave to appetite. I am going deeper and faster. I am drinking. On the last two occasions, with time to kill, I entered a wine shop near Stacia's building and drank absinthe with the laborers and petty thieves who loitered there. There is something deathly about that liquid's bitter astringency which quite fits my mood.

Stacia does not like me drinking. She pulled away from me, angry and confused when I had held her close and told her, 'We are doomed.' I fear she has plans for me. Her intention was not to drag me down to her level, but for me to raise her up to mine (a level whose potential magnificence she is quite deluded about). Within the four walls of that room, surrounded by the lowest squalor of Paris, Stacia tries to foster some grotesque caricature of bourgeois domesticity. Cautiously at first, she is evolving a system of truly awful pet names ('Doggins') and retires in hurt silence when I do not reciprocate in kind ('Lambikins'). When she first tried this out on me, I thought I had misheard; then I all but burst into laughter. Now I accept these endearments as but another aspect of my debasement. How fitting, how quintessentially apt, that the satyr, having penetrated his victim to the core, should hear, as his pagan rapture ebbs and dies, his name hoarsely whispered by his sated nymph: 'Oh, Poopums!'

Gregory's celibacy seems all the more wondrous, all the more saintly, as I consider my own progress. I am thinking of a prank we played at St Sebastian's when we were fourteen or fifteen. The man's real name I don't recall; we called him Brother Lubricius, which must have been close enough to be considered a clever nickname. He was known to all the boys at the school, but not to himself, as a pederast. Not that we felt any moral revulsion or even begrudged him his interest in us – boys of that age are extraordinary in their tolerance of eccentricity in friendly adults. And besides, he was more peeper than groper. I can see him now, ruddy cherubic cheeks, eyes peering over tiny spectacles, gleaming with what could be mistaken for good humor to those who had not yet encountered his boisterous, smoothing hands, which as if by chance . . . 'What have we here?' Brother Lubricius guffaws triumphantly, holding the pose, his arms around Gregory in a loose approximation of a football tackle, laughing at his boyishness, at his engaging in such roughhouse. Only his fingers are moving, restlessly, randomly, as it were absentmindedly. Brother Lubricius is looking around for others to share the good fun, checking to learn in our expressions whether he has strayed. We pass knowing smirks to one another which he cannot fail to notice, except that he fails to notice. (What would the great Charcot make of this? The man knows but does not know what he is.)

It was Gregory (how hard it is to reconcile this mischievous youth with the somber man – he is practically a fanatic) who originated the idea of the salami. The item I stole from the kitchens was gently curved and of modest proportions on the scale of sausages, but as a penis it was prodigious. As all the boys wore cassocks, it was a simple matter of tying a cord about Gregory's waist and suspending the salami so that it dangled appropriately. Brother Lubricius, attracted by the sounds of scuffling boys, soon joined in the game we had arranged, and with the ball passed frequently to Gregory, his particular favorite, it was inevitable that the Brother's roving hand would sooner or later encounter that stallion member. There was no particular moment of insight of which we were aware. After a few minutes, Brother Lubricius quietly wandered away from our game. He was never the same again. He was no longer humorous or fun, and we became aware of an absence in our lives, a spirit we had taken for granted that was gone.

I wonder now what it was that Brother Lubricius's fingers encountered. Not, I think, an awareness of our knowledge of him. It was not an unmasking that he suffered. Rather, I think he touched the gross epitome of his desire — massive, hard, and inevitably destructive in its execution.

There is something around the corner. I can feel it. I am aware of the closeness of some breathtaking fulfillment whose face remains yet in shadow. If I wish (is this true?) I can pull back. But then I will never know what I am. And those who do not grope into the dark corners of their souls are deadened, like Brother Lubricius. I must travel deeper into myself, beyond the maps of custom and convention. The mind is the dark continent of our age. I have embarked on a voyage of discovery with nothing left to lose.

JUNE 11, 1866

My financial situation goes from bad to worse. The tailor has instigated a campaign of systematic harassment. His man is constantly loitering about the courtyard or leaning against the railings across the street. He lies in wait for me, and I have become adept at avoiding him, using tricks, such as exiting by the servants' entrance at the back and even on occasions climbing over walls, which are demeaning. Once, wandering aimlessly and slightly drunk through the rabbit warren of alleyways in the vicinity of Stacia's room, I thought someone was following me. Footfalls echoed on the cobbles behind me and stopped when the sounds of mine ceased. I never saw who it was. If it was the tailor's man, why would he hide himself from me? More likely it was a footpad sizing me up as a prospect to rob.

Finally, when the tailor's man turned up at the hospital and asked the porter at the front gate for my whereabouts, I had had enough. And so last week I put on my magnificent suit and my most haughty, noble manner and deposited a significant fraction of the outstanding balance on the tailor's polished mahogany counter. He appeared gracious and grateful, as if there had never been any trouble between us, and no mention was made of his man's impudent persistence. I hope he was impressed, because now I have nothing with which to pay the rent for this month. And I am in these straits as the result of a vice as trivial as vanity!

When I came home today I found Lothar deep in conversation with Madame Thébauld at the foot of the stairs. They stopped abruptly when they noticed that I had come into the courtyard, and Madame Thébauld was at pains to convey to me that Herr von Pick had only that moment arrived himself and had been inquiring as to when I was expected to return. The sight of him reminded me that I have been so obsessed with Stacia that I had entirely forgotten to attend the Berthier's weekly reception.

Madame Thébauld had an envelope in her hand that she passed to me with some hesitation, as if I might wonder why it was that she carried it about with her, which indeed I did, especially as it appeared to have been tampered with. It contained a statement of my account from the tailor. There was also a note in which he respectfully requested the honor of my earliest attention to the matter of the remaining balance.

'A nosy individual,' Madame Thébauld sniffed, referring to the bearer of the note. 'Asked a lot of questions about you, Count. Persistent. 'Course, it's not my place to answer questions, and I didn't. Not one.' She couldn't help glancing at Lothar, which I took to be the sign of a guilty conscience from having answered every one of the questions he had put to her.

'And quite right, too,' Lothar declared. He turned to me and murmured, 'There is a small matter I have to discuss with you.'

I waited for Madame Thébauld to excuse herself so that we could talk privately, but she found some chore which kept her in our vicinity, and I had no option but to invite Lothar up to my humble rooms.

'I was having quite a nice chat until you showed up,' he said as we climbed the stairs.

'So I saw. I didn't know Madame Thébauld was such a conversationalist, but then I suppose that would depend on the topic.'

'And what could be more interesting than one's friends? We missed you by the way.'

'We?' I asked unwarily.

'Nichole was quite upset that you didn't show up at their at home. She rather took it out on me, which I thought unfair. She seems to think I have some influence over you and therefore holds me responsible for your not being there. I'm in the doghouse. I wish you'd put in a word for me.'

'Do you really care what she thinks of you?'

'More or less. On the whole, yes. But then, I don't care what she thinks of me nearly as much as you do. Or did.'

'I've been busy.'

I opened the door and ushered him in, and he winked in a conspiratorial way as he passed by.

'That's what Madame Thébauld says. She's almost as curious about your nocturnal pursuits as I am.'

'I'm kept late at the hospital.'

'What interesting work that must be!'

'I find it so.'

'But surely you don't . . . I mean, you know, in the hospital?'

'I wish I could offer you some refreshment. If you like, I can send out for some wine.'

'Why so evasive?' he laughed. 'It's just conversation, for goodness sake. Unless you've fallen in love with her.' He scrutinized my face, and I averted my eyes as if this could prevent his astute gaze from winkling out my secrets. Lothar feigned shock. 'Oh, my God! Don't tell me it's serious?'

'No, of course not,' I said, angry and embarrassed, so that my manner revealed everything he wanted to know.

'I envy you,' he said in a voice without irony. I turned to him in surprise. I thought he might even be telling the truth, in so far as Lothar was capable of any mental stance which approximated earnestness. Perhaps such an event could occur only by accident. I have never seen him look so vulnerable. The expression was gone in an instant, replaced by his customary urbanity. But for a moment I glimpsed eyes filled with an uncomprehending yearning, the longing of a man for something he has no feeling for. As I think of it now, I wonder whether Lothar's emotions might be like those of a deaf mute who observes the tears of someone who has surrendered to the sublime poignancy of a Beethoven sonata. What can he know of those tears? What can Lothar know of a passion which consumes a man's being?

'I don't think that can be true,' I said. 'You have everything you need, and more. I'm' – I gestured about my room – 'struggling, as you can see for yourself.'

'I'll give you some of what I have, if you'll share yours.' There was a devilish glint in his eye. I have noticed that Lothar is at his most perverted when he is provoked by some awareness of his emotional shortcomings. 'Aristide's tip on Occidental Traders has paid off magnificently, and I've sold the lot. The stock quintupled! Can you imagine that? And today it crashed! It's practically worthless.'

'I don't see any difference between these stock manipulations and embezzlement. They're both varieties of stealing.'

'This wasn't a manipulation. Or, at least, half of it wasn't. Uncle Aristide and his friends may have helped Occidental climb, but Bismarck was its downfall. The Prussians are going to war with us. Don't you read newspapers anymore? The bourses have collapsed in all the capitals of Europe. We were lucky. We got out in time. And, of course, war is wonderful for the uniform business.'

'You pretend to care about nothing.'

'But is it pretence? That's the dilemma which intrigues people. They can't seem to make up their minds. Can he really be such a monster, they ask themselves? Anyway, I care about you – enough to buy some Occidental Traders on your behalf, and to keep my part of the bargain.'

'Really, you owe me nothing.'

'Come now, it'll give you a tidy sum to squander as you see fit – on that mistress you've hidden away somewhere, if you want to – even if you insist on paying off your tailor's bill, which by the way no one really expects you to do.'

'How do you know what I owe the tailor?'

'Because I looked at his pompous bill, you fool.'

'You feel free to poke into whatever corner of my life interests you. Don't you respect privacy?'

'You don't mind too much. And besides, how nice it is to know that you'll appreciate our ill-gotten gain.'

'I want no part of it.'

'Aren't you letting this "Count" stuff go to your head? Only tradesmen and the French take it seriously, you know. Of course, it goes without saying, it's quite all right with me if you want to pass yourself off as a nobleman.'

'Your offer of money is deeply insulting,' I said coldly, turning away.

'Of course it is, which is the very reason that I'm not giving you any.' I looked back in surprise and cursed myself for rising so predictably to his lure; he had dangled it lazily before me with no result for several minutes, but he had managed to make me jump by threatening to whisk it away. 'I realize it would be unbecoming for you to receive a gift of money.' He held up a hand to forestall further protest. 'What I'm proposing is a business deal. Strictly business. You need to keep that in mind when you hear what I have to say.'

'I'm listening,' I said warily.

Lothar smiled almost shyly, a sure sign of complexity, of wheels within wheels, of feints and bluffs. 'I wish to buy Stacia from you,' he declared.

'Why?' I asked, before I could fully comprehend the monstrousness of his proposal.

'A whim. Let's call it that.'

'A whim? Are you capable of nothing more?'

'A fancy. A peccadillo. Call it eccentricity if you want.'

'Are you mad?' I cried, trying with a show of outrage to regain the moral high ground. But for some reason I didn't feel the strength of my position, as if by some oversight I had already conceded the most precious principle. 'You can't buy people here,' I blustered. 'Do you think this is America?'

'Of course you can. With enough money, you can buy anything you want.'

'You're right. If you want a body, you can buy almost anybody.' He could probably buy Stacia without too much difficulty, I thought. Did I even expect her to be loyal to me? I already suspected she had other lovers. The thought had passed through my mind several times without causing much disturbance. And yet I experienced a powerful sense of duty toward her. I must be her true protector.

'Why involve me?' I asked.

'Because it amuses me.'

'Because you want me to be involved, that's why. You do this purely to make mischief.'

'There are worse motives.'

Nothing came to mind for me to say. No defense of basic truths or arguments from self-evident rights, no fervor rose within me. Instead my mind, unbidden, of its own accord, in something like a perfidious daydream, turned lazily to the thought of rent. In that silence I felt my full moral bankruptcy.

My hesitation was to Lothar like a bared throat to a wolf. 'Mind you, I don't want her when you are bored and finished with her,' he said.

'You talk of this woman as if she's a block of stock to be traded back and forth on the bourse.'

'That's because I'm shameless.' He had intended it in a wry, humorous way, but I had the feeling that I was again observing Lothar in a rare moment of transparency. 'That's what sets me free,' he said.

'I can't believe you're serious.' But I could.

'I want her fresh, now, while she's desired.' There was a gleam of animation and hunger in his eyes. This was the crux of what he wanted.

He had taken a leather pocket case from deep within his coat. If I had cared to think more clearly I could have anticipated what he was about, but I did not, and so I was not prepared when Lothar placed two large banknotes on the desk.

'A down payment,' he suggested quietly. He stared at me for a brief moment, and I fancy he gauged my expression in a most professional way, as I have seen animal trainers at the circus scrutinize their charges, to see if I would balk.

Not being prepared (do I now need preparation because I can no longer trust my intuition, my moral impulses?), I was too slow to respond. I rounded the table and grasped the money.

'No!' I protested, with a pathetic lack of conviction.

But Lothar had already opened the door. He turned as he adjusted the angle of his hat upon his head. 'Till tomorrow?' he suggested in a matter-of-fact manner and started down the stairs.

I could have run after him and argued further. But what was there, really, to discuss? I could have run after him and seized him from behind and stuffed the banknotes down his throat until he choked on them. But first I glanced down to see the size of their denomination.

Stacia has told me that she would not be able to get away from the hospital tonight. With great difficulty, I managed not to ask her why. She is given to wild rages on the slightest pretext, particularly when I give any hint that I suppose I have some call upon her time, particularly when I do not make myself available to her as she demands. It is part and parcel of the passionate nature which so excites me.

After Lothar left, I wandered about the city. I must have some instinctive affinity for squalor, for I am drawn to the most wretched drinking places. Naturally, as it came close to nine o'clock, I found myself close by Stacia's building and could not resist turning down that familiar street. I believe a light burned in her room, although I cannot be sure. On previous occasions, I have never been bothered by the possibility that she would have other men. In fact, from time to time, in an apparently casual way which she does not carry off very well, she has alluded to admirers. She sulks when she does not succeed in making me jealous and gives me to believe there is a rich man who is more than ready to show her his full appreciation if I do not. All her artifice had been lost on me, and yet I am troubled now by this light in her window. What has Lothar done? I feel subtle tentacles tighten about me, binding me closer to her than ever before.

JUNE 21, 1866

My life is a labyrinth, and I grope my way in darkness. Once, a long time ago, it seems, I assumed that I was moving toward the light. I knew myself to progress at times slowly, with some backtracking and false turns, but tending always toward truth, knowledge, decency, family. This afternoon I learned that that route, that kind of life, is forever closed to me. Instead, I am following some instinctual destiny which is like a fine, scarcely perceptible thread that has been laid through the passages of the labyrinth. I do not know where the thread leads or what I will find at its end, whether the heat of Hell, the roar of the Minotaur, or, worst of all, silence, satiety, nothing.

This afternoon I went to the Berthiers'. My aunt Sophie greeted me with a forced, nervous gaiety which at first I thought was to hide her offense that I had missed their 'day' last week. I have been so self-absorbed of late that now I relate every small occurrence to myself. I suppose that it is because she is my mother's sister that I am especially conscious of my loathsome infection as I stoop to kiss her cheek. I was so filled with shame that I could hardly bring myself to mouth the conventional pleasantries, and I had to excuse myself awkwardly.

I found Aristide talking to Lothar and was about to turn away and find another opportunity to speak with my uncle, but at that moment he raised his head and spotted me, and so I had no choice but to go over and join their conversation. Lothar was rather more full of himself than usual.

'Austria-Hungary's position,' he was telling Aristide, 'is that winning or losing a war is not so important as fighting it. We can't let Bismarck trample all over treaties with our allies. Win or lose, we have to stand up to the fellow, even if all we do is bloody his nose.'

'I take it you won't be doing the actual fighting?' Aristide inquired. He seemed tired and looked about the room distractedly as if his mind were weighed down by other matters.

'My country believes I can most usefully serve the Empire in my present capacity,' Lothar said smoothly.

'Spoken like a true diplomat,' I said. Lothar treated this as a compliment.

'I think you're far better off here, both of you,' Aristide said. 'The Mausers the Prussians have can deliver a deadly rate of fire. That's what it comes down to more and more – not courage but bullets per minute. They say war is becoming a science.'

'And the stock market is the first casualty,' Lothar said. 'Especially Occidental Traders – what a bloodbath!'

I thought I saw a look of pain cross Aristide's face, but it could have been only fatigue. 'Occidental Traders,' he breathed as men do when a phrase has taken on some profound, private meaning for them. 'I hope you boys weren't in too deep. I did warn you, didn't I?'

He looked at our faces anxiously for signs of disaster.

'Yes, indeed,' I said, nodding my head vigorously to reassure him.

'If it's any consolation, I got caught in the collapse myself. I saw it coming, thought the stock would ride it out . . . and you know the rest. Lost more than I care to mention, actually.' He chuckled to try to make it appear that Occidental Traders and losing money were things that do not matter to a man of his resources and experience, but the sound came out tight and self-defeating.

Lothar, the perfect diplomat, changed the subject, and I found an excuse to wander away in search of Nichole.

She was surrounded by her sycophantic friends and did not see me approach. I think I must have startled her, coming from behind and appearing suddenly in her field of vision, because she stopped in the middle of what she was saying and appeared briefly disconcerted before recovering her poise. Something about the fresh, pretty faces of the girls in their white dresses, and the decent, untried faces of the men in attendance, made me feel out of place. I felt old and corrupt among them. I belonged more properly with Lothar.

But Nichole was trying to include me in the conversation. She was the light, and I looked at her from my dark place as if this was the last time that we would see each other. I listened as she spoke, not to the words, but to the music of her voice, and tried to remember it, yet there was no place for her memory to reside within me. I joined them in their repartee, for what passed as wit; I listened to stories and critiques of plays and descriptions of who sat with whom at the theater. Nichole glanced at me from time to time to see if I was growing impatient with this silliness. And all the while the sadness grew in me like a sickness. I was taking my leave. I was going on a long voyage. No, I had already left. Part of me had already hardened to those tender emotions as a frost nips off green shoots. I grieved for the life I was leaving and for the passing of feelings which would soon no longer matter to me.

I would have taken my leave, but it was too early for me to do so politely, and so I went out to the conservatory to be alone. It was a place where men would go in order to smoke a cigar and talk of business matters without annoying the ladies, but today the miniature jungle was empty. I stood next to a plant with large, leathery leaves which seemed so alien to me that they could have come from another planet, and I imagined a life of service and self-sacrifice in the tropics as a medical missionary. I could not face the alternative, returning to Hungary to wait in loneliness and boredom for the disease to run its course.

Lost in such gloomy contemplation, I did not at first hear the door open and softly close, and I do not know by what process I became aware of her presence behind me. I turned, not knowing the reason, until I saw Nichole.

'I didn't want to disturb you,' she said.

'Really, you're not,' I replied as she came toward me.

'You looked as though you were deep in thought.'

'I suppose I was.'

'You're such a deep person, Laszlo. So much of the time I haven't the faintest idea what you're feeling.'

'I was thinking about life. How you come to a point where you have to make a choice, where you can go one way or another way.'

'I know.'

I looked at her in surprise. I had assumed, without thinking about it, that Nichole's life was unblemished, that it proceeded without impediment or risk and so without the necessity of any decisions more wrenching that the choice of fabric for her newest dress.

'Sooner or later, everything changes,' she went on. 'All good things come to an end.'

'I suppose so,' I said, although I was not at all sure what she was alluding to.

'Like childhood. That's something that comes to an end. Do you remember?'

'Childhood coming to an end? I'm not sure there was an actual moment when I was aware of that happening.'

'When do you become aware of things? When do you know something about yourself and realize that you're not a child anymore?' She had a far-off gaze in her eyes.

'When innocence no longer serves?' I suggested. 'When you know what you know?'

'Yes, that.' She looked down as if considering the risk of putting something into words. 'I was thinking of the time Mama and I visited you at the castle,' she said without raising her head. 'The poem . . . the infatuation.'

'I loved you,' I said, more to correct a misconception than to declare myself. Nothing mattered now. History had no value. This was not a road I was to take.

But she looked up suddenly, and there were tears in her eyes. 'I know,' she said. 'I know you did. You were so intense, so serious, so determined.'

'And you?' I asked. I might have been practicing for my new occupation as an anthropologist on the Solomon Islands.

'I'm ashamed.'

'Don't be,' I said. 'It was all a long, long time ago. Another world. Those things have no relevance for us today.'

She looked stricken. 'Don't say that!' I thought she would raise her hand to my lips to shut off the words. 'I was cruel to you, but don't throw those times away.

I teased you – you know that. I drew you on, I cut you off, I raised your hopes and then dashed them with my coldness. You were supposed to think that these were actions of a moody young girl who hardly knew what she was doing. But everything was calculated and deliberate. I really wasn't innocent at all.'

'Why are you telling me this?' I said. I had no further need of pain.

'No one had ever loved me,' she told me with a desperate expression on her face, as if she would be damned if I didn't believe her. 'I'd never experienced it before. I didn't know what to do with it.'

'You concealed your feelings well.'

'I had to. I was afraid. Mama and I were in awe of your family. In those days we didn't have all this.' She indicated our surroundings with a peremptory wave of her hand, and then I thought she caught herself, as if she were noticing the opulence of her home for the first time. 'We lived quite modestly then.' She sighed. 'It's all so ephemeral.'

'But we live in an old, tumble-down ruin,' I said.

'I saw a venerable, ancient monument which had been in your family for centuries. You don't know how the romance of it affected me – just the thought of it. For weeks before we set out, Mama coached me on how I must behave among the aristocracy, which glasses I must drink wine from, which forks I should use with each dish. By the time we arrived, we'd worked ourselves into quite a state. But long before we set out I had made up my mind to captivate you. You were to be my prince, just like in the children's stories. Mama hinted that you should fall in love with me, even though I didn't really know what that was. You were the Count's son. You see, I was thoroughly intimidated.'

While she was talking, I had been thinking of the drafty old castle with its stagnant moat and dilapidated roofs. With some stretch of the imagination, on a sunny, cheerful day, one might say it possessed a certain medieval charm, but that a visitor should view it as imposing or in any way noble seemed to me astonishing.

'How far apart we were,' I said with a bitter laugh. 'And I thought you were disdainful of my decrepit home and our provincial ways!'

'I thought, if I could entice you, you'd never notice how ordinary I was.'

'You have never been ordinary, Nichole.'

'I worked to draw you in.'

'I never noticed.'

'You weren't supposed to see the artifice, only to feel the attraction.'

'How did you know what to do?'

'I guessed. I tried to remember things I had heard Mama say to her friends when she thought I hadn't been listening. And then it all came naturally, without scheming – '

'Scheming?' The word stung me.

'I'm sorry,' she said, and I saw in her face an expression of pain that could have been no less than my own. 'I want to tell you: that was how it began. But that wasn't the whole of it, or the most important part of it.'

'You make me feel like a fool.'

'No!' She reached out and grasped my arm. 'Please!' I was surprised by the tenacity of her fingers, by the urgency of her emotion. 'That wasn't how it really was.'

'Then how was it?' I asked, blundering ahead like a wounded rhinoceros, mad with pain, charging full tilt toward the coup de grâce.

'I loved you.'

'Oh, no!' I turned involuntarily from her.

Nichole came close behind me. I could hear her rapid breathing and I took in the fragrance of her perfume, which had been infiltrated with the musky essence of her skin. Tentatively, then more firmly when I did not shake her off, she pressed her hand against my back, and I felt her warmth spread and suffuse my body with a glorious, aching presence. Her head was at my shoulder, almost resting upon it, and she whispered in my ear. 'I was afraid.

I was afraid to love you. I couldn't tell you what I felt. I couldn't even hint to you at the possibility. I was afraid to admit it even to myself. I flirted. I teased you with the mirror.' Perhaps she felt me stiffen, for she added, 'Forgive me!'

I was afraid to ask her what she meant. My head was spinning with the implications of what I feared. How had Nichole found out about the telescope? Had she known about it during her visit to the castle? If so, then she had known that I was watching while she walked naked before my mirror. And that meant that she had willingly revealed herself to me. Here was a sensual element in her makeup of which I had had no inkling. And if that was so, then who was this complex, mysterious woman? And who was the person I had loved? These questions swooped like bats on a summer night, sensed at the edges of consciousness more than seen.

'I hope you will forgive me, as I forgive you,' she whispered.

'For what?' I persisted, though I was sure she knew.

'For showing myself so shamelessly.' I think she sensed I could not bring myself to admit what I had done. She said, 'I noticed that the mirror was always turned to an awkward angle. Even after I'd adjusted it, the next time I'd find it set again in the same position, even though it couldn't have been any use to someone there. One day I sat on the side of the bath and I looked to see what it did reflect, and I saw the sun glint on your telescope. I knew you were there.'

There was a firmness of purpose about her, a determination to reach the truth, which was also new to me. Had I been blind and deaf not to see this person?

'Then, why . . .?' I began.

'Because I wanted you to see me.' I felt like a confessor as she spoke, a hurried, invisible voice from close behind me, into my ear. 'In the beginning, I just wanted to affect you,' she said. 'I was a girl trying out my power over a man. Would you desire me? It was a secret bond neither of us could acknowledge. Nothing was said. We were hidden from one another. I could act like a slut and still pretend to be a lady at teatime. You treated me like a lover, and I responded like a girl. I was ashamed. I wanted you to see that I was a woman.'

'I don't deserve you,' I said, managing with difficulty to control my shaking voice. I was glad that she couldn't see my face. I had moved beyond shock to a deep sadness that we should have been separated by nothing more substantial than mere fancies.

'No,' Nichole said. 'I don't deserve *you*.' I thought that she rested her head on my shoulder at that moment, but I cannot be sure, since her touch was so subtle. I did not turn to her because I sensed there was more that she was preparing herself to say. 'And now . . .' she began. I started to speak but she cut me off, and I realized that she was making a statement, not asking me a question. 'And now you have come back into my life, a man showing all the sensitivity and nobility of spirit that I could have hoped for.'

'You do not know me,' I said in despair. I would have severed my hand with a hatchet if the bargain would have let me take back time.

'But I do!' she cried, and I felt her press against me along the length of our bodies.

'Anyway, it's too late.' There was a curtness to my tone by which I wounded myself as much as I hurt her. I felt her stiffen and pull away.

'You love someone else.'

'No,' I said, with a weariness almost of life itself. 'I loved you then, and I love you still. No one will ever take your place in my heart. I belong to you.'

She didn't believe me, even though what I said was the sacred truth. And why should she, when I did not take her in my arms there and then and press her to me in a rapturous kiss? A leper's kiss!

'I've been my own worst enemy,' she said as if to herself. 'I've played with you. You've meant so much to me I couldn't bear it. I flirted with Lothar to make you jealous, and now he wants to marry me.'

A chill ran through me, like a bolt of emotional lightning cleaving its jagged path through my very tissue. I felt unable to recover. Something in my heart was smashed, but I mustered all my self-control and asked her with a studied nonchalance whose every syllable seemed like the exercise of a supreme linguistic skill, 'And will you?'

'Only if you won't have me,' she said.

I was touched to the core by her courage, and a sob would have broken from me if I had not stifled it in time.

'I have nothing to offer you,' I said coldly.

'And I have nothing to offer you,' she replied. 'Only my love. I have no dowry to speak of – yes, I know,' she said as if I might dispute what she had just told me. 'You would not think it to see how we live. But our circumstances have changed. It has all been very sudden. A sudden, unfortunate turn of events.'

'Lothar is a wealthy man. He will be able to keep you in the style to which you are accustomed.'

'Yes, Lothar is rich. He has already told my father he doesn't care about the dowry. But I don't love him.'

Is there a moment such as this, the keen blade raised in one hand, a pause of infinite intensity, before one strikes at one's own flesh? I said, 'I cannot love you.' And it was done.

I heard her abrupt intake of breath. Tears flowed from my eyes. I could not turn to her.

'I have destroyed the only thing I ever cared for!' she sobbed. She held it back and would not surrender to her grief.

I felt her fingers linger on my back, as if breaking contact would magically usher in a new, bleak era called 'forever' or 'the rest of our lives.' Then suddenly she was gone. I heard the rustle of her skirts and the sharp sound of her heels on the tiled floor as she walked swiftly away from me. From the opposite direction came the approaching sound of gruff, masculine voices, and I retreated deeper into the conservatory to find a place among the palms for my heart to die in private.

But life goes on. I am not dead. On the contrary, I am a man with nothing to lose. That is an entirely different phenomenon. I do not intend to make a career of despair or a philosophy of what might have been. The thing to do is to stamp out the remaining embers of tenderness and to do it systematically. For now, I want to submerge in oblivion, to get drunk, or, the same thing, to waste myself in Stacia. Why can she not see me tonight, or tomorrow night, or the night after?

EARLY MORNING, JUNE 30, 1866

When I began this diary – God, with such good intentions and lightness of spirit that now I hardly recognize the writer! – I could have had no inkling that I was writing my own case study. Case study or confession? Sickness or evil? Let the competent authorities judge for themselves. I am numb. I am dazed. I suspect that if I were to entertain emotion I would feel an eerie exhilaration. That is enough introspection. Just enough for the proper degree of clinical detachment and no more. It will all be over soon.

The dawn is breaking over the rooftops. It seems that it was a year ago, but it was only last night that I went to Stacia's building. I did not go straight there, of course, since she had already let me know that she would not be able to receive me. She never gives a reason, and her tone makes it clear that I have no right to ask. This irks me, as it is no doubt supposed to. I have no call on her. She indicates that she has other lovers, but somehow I feel that I am her only chosen companion, and that the others are paying customers. This was the state of sulky, drunken truculence in which I waited beneath her lighted window. Let us add a dash of self-pity to the mixture. How that ingredient adds spice to the other emotions! But 'self-pity' perhaps understates the high moral pathos with which the evening began, as I returned to my lodgings from the Berthiers' reception. I think I can say that at that point I was experiencing a despair of truly heroic proportions.

First the man for whom I now feel no compassion completed the entry in this diary. Then, as darkness fell, I made my way to that squalid corner of the Latin Quarter where Stacia has her secret room. It was still too early to expect her to have come from the hospital, and I debated whether to conceal myself in a place from which I could step forth and accost her as she made her way to the dilapidated tenement, or whether I should drink until I could expect her to be alone. I chose absinthe. Is it the bitter taste of wormwood that makes the oily liquid taste of death? Or is it the drunkenness it induces that gives one a foretaste of the lethal idiocy absinthe causes in those who fall under its spell? (I chuckle to myself as I spin out these speculations: Does the condemned man grope for new sins to tell the priest in the hope that he will delay his execution and so gain one minute more of life?)

Late, oblivious of time, I stumbled from the doorway of a wine shop. The streets were empty of honest citizens. I concentrated on walking without staggering, and this took much of my mental abilities. I could see that a dim light glowed in Stacia's room, and I passed on without stopping to a place in the shadows beneath some steps from which I could observe those who came and went from her building. It was a spot from which I had spied before, without success. Crouching soon became too much to sustain, and so I sat down in that dank corner. I fell asleep. If anyone saw me, they must have assumed I was another drunkard. I don't know what woke me. At first I didn't know where I was. I was more sober than I had been when I fell asleep, in that painful state when drunkenness and hangover coexist.

From where I sprawled I could see that there was still a light in Stacia's window, but I could not see the entrance door to the tenement. In some pain, I moved my stiffened legs to achieve a crouch and then a cautious stoop so that I could peer over the steps which concealed me from view. Lothar stood before the closed door. He looked carefully left and right. Was he on the watch for footpads, or did he suspect that Aristide's agents shadowed him in order to check up on the activities of the future son-in-law? Apparently he was satisfied that the way was clear, and with a jaunty swing of his cane he set off down the street.

At that point, my curiosity satisfied, I should have returned home. Can there be any human faculty more fatuous than hindsight? Instead, drunk, maudlin, aggrieved, lonely, and with a smoldering rage I did not acknowledge, I climbed the familiar stairs to Stacia's room, feeling my way in the darkness by the familiar landmarks to the landing at the top.

I knocked. There was an exclamation of pleasure within and the sounds of her hurrying across the room. The door swung open.

'I knew you would . . .' Stacia began in a bantering tone, but the gaiety fell from her face when she saw that it was I. 'Oh,' she said as if this were a statement of greeting. She made no attempt to hide a look of puzzlement and displeasure as she stepped aside, after a moment's hesitation, to allow me to enter the room. The air was humid with the intimate smell of two people who have been enclosed together for some hours.

She was wearing a new dress that I did not recognize. It was a stylish evening gown which ensheathed her in black satin and its sleek sophistication struck an odd contrast with the shabby furnishings of the room. With her fair complexion, Stacia appeared pale and unearthly, physically tentative, within its dense, uncompromising black. Evidently she had started to undress when her visitor had left, for some of the fastening at the back was undone, and where the gown was designed to fit taut across her shoulders, it hung slack, inviting a stealthy, insinuating hand to wend its way under cover of the loosened fabric toward its warm, sensuous goal. Or a fist to grip and tear the rich material from her. Out of the corner of my eye, I saw Stacia begin to fasten the dress and then change her mind, as if her dishabille might give her an advantage over me.

She stood with her back resting against the closed door and sighed. 'I thought I had made it clear – '

'Perfectly,' I said. 'You made it perfectly clear.'

'I thought we had an understanding.'

'That all depends on what you understand to be the understanding,' I said, a ridiculous statement which immediately revealed my drunkenness, if she had not already smelled it upon me.

Feeling like a policeman, I paced restlessly about the room, seeking details from which I could reconstruct what had occurred in this space while I had slept below. On the table, among the remains of a meal, Stacia had discarded a bunch of yellow orchids which were wilting from lack of water. A knife with a bone handle rested within the perfect spiral of an apple's green skin, pared with all the precision of a demonstration in geometry. How typical of Lothar's facility with the surface of things! I imagined him feeding her moist slivers of the flesh, insisting in his perverse way that she let him place each morsel between her lips.

'I'm a free person,' Stacia said. 'I come and go as I want. I'm not your patient here.'

'You're not my patient at all,' I corrected her hurriedly.

'This is my place here. I see who I please here.'

'He is going to be married – did you know that?'

'Who is that?'

'Herr von Pick. The man who was here only a few minutes ago. Surely you have not forgotten him already?'

Stacia sighed impatiently. 'What he does with his time when he's not with me is none of my concern.' I thought I saw a calculating look upon her face, a quick appraisal of the value of each new snippet of information. 'It's none of your business either, is it?' she demanded.

'As a matter of fact, I think it is.'

'And how does that come about?'

'Because I happen to know the young lady in question,' I said, blushing with some residue of shame that I thought I had completely exhausted. 'I care for her deeply.'

'Aren't you the knight in shining armor!'

This seemed very funny to her. It built in her until she threw back her head to give free reign to her laughter; she held her sides and her shoulders shook with merriment. I had not noted her for a developed sense of humor before. Moreover, I was at a loss to understand the source of her amusement, though I knew it was at my expense. She found me ridiculous. She found the whole notion of the sacredness of marriage absurd. She laughed on and on, and I began to wonder if she had lost control of herself. Clearly her laughter sprang from some cathartic vein which gathered force from itself and from the counterpoint of my seriousness.

I stared at her bared throat with a peculiar sense of detachment. That, I believe, was the start of it.

'Does it not trouble your conscience?' I demanded.

'No. Should it?' she asked lightly.

'That you should affect an innocent woman in this way?'

'I don't mind sharing. Why should she? The gentleman concerned has more than enough for both of us,' she goaded me. 'Besides, he's going to make an honest woman of me and get me a position as a lady's maid.'

'For God's sake, don't you care that you'll infect her?'

Her angelic face was transformed into a mask of the utmost ugliness. 'What!' she screamed.

'You know very well what I mean.'

She scoffed. 'You've been talking to Roland.' Her anger vanished now that she had located the source of the charge.

'He told me a man killed himself because of you.'

Was there a hidden look of satisfaction, of conceitedness even, that I caught upon her face just before Stacia turned from me?

'Roland is insanely jealous,' she said. 'He says all sorts of things.'

Her equanimity was restored; her good humor had returned. She stood before her mirror humming a tune to herself as she turned this way and that to admire her new gown. Suddenly she looked up as if a random thought had reminded her that I was still in the room.

'Oh, Laszlo!' she exclaimed with a mild fondness which already contained a hint of nostalgia for times which were past. 'For you, everything is so serious, so intense! Let me give you some advice.' She was lording it over me, rubbing in the humiliation which was part of the pleasure of her triumph. 'Nothing really matters. It's all a game. Like at the hospital, at the professor's demonstrations: Everyone so serious, waiting to see if I'll remember, if I'll forget. It's just theater.'

I must have stared at her stupidly. 'Did you think it was real?' she asked me pityingly. Her laughter began again. It was laughter one hears on the stage at the opera, laughter set to music. Perhaps Lothar had taken her. 'You men think you're so clever!' She twirled in delight before the mirror. 'The professor tells me with his questions what he wants me to do, and then he believes he's made a great discovery when I play it out for him! Did you think I didn't recognize you at the house on Rue de Londres? Do you think I wouldn't have recognized the man in the second row who asked his question?'

She began to mime a bewildered hypnotic subject who walked like an automaton toward the table and, as it were, against her will raised the wineglass to her lips and drank. I had come toward her, but she whirled away from me.

'Now tell me,' she said, leaning forward to taunt me, 'who is the actor and who is the director of the play?'

I wanted her to stop, and my hand closed around the knife among the apple parings.

'Enough!' I shouted.

I shook the knife like a pointed index finger, for emphasis, but I couldn't get her to pay attention. Stacia had begun to laugh again, trilling up and down the scale to show that even in mockery she was an artiste of accomplishment. Now she pirouetted on her toes, and as she spun toward me it seemed natural that I should anticipate her rotation with a purely mechanical thrust of my arm which seemed to have nothing whatever to do with what I was thinking at the time. The knife struck her in the throat. I felt it catch, and then her momentum forced the blade through the resistance, and she fell away from me.

Dazed, I watched her heart continue to pump blood through the wound for several more seconds, and it was not until the flow finally petered out that I began to realize what I had done. Her eyes were open when I knelt beside her, her hand warm. After several moments, I found that I had been studying the mesmerizing reality of a strand of her hair.

Now that I was so close to her, I no longer thought of Stacia as dead, but in some state other than life in which she had wielded power over me. I hesitated to look at her face. I avoided those staring eyes as if they might possess me. I bent to kiss her lips, but instead I extended the movement. Gently, I pressed my lips against the soft, surrendering edges of the wound and tasted the still unclotted blood which welled there.

I believe I was unseen, except for Madame Thébauld who was roused by the creak of the gate. The curtain of her window twitched back as I entered the courtyard. Whether there were witnesses or not makes no difference, since I intend to surrender myself to the authorities once I have had some sleep. This diary is my confession. I can think of no defense which mitigates my action, and I do not intend to plead for mercy. Strange, the tricks of the mind! At various moments I find myself wondering whether Stacia will attend my trial, how she will comport herself, whether she will feel compassion when I am condemned, if she will forgive me when she hears that I am to forfeit my life.

JULY 1, 1866

We have just crossed the French frontier; I am safely beyond the reach of the law, if not justice.

This morning I was woken by a loud hammering on my door, and I thought it was the police come to arrest me. Outside stood Uncle Kalman with an agitated and ever curious Madame Thébauld hovering in the background. George has been killed in the first engagement against the Prussians. We are to return to Hungary for the funeral, after which I am to be invested as the new count.

Uncle Kalman sits opposite me now; his ramrod posture will make no allowance for the sway of the train. At intervals, absent-minded tears roll down my cheeks as I stare at the landscape which unfolds outside our carriage window. At other times, I am overcome by the absurdity of the rescue Fate has contrived, and a mad, uncontrollable guffaw breaks loose from me. The gruff old soldier is uncomfortable with these displays of emotion and retreats with noisy throat clearing and much rustling behind his newspaper. He assumes I am distressed by my brother's death.

8

MAY 17, 1887

Twenty years have passed since I wrote those last words. During that time this diary has remained closed in its hiding place in the library, sitting unobtrusively on a shelf among my grandfather's collection of theological treatises. There have been times when I was tempted to slip my finger into the groove between its boards and feel again the smoothness of the tooled leather and the flick of these crisp white pages, which seemed intended for only the most portentous thoughts. I have gone so far as to slide the ladder on its brass rail to a point below which the diary sat, mount a step or two, and stand irresolutely in limbo before turning back to safer ground.

The diary is like an itch. I have reasoned that if I make the effort to ignore the sensation, if I leave the book unread, the impulse will, in time, fade of its own accord. But if I scratch at it, if I pander to my nostalgia, I gratify myself only at the cost of creating a further and greater need to scratch; soon the itch intensifies to a distracting, nagging thirst for touch, to an obsession for the caress which will provide a fleeting but voluptuous fulfillment. It will end as a craving, without the possibility of pleasure, which consumes all awareness.

Today, after lunch, I gave Brod orders that I was not to be disturbed and sat down to read it through for the first time. I had hoped to find that the young man who began the diary was dead, but it is not so. Of course, the young Laszlo was a fool. Stacia and Lothar manipulated him with ridiculous ease. Perhaps Nichole did, too, but perhaps that is merely the cynicism of the person I have become. I have not lost his curiosity or love of life, although I have spent much of the last two decades in a monkish kind of existence in order to extinguish these qualities. More or less, I have been trying to kill myself without actually dying. I am afraid that neither of the Laszlos has been particularly courageous on that score, on 'doing the decent thing,' as George would have said.

I certainly did not marry George's wife out of spite. I tend to think of it as a kind of penance, even though the union was dictated by purely dynastic – that is, business – considerations. George's marriage to Elizabeth was something for which Uncle Kalman had wheedled and schemed for years. Elizabeth is the only daughter of one of our neighbors and a distant relative, and she brought in her dowry substantial tracts of land which bordered our own. A covenant in her father's will promised that all of his land would eventually follow her marriage, as long as our families remained united. In a state close to emotional collapse on my return to the castle from Paris, afraid that I could be summoned at any moment to account for Stacia's death, and convinced that I was utterly undeserving of the position into which Fortune had thrust me, I had no heart to resist when Uncle Kalman broached the subject in his usual blunt fashion soon after George had been buried.

It is certain that I do not deserve a woman of Elizabeth's goodness. No man does. She is a saint. She is generous, forgiving, pious, and kind. She has the eye of an eagle for all that may be good in a man, be it no more than a single atom of altruism, and she is blind to human faults which she will argue, with an ingenuity bordering on sophistry, derive from good intentions subverted by misfortune. Is it not proof of the Devil's mischief that I have prayed for some fatal accident to befall this excellent woman – for dear Elizabeth to encounter some unthinking, inculpable agent of chance such as the loose tile which, falling from the height of the tower, ten years ago mangled a horse?

It is no small thing to contemplate carnal relations

148

with the wife of one's dead brother. Elizabeth is not unattractive. She has an oval, open face which beams forth honesty and optimism, although her complexion is somewhat colorless. Her fine, pale hair has a curling tendency which is a trial to her. Once she told me that as a girl she prayed that God would make her hair straight and at confession was fiercely admonished by the priest for such vanity. She is not plump, but there is a softness about her body which, while others might find it comfortable or even desirable in a slightly Rubenesque way, is not to my taste. I have not made love to her. I have been afraid of the risk of infecting her with syphilis and of impregnating her with a series of idiots and madmen. Consequently, we have no heir. I have not discussed with her the reason for my lack of attention, since I confide in her very little; rather, we lead our lonely, secret lives in parallel. She is inherently maternal and longs for a child. In addition, Elizabeth is strongly sexed, much to my surprise early in our marriage, since I had supposed that someone so pious would have no truck with lust, even within the conjugal bed. I quickly learned to recognize in her the signs of impending seduction – restlessness, sighing, incessant, nervous fanning of herself in summer, in winter hot glances across the table at dinner – and used the expedient of the so-called solitary vice to induce in myself satiety to the point of impotence. Then, when I dutifully visited her bedchamber, the obvious cause of the unconsummated state of our marriage lay limp and palpable between us. On reflection, these arrangements seem not so much sordid as impossibly lonely. Yet I represented my actions to myself as chivalrous.

Instead, I have busied myself in managing the estate, which had been run into the ground by Uncle Kalman, my father during his brief tenure, and by my grandfather, the theological dabbler. We have been poor country squires for generations, yet the lands we held have always been potentially prosperous, given consistent attention and a firm hand. The small town which sits at the bottom of the hill below the castle has grown enormously since the arrival of the railway. I am generally given credit for that development, though no one in the town is aware of the substantial bribe I placed with the railway company's chief engineer so that the line would run through our valley.

I have taken up the diary again now that Uncle Kalman is dead. It would be difficult to exaggerate the influence of this man within the castle. He was himself a kind of bastion, a towering, glowering man with an enormous mustache coming to points almost level with his earlobes which he would sweep between finger and thumb at times when he became emotionally exercised. He meant well, but he was used to dealing with recalcitrant soldiers, and his military manner struck terror into George and myself. George was quick to learn how to earn his favor, but I did not gain his approval until I had gone to boarding school after mother died, and so I suffered during my formative years under his stern and disapproving gaze.

It was through Gregory that I at last gained some measure of respect from my uncle. I had brought my new friend home for the holidays, because Gregory, an orphan like myself, was also a scholarship boy and would otherwise have had to remain during Christmas with the fathers at St Sebastian's. Uncle Kalman asked Gregory if he wished to accompany George and himself hunting. I think he invited Gregory more out of politeness than in any expectation that he might want to join them, since Gregory was my friend and I had consistently voiced my opinions on the cruelty of the sport. Gregory accepted the offer at once. Feeling vaguely betrayed, but also left out, I volunteered my company 'for the exercise'. The exhilaration of hunting has never left me from that day. I developed a passion for stalking animals and a skill for closing on them which even my uncle could not match. From that day on, Uncle Kalman and I would walk forth into the woods together. It was the single activity in which we achieved any kind of harmony. In later years, for variety – I believe he was never aware of this – I would separate from Uncle Kalman in the forest in order to stalk him.

We disagreed on all other things. I think that in his heart he did not recognize me as the real count. I was the representative of a modern world he would have no truck with, a world which had brought machines and change into the settled arrangements of the valley. The railway was a striking embodiment of this process, and he blamed me for what he perceived as the rape of the landscape, the movement of the young people into the cities, the breakdown of discipline. I was the count, but he had the loyalty of many of the families, and he had commanded the men when they had been in the army during their two years' service. His stubborn disapproval should not have bothered me, except that the tone of his voice evoked within me echoes of the cowed attitudes of boyhood.

He died four days ago. Gregory presided at the funeral yesterday. Uncle Kalman always had a soft spot for Gregory. When he was a boy, our uncle bestowed on him small gestures of tenderness – a hand resting momentarily on his shoulder, unusual fussiness about the piece of meat he carved for him at the dinner table – which George and I never knew. Strangely, we did not begrudge him this special treatment; without speaking about it, I think we both believed that Gregory had so little and had accomplished so much with none of our advantages, that he had a right to some kind of compensation. George, anyway, was so eager to win Uncle Kalman's approval that he could not have brought himself to question his uncle's behavior even if he had thought the favoritism unfair (there were times during George's early adolescence when he reminded me of an eager setter, forever rushing off to fetch the stick, returning with wagging tail, never once questioning the wisdom of his task, even though Uncle Kalman would seem to have a penchant for landing the stick in the metaphorical equivalent of a muddy pond). After Gregory's ordination, Uncle Kalman's relationship with him changed; he treated Gregory with a rare respect and with a deference I think it is unlikely he had accorded even his commanding general. Gregory, in turn, revered him, but in a quiet, discriminating way which was in contrast to George, and Kalman appeared to value his love all the more that it was not given easily. Mine, of course, was not given at all. I was my mother's boy and had no use for a surrogate father. Uncle Kalman at least had the good sense not to inflict his sense of paternal duty on me, except in matters of discipline, and he tended to leave me alone to my reading and daydreams in the library, a room he rarely entered because it made him feel ill at ease.

In Gregory's hands, the funeral mass was a strangely spiritual occasion with which to mark the passing of this man of no nonsense. A vast crowd filled the church, and all of the spaces in the pews were taken with ancient grandees in fur cloaks slung from one shoulder, with swords and sabers worn even by those who required a young retainer to help them hobble to their places. All the old families had sent a representative to honor my uncle. So little room remained that the burghers of the town and the workers of the estate had to stand. They filled the aisles and overflowed onto the porch, and when the time came to pray, they knelt on the cold stone flags on which memorials to our ancestors had been carved. Above us were unfurled the banners which had led our men into battle since the time of the Crusades. It was a grand dynastic pageant which filled the mysterious gloom of our church; the massed voices of four hundred were a resounding demonstration of solidarity for the reactionary ideas of noble prerogative which my uncle espoused. How he would have relished the occasion!

Gregory – Father Gregory, that is, not our teatime companion who regales us with gossip – did him proud. Not that Gregory embellished Kalman or said anything that was untrue in his oration. The man he recommended to his Maker was the man he had experienced, someone who might have existed for George or even myself. This

Kalman was the person divined by the pure spirit and starry eyes of Elizabeth. He was not a saint or anything even close to that state of virtue, but a man of heart who had invested his modest talents, and large passion, and vast energy to further all those with whom he felt bound by reciprocal ties of loyalty. Loyalty, not goodness or rightness, was the guiding principle of Kalman's life. These were the kind of things which Gregory said. I suppose he was right, though from the perspective from which I had viewed Uncle Kalman, he described a man I scarcely recognized.

I was pondering these thoughts as I strolled a short distance along the path from the church – Elizabeth had lingered at the door to talk to Gregory about his oration – when I was startled by a sudden sharp sound at my feet. Someone had dropped a prayer book as I passed, and it hit the flagstone of the path with a slap. I stooped to pick it up. It belonged to the mayor's daughter, and she curtsied as I handed it back to her. But instead of looking bashfully at her toes as I was accustomed to the girls of the town and the farms to do when I addressed them, she fixed me with a direct and penetrating gaze such as I am rarely subjected to today. I am the count: My people look to gauge my mood or inclination, as a peasant might scan the clouds to see if it will rain on his hay, but they do not look far into my face. Even when I am shaving and look in the mirror I scarcely notice myself. In some sense, I have ceased to exist in my own awareness. This has come about as a creeping numbness of the soul that has been so gradual that I have barely noticed it.

I have been on the alert to detect in myself the numbness, the *tabes dorsalis*, of syphilis. For several years, on the first day of each month, I have pricked each finger and toe with a needle I keep for this purpose among my cuff links. Each month, I ask myself if the prick felt quite as sharp as it had a month ago. I have developed no rashes or gummas. My cognitive faculties are as acute as one might expect in a man who has been buried for twenty years in this rural backwater. As far as I can tell, I am not mad – in fact, quite the opposite. I am sober and industrious to the point that I no longer recognize how bored I am by my existence. In other words, I have survived so long without the slightest sign of infection showing itself that I can say without a shadow of doubt that I do not have the disease, have never had the disease.

If the castle has been my prison, and Uncle Kalman my jailor, and syphilis my sentence, then the slap of the prayer book on the flagstone was the moment at which I was set free.

MAY 19, 1887

The receiving line at Uncle Kalman's funeral had been endless, and I spent several hours greeting the procession of Magyar noblemen in national costume, each one seeming to be a caricature of himself – wizened horsemen in high boots, britches, and fearsome mustaches; slick courtiers from Budapest with silk panels to their tunics and tassels dangling from every corner of their dress; and grand magnates hung with furs like latter-day barbarians. They passed as a blur before my eyes, each achieving a startling individuality which was then canceled by the next fellow. I had long regarded them as colorful, but rather comic anachronisms when they had visited my uncle. They are part of an old Hungary which has no relevance now. The future lies with the towns, with the railways and industry, and with the merchant classes, not we land-owners.

I recollected that one man had introduced himself to me as George's colonel. He spoke warmly of my brother, as many did on that occasion. George's own funeral had been overshadowed by our defeat by the Prussians, and the ceremony had been without the pomp and pride which so marked Kalman's leave-taking. But over the years, like a fire gathering force from its own heat, George's reputation had grown to the extent that he had reached the status of a martyr. These men in the receiving line fitted George into a family tradition which had begun in the distant, dim, and entirely unverifiable past and came to culmination with my father, a true martyr to the cause of Hungarian nationalism. I am not sure how George truly fit into this scheme of things, since he died fighting the Prussians for the Hapsburgs, but I sensed in these Magyar noblemen a need to create heroes, as if heroes constituted the political fuel that drove their cause.

Uncle Kalman had carried this torch. Soon after I had been invested as count he had begun a conversation with much throat-clearing and false starts in which he had tried to interest me in something called the Magyar League. His attempts to enlist my support were limited by the fact that the League appeared to be some kind of secret society whose nature he was not at liberty to reveal to me unless I first promised to join. I was reminded of his earlier, and astonishingly inaccurate, attempts to explain to George and myself the facts of life. Both talks revolved around some statement by Uncle Kalman which seemed to have been taken from the midst of a conversation he had previously rehearsed with himself, quickly followed by a gruff 'Don't you agree?' or 'That understood?' As a man with a thoroughly military cast of mind, my uncle acknowledged the mental states of assent and incomprehension, but not disagreement. Since he thought it was essential for the count to be an active member of the League, I followed a policy of procrastination. When this wore thin, I questioned him on matters on which I guessed he was sworn to secrecy, and then he would mutter dark threats of what would befall those who were not part of 'the coming order.' Perhaps if I had known Colonel Rado better I would have taken the League more seriously.

The reason I had not remembered Colonel Rado when he had paid his respects is that he did not fit the stereotype of the Magyar nobleman. He is a man of slightly less than medium height of, I would guess, fifty-five years of age, but with a sprightly bearing and a rapidity of movement that would suggest a younger man. His hair is still black, brushed back from his forehead, with gray spreading from the temples. His face is complex, changing in expression frequently, so that I feel I have no confidence in discerning his inner life. The colonel sports the obligatory cavalry mustache, but is otherwise free of the swagger and affectation which have come to seem as much a part of an army officer as his uniform. He listens attentively, and his eyes flick back and forth from one point of fixation to another, as if one cannot speak quickly enough to keep his mind fully occupied. It is this attitude of thoughtfulness, incongruous in a military man, which makes him so formidable.

Colonel Rado visited me today. In the library, over a bottle of Tokay, we talked of hunting and discussed the relative merits of different rifles. (I wanted to tell him of my experiments with an ancient spear which hangs in the billiard room; I thought the colonel was the kind of man who would appreciate the principle of a kill at close quarters, but I held back. Uncle Kalman had prevailed on me to keep quiet about it; in his view, the method wasn't quite sporting.)

'Your uncle was a great man,' the colonel said, holding the amber liquid to the light reflectively and turning the glass.

'He was unique, the last of his kind. We shall all miss him greatly,' I replied. By now, whatever small quantities of affection that had once informed my expression of regrets have been worn down by repetition.

'He was great in ways you may not have known about. Much of his work cannot be recognized openly.'

'But his deeds are remembered by all those he has quietly helped.'

'Yes, indeed. However, I was referring to his political work.'

'He was a strong believer in an independent Hungary,'
I began, 'but as far as I know, he didn't take it any
further than that.' For some reason, I didn't want to be
the first to mention the League in this game of cat and
mouse.

'In fact, he was very active,' the colonel said.

'That wasn't something of which I was aware.'

'No? He never mentioned the Magyar League?'

'In passing, perhaps,' I said casually. It was becoming
clear that his visit was a recruiting drive, or an attempt to
solicit contributions, and I resented it.

He laughed aloud. 'But I know for a fact that he tried
many times to get you to join!'

I thought of telling him coldly that he was mistaken,
but his good humor was infectious; moreover, there was
a glint in his eye which suggested that this was not a man
who tolerated games. I don't know which aspect won
me over.

'We meet in Budapest once a month. Next time you're
in town I'd like you to call on me. I'll introduce you to
some people.'

That was all. It was not so much an invitation as
an expectation. There was no further mention of the
League, and the conversation passed easily, through a
more general discussion of our political situation, to
other subjects. He is an avid reader and took some
time to peruse the books in the library. It may have
been my imagination, but I fancy that his gaze, passing
across the theological section, paused briefly as if checked
by this book high on its shelf. No one has ever noticed
it before. Later, when I looked myself, I think it is just
possible, from a viewpoint standing on the floor, in
the late afternoon sun, to make out that the binding is
slightly different from the other books which surround
it, in spite of my efforts at disguise. I used to like the
sight of it up there, my confession hiding in plain sight,
but now I feel I have something to lose, and I must find
a new place.

MAY 23, 1887

I have a dilemma: Since we are in mourning for Uncle Kalman, we cannot celebrate Elizabeth's birthday. Yet there are precious few occasions on which she will permit us to show her the appreciation her goodness deserves. This is just the kind of situation which Uncle Kalman, with his unquestioned authority on the right and the proper, would have decided for the household days ago. I am afraid that if the servants are involved there will be a tremendous hoopla, which is exactly what I want to avoid, since it will occasion much muttering among the Kalman diehards on the estate who are offended if we so much as smile while their hero lies fresh in his grave.

The solution I have devised is that we shall have an entirely private party – Elizabeth, myself, and Gregory, who is really part of the family (we are pathetically few). But there can be no birthday party without a birthday cake. True, cook could assemble one of her monstrous constructions, complete with layers of marzipan heavy enough to sink an ironclad and a crust of frosting as hard as arctic ice, but I want to bypass the domestic establishment, I want something dainty for Elizabeth, and above all I want a surprise.

To this end, I made an excuse to take the trap into town. The sun was shining brightly as I drove along the road which winds through orchards down the hill to town. The trees are filled with blossom (except for the apple trees, which have not fully recovered from last year's canker and appear quite sparse); the birds sang, and I whipped up the horse to a brisk trot so that I could feel the clear spring air across my face. I felt as though I were awakening from a slumber. I was aware of life as an actual sensation and I felt a sense of freedom and possibility that I have not experienced since I returned from Paris.

In the days of my childhood, members of my family were treated with deep and universal respect on those rare occasions on which they would walk in the town:

Men removed their hats when we passed by, and women curtsied. Today, the town is a different place. There are immigrants who have had no relationship with us and can have no knowledge of what we have accomplished for them. There are socialists who hate us for what we have, while others see us merely as a source of profit. Generally, though, the townspeople give every indication of warm feeling toward me, since most know that I have worked for their prosperity.

Theissen the baker is also the mayor. In fact, he is somewhat more than a baker and has a finger in a number of pies, but spends most of his time presiding over his shop on the main street just before the market square. Recently, he has installed windows with large panes in the front of his shop so that passersby can see the pies and pastries arranged in tiers. It was this which gave me the idea of commissioning a birthday cake for Elizabeth.

I rarely set foot in shops. When I need something I make out a list, and Brod the butler fetches the items. To tell the truth, I am uncomfortable in such places and am at something of a loss as to how to conduct myself. A shop is an essentially democratic institution, but when I am recognized the manager immediately bustles forward to serve me himself, before all the other people who have been waiting; on the other hand, on those rare occasions when I am not recognized, I am concerned that no slight is seen to have been intended against my family by my having to wait for service along with the common people. Without sounding like Uncle Kalman, I must say that the dignity of our name is paramount and must be preserved from the slow, leveling erosion which seems part and parcel of the modern world.

There was a bell on a spring perched on the corner of the door which tinkled when I entered the baker's shop. The mayor is a stout man, bald, with a jolly, florid face and calculating eyes which appraise one's boots, trousers, coat, and cravat all the while that his mouth keeps up an unending stream of obsequious chatter. I have dealt with him on several occasions when he has called at the castle on the official business of the town: petitions from the Town Council, delegations to discuss widening roads which run on our land, and so on. He was mortified by my seeing him in an apron, in his more menial incarnation, and hurriedly removed it.

'An honor, Count. A great honor,' he said, advancing and bowing at the same time with some difficulty. His small eyes were flicking about as if he had a guilty conscience, surveying his shop for anything out of place.

'You have a remarkable establishment, Theissen,' I said, looking about. There were delicious-looking cakes dusted with icing sugar and succulent fruit tarts and biscuits with candied peel, all beautifully presented on paper doilies and arranged with the care that the old Dutch Masters would have given to a still life, an artful profusion seemingly spilling forth. 'I haven't seen anything like it outside Budapest.'

'I would like to believe we are the equal of any baking establishment within a hundred miles,' he declared. 'But Your Excellency honors me by your presence in my humble shop.'

I could see that Theissen was intensely curious to know the reason for my visit, and his obliging smile was showing signs of strain.

'The pleasure is mine,' I said. With such marvels on our doorstep, I wondered, why did we persist at the castle in struggling through confections from the Dark Ages? 'Really,' I said. 'First rate.'

While we had been talking, the sound of rustling and whispered conversation had come from the other side of the curtain which separated the shop from the rear of the premises. Now Theissen's wife, a woman with genteel pretensions who made a point of nodding to me at church whenever she managed to catch my eye, stepped into view. Behind her was their daughter who was introduced to me as Estelle. Estelle appeared shy in the presence of her parents, though I believe her demure manner was a sham, since I know her to be an accomplished actress.

'I believe we have already met,' I said.

She looked up at this. 'You were kind enough to retrieve my prayer book last week,' she said.

I am almost sure that she dropped it at my feet deliberately, the young hussy, and she gave me a secret, inward smile, as if she knew I might be aware of this and didn't care.

'I was thinking of your stage performance in *Salomé* last winter,' I said.

In lieu of any personage of real distinction in the arts, I had been enlisted to present bouquets to the cast at the conclusion of the town's amateur dramatic society production, mainly, I think, because I had once lived in Paris. Estelle had been a point of light in an otherwise bleak and wearying evening, almost as much for her acting ability as her looks.

'Oh, Count,' the mother gushed, in raptures that I should remember her daughter's performance. 'Was she not divine?'

Estelle looked irritated by her mother's invitation to praise and hid beneath an air of boredom. To tease her I said, 'A performance worthy of the divine Sarah herself.'

'And did you see Miss Bernhardt when you were in Paris, Count?' Estelle asked.

I regretted bringing the subject up now, since I think it better to gloss over my sojourn in France and leave to people's imagination how I had spent my time there.

'Unfortunately not,' I replied. 'I was much taken up with my medical studies and had little time for the theater.'

'But we are detaining you, Count,' said Theissen, who still had not had his curiosity satisfied as to the reason for my visit.

'I am in need of a birthday cake,' I announced.

I could not have pleased this family more.

'I have not the slightest doubt we will satisfy your most demanding requirements,' Theissen said proudly.

'I want something rather special.'

'Yes.'

'Quite . . . elaborate.'

'Yes!'

'Something pretty, and decorated, which will please my wife,' I stammered.

Mrs Theissen wrung her hands in pleasurable anticipation. The baker listened to each new requirement with eyes narrowed by the intensity of his concentration. His fingers twitched in rehearsal. He could have been a sculptor intent on translating the mythic allusions of his papal patron into a marble which would stand for eternity. Estelle, to my disappointment, wandered away.

'I shall make you a masterpiece,' Theissen said. He spoke with such fervor that I feared he would clutch me by the shoulders and shake me.

'Estelle!' Mrs Theissen called out. She had disappeared behind the curtain. 'She is an artist,' her mother said proudly, but I think also part in explanation and justification for her behavior.

Estelle rejoined us, and I saw that she had left to fetch a sketch-book which she now laid on the counter and invited me to view. Her talent was indeed extraordinary, in the sense that she was very accomplished, but also because of the subject matter of her drawings. Where poets might describe worlds which have never and could never have existed, and artists might paint sublime landscapes of the imagination, Estelle had drawn cakes. They were extraordinary cakes, of another age or another realm. Some were elaborate fantasies in a romantic, rococo style; others were architectural extravaganzas with Gothic elaborations and intricate detailing which seemed to defy the engineering possibilities of dough, icing sugar, or almond paste.

I was speechless. 'I had no idea,' was all I could say.

Her parents exchanged a glance of pride, a confirmation of previous, similar reactions to their daughter's work.

'Now you know what I meant when I said she's an artist,' Mrs Theissen said.

'But can these wonderful cakes actually be made?' I ventured cautiously.

The baker laughed. 'She is the architect, and I am the builder,' he said. 'She likes to test me, but she has yet to better me.'

'If you would permit me, I could design something especially for you,' Estelle offered.

'For my wife,' I corrected her.

'I would have to get some idea of what you have in mind and what your tastes are.'

'Just as you might sit for a portrait, Count,' her mother put in.

'Well, I think that would be marvelous, but do we have time? – her birthday's in a week.'

'If you can spare the time to instruct me while I draw the design, I'm sure we can have it ready.'

There was an ambiguity to her invitation, perhaps it was a slight huskiness in her voice, which made me envision myself standing over her while she sketched, leaning over her shoulder to point out a detail on the paper before her, the scent of her hair in my nostrils, the soft skin so close that I could see the gleam as the sunlight picked out the tiny blond hairs on the back of her neck. Was this her magic working upon me? Or the coming of spring which makes all sap rise? Or is it the resumption of my life which has come with the opening of this book?

'I will find the time,' I promised.

MAY 24, 1887

We have arranged that I shall return today to give Estelle directions on how the cake is to be styled. There is a flutter of excited anticipation in my stomach which I have been trying to deny to myself all morning. Nevertheless, the signs are there (I only hope no one else notices them). I have had Brod trim my hair, since it was becoming long and unkempt. I took a pair of sharpened scissors to my mustache so that the line above my upper lip was straight and crisp. I was intent on this task when, as it were, I caught my eye in the mirror. It was one of those occasions when one looks at a familiar face and sees in its place someone strange, as if he might be an impostor.

I found a roguish twinkle in the stranger's eye, but the mouth does not move to form the debonair grin which (I am told) was such a charming feature of the young man who wrote the first part of this diary. The mouth is frozen. The lips are stern. The high, Slavic cheekbones are more prominent than before, and there is a furrow, almost a slit, in the skin that runs in the hollow of the cheeks to the line of the jaw, which gives a severe look to this face, the look of a man who has grown accustomed to self-denial and expects the same of others. Only the glint in the eyes, like a candle in a window, shows that someone still lives here.

The flutter in my stomach is the thaw of spring. I am coming back to life. I have been browsing the earlier pages of this book. I am wiser than the young fool who fled Paris. Stacia could not trap me now, nor am I the man to allow himself to be manipulated by Lothar. Only, I am afraid I may have waited too long.

Estelle was waiting for me in the front of the shop. I noticed color high on her cheeks. Stacia would have been invisible and unavailable at the back of the shop for several minutes and then would have pretended to be momentarily surprised by my arrival, as if our appointment had slipped her mind. Estelle is much more forthright. Indeed, she is so openly enthusiastic about my arrival that I was afraid her parents might suspect there was something amiss. They stood in attendance, bowing and smiling, thoroughly proud of the illustrious attention their daughter was receiving.

She was dressed in a charming frock of pale blue muslin which set off the soft gold of her hair. There is something attractively soulful about her eyes. There is a hint of darkness beneath the lower lids which has the effect of deepening the setting of her eyes, although I suspect its cause is that she does not sleep well. She is very active, and constantly in motion, fetching sketches or skipping quickly over to the glass display case to show me a cake which is decorated with the kind of icing sugar she has been describing to me. I was captivated.

I said, 'I had no idea that cake decoration could evoke such enthusiasm,' and Theissen and his wife beamed with pleasure. Estelle saw that I was teasing her and gave me a covert look of reproach. I like her quickness of understanding.

'And this is just one of her accomplishments, Count,' her mother told me.

Estelle turned the pages of her sketchbook for me. It was becoming hard to continue representing our intercourse as merely the commission of a cake. I leaned over her to point to a detail on one of the drawings and breathed in the scent of her young body, the faint spicy fragrance of the pomade which must hang in her wardrobe. She cannot be more than twenty years old.

'Goodness,' I exclaimed to break the spell she cast on me. 'This one is more elaborate than my grandfather's mausoleum!'

They laughed nervously, wanting to show appreciation of my joke, but afraid that unrestrained laughter might show disrespect for my forebear. I willed them to disappear so that I could have her to myself.

Reluctantly, dragging out the process until I could waver no longer, I settled on one of Estelle's creations which resembled a Gothic monument. We agreed on the substance, or as it were, the foundation, of the cake which would support this superstructure. I chose the colors of the icing sugar, we discussed the filling of raspberry jam, and we made precise arrangements for this masterpiece to be delivered to the castle. Finally, there was nothing further I could reasonably accomplish and I was forced to withdraw.

MAY 25, 1887

Elizabeth senses a change in me. 'You're so restless, Laszlo. You pace. You can't read the newspaper for more than five minutes at a time.'

I managed a sheepish smile as she looked up from her embroidery. She is an acute observer, and I cannot altogether hide from her. She is aware that I am up to something. I have scattered hints, minor 'mistakes', lapses, and so on, which should lead her to the suspicion that I have a surprise in the offing. I would like her to believe that my suppressed excitement has something to do with her birthday, then she will look no further into the causes of my distractibility, because she would not want to spoil the pleasure of the surprise – my pleasure at bringing off the surprise, that is, not her pleasure as the recipient, since it is the feelings of others which are of paramount importance to Elizabeth.

'Perhaps you should go to Budapest for a visit,' she suggested. 'The change would do you good. It's not good for you to be cooped up in this old place year after year. You need stimulation, more educated company.'

'Perhaps you're right,' I sighed in a tone which implied I wished to avoid disagreement but had not the slightest intention of following her advice. Such is the placid surface of our marriage. Elizabeth deserves better than to serve as my penance. I must not hurt her, at least. I must not, in whatever I am about to do, harm her dignity. I will not bring her low.

166

But Elizabeth had sent my mind down a track which I had not allowed myself to explore. Budapest is not Paris, but it is an Aladdin's cave of delights compared to my present situation. I have cut myself off from all the interests which I had pursued with such passionate intensity twenty years ago. Journals from the medical societies lie within a cupboard still in their original wrappers. There is nothing here for me. I have come to a complete stop. Even hunting is beginning to pall. But Budapest . . . I found myself considering the feasibility of setting Estelle up in an apartment there. It could be done. The estate is making money consistently for the first time in a century. I have paid down debt and now have a sizable balance on account at the bank. In short, I concluded, I had the resources to maintain a mistress. It was simply a matter of resolve, of opportunity, of stalking my prey and closing upon her.

'Perhaps I should,' I announced several minutes later.

Elizabeth looked up, puzzled, from her needlework. She had been thinking her own thoughts and was momentarily at a loss to know what I was talking about.

'Yes, you should,' she said encouragingly once she had recollected herself. 'I don't know why you haven't done it sooner.'

'I might go to some meetings of the Medical Society,' I tried, but she didn't respond. This is the closest Elizabeth will come to disagreement. 'Or even to some of the lectures at the University,' I said, more to myself, as if mulling over a possibility aloud.

When I had returned from Paris and we were first married, I had wanted to throw myself into the practice of medicine. It was the way in which I would make some restitution to the human race. I thought I could lose myself in the bustle of activity and fatigue. Instead I have been forced to wait out my sentence in more or less enforced idleness. Doctoring may be an adequate profession for a younger son, but it is not a seemly activity for a nobleman to engage in. Uncle Kalman was quite outspoken on the subject.

'I think a scientific interest is a fine thing,' Elizabeth offered after a few well-considered moments. Her faint enthusiasm is meant to indicate to me that dabbling in the sciences may pass as an endearing eccentricity, but practicing as a physician is beneath the count.

'I suppose I could speak to Colonel Rado,' I suggested.

The room in which we were sitting is the only one which ever receives the spring sun in sufficient quantities for us to feel its natural warmth, but a slight chill fell over us, as it does whenever the conversation touches upon George. He is an unacknowledged ghost between us that we cannot bring ourselves to speak of, except in the most vague and mythic terms. It makes for some curious twists of speech.

'George's commanding officer?' Elizabeth asked carefully. She did not look up, although she must have been curious as to the nature of my connection with this revered warrior.

'We spoke at Uncle's funeral. He wants me to get involved in some sort of Magyar club.'

'I didn't know you were interested in politics.'

'Well, I'm not, really. But I think I ought to be.'

There was no answer from Elizabeth, who seemed to be involved in an especially intricate piece of stitching.

'Don't you?' I persisted. 'We can't let ourselves be pushed around by the Austrians forever.'

She looked up and stared at or through the window, I'm not sure which. I wondered if she was becoming shortsighted, but it may have been that she was looking into the past. 'Yes, of course,' she said finally, in a tone she often used to suggest that she might as well acquiesce with grace to something she had no say in anyway. This was followed by a small smile which indicated her complete acceptance of the status quo. I suspect that she thinks of this self-suppression as being 'faithful', but I will never know for sure. We are separate containers whose contents never mingle. What do you dream of, Elizabeth, while your fingers are busy with needle and thread and your mind is free to wander where it will? Sometimes I see a fond smile on your lips as you look down at the piece of stuff you cradle in your hands, as a mother might dote upon her baby.

MAY 26, 1887

Gregory joined us to celebrate Elizabeth's birthday. The cake was splendid – so much so, in fact, that none of us at first would cut into it. Instead we circled about the edible edifice, pausing from time to time to peer at some scroll or other architectural detail, and exchanging speculations as to its real purpose.

'An altar to the new paganism,' Gregory proposed.

'A memorial to a departed prince,' Elizabeth offered softly.

'The housing for a plaque commemorating the discovery of a new land,' I said.

Elizabeth was enchanted with the cake and quite touched that I had taken so much trouble on her behalf. She looked at me with such intense fondness that I was reminded that it was high time for me to make another attempt at conjugal duties. It was I, finally, who cut the Gordian knot and slipped the knife into the pristine white of the cake's body. Inside, it was rich and dark, full of moist currants, fragments of nuts, and slivers of candied peel which released in the mouth the essence of summer.

'Elizabeth tells me you're becoming interested in politics,' Gregory said. He has a habit when he takes tea of wandering about the sitting room with a cup and saucer dangling in one hand, or in this case, with a plate full of cake which he held close to his chin so that he could fork pieces into his mouth without having to pay attention to the process of eating.

'I think it's time I became more involved in how things

are run.' I asked myself when they had had a chance to discuss our conversation of yesterday and wondered, with annoyance, how many of the details of my life Elizabeth confided to Gregory in the confessional.

He smiled at me skeptically. 'I just don't see you mixing it up with the Magyar old guard.'

'But I'm not going to be mixing it up with the magnates; I'd be on the same side they are.'

'I assumed you'd be on the side of the angels.'

'If you mean the progressives and the socialists, the answer is definitely no.'

'Somehow, I can't quite see you allied with those old fossils.'

That's the difficulty of trying to put one over on someone who has been your friend for thirty years: He knows you too well to be entirely taken in, even if he doesn't know exactly which part of the story is out of character.

'I think we Hungarians have to stand up for ourselves against the Hapsburgs,' I said.

'But that's ancient history,' Gregory insisted, waving a pillar of icing sugar in the air. 'We have to think beyond nationalism.'

'To socialism?'

'No, I didn't say that.'

'But if you're not a nationalist, what is there but socialism?'

'I think you can have concern for the welfare of your fellowman without being a socialist.'

'In material terms, my people have never been better off.'

'That's not what I hear,' Gregory said.

'There are a lot of things you hear in the confessional –' I thought Elizabeth was avoiding my eye, but I couldn't be sure. 'But you haven't the slightest idea whether they're true.'

Gregory threw back his head and laughed good-humoredly. When we argue, he is always the one to anticipate an impasse, or to recognize that our exchange is veering into areas where our playful verbal fencing would turn to slashing in earnest.

'All right, I don't know if people tell me the truth. I've never made any attempt to tell the difference. If people lie to me, so be it. In the end, I don't think it matters.'

'Because, in the end, truth will prevail,' Elizabeth said. There was a strange light in her eyes.

Gregory and I have been debating each other for so long that we know each other's moves thoroughly. When we were boys at St Sebastian's we would sometimes stop in the middle of an argument and switch sides so that each would argue the point of view he had just opposed. We were both idealogues, both enthusiasts of ideas, and I think it was one of the things that drew us together. It was in the divinity class of Father Ignatius that we discovered this affinity. The father was a man supremely confident that his doctrine – he referred to it as 'the truth' and to everything else as 'hypothesis' – would prevail, and so he had no hesitation in allowing all points of view, short of outright apostasy, to be expressed. When I tested the limits of his tolerance, Father Ignatius challenged me to invent a heresy which had not already been thought of, and when I come up with some tortuous ideological perversity, he took great pleasure in telling me the name of the heretic who had preceded me and the year in which Rome declared his belief anathema.

'As you will no doubt discover for yourself, there is no new abomination under the sun,' Father Ignatius had intoned cheerfully.

Gregory and I fancied ourselves the Devil's advocates, and I think the father enjoyed our sallies. Perhaps he saw that we were closer to orthodoxy than we realized: to argue is to share assumptions. If a man will swallow a premise, the entailment will surely follow. A subtle, patient man was Father Ignatius. Gregory, at least, fulfilled his expectation.

Last night, after we had retired and the castle was quiet, I allowed a suitable interval of time to pass before I crept softly along the cold stone passageway to Elizabeth's bed-chamber to enact our grisly ritual. At her door I hesitated. It seemed unkind to disturb her sleep solely to perpetuate the illusion that our marriage was anything more than a dynastic convenience. Does this futile behavior really lead her to believe that I care for her? I doubt it. It is part of my penance. I am to maintain the illusion just as the prisoner from time to time is made to whitewash the walls of his cell.

Just as I was about to knock on the door, it opened. Elizabeth stood there in a long cotton gown with a taper in her hand, the light falling from an angle which accentuated her heavy breasts and the dark, shadowed cleavage between them. Silently, she stood aside for me to enter the room. I closed the door and turned, expecting to find that she had climbed into her bed, but she had placed the taper in a holder and stood waiting for me to come to her. In the dim light of the flickering flame, with her hair let down around her shoulders, she seemed unfamiliar to me.

I kissed her on the lips. We lingered far longer than I had intended, long enough for me to become affected by the curves of her body through the thin fabrics of our robes. It was she who blew out the taper, and then I heard a rustling in the darkness as she slipped between the sheets. She had left a window open, and I shivered slightly in the coolness of her room as I threw off my dressing gown and groped my way to her bed.

The birthday cake had evidently released some hidden reserve of affection for me, because Elizabeth grasped me as soon as I entered the bed. She worked her body against me with a fervor and an urgency I had not experienced in her before, and perhaps, in retrospect, there was also an element of desperation, as though this might be her last chance at fulfillment. Somehow (I do not know by whose hand) our nightgowns had become hoisted above our waists, and before I knew what was happening I was inside her and thrusting in time with her breathless endearments. The idle imaginings in which I have seduced Estelle in a hundred different ways had undone me.

Elizabeth herself is changed. I awoke to a strange sensation, and for several moments did not know whether I had really awakened, or had merely dreamed it. What had aroused me from sleep was the sensation of sexual climax. That might seem a delightful way to begin the day, but in reality it was profoundly disturbing to move from the depths of sleep and to break surface at that peak moment of selflessness.

I must have cried out. Elizabeth, who was astride me and was evidently in her own last throes, placed her hand across my mouth to stifle the noise. And there we were, frozen like a tableau, my eyes coming to a focus as I began to comprehend the nature of the situation, Elizabeth becoming more aghast as she saw wakefulness and then understanding dawn upon my face. Collecting herself, she took her hand from my mouth and eased herself off me with as much decorum as she could muster. She was mortified with shame, but did not cry. I suppose I had caught her *in flagrante delicto* committing a species of adultery. Gregory has told me, and I assume she holds to his doctrine, that lust within the marriage bed is fornication nevertheless.

She had turned away and sat on the other side of the bed with her back to me.

'You must go now,' she said. 'The servants will soon be up and about.' How maidenly she is to worry that the servants would find out that their master and mistress had spent the night together! 'Yes, of course,' I replied in a matter-of-fact tone. As ever, we were beyond speech.

I sat up and began to shift out of bed, but Elizabeth had turned noiselessly and swiftly like a cat (another surprising potential I had not known lay within her) and she took hold of my wrist in an impulsive, tender gesture as if to stay my departure. She quickly withdrew her hand, but before she could turn away, I saw on her face a look of such simple and defenseless joy that I am forced to admit that in spite of all my preventative measures and all my attention to emotional hygiene, I have infected her with the most troublesome and wounding of all bacilli: love.

9

MAY 28, 1887

I am at sixes and sevens. I am fifteen years old. I am a stallion who sniffs on the wind the maddening scent of a mare in season who grazes in a pasture two miles distant. Nothing perverts a man's intelligence so much as love, but lust follows a close second. I can scarcely think without that ridiculous tumescence in my britches raising his monstrous head. I have learned nothing from my life, since I am still a slave to passion.

I think of Estelle night and day. My imagination focuses, like a lens which brings the rays of the sun to a fiery point, upon a tiny mole on the side of her neck, just below the left ear. Why my mind has fastened itself to this erotic talisman, I do not know. It is a pinpoint of longing.

But I have not yet found a way to declare myself to her. Or rather, I have concocted a thousand schemes to bring myself to her side and rejected each one as rash, hazardous, brazen, presumptuous. It's not as if I have had any clear expression of interest from her. But then, why should I need that to proceed? I ought to seize the moment. What species of lover is so easily daunted? True, she was especially effusive when I presented her with the bouquet at the end of the play, but perhaps that was only the afterglow of the applause. True, the fall of her prayer book at the very moment at which I passed by was contrived to bring her again to my attention. And was this my fancy, or did her fingertips brush the back of my hand when I gave it back to her?

In rare moments of objectivity, these questions seem

utterly puerile. Can these really be the thoughts with which a forty-four-year-old man occupies himself? I do take some satisfaction from the birthday cake. That showed ingenuity. But it was such a devious maneuver that my true thinking was obscured by entirely hypocritical sentiments: Much of the time even I believed that I was commissioning the cake to bring happiness into Elizabeth's life! And yet I also knew that she would far prefer her birthday to slip past unnoticed.

Since the night before last she follows me from room to room like a schoolgirl with a crush, full of shy glances and implausible reasons to be in my company. Her docile, adoring love should make me feel ashamed of the adultery I am plotting. The truth is that I do feel guilty, but it is a paltry emotion, closer to a legalistic consideration than any kind of anguish. I wonder if in some subtle way I have become morally defective during the long years of my imprisonment when I had no cause to exercise this faculty.

The plan I have decided on is a most simple one and stands the best chance of success. I shall simply, entirely impromptu, perhaps even giving the appearance of having acted on impulse, enter the shop with the stated intention of thanking Estelle for the cake she created. If I find her alone, well and good; I shall engage her in conversation, and gradually, imperceptibly, the talk will turn toward matters of – what? I shall improvise. If, on the other hand, her mother is present, I have a perfectly decent reason for being there, and they will no doubt be gratified that the count has taken the trouble to express his gratitude in person. I have chosen Tuesday as the day. The Town Council will be in session, and so that disposes of Mayor Theissen as far as his presence in the shop in concerned.

AFTERNOON

God has intervened. Or, at least, Gregory, his instrument, has.

Gregory has given himself over to his church body and soul. There is a growing severity about him, although this is directed mainly at himself rather than toward the moral harassment of other people. His hair is iron gray now, and he wears it short – cropped, one might as well say, for he takes little trouble to give any finesse to his appearance. He has two black cassocks, both of which are worn and even frayed in places. I have told him that he must pay more attention to his dress, if for no other reason than to retain the respect of his flock, and on several occasions I have gently offered to bear the expense of a new outfitting, but he will have none of it. He has no use for material things. With his energy and ability, and Uncle Kalman's influence, he could have been a bishop by now. The fact that he is here with us, working as a priest in an obscure parish far from the center of things, with no interest in advancement, is a measure of his fanaticism. And yet for all that, he has not lost the human touch, although I fear he will, for there are times that I think he sees the eternal soul and looks plain through the mortal man or woman.

This is why I feared the worst – hellfire and damnation – when he broached the subject of Estelle. We were having tea, our afternoon ritual in the English style.

'I wanted to ask you something about the mayor's daughter,' Gregory began with unusual diffidence. My heart sank in irrational fear. Would this be a warning he was about to deliver, I wondered? Had he divined my intention and was now jumping ahead of me to prevent my journey down the road to sin? Had he pieced together a jigsaw of intelligence from all the fragments brought to his confessional? These are the mad thoughts of a man who has spent too long within the confines of a deadening morality and now ventures to live.

'Our cake artist?' Elizabeth asked.

'Estelle,' I said to have the pleasure of speaking her name aloud.

'She's an extremely talented girl, as we know,' Gregory went on. 'Her father feels that in order for her to be brought on she needs something more than our small town can offer. Something broadening, something more sophisticated.'

'You mean further instruction? Training of some kind?' Elizabeth asked.

'I don't entirely know what her parents have in mind.'

'Aren't they concerned Budapest will spoil her? I assume that's where they're thinking she would go,' I added quickly, lest they have any suspicion that a cozy apartment in Budapest was what I had in mind for Estelle.

'That's what they're concerned about. They want their daughter to be exposed to culture and better society, but they want her to have safeguards. It's understandable.'

'Wasn't she in the play the Drama Club put on at Christmas? Golden hair, extraordinary features – I remember her. She's absolutely beautiful,' Elizabeth said generously. I have often marveled at her capacity to be an objective observer, even an admirer, of other women's looks. 'Of course her parents would be worried about her falling in with the wrong company.'

'And that's where we come in?' I prompted him.

'I was hoping you'd be able to help. If you knew of a good family who need a governess–cum–nursemaid, something of that sort. She'd work, but she'd pick up a bit of polish in the process. She's quite an accomplished young lady, I gather. She needs someone to take her under their wing.'

'We're so out of touch,' Elizabeth said, turning to me.

'Well, actually,' I found myself saying, 'I thought I'd go up to town for a couple of days next week. Take Colonel Rado up on his offer.'

'I think that's a wonderful idea,' Elizabeth said. For a moment I was afraid that she'd propose to come along with me. 'There must be hundreds of people you've lost touch with who are wondering whatever became of you.'

'As a matter of fact I was planning to look up a few old friends.'

'Though I doubt they would have children of the age

in question.' Elizabeth's childlessness is a sore spot she is unable to stay away from, and a look of sadness followed by fortitude eclipsed the pleasure she took in my emergence from the social isolation I had imposed upon myself.

'Anyway, I can ask around,' I added casually.

'I don't mean to burden you,' Gregory said.

'Not at all,' I insisted.

'I think she's worth the effort.'

For another crazy moment, I looked into his eyes to see if it was a trap. But there was no cause for concern. Why shouldn't Fortune smile upon me?

'Glad to do it,' I said.

'I'll speak to Theissen,' he offered. I began to protest, but he cut me off. 'No, don't worry,' he said. 'I won't make any promises. I'll tell him you're considering the matter; he'll be pleased that his request has gone even that far. As for Mrs Theissen, she'll be over the moon. She has certain aristocratic pretensions, and I think, at the back of her mind, this is all part of her secret dream for Estelle to marry into the nobility.'

'I hope we're not getting into something over our heads,' Elizabeth cautioned.

I assumed a burdened and dutiful demeanor which I hope was not overdone. 'I rather think this is something I should handle myself,' I said. 'After all, how am I to know what the girl wants if I don't talk to her directly?'

And that is how we left it. Gregory will speak to the Theissens, and they are to present themselves at the castle at eleven o'clock on Monday morning.

Elizabeth has been giving me longing looks. This afternoon, after Gregory had left on his calls, she let her hand trail casually across my shoulders as she passed behind the chair in which I sat reading. I pretended to be incensed by an article in the newspaper.

'Now the Austrians want us to pay for their army!' I

exclaimed, smacking the paper with the back of my hand and shaking my head in disbelief.

I have not gone to her since our night of coitus. With the meeting with Estelle imminent, I simply cannot trust my body to remain impotent, even when I remind myself over and over again that she is George's wife, and imagine my brother in this same position before me, or – a scenario I reserve only for that direst emergency, the first, undeniable stirring of tumescence, in order to maintain the freshness and efficacy of the image – that Uncle Kalman stands at the bedroom door saber in hand. Unaccountably, I failed to use these ploys two nights ago, and it was this dereliction that is responsible for the erection which, like rain on the desert, has woken Elizabeth from her state of pious resignation.

MAY 30, 1887

Theissen was nervous. He was sweating, and his collar looked very uncomfortable. Mrs Theissen was nervous in her own way, effusive and silly. Estelle was cool, composed, confident, and divinely beautiful.

I was tired and on edge, having had little sleep last night. Elizabeth had taken it upon herself to visit me in my bedroom, and I had had to invoke Uncle Kalman's ghost three times before she gave up and allowed me to return to my slumbers. But my suppressed irritation set a good tone for the interview, since it put the Theissens on the defensive and affirmed their ideas about what it would be like to be supplicants in need of my noble largesse.

I received them in the library. They sat in a semicircle, upright and stiff in straight-backed chairs, while I lounged in the old count's chair, an oaken throne smoothed and blackened with age.

'I don't want her to be a domestic, mind,' Mrs Theissen was saying. 'Not a lady's maid or anything of that nature. Estelle's far above that.'

'But we are grateful, truly, Count,' her husband put in hastily, lest I be offended, 'for any assistance you may see your way to giving us.'

I looked over Estelle openly, as if I might be sizing her up to see if she possessed the moral fiber for some possibility I had in mind (which indeed I was). Every time I see her I am impressed by her self-possession and poise. She looked back at me calmly, without offense or a protective insolence, but with the same interest with which I appraised her.

'You may not know this, Count,' Mrs Theissen began with a simpering smile, 'but Estelle is related to the Esterhazys.'

'Indeed? I was not aware of that,' I replied and turned back to Estelle as if this fresh information made necessary a second look.

'Through my mother's side,' Mrs Theissen added proudly. I had the impression that it was a culminating moment which she had been eagerly anticipating.

'Of course, the relationship is a very distant one,' Theissen said. He gave his wife a meaningful glance which seemed to contain a hint of malevolence. 'It's not as if we're claiming any blue blood.'

'The relationship occurred a long time ago and it was never officially recognized,' Mrs Theissen said delicately.

'It occurred a long time ago and it's not relevant to the present proceedings,' Theissen growled.

'Count, I mention it only because I believe Estelle is destined for greater things, and part of it is that she has it in her background.'

They seemed on the verge of setting off before me a well-worn family argument, with escalating tempers and no resolution in sight. Estelle seemed not to hear. She had eyes only for me and seemed to light up whenever I looked her way.

'Still, blood is blood,' I said, as a judge might pronounce a verdict.

They waited expectantly for me to guide them. It was

impossible. They wanted their daughter to be in the employ of a good family, and yet for this family to treat her as one of themselves. Did they think that the social gulf which separates master from servant disappears in the exotic strata of Budapest? They wanted her to acquire culture and knowledge of the greater world but to be safe and sheltered. They wanted her to gain savoir faire but to retain her virtue. What they really wanted was for Estelle to find a husband for herself in Budapest who was a few steps higher up the social ladder than themselves.

Finally, I said, 'I wonder if I might talk to Estelle?'

They readily agreed, but did not budge. For several uncomfortable moments I smiled politely in their direction while they looked back at me in bewilderment. At last, Mrs Theissen realized that I wanted to speak to their daughter alone, and they stepped humbly and carefully, as if their shoes might hurt the floor, from the room.

Their trust is touching. It is based entirely on the aristocratic principle: I am noble, therefore I possess a superior moral capacity, therefore they can leave their daughter alone with me unchaperoned. I am a cad. In George's regiment, fellows were expected to blow their brains out if they abused their family's standing by taking advantage of decent folk. I know this, I appreciate this, and yet I am not deterred from my course. I feel for the Theissens, for their clumsy bodies and their snobbish pretensions and their fond hopes for their child, and all the other human, heartbreaking qualities which make them such easy prey: Yet I will ruin their daughter.

I closed the heavy door behind them and turned to Estelle. There was something in her posture as she stood with one hand resting on the back of the chair in which I had been sitting, in the rapidity of her breathing, in her glowing eyes and the way she held her lips, slightly parted, that signaled her receptivity without a word passing between us. I considered taking her there and then.

'I'll do anything to get away from this town,' she said. 'Anything.'

It was more a breath than speech. I never knew a single word could be so intoxicating.

'Would you like to go to Budapest?' I asked her.

'Yes. Then Paris.'

I laughed and felt relieved. My chest had grown tight and I was having trouble breathing. 'You have bold plans.'

'I do. I have all sorts of plans. Life isn't worth living without ambitions.' She searched my face to see if I would make fun of her. I thought how young she was, and intense. It made me feel vital to be with her.

'Perhaps we should start with Budapest.'

'If you could help me find a position in Budapest, I'd be eternally grateful to you.' Again she spoke in a voice close to a whisper, with a wonderful, sensual huskiness which seemed on the brink of surrender. I felt weak with lust.

'Do you want to be a governess?' I had taken a step closer to her and she held her head back and stared into my eyes.

'No,' she said.

'Then what do you want?'

She was staring at my lips and she sighed at the last moment as my mouth closed on hers.

JUNE 7, 1887

It is a long train ride to Budapest with few amenities in the coaches. When I boarded, the station master insisted that I should have a private coach, although I had not engaged one. I suppose he feels he owes his job to me and is trying to show his gratitude, but the result is that I have had to endure this tedious journey in splendid isolation. I am impatient, irritable, and cannot rest contentedly with a book as I was able to do only a month ago.

On the rare occasions on which I have visited Budapest since my return from Paris, I seem to have gone about my business like a sleepwalker, without noting the changes which have taken place. Now that I am awake, I see that the city has taken on a modern air. True, the cobbled streets of Buda that wind their way up from the Danube to the towering castle which dominates this side of the town retain their antique charm, and the buildings speak of our feudal past, but there is a bustle and haste about the city, a swaggering, fashionable air, which reminds me of Paris twenty years ago. Now that it is warm, the cafés have spread beyond their glass fronts onto the sidewalks; students argue politics and men about town appraise the passing women as they linger over coffee.

As I wandered about town, I passed the office of an estate agent and had half a mind to enter and inquire about renting an apartment, but I considered that premature. Estelle has given every indication that she would like to be my mistress, but I do not want to rush her into formal arrangements in case she gets nervous and bolts. My task on this trip is to lay the groundwork, to establish contact with the Magyar League which will be my alibi and the excuse for frequent visits to Budapest in the future.

I had time to kill before my meeting with Colonel Rado in the evening, and so I strolled at dusk along a promenade high above the river. It seemed to be a popular spot for lovers to walk and loiter at the parapets to admire the view and find some excuse to draw closer, to touch hands. The sun was setting in fiery splendor, obscured in part by a few dark clouds, so that it shot rays which reached like divine commands focused on some single house or field into the countryside. At any moment I felt it possible that the clouds in the heavens would make some slight shift so that one of these rays would pick me out, that I would be blinded by a light so powerful that it would stop me in my tracks for one epiphanous, destiny-deflecting moment.

Rado's house was quite grand. I should not have been surprised, since his regiment was one which was regarded as extremely smart, and George would not have got in if Uncle Kalman had not persuaded them to waive the usual bribes and commissioning fees. As it was, my brother was able to keep up with the fast crowd of young officers only by borrowing heavily against the estate, as I discovered when the promissory notes were presented to me soon after I became count.

A silent and impassive butler showed me to the colonel's study where he was waiting for me. Rado greeted me in a courteous manner but with a watchful reserve. The butler served us and left the room.

I sipped the cool white wine, which was immensely refreshing after the walking I had done during the afternoon. When I looked up, I found his eyes upon me.

'How do you find it?' Rado asked.

'Excellent.'

'It's last year's, from my estate. I think it compares with some of our best vintages.'

'Exceptionally fine.'

'You come highly recommended.'

'I'm glad to hear it,' I said, a little puzzled, since I have lost contact with so many of my former friends and couldn't think whom he would have asked about me. 'May I ask the identity of our mutual friends?'

'Your ancestors,' he replied, laughing. Then he added, 'And our Father Gregory.'

I couldn't have been more surprised. 'You know Gregory?'

'Yes, of course.'

'And is he a member of the League, too?' I asked.

'As a matter of fact, he is.'

Gregory had never told me that he was on terms with Rado, even when I had mentioned at Elizabeth's birthday party that I was coming to see him, and I felt rather hurt at not being taken into his confidence.

'Our families have fought alongside each other for generations,' Rado was saying. 'I served under your uncle, of course; and I knew your father. I was a lieutenant at the time he died so heroically. A great patriot. And George, too. You come from a family of great Hungarian patriots.'

'I'm very much aware of it. Sometimes the responsibility weighs on me.'

'And now the time's come for you to do something for your country. That's why you're here, isn't that right?'

'Yes, that's why I'm here. After we talked, I wanted to think over what you said. I didn't get in touch with you right away, because – '

Rado held up his hand to interrupt me. 'You thought it over. You took your time. That's good. We're not looking for hotheads or martyrs. Although, as in any worthwhile enterprise, there are dangers enough.'

'I'm not entirely clear what it is you do,' I began hesitantly.

'The first thing you need to know about us is that the Magyar League does not exist. Nothing we speak of tonight can leave this room. Is that understood? If you claim I mentioned the League to you, I'll call you a liar.' He had become quite irate and, catching himself at the last moment, forced a smile to show that he meant no offense. 'Excuse me, please. Forgive me. I get rather exercised on the subject of secrecy. We are a clandestine group. The authorities would suppress us if they knew we existed, if they had any inkling of our aims, even though we number among our members many of Hungary's most prominent statesmen. The Austrians – or worse, Hungarians who are Austrian sympathizers – are constantly trying to infiltrate us, and lately they've had some slight success in that direction.'

'I see,' I said in a tone which I thought soothing, but Rado looked at me sharply – he was still bristling with indignation at the thought that there were countrymen of his who were Austrian sympathizers. I told myself that in future it would be prudent not to show too quick a comprehension when I dealt with this suspicious, prickly man. It crossed my mind that I might be dealing with a madman, or at the very least a fanatic.

'This is, of course, beside the point.'

I was about to agree, but managed to hold my peace.

The man could change in the blink of an eye, and the less I said the better.

Rado was attempting to calm himself, and with an effort resumed his customary charm. 'You're not a military man, are you?' he asked with a courtesy tinged with patronage.

'I'm afraid not.'

'How'd you manage that?' He was watching me carefully, and I had the feeling that he had researched my case and already knew the answers to his questions.

'I was a surgeon in the reserves,' I replied. 'I still am, I suppose.'

'A doctor . . . yes, I think I knew that. Well, at least you're no stranger to the sight of blood. But if I recall, you weren't with George in the campaign against the Prussians, were you?'

'I was studying in Paris.'

'Ah.'

There was sarcastic intent to that soft expression of regret, and I was irritated by the implication that I had shirked my duty by not dying like my brother in that rapid and ignominious defeat. 'The war was over before I had a chance to get into it,' I replied.

If he saw my anger, he passed it off with a shrug. 'Well, what can one expect with Austrian generals? Next time we fight the Prussians, we'll be led by our own. You know how to handle a weapon, of course.'

'I do a good deal of hunting.'

'Not quite the same thing, though, is it? Killing an animal, killing a man.'

'Is that an ability I'll need in the Magyar League?'

'When the time comes, yes. The Austrians aren't just going to give us our independence. We'll have to take it from them, obviously. Does that bother you, spilling blood?'

'In the right cause, no.'

'Are you sure – I thought you looked just the slightest bit put out?'

'No, not at all.'

'Something for you to think about, anyway. It's not a boys' club. And by the way, we don't accept resignations. Once you're in, there's no way out.'

When I left him that night he seemed satisfied and bade me good-bye with a firm hand clasp and an unexpected warmth.

'You handled yourself well, and we'd be glad to have you join us. But give the matter some thought first.'

As I write this on the train on my way back to Transylvania, I am still not sure how much of Rado's cloak and dagger stuff is real and how much is the wishful thinking of a soldier who longs for action and intrigue to bring meaning to his life. There is something rather formidable about Rado, but does he really have an organization of conspirators, or has he blown up the importance of a group of old buffers who get together over brandy and vie with one another in growling anti-Austrian slogans? Either way, I plan to stay at the fringes of the Magyar League and not get involved in their machinations.

JUNE 11, 1887

Today I paid an impromptu visit to the bakery. At first I was confused by Theissen's reference to a previous visit, thinking he meant the time when I had come to order the cake for Elizabeth's birthday.

'We are so grateful that you are looking into something for Estelle,' he said, pumping my hand up and down.

'I'm glad to do what I can,' I replied, unaware that I had done anything to warrant such effusiveness. Estelle, at the back of the shop, smiled at me with uncharacteristic shyness.

'I understand the family is in the diplomatic service and travels a great deal?' Mrs Theissen asked.

I was at a loss as to how to reply. Estelle came to my aid.

'I've been telling my parents about the du Barry family,' she said.

Mrs Theissen fluttered about me excitedly. 'They sound absolutely charming, Count. I am sure they are most refined. Monsieur was recently the ambassador to Siam, Madame the last of a noble line which was all but made extinct in the Revolution. How cultured they sound! And the children . . . darlings, absolute darlings, I'm sure!'

I must have looked nonplussed. Estelle approached me with an uneasy, guilty smile. 'I know you didn't want me to say anything until the details had been worked out. But when you came into the shop yesterday and told me, I just couldn't keep it to myself. It was just too exciting. Then, right after you left, Mama returned from her visits, and I weakened and told her.'

'They are most excellent people,' I improvised weakly.

'And old, old friends of your family,' Mrs Theissen gushed.

'Well, I'm not sure I'd go as far as that,' I said, feeling that I should take some authorial control of the burgeoning fabrication before it got hopelessly fantastic. 'Due to Monsieur's travels on behalf of his government, I haven't seen as much of them of late as I would care to.'

'Forgive me, Count, if I am forward in asking questions which would not otherwise be my place to ask, but if we are to entrust our only daughter . . .'

'I quite understand,' I said quickly, hoping that Estelle had left me sufficient room to invent without contradicting what she had already told her parents.

'I understand that you and Monsieur – or, to give him his true and noble title, Monsieur le Duc – were students together in Paris?'

'Monsieur le Duc?' I asked, turning, in the hope of clarification, or more inspired invention, to Estelle. She seemed to be caught in a fit of giggles, unable to appreciate the precarious position in which she had placed me.

'Why, the Duke of Barry!' Mrs Theissen exclaimed.

Like a man who inches along a plank high above the

street, I felt a sudden loss of nerve at the halfway point and was seized by an overwhelming desire to grope my way back to the solid ground of truth. 'I'm afraid there must be a misunderstanding,' I said.

Mrs Theissen looked downcast. 'I had been led to understand' – here she cast an accusing glance in Estelle's direction – 'that the family was one of the noblest of all the French nobility.'

There was an awkward silence which I felt considerable pressure to fill. I turned to Estelle and saw that she would do nothing to make my exit easier. On the contrary, her face held a challenging look: She would stand firm. If I was to have her, I had to win her.

'Due to the delicacy of Monsieur's mission,' I began, having not the slightest idea how the sentence was to end, 'and on account of the constantly shifting political configuration in France, there are many aspects of Monsieur's past which must be handled with the greatest discretion.'

I could not have pleased them more. Theissen puffed up his chest proudly like an old soldier. Mrs Theissen's mouth had fallen open in anticipation of secrets being divulged which were orders of magnitude more momentous than the gossip she exchanged on her calls.

'You will understand that there is little information I can impart. Suffice it to say that Monsieur le Duc' – I nodded in acknowledgment to Mrs Theissen – 'must remain incognito. The situation necessitates that he cannot be called by his real title. We will refer to him henceforth simply at Monsieur du Barry. I'm afraid I must insist on that. Plain citizen du Barry.' I could tell they wanted more, but my intuition told me that any details I gave them risked breaking the spell of intrigue which held them credulous. 'There! I have taken you into my confidence,' I went on briskly. 'I must beg of you, not only to keep this information to yourselves, but to excuse me if I am circumspect in answering your questions.'

'Of course. Of course.' Theissen waved away any remaining reservations.

Mrs Theissen had lapsed into a complacent silence, no doubt calculating the tidbits of information she could let fall during unguarded moments to pique the curiosity of her acquaintances as they took tea together. A sudden thought struck her. 'But there is no danger, surely?' she asked, looking apprehensively, but also I thought with a hint of envy, toward her daughter.

'Absolutely not,' I said with authority. Then, as an after thought, I added, 'Providing of course, that everyone concerned is discreet and is able to restrain their curiosity.'

'I can hardly wait,' Estelle exclaimed excitedly. 'Count, every evening, as I walk by the riverbank, I think about the day that has gone by and I dream about the future. But I never thought I'd ever have an opportunity like this!' She held out her hands in a gesture which would have welcomed me to embrace her and hold her tightly to me had we been alone. I think it could have passed for gratitude.

'Then let us hope today brings all that we wish for,' I replied. We gazed at one another in a rapture of love, until I was forced by propriety to tear my eyes from her.

EVENING

I could hardly contain myself at dinner, glancing too frequently through the window in case I should be detained past sunset, and I aroused Elizabeth's curiosity.

'Are you expecting someone, Laszlo?' she asked.

'I was wondering if it was going to rain, that's all.'

'Surely you're not going out again?'

'I thought I'd go out for a bit with a gun.'

'You're restless since you came back from Budapest.'

Elizabeth has been so well brought up that she considers it impolite to ask questions on any matter that the other person does not first offer information. I have told her something about my talk with Rado, but I have a feeling there is more that she would like to ask me about my visit.

'I'm a bit uneasy about the club Colonel Rado wants me to join,' I said with a frown.

'How so?'

'It all sounds a bit more intense that I bargained for. I'm not sure I really want to be involved.'

'There must be others.'

'But they're not quite the same,' I said.

'You could give it a try, and if you don't like it, then you can always resign.'

Elizabeth is not interested in politics. I can see that she wants to engage me in a deeper conversation about ourselves but, mercifully, doesn't know how to begin it. Her upbringing does not include such exchanges as part of the repertoire of graceful accomplishments. Her lingering, longing glances toward me have passed away. She looks tired now and goes about her business with a tight-lipped, frozen expression. In moments when she has not been aware that anyone was watching her, she does not hide a stricken look. Once, in a mirror, I caught her gaze upon me: sad, loving, reproachful – above all, uncomprehending. I would prefer it if she had grown angry; then she could have learned to hate me. That would have been a relationship which I could have sustained. But who is capable of hating the saintly Elizabeth? Not I. She keeps all this to herself, suffering in silence, without a sign. I believe her religion is some solace to her. I have no more to give her than I ever had: courtesy and kindness. These are poor substitutes for her heart which I know to be capable of a fullness of feeling, and which yearns for love.

I had instructed Jacob, my chief groom and gun bearer, to have the black gelding saddled and ready, and as soon as I had finished dinner I took off in the direction of town and the river. Halfway down the hill, I realized I had forgotten to take my gun and hoped that Elizabeth had not been watching my departure.

The railway line follows along the course of the valley beside the river and diverges outside our town, so that the station is on the northern edge of town and the river runs through its southern outskirts, closer to the castle. In olden times, my family's land extended all the way to the river, and one of my ancestors had planted an avenue of chestnuts along the river's bank in what had been the castle's park. Now it is public land – a bequest to the townspeople by that same count who planted the trees – and it is a quiet and pleasant place to stroll, though I had not visited it since I played there as a boy.

The avenue is bordered by the river on one side and on the other by a thin strip of meadow separating this public land from a dense copse of trees. I took Sabbath a little way in among the trees and tethered him there. He was not happy with the enclosed space, and I made a mental note to have the foresters attend to this patch of woodland which badly needs thinning, for the trees were thin and spindly and little light reached the floor. But it was ideal for my purpose, which was to keep a watch on the avenue for signs of Estelle – and for other strollers, since it would not do for the count to be seen alone with her.

I crouched beside a young oak tree and waited. I was afraid that I had left too late and that Estelle had already taken her walk and gone home, for the light was beginning to fade and the cows in the pasture were already beginning to settle. But this morning she had given me a veiled but unmistakable invitation to meet her here, and I was learning that she was a determined and resourceful young woman.

Looking obliquely along the avenue, my view of the bridge was largely obscured by the row of chestnuts, so at first I could not be sure whether the white shape I spied for one tantalizing second could be her. I glimpsed the shape again and knew it to be a woman. Gradually Estelle came into view. My heart thudded with excitement. She sauntered between the massive trees, trailing an umbrella and turning about from time to time as if in the midst of a dance to look behind her, and giving a wonderful facsimile of an empty-headed maiden given to sighs and poetic whimsy. I saw no one else.

I wondered at the freedom she was allowed to walk alone, without companions. Was she so adept at excuses, at alibis and stories to cover her real movements? Was she experienced? From there I began to speculate as I had many times before on whether there had been other lovers. I am not sure what I wanted the answer to be. If I was not the first, then I need not feel responsible for leading her astray. Yet there is part of me which wants her pure.

I could have called out to her as she drew level with my hiding place, but I was captivated by her existing unaware of me, by the impatient stabs she made at the ground with her umbrella, by the toss of her head, then by the gentle curve of her neck and her pursed lips as she appeared lost in thought a moment later.

When Estelle had passed by, I quickly climbed the fence and ran across the pasture to the cover of the nearest chestnut tree. The cows regarded me with boredom. I looked in the direction in which she had come and, seeing no one, flitted to the next tree and then the next, and another, until I had caught up with her. She heard nothing. She was humming to herself – a music hall song, I think – and the sound blended with the swirl of the river behind her. I heard her sigh with a mixture of impatience and gathering disappointment. It was a possession of sorts, to be in her heart, to be in her presence, but to be invisible. I felt her in my power.

Estelle looked back, sure that she was alone, and while she waited for me to appear at the other end of the avenue I stealthily crossed the ground behind her so that when she resumed her walk, there I was, standing before her where previously the avenue had been empty. For a second we regarded each other in wonder, then she ran to me and I swept her off her feet in my arms and held her, oblivious to the world about us.

I don't know how long we stayed like that. Slowly, I lowered her to her feet. Her eyes opened, but they were dreamy and unseeing as I touched my lips to hers and felt the first, careful pressure of her lips in return. The rush of the water filled my consciousness. I felt her yielding to me. Her mouth relaxed, and I felt the wet, inner surface of her lips as we pressed against one another in a rhythm whose flux bore some unknowable message from one body to the other. Her hands about my neck became fingers which explored and caressed. She let me pull her body to me and we molded to one another. I was lost.

It was she who pulled away, breathless, averting her eyes in case I saw there what every other part of her had already told me. It was Estelle who glanced up and down the avenue to ensure we were not observed. I returned to consciousness with my awareness clotted, like a bewildered epileptic recovering from a fit, like a dreamer who shakes off the previous reality only with reluctance.

'We should walk,' she said.

It seemed safe enough. We went in the direction away from the bridge, toward the point where the avenue ended and a trail which was mainly used by fishermen continued along the river's bank. If anyone entered the avenue, we would be too far off to be recognized and could slip away without difficulty. I took her hand; she glanced at me shyly but didn't take it away. It was a precious thing I held, a miraculous object such as one reads about but never expects to see or touch. I remember such a feeling of strangeness and reverence when I first saw, within the shadows of an opened thorax, a human heart.

The river was dark and swollen with the recent rain. Its powerful flow moved rapidly with us, and we heard the suck of eddies and the tumult in those places where it swirled around the large rocks which lay in its path. It was a living presence which moved beside us, inexorable, mysterious, and callous.

'I come here often,' Estelle said after we had walked for a long time in silence. For my part, I was too intoxicated by her presence to feel the need for words.

She is smaller and more delicate than I had appreciated until then, when I walked beside her. Because she is fine-boned and her limbs taper to tiny hands and feet, she reminds me of a Dresden shepherdess. When I gazed at her, she grew uncomfortable and inclined her head in a charming attitude of modesty. I wanted to reassure her that I looked only in adoration, for I was afraid she would see the hunger in my eyes and become frightened. Stealthily, almost guiltily, I stole a glance at the tiny mole on the side of her neck (it is a secret place even she does not know about). I was overcome by the softness of her skin, by the wondrous, vital flux of her changing expressions. It was a moment when assumptions break down and leave one in a primordial state akin to madness: I was confused that such a body should also have a soul, that her spirit could also be possessed of such a carnal form. That she should exist!

'If I'd known this was where you came, I'd have found you sooner,' I told her.

'Would you really?' she asked, stopping and turning to me as if this was the most important question in the world.

'Yes,' I said. I felt the sincerity like an ache in my chest. I would have kissed her again, but she turned from me and urged me to walk on. Her head was down in a veiled, thoughtful manner. 'I think of you constantly,' I whispered – anything that would raise her head and bring her eyes again to mine. I saw a small smile of pleasure play upon her lips.

'Do you?' she asked, turning her head partway toward me and away again quickly, like a bird.

'I think about talking to you alone like this, walking together, touching you.'

'I've thought of you when I've walked here,' she said diffidently. There were dark shadows beneath her eyes, and I wondered if she had lost sleep over whether she should go with me to Budapest. But she seemed confident enough now, in my presence.

'You must be sure you want this,' I told her. I meant to be considerate, solicitous, but it was a stupid thing to say, and I knew it as soon as I saw her face.

'Aren't you sure?' she asked. Her eyes flashed in challenge and, I thought, anger.

'Yes, yes, absolutely. I've never wanted anything more in my life,' I lied, but with enough conviction that at the time I believed it myself.

'Then that's all there is to it.'

'I was concerned that you . . .' Did she know where this led, to leave her family, to go to the city, to be kept by a man as his mistress?

'I care less about all that than you do,' she said with a toss of her head.

We walked in silence again. I was afraid my clumsiness had broken the spell.

She touched my arm as if to wake me and laughed lightly. 'Did you think I was naive?' she asked.

'I had no way of knowing,' I said.

'Well, I'm not.'

'I'm glad of that.'

'Do you believe me?'

'Yes, of course.'

By way of proof, she stood on tiptoes to kiss me. Immediately, she opened her mouth to invite my tongue into her. I felt her fear as I ventured very slowly forward. Her tongue was soft and hesitant, and when I touched her, there was a catch in her breathing that could have been either passion or panic. I held her tightly to reassure her, to transfuse her with my will, and I felt her respond to me with a returning pressure, and with a boldness and rising excitement that made me heedless.

And then, all of a sudden, she disengaged. She pressed her face into my shoulder. 'I'm afraid someone will come,' she said.

We had come to the point where the avenue ended and a narrow path wound its way through thick undergrowth that bordered the river. We turned, although my impulse was to take her farther into that dank, green tunnel. We walked in the opposite direction, through the spacious aisle formed by the soaring chestnuts, toward the spot where in the distance the white stone of the bridge gleamed in the last of the day's light.

'This thing with the du Barrys,' I began.

She giggled mischievously. 'Did you like it?'

'I did. Very inventive.'

'I've told them that you've said the du Barrys definitely have a position for me, and that I'm starting in two weeks.'

'Two weeks?'

'I know. I can hardly wait. But we have to make it believable. We can make it one week if you absolutely can't wait.'

'No, two is better. It's just that it doesn't leave us much time . . . to make arrangements.'

She closed her eyes and a beatific smile filled her face. 'I've set my heart on drapes, in the parlor, of cerise, or else of deep, deep rose.' Her eyes opened suddenly. 'Don't you think that would be lovely?'

'Any room where you are would be beautiful.'

'You just say that!'

'Won't you call me Laszlo? It's my name, you know.'

She seemed quite touched. 'Laszlo,' she said shyly. I think we both had a feeling that a threshold had been crossed. 'Laszlo,' she said, touching my lips with her fingertips, as if she were a blind woman learning the meaning of a new word. 'Now I have to go.' I wanted to hold her to me before we parted, but she was looking in the small beaded pocketbook she carried. 'I'm late. I must hurry,' she said. 'This is a letter I wrote from Madame du Barry. But it must be posted from Budapest.'

I looked at the envelope and saw that it was addressed to her parents. When I looked up, Estelle was already running toward the bridge; with her dress picked up to free her legs and the lower regions of white knickerbockers in view, she was elegant and graceful even in that awkward, encumbered state.

10

JUNE 18, 1887

The timing is excellent. Colonel Rado has sent a telegram to inform me of a meeting of the Magyar League which I am to attend. Not 'would be pleased to have the pleasure of your gracious company', or 'by all means come if you can, old chap'. No, I am commanded. This thing is altogether too militaristic. I am afraid that Rado and his friends take themselves a bit too seriously; but on the other hand, what a perfect excuse the League is for frequent, unexplainable absences in Budapest! Apparently he has convened a special meeting for my benefit and there is to be some induction ceremony, oath taking, and God knows what other mumbo jumbo. My main worry is that I won't be able to keep a straight face during the proceedings.

I am wearing the traditional Magyar costume of my rank, rather than the frock coat and top hat which is my usual dress when I go up to Budapest. I have a distaste for these clothes, and rarely wear them, except during holidays and solemn occasions when I am expected to show the flag, as it were. The furs are damnably uncomfortable in the summer, and the colors of the silk facings remind me of nothing so much as a joker's motley. It is all so medieval. However, I remind myself, it is a means to an end, and I must admit that my dress does bring out a certain eagerness to please in the otherwise sullen employees of the railway I encounter at the East Station in Budapest and in the servants at the hotel.

Rado's ceremony is tomorrow. In the meantime I am

scouting out suitable locations for a 'love nest'. I would guess from the reactions of the estate agent I consulted that my predicament is a common one.

'I am looking for a pied-à-terre in town,' I told him. 'Nothing too fancy.'

'Will it be for yourself?'

'Yes,' I said vaguely, wondering if I should tell him it was for my niece.

'A bachelor apartment?' he asked straightaway. His name is Wlassics. He is unctuous and devious and will not look me squarely in the eye. At any moment I expect him to forget himself and rub his hands in avaricious satisfaction.

'Something of the sort,' I replied. 'My wife may stay on occasion.'

'And will you be bringing servants, Count?' Here was something I had not thought of. 'Or perhaps a live-out maid could be engaged for those occasions when you intend to be in town?' he suggested, seeing my hesitation.

'That will do nicely.'

'We have properties for lease in all the best locations. Was there any particular part of the city that you had in mind?'

'I would think a quiet neighborhood.' I wanted to say, 'Something on a street where I'm not going to run into people I know and have to explain myself.' I said instead, 'It doesn't have to be in a fashionable area, but somewhere close to a park or on a square where there are trees would be nice.'

'I think I see what you mean, Count. We have just the thing on Maria Theresa Street. The building is quite private and entirely discreet.'

Like dealing with a pimp, one is grateful to be able to speak in general terms and not have to spell out explicitly what one wants, but it is an uncomfortable situation to have a stranger whose only interest is mercenary privy to one's intimate business, especially Wlassics. I worry about blackmail. But really, is this a valid concern? Everyone does it! At least, they did in Paris.

The apartment is on the second floor and looks into the branches of linden trees which border the square. It is quiet and discreet as Wlassics promised, and receives the morning sun. I have taken it for a year. Can the affair last that long? I haven't even begun it, and already I am thinking of its end. That is because I am worried about entanglement. If we don't hit it off, can I simply send her back to her parents? Enchanted as I am, I know that sooner or later one of us will become bored with the other. I am as afraid of her power over me as I am of her becoming dependent upon me.

NIGHT

The same impassive butler showed me into Rado's study this evening. The colonel was in full regimental dress of scarlet tunic crossed with gold braid, and a fur-fringed cloak of canary yellow was flung back over one shoulder. He came across the room to greet me with his right hand on the hilt of his saber.

'I'm glad you decided to come,' he said.

'I never gave it a second thought.'

'Perhaps you should now.'

'I don't know what you mean?'

'I mean this is your only chance to back out.'

'I don't want to back out. I want to go forward.'

'You understand that once you're an initiate, once you know the identity of the other members of the League, you will not be permitted to leave our organization?'

'Yes, I understand.'

While we were talking, I had been aware of the thump of boots and the scrape of shoes as perhaps two dozen people had walked together past the door. Now it was again quiet outside the room. This seemed to be the moment Rado was waiting for; there came a soft knock on the door which he did not acknowledge.

'Then I think we should begin, don't you?' he suggested.

'Absolutely,' I replied. I had tried to maintain an enthusiastic tone, but I must admit that his stern manner and the absence of any exit once I had committed myself was beginning to make me a trifle anxious.

There still remained some light outside, but the room into which Colonel Rado preceded me was dark. As soon as I entered, the butler closed the door, although I fancy he did not retire as he had on previous occasions, but came into the room behind me. The space was pitch black and silent. But perhaps not entirely silent, because I was aware that I was surrounded by a human presence. The air was cold and musty. Not a gleam of light showed from any corner. I thought to clear my throat or shuffle my feet – something to indicate that I was there, that I existed, that I was not overawed – but the truth of the matter was that I was intimidated. The stillness continued for several minutes. It could have been longer. It could have been no more than sixty seconds. At one point, far off, I fancied I heard the sound of a low murmur, as if two old men were consulting one with the other. Then there was another long silence. Was it a test? And if so, was I supposed to prove myself by enduring the darkness in silence, or was I to show that I was not afraid to speak out?

I was about to laugh it all away, to treat it as an overdone prank, when I was startled out of my skin by the sudden crisp grating of a match. The flare illuminated Rado's face from below and gave his features a fiendish, unearthly cast as he pressed the match to the wick of a candle. My eyes were instinctively attracted to the flame, so that when I looked about the room at the dim shapes of figures who sat at some distance on either side of me, I was dazzled and could make nothing out.

'You need concern yourself only with me,' Colonel Rado said in a clipped, military tone.

'Very well,' I replied, as if I had some say in the matter. I wanted to indicate that even though he could set the scene to his advantage, I would not be cowed.

'We are willing to lay down our lives for a great and independent Hungary. We would free our nation from Austrian interference. We would extinguish the influence in our national life of interlopers such as Wallachs, Saxons, and Ruthenians in order to restore Hungary to the Magyars. And we will place on the throne of St Stephen a man who is worthy to be king. Are you willing to dedicate yourself to this great cause?'

'Yes, of course.'

'Do you swear?'

'I swear.'

'Do you swear never to reveal the identity of any member of the Magyar League?'

'I do.'

'On pain of death?'

'Yes,' I responded promptly, although I thought the provision rather melodramatic.

'Are you willing to spill blood for our cause?' he demanded.

'If necessary,' I replied after a moment's thought.

'Good.'

There was applause in the gloom about me as Rado stood to shake my hand.

'Welcome,' he said. As he leaned toward me over the table on which the candle sat, his face was all but eclipsed, the light catching only his chin, nose, and the underside of his eye sockets, making him appear insubstantial and ghostly. The effect disappeared immediately the butler lit the gas lamps.

I saw that I was in a chamber that must at one time have been the private chapel of the family. In place of the altar was a substantial oak table with a thronelike chair behind it in which Colonel Rado sat. There were benches much like choir stalls which faced each other across a central aisle in which I had stood before him. These, I now saw, were filled with noblemen in traditional Magyar dress, men in military uniform, and here and there, a priest in black cassock. They pressed forward to shake my hand and congratulate me. There was something dreamlike in having men whom I had known many years before in diverse contexts emerge from the sinister darkness to pat me on the shoulder. One was a professor of anatomy who had taught me at the Medical School. Another man had been a childhood friend of my father and would occasionally visit me at St Sebastian's to see how I was getting on. Another was the brother of a friend from the University. The sight of the familiar faces reminded me how I have cut myself off from my past and how, associating only with bailiffs and servants on the estate, I have deprived myself of the company of my peers.

At first I couldn't believe that at the back of the throng of men I had seen Gregory's face. As the crowd thinned, I caught sight of him again, grinning from ear to ear. Eventually he, too, came forward to shake my hand.

'Now you understand why I couldn't say anything,' he said by way of apology.

'Then let there be no more secrets between us,' I said, although what I meant was that I wanted him not to keep anything else back from me.

MORNING, JUNE 20, 1887

Now that I have returned, I cannot bear the unreasonable calm of the castle. Outside our valley the world is bustling. Here, all is stagnant. I am dying of inactivity. I cannot wait to return to Budapest, because there we shall be together.

To my intense anger, the train was halted in the middle of nowhere, because, as the conductor later told me, of a signal failure farther up the track. As a result, I arrived at the station too late for the rendezvous with Estelle by the river. I was greatly disappointed, since I had been looking forward to seeing her with an intensity fired by the daydreams with which I had whiled away the time on that long and tedious journey. This is the only way I can account for my lapse last night during which I visited Elizabeth and committed coitus. It is all very well to say this in a calm and detached tone after the fact. Now the act would seem to have no more significance than the discharge of pent-up steam from a locomotive, were it not for the effect upon Elizabeth.

'You can visit me more often, if you want,' she whispered shyly when we lay spent and each in our own way guiltily sated.

I had made a halfhearted and inevitably futile attempt to stem my pleasure at the moment of no return. Elizabeth is beyond child-bearing and so the act can have no significance in her religion beyond lust pure and simple, and yet she accepts the tax of guilt on her pleasure far better than I. This morning I sense she is confused. There is a hesitation about her which I interpret as her uncertainty as to whether she is to hope any further for love. I wish she wouldn't, but I am in no position to advise her.

AFTERNOON

Instead of a stroll by the river in which I could tell Estelle about the splendid apartment I have arranged for us, I had to content myself with a visit this morning to the cake shop. Evidently, Mrs Theissen had seen me coming, or for some reason had been expecting me. (This makes me uneasy; if I am becoming such a predictable visitor, then others may also have noticed my special interest in the Theissen family. This is how gossip starts.)

'Oh, Count! We are so thrilled! How can we ever thank you enough?'

I smiled benignly, confident that they would mistake

my uneasy ignorance of Estelle's latest foray into creative fiction for a modesty which prevented me from passing any comment on my own good deeds.

'We've received a letter,' Mrs Theissen said in a teasing, sing-song voice as she wagged her finger at me in a manner which in any other circumstances would have been grossly overfamiliar. But I was distracted by the radiant appearance of Estelle through the curtain which separated the front of the shop from the working area at the back. It had not occurred to me until that moment that it would have been expedient for me to have read the letter she had written for the du Barrys before I posted it in Budapest. But it was too late now.

'From Madame du Barry?' I inquired.

'You guessed!' Mrs Theissen said. Whatever Estelle had written, it had sent her mother into throes of delight.

'No, I have to confess that I was speaking to Madame only yesterday, and she said that she had written to you. In fact, I suspect that the letter and myself may have come from Budapest on the same train.'

'Madame wants me to start just as soon as they have their new home in order,' Estelle said.

'Really?' I said surprised. 'I received the impression that she was hoping you'd be able to join them in a little over a week.'

'Are you sure?' Estelle jumped up and down with excitement. From time to time I have to remind myself how young she is. 'Are you really sure?' she insisted.

Our eyes met in the significance of the moment, as if we could communicate by telepathy without other people in the room knowing what passed between us.

'Yes,' I said. 'They are ready and eagerly looking forward to your coming. I have told them much about you.'

'I do hope Madame will confirm the arrangements,' Mrs Theissen said anxiously. 'Everything is happening so quickly, it's making my head spin.'

Estelle made a hurried excuse to disappear behind the

curtain, and I was persuaded by Mrs Theissen to try some almond cake. It was so delicious that when Estelle returned she insisted that I take some back with me for tea, and she wrapped it herself in a neat flat package.

JUNE 26, 1887

I am in Budapest again, under cover of a fictitious meeting of the Magyar League, to post the letter which Estelle thoughtfully included with the almond cake. I took the opportunity to order furniture for the apartment, including a massive bed with putti and bunches of grapes carved in the headboard. I have been rather extravagant, but there it is. My heart is beating with an excitement which is not entirely anticipation. As I circle the empty rooms, my footfalls echoing off the bare walls, I am tightly coiled, self-possessed, and with an inner stealth which is at odds with the confident, noisy movements I make.

When I arrived, Wlassics was waiting for me so that he could explain one or two things about the building. I paid little attention, except for noting that he went on and on, describing details with which I would never have concerned myself, and it occurred to me that there was something else he wanted to say. With some impatience, I maneuvered him toward the door. He hesitated as he was about to place the key in my waiting hand.

'I do hope you will be happy here, Count,' he said.

'I have no doubt on that score,' I replied and opened the door for him to leave.

'You can count on my discretion absolutely,' he said with a significant look which I chose to ignore.

'Of course.'

'And if I can be of any further assistance, I hope that you will not hesitate to inform me.'

'You have been of great service, Mr Wlassics. I shall impose on your valuable time no longer.'

He left without any further comment, but the exchange left me with an uneasy feeling. Was the fellow angling for a tip? Surely not, since he would have collected his commission from the owner of the property. Am I supposed to divine his intention from the allusion to 'discretion', his slight hesitation, a momentary sense of dis-ease or embarrassment? I do not like it when I think I may have missed something. If this is blackmail, it is far too subtle an attempt, for I experience no threat.

And yet there is something going on about me. Or, at least, I think there is. This morning the sun shone brightly in a blue sky and I decided to walk from the railway station to my appointment with Wlassics at the apartment. Consequently, I told the porter to place my bags in a cab and gave the driver instructions to deliver it to the hotel. I had gone only a short distance when I remembered that I had left with the baggage a hunting knife whose handle was broken, and which I had planned to leave for repair at a store I would pass on my way to the apartment. But when I turned back I saw a man in earnest conversation with the cabdriver, after which the man tossed the cabby a coin, and the cab drove off with my baggage still intact in the back. It happened too quickly for me to cross the street and retrieve the knife or to question the cabby as to the nature of the man's inquiries. The fellow himself, noticing all of a sudden that I was watching him, turned about quickly so that I would not see his face and slunk away, and I soon lost him in the comings and goings outside the station.

At least, this is what I thought had happened. I do not know whether the exchange really had anything to do with me, and since I was viewing the scene from the other side of a busy street, I do not know for sure if the man questioning the cabdriver was really reacting to my spotting him, or whether he was simply going about his business entirely unaware of my presence. Except, later, as I stood at the door doing my best to get Wlassics to leave without actual discourtesy, I saw a man leaning against the cast-iron railings which border the square. He was reading a newspaper – not a particularly sinister occupation, but why was he doing it in that spot when he could sit more comfortably on one of the benches? As soon as Wlassics left, I went upstairs to get a better view of the man, but he had tucked his folded paper under one arm and was ambling off in the same direction which Wlassics had taken, which indicates, I think, that whatever his purpose may have been, it has nothing to do with me.

I am getting jumpy. My nerves are on edge. I am not the hunted. This is a product of sexual tension and an overworked imagination. I cannot settle until I have the reality of Estelle in my arms.

NIGHT, JUNE 27, 1887

I am writing this as I sit beside the open window which looks out onto the small park in the square. A half moon has risen, and the whole city of Budapest is asleep. There is a stillness to the air that is broken from time to time by a breeze which rustles the leaves of the lindens in a most delicious way. I am at peace with the night.

I have what I desire. In the bedroom next door, in the massive bed with the carved headboard, tangled in sheets like a Tiepolo angel, Estelle sleeps fitfully. I watched the regular rise and fall of her chest, the sigh of her breath, the moan which precedes an adjustment in the disposition of her limbs revealing some new, milky softness of her. I hover above her, balanced between a loving, fatherly solicitude for the fragility of this young girl, and some inchoate, animal impulse to consume her. She stirs. I step back into the shadows. She does not know that it is the light of the moon which troubles her.

This morning I had intended to meet Estelle at the station. I spent the night alone in the apartment, waking at four and pacing aimlessly through the rooms like a caged animal as I waited for the sun to rise, watched at the windows for signs of activity to begin outside, and returned again and again to see if the hands of the clock had crawled closer to the time when I might reasonably leave.

At the station, they assured me that the train would be on time. I was an hour early and drank too much coffee while I attempted to read the newspaper. Finally, with infinite deliberation and pumping of steam, the locomotive pulled into the platform. I waited in an agony of anticipation through that hiatus between the moment when the train appears to have come to a standstill and the carriage doors fly open along its length.

Halfway along, not far from where I stood beside a pile of luggage, Estelle alighted from a carriage. She was wearing a new outfit in pale blue I had not seen her in before. She looked around hurriedly but did not see me, and I, enjoying the sight of her from within the crowd, did not signal my presence. Then she turned to look into the carriage from which she had come, and to my surprise a young man stepped down and stood beside her. He was talking to her as if they were on good terms, as if, in fact, they knew each other passingly well. She nodded at something he was saying, and smiling, looked around and caught sight of me. I was of two minds as to whether I should come forward to claim her from this young interloper, but I was alerted by her decision not to acknowledge me. A moment's reflection reminded me that there were passengers on the train from our town who might recognize me, even if I did not know them. Quickly I averted my head to study a timetable in a glass-fronted bulletin board. With mounting rage, I watched their reflections as he engaged a porter for her luggage and followed their ghostly images as they passed behind me. There was no undue familiarity. If he had laid a hand on her I believe I would have killed him there and then before a hundred witnesses. I dawdled the length of the platform ten feet behind them, swinging my cane in leisured insouciance while I strained to make sense of the scraps of their conversation which came to my ears.

I will own that he was a handsome young pup, with a somewhat oafish, eager, and overly honest manner about him. I took him to be a clerk or at best a student of the law. I was pleased to see that Estelle gave him no encouragement, but for his part he seemed to have a thousand reasons to lean in her direction or gesture with his hand close to her person. They gave up their tickets and passed through the barrier and then stopped in some awkward leavetaking which I was prevented from eavesdropping upon. I was forced to stand where I was, with nothing to contemplate other than the ridiculous persistence of a male pigeon who was attempting to attract the attention of a female entirely preoccupied with foraging for crumbs. When I looked up from this dispiriting metaphor he was gone, and Estelle stood radiantly before me. Her eyes were moist with emotion, and I succumbed in some instinctive way and wrapped my arms around her then and there – the devil take the scandal!

'At last,' I sighed, hardly able to breath.

She was pale, and I was afraid she would faint away.

'Come,' I said, putting my arm about her and drawing her from the place. I beckoned the porter to follow, and in no time we were seated in the back of a cab jolting toward our secret place. Her hand was cold in spite of the day's warmth; I held it to my lips and felt her fingers warm under my influence. By the time we had arrived she had recovered considerably (although I still did not think it timely to ask her about the young man she had traveled with), and when she saw the apartment and went from room to room exploring the space which was to be hers, she was entirely revived by her excitement.

'There is still more work to be done,' I said modestly.

'Oh, but it's marvelous! Oh, Laszlo!'

She hesitates still before she can pronounce my name, and I find something charming and tender in this, as if the syllables hold a new and fuller significance. As if I have a new and fuller significance. When she speaks my name in that shy way, I feel I am called fresh into existence.

'I've ordered more furniture, but it won't be ready until next week,' I told her. I watched her face as I disclosed each new item; as if I were dropping pebbles into a pool, her spreading smile was like the concentric ripples across the surface.

'More?'

I thought she would clap her hands together in glee like a schoolgirl. 'Well, we must have a table and a set of chairs for the dining room.'

'Yes?'

'And a sofa and easy chairs for the parlor.'

'What color will they be?'

'That's the reason why they're not ready. I told the merchant that you would have to decide on the fabric to go with your cerise drapes.'

'Oh, this is too, too wonderful!'

I did not realize how easy it is to make someone happy, nor was I familiar with the simple pleasure which derives from such an action. Estelle babbled on, but I fancy I was listening to the sound of her voice as one might to a piece of music, for I cannot recall one word she spoke. I followed after her, pleased by her pleasure, smiling indulgently, perhaps slightly bemused by the effects of my beneficence. And all the time, another lurks here, in the shadows of my self, peering out at Estelle through my eyes. He awaits, like a hunter blended carefully into the overgrowth of a thicket (my thoughts, my actions), his moment.

She came to me. It was a spontaneous burst of affection which drew her to me in a sudden patter of feet, her arms outstretched, lips open, to be kissed. At the last moment she hesitated at the social gulf she sees between us. It is an illusion, a mirage. I swept her up and pressed her to me along the length of our bodies to show her that nothing lay between us, and she gave herself to me with a small whimpering sound of surrender and desire.

'My love,' I whispered to her when our lips at last parted to draw breath.

'Oh, yes!' she answered me with an urgency that made her voice sound hoarse.

She held me tight about the neck, and it was a simple thing for me to sweep her off her feet and carry her to the immense bed. I laid her down tenderly and stepped back, although another part of me would have torn at the buttons and ribbons which fastened her bodice and routed beneath the lacy abundance of her petticoats with the abandon of a hungry animal.

Instead, I behaved like a gentleman, for there is no decorous way in which one may make love to a fully clothed lady, unless the lady in question is, like Stacia, experienced and has anticipated the encounter by coming to the assignation entirely stripped of clothing beneath the tent of her crinoline. So I kissed Estelle's hand and gently disentangled her other arm from about my neck. She was breathing heavily and was obviously discomposed, with a feverish glaze to her eyes.

'Only call when you are ready, and I will come,' I declared.

'No!' she cried as I went toward the door, and I was afraid that she did not take my meaning.

I should not have been concerned. I undressed quickly and put on a silk dressing robe which I had placed strategically for the occasion. Impatient as I was, it seemed that I waited only a few minutes before I heard her voice.

'Laszlo, I'm waiting for you.'

I had expected that she would retain a cotton shift or some such vestment with which to clothe her modesty. But when I turned back the sheet, I found her naked. She did not flinch from my admiring, devouring gaze. Her body is lithe and slender, and the darkness of her nipples stands out shockingly against her fair skin. When I stripped off my robe she looked quickly away, a maidenly gesture. I slipped in beside her and buried my head in her neck, between her breasts, on the inner, secret surface of her arm, breathing in the intoxicating summer scent of her and catching the faint hint of that more acrid perfume from below. She quivered when I touched the soft, downy hair there, and I felt her loosen and relax and sigh.

When I eased myself on top of her, she clasped me to her with a ferocity which I thought was eagerness, but I now known was born of fear. I was not prepared for the resistance; it gave suddenly when I entered her more deeply. She let out a cry of pain. I paused, but she clutched insistently at me in case I drew back.

'No!' she pleaded.

I continued, pressing against her halfheartedly, exquisitely sympathetic, obsessed with each stab of pain I caused her. I was hurting my beloved with each step of my loving her. I felt her tears at the spot where our cheeks touched. But I went on nevertheless. It was the way. Shudders ran from my chest down the back to my hips. A beast possessed me. There was a stranger within who was intent on only one thing and drove with single-minded purpose toward his savage delight. I raised up on my arms above her. I reared up like a centaur and flung back my head and if I had been in the forest I would have roared with the release of the mindless, wild bliss.

It ebbed, with endless gradations of delight, from me, and by degrees I almost returned to the man I was before. Below me, Estelle looked up with a half-relieved, uncertain look in her eyes. I reassured her with a kiss – our lips can lie in so many different ways – holding her, gentling her, steadying her. I slipped lower to circle with my tongue the dark areolae, searching for some last echo of the moment that lingered on her surface. Her fingers brushed through my hair tentatively, contemplatively, but I had not returned to a state of tenderness. I was a monstrous python that made his sinuous way still lower, that coiled himself about her waist and thighs to nose deeper into the hidden cleft to lick and suck and taste the slime and gore of life itself.

The next morning – this morning – I came slowly to

my senses in the strange bed. The light was different from my gloomy castle; instead of shadows and damp, sunlight streamed in through the huge windows which of course have no drapes, cerise or otherwise. Like a drunkard, I tried to recall the events of the previous day, and they came gradually to me, alien actions perpetrated by a stranger. Their memory made me wince. I had ravished Estelle. I turned and found that she was not in the bed. I lay still and listened for the sound of her movement elsewhere in the apartment, but heard nothing. Nor were her clothes in evidence about the room when I sat up and looked about me.

I felt sure she had gone. I had disgusted her, hurt her, degraded her. I believe I felt some remorse, a sudden pang such as one experiences when an unaccustomed movement reveals in a spasm of pain an old vulnerability one has forgotten. Mostly I felt panic-stricken that I had lost this precious person who alone was capable of restoring me to life after my sleep of twenty years.

I leapt from the bed, and snatching up my robe strode through the sparsely furnished rooms. I was afraid to call her name in case I received no answer. What could be lonelier than to hear my own voice evoke all the magic of that sound without the reality of her presence? I went first to the bathroom, hoping to find the door locked and Estelle within preparing to emerge radiant and refreshed in response to my gentle knock, but the door was open and the room empty.

I came upon her at last in the small room I have taken as a study, although presently it contains only a chair and a desk. It is the room where I sat last night to write the last entry in this diary, looking out on the square in the light of the moon.

'Ah, here you are,' I said.

'Where did you think I'd be?' she asked mischievously.

I suppose I was visibly relieved, and she was not averse to taking advantage of the situation. We scarcely know the outlines of each other's character, much less each other's

216

hearts. Revealed in an unguarded moment, my anxiety at the thought of losing her carried the ring of truth, and who can blame her for vying, as new lovers will, for these outward trophies of affection?

I came to her where she sat and put my arms about her. Her arms crossed mine to hold them there, and she gave a small shrug in order to fit more comfortably to my embrace. And so we remained, cheek to cheek, breathing in time, empty-minded, staring out the window at nothing in particular. Such a simple, quiet pleasure; so close to bliss! Yet I could not help wondering whether, if life had taken a different form, it could ever have been Nichole whom I cherished this way in my arms.

As Charcot never tired of demonstrating to us (he is discredited now, I learn) the mind is a paradoxical instrument. By what impulse did my eyes move from their idle contemplation of the sunlight on the dappled trunk of the lime tree outside the window to the desk immediately before us? How was it that my consciousness narrowed from its relaxed panorama to sudden, focused scrutiny? With alarm like a physical sensation running through my body, I realized that my diary lay in plain sight on the desk before us. How long had Estelle had been sitting there alone? God knows! Long enough to browse through it and come upon my confession to Stacia's murder? My change in mood must have communicated itself to Estelle, for I felt her tighten in my arms (why so sensitive? a bad sign). I nuzzled her affectionately and felt her blend again into my embrace (a good sign, indicating that she was not on guard).

In unfamiliar surroundings, being off-guard and distracted, I had not thought to find a hiding place for this book. There can be no one to blame but myself. But I reasoned that the fact that the diary lay in full view of Estelle did not make it a foregone conclusion that she had actually read it. However crucial to me, to anyone else it would remain an object of no particular importance so long as they never turned its pages. And so I calmed myself; I attempted to slow my breathing, to drain the panic from my mind, and to find out as much as I could from her without tipping my hand.

'I missed you,' I told her. She purred like a cat inviting further stroking. 'Have you been awake long?'

'No, not long.'

'What time did you get up?' I inquired.

'Who knows? You don't have any clocks!'

'There's one on the mantel in the parlor. You haven't had time to find out where everything is. When you do, I want you to think of this as our place together.'

I felt the grip of her hands on my arms tighten in pleasure. 'Do you really mean that?'

I kissed her. 'Yes, of course, my darling.'

She sighed. 'You've never called me that before.'

'Now we're together, I can say what I feel.'

It was a good sign that I had been able to bring back the feeling of cozy intimacy. If she believed herself to be in the presence of a murderer, she gave no signs of tension or fear. Yet I reminded myself, Estelle was an accomplished actress.

'I had the devil of a job finding you,' I coaxed teasingly, rocking her back and forth.

'Perhaps I didn't want you to find me too easily,' she said coyly in the same tone.

'And why would that be?'

'Because.'

'Because?' When she didn't reply, I had to ask again. 'Because, why?'

I think she squirmed in my arms. 'Don't ask,' she said. If she was acting the part, it was a masterful performance, seamless.

'All right,' I said gently. 'You don't have to tell me if you don't want to, you know.'

I proceeded to kiss her slowly about the ears and the back of her neck, picking each spot precisely according to some intuitive, erotic scheme of anatomy of which I have no rational understanding.

'All right, I'll tell you,' Estelle said. 'If you want.'

'No, I don't want you to.'

'Why not?' She turned halfway around in surprise, but I held her fast. I preferred to listen cheek to cheek, to concentrate on pure sound. As Gregory says of the confessional, faces can be composed, but the voice is harder to disguise.

'Because I don't want you to feel that I command you.'

She was silent for a minute, considering this. 'That's why I wanted you to come looking for me, so you wouldn't take me for granted.'

'I'll never do that,' I said, and gave her a squeeze of reassurance. And that seemed to be the end of the matter as far as Estelle was concerned. Unless she was playing a very sly, cat and mouse game with me. She seemed content to cuddle in silence.

'So you were hiding yourself away in here,' I suggested casually.

'Not really.'

'You had the door closed.'

'I was thinking.'

'You have to close the door in order to think?'

She laughed with such spontaneous gaiety that it was hard to believe that she was anything but happy. 'No, of course not!' she said. 'But everyone needs some quiet to think once in a while.'

'Oh?'

'That's why I walk by the river.' She was pensive, and I wondered if she was homesick. If she was, she seemed to shake it off quickly. 'Besides,' she said, regaining her previous levity, 'there's nothing to eat here!'

'Nothing to eat?' My first impulse was to summon the servant in question and give them a good talking to. But we had no servants.

'You've been hungry!' I exclaimed. For some reason I found this a profound dereliction on my part. 'You should have woken me sooner.'

'I didn't want to disturb you. You were so peaceful, sleeping with your arm curled around the pillow.'

Her fingers stoked the back of my hand. I listened for hesitations, for sudden changes in cadence, for an excess of emotion, for unnecessary explanations, but I detected no signs of deceit. No, she spoke with a tenderness which I found utterly convincing. In spite of myself, I was touched by her image of me. 'When I looked at you asleep,' she said, 'I imagined you were a shipwrecked sailor washed up on the beach of a desert island.'

My mind would be at peace were the consequences of being mistaken not so high. It is hard to believe that Estelle could have responded to me in such a lighthearted and affectionate manner if she had read my history. And yet . . .

I have tried to reconstruct in my mind the exact scene in the study as I opened the door. Estelle turned quickly when I came into the room. (Why would she have been startled by my entrance – surely she had heard me as I walked about the apartment in search of her – unless she had been absorbed in what she was reading?) Her hand was resting on my diary. Her left hand. Can I be sure of that? A minute later I was bending over her and I remember distinctly that her hands came up to hug my arms. Was she startled when I entered the room, or was she excited to see me? It's hard to say. I am uneasy that her hand was on the diary. I am sure Estelle's hand was resting on the diary.

I take her at face value. She knows nothing. Besides, what kind of a woman would read a man's diary? Estelle has, in her dealings with me, given every indication that she is an honest and forthright person. (But did she not trick her own parents? That deception, however, only demonstrates the depth of her loyalty to me.) She is loving to me. I am her sole support in the world now. I know she feels this keenly. I am confident I am safe, as long as I am assured of Estelle's loyalty. (I wish, though, that she had seen fit to volunteer information about the identity of the young man who accompanied her on the train. Has she something to hide, or is it simply that the matter isn't worth mentioning further?)

JUNE 28, 1887

Even if we had food, we have no servants to prepare it, and we cannot live on Estelle's creations. I mentioned that to her as a joke, but it fell flat. I rather think that she regards her work in the cake shop as something she has left behind, something now beneath her. The upshot is that neither Estelle nor myself have any idea of how to engage the services of a maid in this city. I had assumed that she would be more practical in those areas in which I am deficient.

Wlassics must deal with this kind of situation all the time, what with people new to town moving in and in need of help. Estelle jumped on the idea as the solution to our predicament, but I went along to his office only with reluctance. There is something in Wlassics's manner which makes one feel that it would be prudent to exclude him as much as possible from a knowledge of one's affairs. He has an unattractive habit of blinking rapidly when he thinks information of a personal nature may be forthcoming; at the same time, he smiles with an indulgent, faraway look to his face as if he is not really listening. It is not his prying which I find repulsive but his obvious excitement at getting into another person's private business.

'And how many will there be in the household, Count?' he asked, adding hurriedly, 'I only ask so that I may have an idea of how much help you will need.'

'I'm sure one maid will be sufficient for my needs,' I said coldly.

'Yes, of course. But will you need her all day, or just mornings, or should she come for the afternoon?'

I had no idea. Elizabeth handled these details of everyday life. In the beginning of our marriage, she had tried to consult with me on some domestic arrangement or other, but, seeing my impatience with such matters, had never bothered me with them again.

'May I make a suggestion, Count?'

'Of course,' I agreed grudgingly.

'You're much better off with a live-in. Because you never really know when you're going to need someone to do something for you, do you?'

'If you say so,' I conceded. 'Is there anyone reliable who is known to you? It's so tiresome going through references and so on if it's something that can be avoided.'

'I believe I can be of service. Now let me see.' With that same indulgent smile, Wlassics stared off at the far corner of his office, a poet consulting his muse. 'I know just the person!' he said with sudden inspiration. 'And she is the soul of discretion – you can count on that.'

Of course, one doesn't want the help to gossip outside the house even when one maintains an establishment of the utmost propriety, so I don't see why the man needs to harp on the subject.

We had breakfasted on rolls and coffee at a café, and I had promised to take Estelle to lunch on Saint Marguerite's Island in the Danube. The place has been converted into a spa, and there is a spring which spews forth foul-tasting sulphurous water which still retains some faint warmth of its volcanic origins. Since some distant authority once declared that it has medicinal properties, invalids and neurasthenics gather to sip the cloudy brew and discuss their symptoms. Fortunately their delicate appetites do not permit them to frequent the restaurant, which is a far more jolly place.

We were just in time to board the ferry which carries passengers to the island. It is called the *Swan* and is a trim little steamer done up in white, as its name would suggest, except for its tall black smokestack. Estelle was very excited, laughing and clinging to me with every small sway of the gangplank. Today has been the first hot day of this summer, with hardly a cloud to mar the pristine blue sky, and we were glad of the faint passage of air we felt as the boat pulled into midstream and made its way downriver. I urged Estelle to come forward to the bows so that none of the soot which belched from the smokestack would fall on her. She was most fetching in a dress of white muslin with ruffles at the shoulders and a small hat with a blue ribbon, a more petite version of the item a sailor would wear. When I complimented her on her outfit, she told me she had made the dress herself. Remarks like these make me realize how little I know about her. (I must help her fill out her wardrobe, but am leery of giving her money so that she may buy whatever clothes she wishes for herself in case the gesture may seem too crass. But sooner or later I must put cold, hard cash in her hand, otherwise she will starve when I am not here. The point to make – or, rather, to be avoided – is that my giving her money is not part of a transaction. I am not buying her.)

When I returned with some bottles of seltzer, Estelle was leaning against the railing to watch as the mount of Buda with its fortress and royal palace passed by on the other bank. There was something delicate and maidenly in her appearance which made my suspicions of the previous day seem mean and small. She turned to me with an expression which was simply happy.

'Thank you,' she said, and her eyes looked into mine with all the love and gratitude I could have hoped for. She is full of excitement and wants to see and do everything. She is surprisingly well educated, but much of what she knows comes from reading books and periodicals; she has rarely traveled outside our town. Later she confided to me that she had never before been on a boat.

The island is an ellipse a mile long which sits in the middle of the Danube, and the ferry looped around it before docking at a wooden platform which extends a short distance from the shore. Previously, the Archduke Joseph had retained the island for his private use, but it has recently been converted into a park open to the public for a fee. We strolled the paths at ease, grateful for the shade of trees and bowers which were covered with the first rose blossoms. The place was too prettified for my taste, with geometric walkways, rectangular flower beds, and everything in its proper place, but Estelle was delighted and called it the Garden of Eden.

At the restaurant, tables had been placed outside, beneath umbrellas to shade customers from the sun. I ordered some Riesling for us and made sure that the waiter understood that he was to serve it chilled. Everything Hungarian had been banished from the menu. Apparently our robust cuisine is not considered chic in that fashionable eating place. The German influence is paramount. Consequently, we ate Wiener schnitzel, which was soggy. But the wine sparkled.

'See, it matches your hair,' I told her.

We lolled in our seats, and held the glasses to the light to admire the wine's golden tint, and sipped its almost-sweetness, and colluded in those chance encounters between fingers and the backs of hands with which lovers must make do in public places. Before I knew it, I was upending the bottle to pour the last of the wine into our glasses.

'I was afraid I'd never get to see all these things,' Estelle said.

'Oh, there's lots more than this,' I said, waving my glass in an expansive gesture. 'This is just the beginning.'

'What else?' she asked eagerly.

'Well, I think we should dine at Wilensky's, for one thing.'

'Oh, yes!'

'But first, we have to find you a dress that's fit for the occasion.'

She reached across the table to squeeze my hand. 'You're too good to me.' There were tears in her eyes.

'Nonsense, my dear. Nothing's too good for you.'

It didn't matter to her if I was facile. She was completely without her bearings. Anything was possible.

A moment later, Estelle was thoughtful, biting her lower lip. Then she looked at me directly, and I saw that she felt the time was ripe to ask me something which had been on her mind.

She leaned forward. 'Tell me about Paris, Laszlo.'

It was as if a dark cloud had passed across my happiness. What could be her reason for bringing up the topic now, I wondered?

'Paris,' I sighed, as if the sound were something that could be savored like a wine to yield its layers of nuance. I was temporarily lost in thought.

'It must be so romantic,' she offered.

'I was a doctor then. And so I saw a different side of life. It wasn't like a pleasure trip.'

'Of course. I knew that.'

'But there's nothing like travel for broadening one's experience.'

'I dare say.' She smiled politely, hiding her disappointment.

'Why, you yourself must have found that just on your journey here to Budapest.'

'I want to travel everywhere.'

'But just consider a simple train ride – the people one meets.'

'I suppose.'

I let the thought dangle while I considered the wine in my glass, but my elliptical approach seemed not to prompt any further information from her.

'I wonder why you didn't introduce me to that young man at the station,' I said in a matter-of-fact tone of voice. 'Is he a relative?'

She laughed. 'And if he was, I certainly wouldn't want him to meet you, would I?'

'Well, you might.'

'After we've worked so hard to arrange this the way we have?' She put her hand to her mouth, giggling, and looked around furtively as if we might be overheard and hauled away by the police.

'I'm not sure anyone cares here what we do. You'll find Budapest's much more cosmopolitan in its attitudes. More modern.'

'Do you think there are other people like me in our building?'

'I shouldn't be surprised.'

'Then perhaps I shall make some friends.'

'I don't see why not,' I agreed halfheartedly.

'Would you prefer it if I don't?'

'No, not at all. But you should be cautious about whom you associate with.'

The party at a nearby table had got up and was leaving the restaurant. 'I will,' Estelle said absently. The women were fashionably dressed, and she was intent on studying the dresses they were wearing.

'Who was he, by the way?' I asked. My casual tone was wearing thin.

'At the station? He's no one.'

'You mean you would talk to a complete stranger you happen to encounter on a train?'

'He's not a complete stranger,' she replied somewhat huffily. I suppose a tone of disapproval had crept into my voice. 'When I say he's nobody, I mean he's not someone for you to get exercised about.'

'I was just curious, that's all.'

'He was someone I went to school with. Wasn't that a coincidence, running into him like that on the train? I didn't even recognize him.'

'But he recognized you, of course.'

'He introduced himself, and the name sounded kind of familiar, but I had to look and look at his face, and then it clicked into place, and I knew who he was.'

'Did he use to pull your hair in class?' I asked, trying to make up for my false step earlier by injecting a little levity into the conversation.

'No, he'd never have done that.'

'Why not? Didn't the boys use to fool around at your school?'

'Because Paul had a crush on me.'

Why did she have to give him a name? Now the episode is like a fishhook caught in my skin. He has substance. He is a clerk of some kind, or something slightly more than that – Estelle is unclear – and works in the Finance Ministry.

Here is another coincidence. Since we have still not sorted out our domestic arrangements, Estelle and I went out to a chop house near the apartment to eat dinner. After we were seated, a man came in, looked around as if he expected to find friends there, and seeing no one he knew, left the dining room. Now, the funny thing is, and I am by no means certain of this, I seem to remember him as being a passenger on the ferry which took us to the island this morning.

AUGUST 2, 1887

The castle is a gigantic dungeon. I cannot abide the passage
of time here. When I think of the days I must spend until I
can plausibly return to Budapest – to Estelle – I am afraid I
shall go mad. Everywhere, it seems, I am reminded of the
slow drip of time. In the silence of the night, the chimes
from the grandfather clock at the foot of the staircase
punctuate my insomnia. The creaking mechanism of the
ancient timepiece on the mantel of the drawing room
grates on me while I attempt to read the newspaper, and
I cannot shut it out. Involuntarily, I count the days, then
I calculate the hours and finally the minutes until I will
be with her again, and my scalp tingles with an intensity
which makes me wonder if my brain is inflamed.

But I also recognize that I am restless when I am
with her. I am not bored with her – far from it. I am
fascinated by every movement of her body. Whatever
she says delights me. I take the most intense pleasure
in the slightest thing which pleases her. Her whims are
my commands. She is not aware of the hold she has on
me. When we are clothed, I hide my infatuation behind
an urbane blandness of manner: She looks up to me as
her teacher of things sophisticated and her guide to the
culture of a Europe which lies beyond her experience. At
other times, I am a man of the world, a connoisseur of
the sensual, and here, too, she is an eager pupil. There is a
lewdness about her which she suppresses. I think she feels
it would be unladylike to express this side of her nature.
Yet it will out.

I sense she is proud of her charms and would like me to see her, but such a display would be in conflict with the strict rules of modesty in which she has been brought up, and therefore she must find a pretext for nakedness. After her bath on the day of my departure, she returned to the bedroom where I delayed in bed; she had, she said, left some item of clothing on the floor, and stooping before me, allowed the towel to loosen so that as she leaned forward it slipped from her body altogether and fell to the floor. She stood upright as if in shock, covering herself with hands and arms with an adequacy which was scarcely more than symbolic. With a coy smile, pretending to be flustered, she turned to me, her teacher now in manners and mores, for guidance in this moral quandary, for in order to pick up the towel she would have to remove one of her hands from the part which it concealed.

'No!' I commanded, holding up my hand to indicate she was not to move an inch. Estelle froze like an artist's model. 'I will collect it for you. It's the least a gentleman can do.'

I had never seen her wholly naked before. She was slim and lithe, yet with full, womanly curves to her hips and buttocks to which the warmth of her bath had imparted a faint blush. Her breasts spilled over the forearm she held across her chest. I took my time coming across the bed. I suppose my purpose was somewhat obvious. Estelle giggled in anticipation.

I knelt on one knee to retrieve the towel and breathed in the humid fragrance of the French bath oil I had bought for her the previous day. It glistened on the skin of her thigh and outlined every pore and tiny, golden hair. I let the towel fall. I held her hips in my hands and lingered with my lips in that soft fold where thigh and buttock join. I closed my eyes and was lost in reverence for the living flesh. I breathed in the fragrance of the perfume, her own rank scent; my arms encompassed her; my lips glided across her satin skin. It was worship of a kind. It was an apotheosis of the senses, an ecstasy more profound and sinister than lust.

Perhaps Estelle sensed this. I felt her body turn in my arms so that she could look down at me over her shoulder, and I was roused from my trance. I did not want her to see the expression on my face. When I kissed her again she shivered and let out a gasp which she made sound like laughter.

'You're tickling me with your mustache,' she protested without conviction. There was a note of uneasiness in her voice, at the unaccustomed position of a man kneeling at her feet. We were beyond etiquette or propriety, beyond the bounds of society. There were no rules, no principles of conduct to protect her.

But she didn't complain as I followed, with lips made slick with French bath oil, her curves and hollows. My eyes were closed. I was a mapmaker adrift at night upon the ocean of her body, committing her pink, perfumed contours to everlasting memory.

Orgasm is the release, but less and less is it an end in itself. I no longer lose myself in the experience; instead, I feel exceptionally focused in a strangely objective way. Estelle, on the other hand, is noisy and theatrical in the throes of passion and has so little recollection of her climax afterwards that she questions me in great detail about her behavior when we lie, temporarily sated, staring at our ornately plastered ceiling. She is becoming increasingly obsessed with orgasms and requires several of them a day. Presently she thinks that there is only one key which will turn her lock and that I am the one who possesses it. Consequently, she would not let me go until I had satisfied her one more time, with the result that I had to promise the cabby a large tip so that he would drive me to the station posthaste, and even then I only just managed to catch my train. She sees me as fabulously accomplished and worldly, and I wonder sometimes whether that exaggeration doesn't carry with it the risk of disenchantment.

In the same way that, the wind dying abruptly, one becomes aware of another sound in the forest which has been there unnoticed until that moment, I have become aware of my restlessness now that I am not preoccupied by the stimulation of Estelle's actual presence.

Today I arranged to go hunting with Gregory, hoping to tire myself out, or at least to provide some distraction from my pacing and obsessive thoughts. After luncheon I was eager to set out, but Gregory accepted Elizabeth's offer of coffee in the drawing room. He had a surprise for us, he said. We sipped from the frustrating, tiny cups Elizabeth insists on, and made small talk while we waited for the time which Gregory would judge to be the right moment to reveal what he had in store for us. There is so little playfulness in the dealings of my once lighthearted friend that we are inclined to indulge him on these occasions. He shifted awkwardly in his seat and his hand disappeared into one of those innumerable pockets which priests manage to conceal in their cassocks, finally emerging with a white envelope.

'My seed has borne fruit,' he said, flourishing it like a magician.

'You have a new benefactor,' Elizabeth guessed.

'Why would I need a new benefactor when I already have such generous patrons?' he asked rhetorically.

This was something of a sore point, since it has long been my feeling that there are other families in town with substantial incomes who could well afford a bigger share in supporting our church. But I remained silent, since I know that Elizabeth takes great pride in the fact that we essentially underwrite all the expenses. She insists that the funds for this purpose be drawn from her dowry, and when she refers to 'our' church, there is nothing casual about her use of the possessive article. There is a secret symmetry here: her church, my love nest. This is mean-spirited, I know, but I believe that the money she lavishes on a new altar screen or princely vestments in a sense justifies the expense of cerise drapes.

'Any ideas, Laszlo?'

'No, not really,' I replied, for I thought I had heard the clop of the horses I had asked Jacob to saddle for us and wanted to have done with the game. Besides, being a man with many secrets, surprises are not to my taste.

'Really! Make him guess, Gregory. Laszlo's become so moody. He needs bringing out of himself.'

'The bishop has finally agreed to give you another assistant,' I offered.

Gregory shook his head. 'In point of fact, it's Laszlo who's responsible for this letter. It comes from Budapest, from our cake decorator.'

I was on the point of swallowing a mouthful of coffee and almost choked with surprise.

'From the Theissen girl?' I asked.

'Estelle,' Elizabeth said. 'Such a pretty name. Such a pretty girl.'

I nodded my head vaguely while I mastered my apprehension.

'She's taken up her position with the French family you recommended her to and she's written to her parents, who in turn gave me the letter to read to you with their most profound gratitude.' Gregory's voice assumed a deep Germanic bass on the last phrase as he imitated Theissen.

Elizabeth smiled fondly at me as she does whenever she thinks I have performed some good work which may bring me closer to Heaven. She worries about my soul for all the wrong reasons. 'Do let's hear it!' she said.

'Here's what she writes. "Dearest Mama and Papa" – there's some asking after relatives and the family dog and so on – "Madame du Barry has received me most graciously and has made me feel quite at ease in her home. She is extremely fashionable and aristocratic, but somewhat lonely since she is as much a stranger to this city as I. Consequently, she finds many occasions to engage me in conversation. She is improving my French, and I am teaching her Hungarian, which is very difficult for a French person to learn. I have the feeling that she would like us to become friends. Monsieur is very distinguished and tends to speak only seldom, but he is also most considerate. Much of the time he is away on government business. They have taken an apartment in the Leopold District of Pest close to the new Opera House, and Madame has promised that one evening I shall accompany them to a performance there, since she is insistent that her children be exposed to culture from the earliest age.

"'The girls are totally charming; they are well behaved and not at all spoiled as we hear French children often are. Anna is six years old, though you would not think so from the questions she asks and the things she comes up with! Sara, the four-year-old, is always getting up to some mischief or other, so that between the two of them I am kept quite busy, as you can well imagine! Yesterday we went to see an exhibition of paintings by Mihály Munkácsy, who many people say is the greatest artist of this century. Madame is very knowledgeable about art, and I can learn a lot from her, so in between herding Anna and Sara through the salons (they were of course terribly bored) I did my best to listen to what Madame had to say about the paintings, and I must say, the way she explained things, he is indeed a very great painter, with a marvelous sense of contrast. One entitled *The Dying Mozart* fills one with a haunting sadness. How fitting that the greatest musician of his time should be depicted by the greatest painter of his time. We have also visited the zoo, and last week we took the carriage across the bridge to Buda to one of the pretty open-air restaurants there called the Marble Bride. Such a strange name! But so lovely with the Gypsy orchestra playing. The girls fell asleep in the carriage on the way home and George the groom had to carry them upstairs to bed because Madame said they looked too beautiful to awaken.

"'I must go now. At times I am a little homesick. Still, it wouldn't be natural if I wasn't, would it? But I am feeling quite at home here and am treated as one of the family.

Perhaps when I have been here a few months Madame will let me have a few days to come home to visit." There!' Gregory said, looking up with an expression of satisfaction. 'It couldn't have worked out better.'

They were both looking at me as if I was expected to make a speech of acceptance. 'Well, of course I'm delighted it worked out so well,' I said, though the truth of the matter was that I found the letter profoundly disturbing.

It wasn't the hallucinatory clarity of the fiction Estelle had invented which worried me (though on further reflection her capacity for improvisation does bear thinking about), so much as the thoughts of another which I detected mingled among her words. When I left her a week ago I could swear Estelle didn't even know of Munkácsy's existence. 'Marvelous sense of contrast . . . fills one with haunting sadness'? Whose phrases are those? And how had she found her way to a restaurant on the other side of the Danube, this girl who a few days previously had never before even set foot on a boat? I was already searching my mind for an excuse to rush back to Budapest.

'I'm sure you've done far more to make this a success than you've let on,' Elizabeth said without a trace of irony.

'He's a dark one, that Laszlo,' Gregory said.

'I have a wonderful idea!' Elizabeth exclaimed. 'We're always saying how dull things are here.'

'I'm not complaining,' I put in, trying to head off whatever might be coming. 'I like things the way they are.'

'There's always room for improvement,' Gregory suggested.

'Why don't we invite the du Barrys here for a visit?' Elizabeth asked, looking from one to the other for our reactions. She persevered in spite of the sour face I made. 'They sound most cultured, the little girls are charming, and Estelle would be able to visit her family into the bargain.'

For an instant something reckless (not to say suicidal)

inside me considered the logistics of such a deception. (Is this a perverse need to be found out? And if so, is the impulse to confess or simply to destroy myself?)

'They're really terribly affected people,' I said doubtfully. 'Giselle is entirely neurotic, and Hubert's a frightful snob. I once witnessed him put an entire dinner party to sleep describing his family tree. Giselle, on the other hand, is more dramatic; she has fainting spells. When I knew them in Paris, I was still a doctor, of course, and Giselle insisted that I was the only one who could revive her whenever she had an attack of the vapors. It got rather boring.'

I was beginning to understand Estelle's trick of improvising. Beginning was the hard part: overcoming a lifetime's habit of truthfulness. Once one began, it wasn't difficult at all.

'That wasn't the way you described them to the Theissens,' Elizabeth said. There was an uncharacteristic glint of pique in her eye which was immediately extinguished. I have rarely heard her contradict me so directly, and certainly never in front of a third person. Taken aback, I was inclined to compromise.

'There's two sides to everyone, I suppose,' said Gregory in his soothing role.

'I have nothing against people coming to stay,' I offered.

'We never see anyone.'

'That was because I thought you were content.'

'I am.'

'We can have guests. We have plenty of room. Of course, the hunting's a bit limited until the deer come into season.'

'Some of the bathrooms will need attention.'

'I'll speak to Brod about it.'

'Will you really?' She seemed pleased.

'Of course. It's about time. There are all sorts of people I run into in Budapest with this political stuff I'm involved in. Much more amusing people than the du Barrys.'

Improvising is not difficult. In fact, it is too easy, and very quickly runs away with one.

Jacob waited patiently in the courtyard holding the horses by their bridles. I checked the guns in their leather sheaths attached to the saddles. The sun was still high; there were a few scattered clouds, but the light was good. I looked to see the movement of the clouds which would give an indication of how the wind would be blowing on higher ground.

'From the southeast,' Jacob said, anticipating my thought.

He looks at me inquiringly these days, as if to ask why I am hunting so seldom. Even when I do, I leave him behind as often as not, since I prefer to be alone and can get along without a gun bearer for small game. He worries that he has fallen from my favor, but if I tell him that I am not displeased with him, he will think I am trying to placate him and will wonder why I have broken my silence on the subject. Jacob is that kind of man.

Today our destination was a part of the forest where Jacob had seen signs of bear. It was a scouting mission to search out likely spots for next year's season and to bag whatever small game came our way. Jacob was to accompany us on the big chestnut called Trojan, a slow and stupid horse but immensely strong, and not at all skittish about carrying freshly killed deer strapped to his back.

Gregory and I took off together exuberantly, as if we were sixteen again, galloping through the castle gate and swerving around the corner of the driveway on the hard-packed gravel. We cantered on the road which curves around the hill through the orchards and at the bottom rode away from town, following the river road that leads up to the mountains. When the road gave out and became a steep path, we let the horses walk.

'Colonel Rado's a bit of an odd character, isn't he?' I said. We had been riding for a while in easy silence, and I thought it a good opportunity to find out more about the Magyar League.

'Rado? I wouldn't really know,' Gregory replied.

I was surprised. 'I thought you'd been involved with the League for a while. That's what Rado implied when he was trying to get me to join.'

'Not really.'

'But you were there at the ceremony.'

'I joined because of your uncle. He wanted it, and it didn't seem like much to do to please the old man.'

'You never said anything about it.'

'It didn't seem important.'

'But if it wasn't important, then it wouldn't have mattered if you'd told me.' I was surprised how hurt I felt that he had left me out of this corner of his life, that I was superseded by another loyalty.

Gregory glanced at me, sensing this. 'They swore me to secrecy. You know the stuff. You went through it yourself.'

'But you could have leveled with me, surely?'

'You forget, it's my business to hold secrets.'

To provoke him, I said, 'Who knows what dark and dirty secrets scurry through that head. You've probably got something on just about everyone in town.' I snickered, but he wouldn't react.

'Except the Gypsies,' was all he said, with a slight, formal smile that pertained to his role as priest rather than friend.

I realize there are limits to our relationship. Indeed, for Gregory there are clear limits to the importance of anything in the transient, material world. He is committed to transcendence. Sometimes, as this afternoon as we walked our horses side by side, there is a dreamy, far off look to his face, as if part of him has already left this life.

'If you've been a member of the League all this time, how is it that you've never gone up to Budapest to meetings?'

'It's quite loose. They don't expect people to come to all the meetings, especially if you live far away. There's only a small core of people actively involved.'

'That isn't the impression Rado gave me. He more or less told me that once I'm a member, he expects me to participate.'

'But you're special.'

'How so?'

'They really wanted to recruit you. Rado was intent on getting you to join.'

'And you helped them?'

'I thought it wasn't a bad idea. You were in a slump. I thought it would be good for you to be part of something bigger, something to get you out of yourself. I was right, wasn't I?'

'I suppose so.'

'I hadn't heard from them for years. In fact, I'd entirely forgotten about them. And then out of the blue I got a letter with a train ticket saying they'd made a reservation for me in a hotel and would I be sure to come to a meeting.'

'How odd.'

'Not really. They love the aura of secrecy and conspiracy.'

'Why me?'

'They want to recruit people who have a vote in the Upper House.'

'That's funny. Rado's never mentioned anything to me about Parliament.'

'He will. He's playing you like a trout. First he wants to make sure you're hooked, then he'll try to land you.'

'I'm not sure I like the sound of that.'

'He's really a very charming man, and quite innocuous. Humor him . . . maybe there's a place for you in national politics. Why not?'

We dismounted and left the horses at the edge of the trees and lay on the grass bank beside the path to wait for Jacob to catch up with us. Even in that peaceful place I was unable to rest. I got up and walked a short distance to a rise from which I could look back along the valley toward town. I had a fear of Estelle slipping away from me, as if she were something I possess and therefore something which could be stolen from me. I walked back to the bank where I had left Gregory and found him reading his catechism.

When Gregory had come here last week with Jacob, they had found stool from bear in a steep valley beyond the ridge, and we set off in single file to investigate the area further. The day was mild, and although the breeze had gathered strength as we came higher, the movement of air was barely perceptible as we made our way along the narrow trail between the pine trees. Jacob led, and by habit we climbed in silence at a steady pace that we knew from experience was comfortable for all of us. Our boots made no sound on the carpet of pine needles. Where there were rocks or stones in our path, we avoided stepping on them. The leather of our bandoliers was oiled and supple, and our guns were slung where they would not tap against a button or buckle. This was the enduring influence of Uncle Kalman.

'Chatter all you want, boys, on the road and in the fields. Once you enter the forest you must be as quiet as the deer himself.'

The going was steeper and the trees thinner when Jacob led us off the trail in a northerly direction, following the line of the hill's crest. After about four miles he indicated that the place he had been looking for lay on the other side of our hill. Slowly and carefully we climbed almost to the summit. Some of the hillside was steep enough for us to use our hands to climb, and in places the rock was bare of earth. We had to skirt this in order to make our approach silently. We lay at the crest and looked down into the ravine on the other side.

Our hill was merely an extension of a larger mountain, the peak of which marked the boundary between my own land and the estate of my illustrious neighbor, Count Aponyi. Between the hill and the mountain lay a ravine not more than a hundred meters wide with steeply sloping sides and a flat, soggy bottom through which a small stream meandered. It was unusual terrain for this area because of its marshiness, the rest of the vegetation being sparse except for the trees, and it afforded lush grazing. The ravine was fed by a waterfall that splashed from a height over rocks to our right, and I think the rock formation must have provided a basin which held the water. It was too damp for pine so there was little canopy to cut out the sun, and grass and bushes grew in profusion.

It was a tempting but dangerous place for deer. Some of the bushes had grown to the height of a man, but otherwise there was limited cover. More importantly, the ravine was enclosed on three sides, by the side walls of the cleft and at one end by the narrowness and steepness of the watercourse, which ended in a free fall of five meters into a gathering pool.

Jacob signaled that he would enter the valley by the waterfall and that Gregory and I should make our way to the other end, the outlet of the cleft, so that the sound of his movement would drive any animals toward us. But I countermanded the plan and instead signaled that I would take Jacob's place. He was not happy with the arrangement, but the situation did not allow for discussion, and he could do no more than give me a disapproving look as I handed over my gun and bandolier to him and urged them to be off. He grumbles about my methods, particularly the use of the spear, and hints that my desire to close on the animals I intend to kill is unseemly. Of late he has become quite truculent and mutters complaints to other servants just out of my hearing. He is most insistent on the distinction between man and beast, on a proper distance between hunter and prey.

I set off to work my way around the shoulder of the hill to the place where the stream fell into the ravine. This part was thickly wooded, and I could not look down into the area to see if animals were there. I traversed a rocky ledge which brought me farther away from the blind end of the cleft, and then descended slowly, using the trunks and roots of trees for handholds, and pausing at intervals to listen and scan the undergrowth below. The clatter of the water on the rocks hid whatever sounds I made.

At the bottom, I waited immobile for several minutes behind a bush which screened me from the flat area on either side of the stream. There was little movement of air at the valley bottom, but enough to carry my scent slowly along the length of the ravine toward any animals there and to drive them toward Gregory and Jacob. The air was filled with the moist, earthy fragrance of the moss which lived off the waterfall's spray. The water splashed irregularly, and I listened in those fragments of silence for the sound of footfalls or grazing.

I had worked my way to the edge of the bush that hid me and was about to move to the next, which would bring me closer to the stream, when a deer emerged from behind it. She was a full-grown doe and she stopped chewing on a mouthful of grass to turn her head with an abrupt, intent focus in the direction of the mouth of the ravine. I thought perhaps she had caught some faint sound of Gregory and Jacob getting into position a mile away. She pricked up her ears, and her tail twitched nervously. But no further sound came to her to cause alarm, and after fixing her gaze on sectors to either side of the original direction, she resumed her browsing.

I wonder that this one did not smell me. At one point I thought I caught a trace of her musky scent, but I must have imagined it. With almost unbearable anticipation, I listened to the crisp snap as she pulled at the grass and watched through the leaves of my cover as she rechecked in the direction from which the suspicious sounds had previously come. Perhaps that is what distracted her from her present danger – for I meant to kill her, season or no season, now that such a splendid opportunity had presented itself.

Something, however, had made her skittish. She spent more time with her head up listening and watching, frequently stopping her chewing to turn her head to one side or the other. Infinitely slowly, I moved my hand down my side toward the hunting knife at my hip and eased it from the sheath. The twenty feet which separated us might as well have been the Pacific Ocean. But by some uncanny force, she took several steps toward the bush where I hid as if she intended to browse it. And then in mid-course she checked. Her nostrils flared, and she raised her front hoof from the ground, lowered it uncertainly, and raised it again. She seemed to stare right into my face, a sad, reproachful gaze.

Then she bolted. There had been no change in the wind, or shift in my position which might have alerted her to me. I stood upright and was for the first time aware of my heart thudding within my chest and the sensation of my shirt sticking uncomfortably to my body. I was panting. My hand trembled as I sheathed the knife. To my left I heard further thrashing in the undergrowth as another deer, perhaps the buck, made off in a hurry toward Gregory and Jacob. Then there was silence in the bright sunlight, except for the buzzing of a bee going about his business. For reasons I cannot explain, I felt fear ebbing slowly from my body, as if it had been my life which was in danger.

AUGUST 30, 1887

I have been concerned that Gregory might want to accompany me to meetings of the Magyar League, but so far he has shown no interest whatsoever, and Colonel Rado has made no further mention of him. My train to Budapest was late again, and to my intense chagrin I had no choice but to endure a meeting of the Magyar League before I could join Estelle at the apartment off Andrassy Avenue.

It was late in the evening, and I expected that Estelle had been waiting for me for several hours. I had never before had occasion to disappoint her, and I was afraid I would be met with pouting, or recriminations, or chilly silence à la Stacia. As a precaution I had detoured the cab to pass by the Opera, where I had bought an enormous bouquet of deep red roses from one of the old peasant women who sold flowers there.

Our porter at first pretended not to recognize me. This gave him the opportunity to ask me a host of impertinent questions, and I had to go through a long description of who I was. I had, during the heat of the discussion at the meeting of the League, drunk more than I am accustomed to, and I now found it difficult to restrain my impatience with the man. Finally, at the point when I had decided to give him a good dressing down, the porter 'remembered' and with profuse apologies allowed me to enter. Confound the prurient curiosity of these fellows! Take so much as a single step outside the bounds of polite society, and one becomes vulnerable to all manner of familiarity from common people who would take advantage.

I let myself into the apartment in order not to disturb the maid and called softly for Estelle. There was no answer. The lights in the parlor were on, but the room was empty. I thought perhaps she had dozed off while waiting for me, and intending to waken her with the surprise of my arrival I slowly eased open the bedroom door. She had draped the single lamp with a red woven shawl, and the pink light suffused the room, casting long, distorted shadows across the walls and bed where Estelle lay. I was immediately alarmed by her sickly appearance. She did not appear to be sleeping, but lay in a contorted, uncomfortable attitude as if caught in the middle of a spasm of stretching, or, and this was a realization which hit me like a blow, she had succumbed to an agonizing death. I came quickly to the bedside and almost stepped on the fragments of a smashed wineglass which lay on the floor where it must have fallen from her fingers. Her complexion was gray, her lips pallid, her cheeks sunken. No inspiration moved her breast. I felt hurriedly for signs of life in her outstretched wrist; the bounding of my own heart almost obscured the rapid, thready pulse I felt there.

'Thank God!' I breathed, and as I spoke I thought I saw her stir.

That gave me hope, and I took her by the shoulders and shook her, calling her name again and again, trying to wake her from her slumber. She showed no signs of animation. When I put my ear to her mouth I could feel the soft, reassuring sensation of her breath, but I also encountered a chemical odor I did not recognize. I drew back in horror. Distractedly, I began to look about the room for a bottle or vial which would confirm my suspicions, and it was then that I saw the paper, neatly folded and addressed to me, clasped in the fingers of her other hand.

My dearest, dearest Laszlo, [I read] I can wait no longer. An hour without you is an eternity. An eternity without your love is death. If you cared for me, you would know this. My life has no meaning without you, therefore I give it up without sadness. I believe and hope that our spirits shall meet again on another, more perfect Plane of Being. Farewell. Estelle.

I fell on my knees at her bedside. 'Oh, Estelle, no!' I groaned aloud, my face pressed against the bouquet of red roses I had brought for her.

But it was not a moment in which to indulge grief, and I caught myself up and began to think like a doctor. The remedy lay in either purge or emesis. I went in search of the maid, but she was nowhere to be found, and I reasoned that Estelle had sent her away so that Lucy would not thwart her plan. In the scullery I hurriedly mixed salt with some warm water in a glass and found a basin for Estelle to vomit into.

When I returned to the bedroom, I thought I had gone mad. Where Estelle had lain in her contorted position upon the bed, there was now only a bouquet of crimson roses propped neatly against the pillow where her feverish head had lain. For a single crazy moment, my mind considered the possibility that I was in fact living out one of those Indian stories of metamorphosis in which a person at the moment of death is transformed into a plant or an animal. I put down the basin and the glass of brine. It was conceivable she had rolled off the bed, but she was not on either side or beneath it. Perhaps, I considered, she had partially regained consciousness while I had been looking for Lucy, and wandered in a state of delirium to another room of the apartment. I searched every one without finding her.

Puzzled and disturbed, feeling I had blundered into the realm of the occult, I returned to the bedroom. Now I found Estelle once again on the bed, laid out symmetrically like a praying corpse, wearing nothing but a bouquet of roses. I crawled across the bed and tentatively touched her cheek. Her shoulder jerked once and a shudder went through her which I thought at the time might be a sign of impending seizure. A spasmodic tightening of her lower face, particularly about the mouth, caught my attention. Then one eye opened, regarded me at close quarters for a second, and closed again.

I stepped back for a change of perspective. The pink glow of the lamp confused the picture, but now that I could view her naked, I could see that there was something distinctly odd about her appearance. The color of her face was artificial and did not match the far healthier hue of the rest of her body. Her respirations were deep and rapid now, and her toes and fingertips were warm and well perfused. On an impulse, in a state of perfect uncertainty, with my verdict balanced evenly between disaster and prank, I caressed the breasts and noted that the nipples of this comely corpse were soon erect.

I undressed quickly and as noiselessly as possible, all the while watching to see that Estelle did not open her eyes and always keeping one hand moving across her body so that she might think I was entirely engaged with her. I moved the flat of my hand with exquisite slowness along the length of her belly: down the incline from her chest, across the plane of her upper abdomen along the suggestion of a groove between the bands of muscle, to her navel, and then over the slight rise before the dip down, through her downy hair, to the moistness, like a sweet decay, between her legs. The stiffness of death had been replaced by a new pliancy. I encircled the corpse with a strong embrace which encompassed the praying hands and crushed the roses, thorns and all, between our bodies; and when I eased myself between the thighs, they yielded with the indifference of inanimate matter. I entered it. I held it to me and writhed against it and ground the roses between our chests and lived within the pungent smell of broken leaves, the perfume from smeared petals, and the vital, consuming burn and ache of thorns driven beneath the skin. And thus I restored her, with a cry at last, to life.

I eased myself off her gingerly. One rose was stuck by a thorn to my chest, and I plucked it off. Estelle, I saw, was in some pain. I began to lift the ruined roses from her body one by one, as one might the bandages from a wound.

'How could you do that?' she asked plaintively. She wasn't looking at me, and she appeared pale and disturbed. I thought that I might have frightened her.

'It was part of the game,' I said. 'I was playing along.'

'That wasn't how it was meant to be.' From her tone of voice, I wasn't sure whether she was about to cry or withdraw into a sulk.

'But it was very good,' I urged her. 'Really, it was awfully good. You were simply marvelous. I had no idea at first – you had me going completely. I thought you were dead!'

'Well, now it hurts!'

'That proves you're alive, at least.'

'Please do something!' she cried, fluttering her hands helplessly.

Parting the flattened leaves, I found that a thorn had penetrated the soft white skin of one breast.

'Be brave,' I said and with infinite care began to pull it from her. The thorn was curved like a Turk's dagger, and my motion followed its line as I slowly withdrew it. I heard her suck in air, and then she remained rigid, wincing only as the very tip emerged. A bead of dark blood welled and gathered, and at the moment when it would have run into the hollow between her breasts, I stooped and kissed the spot, drawing the drop into my mouth.

'Look at me!' Estelle protested, much put out. I think I had frightened her. There were indeed scratches and blotches where the flowers had been pressed too roughly against her chest, but my mouth was filled with her salty, metallic essence, and in the act of swallowing I seemed to dip and almost swoon.

'Whatever will people say?' Estelle cried.

'But whoever will know?'

'Lucy, for one.'

'How so?'

'When she pours my bath, naturally.'

'And . . . are there others?'

'Of course not. How could there be others?'

'Then I'm sure you can think of something ingenious to tell Lucy. You're so inventive in that department.'

'How do you mean?' She had turned to me, almost smiling now, in anticipation of praise. She is proud of her ability to improvise, to turn a tale on the spot to fit the needs of the occasion. She insists that such a capacity is an essential component of an actress's repertoire, but she is also aware that her talent is only a hair's breadth from the more common and far less praiseworthy proclivity to lie.

'You have a gift,' I told her, glad that she was not going to sulk. 'I particularly liked the part in your letter about the two little girls. That was most creative.'

'How did you come to hear about that?'

'Your grateful parents gave it to Father Gregory so that he could read it to me.'

Estelle held her head on one side, considering this. On

the whole, she seemed pleased that I should be in a position to appreciate her literary endeavors.

'Did he read you the one in which Anna and Sara catch chicken pox and I nurse them?'

'No,' I said with rising apprehension.

'They were really ill. Even Doctor Bernhardt from the embassy was worried. I was up all of one night sponging them to keep them cool, but I didn't mind, because they are such charming, affectionate little girls. The sad part was that they were too sick to go to the opera, Madame said, even though they were feeling much better and had been looking forward to going for weeks.'

'Estelle,' I said gently, trying to interrupt the flow.

'But Madame said that I shouldn't miss it on account of the girls' illness and told Lucy that she was to stay with them while we were out.'

'Sometimes I think you believe these stories yourself.'

'But they are partly true. That's the trick of it. That's the art of being an actress: You start with something that's true – it could be an emotion, it could be something you read about – and then you develop the story from there.'

'But don't you find yourself getting lost sometimes?'

'Lost? How?'

'I mean, what's real and what's fantasy . . . confusing them.'

Estelle turned to me with a most solemn expression. 'And who's to say where the one ends and the other begins?' she asked.

It was one of those questions which set off profound philosophical reverberations in the soul of a twenty-year-old; for my part, it served only to illuminate, like distant lightning, the abyss two decades wide which separates us. And yet I was a man who had once eagerly immersed himself in the mind's mysteries in order to trap some proof of magic. And what is magic but that point of experience at which fantasy becomes reality? Skepticism is a wasting disease which leaves intact the mind while it insidiously hollows out the soul. Perhaps it is already too late for me.

I held my peace, and she took the silence to mean that she had forced me to reflect on my assumptions.

'Are you so sure you know?' she asked, imagining she was pressing home some rhetorical advantage.

'I think I am,' I replied.

'But that's the point: If you only think you're sure, then you can't be completely sure – and that leaves just the smallest chink for doubt to enter in.'

'Are these your own thoughts?'

'Of course they are!' She laughed musically, fondly, as if I were a dullard in need of reassurance that the world was in fact simple and manageable. 'They must be my own thoughts, otherwise how could I tell them to you now? Sometimes you're quite silly, Laszlo! I know you want me to think you say things like that on purpose, but sometimes I wonder.'

'Who else do you talk to?'

'Lucy mostly.'

'Lucy?'

'Why not? She's a good listener. And she's got a good head on her shoulders.'

'But you can't talk to the maid.'

'Why not?'

'For goodness sake, because she's the maid, that's why!'

'Well, I have to talk to someone, otherwise I shall go mad!'

'There must be . . .' I cast about helplessly for some solution.

'Other people in similar situations,' I suggested lamely.

Estelle said nothing.

'It's just that, from your letter . . . I mean, going to Munkácsy's exhibition, and so on . . . it sounded as if you'd found somebody to show you about.'

'And whoever could that be?' she asked archly.

'I don't know. Who knows? An old friend you'd run into, or someone.'

'Well, I'm lonely, and when you read the next letter, you'll hear that Madame has given me a week to go home to visit my family.'

'Don't you think that's something you might have discussed first with me?'

'Indeed? Why? I think it's a matter entirely between myself and Madame.'

I believe Estelle is teasing me. There is a playful side to her which I find very attractive. Nevertheless, I have an uneasy feeling that this affair is rolling beyond my control – that is, if it has ever been within my control. I cannot shake the suspicion that I am being used. I will be nobody's fool.

MORNING, SEPTEMBER 16, 1887

Estelle is to arrive home today. She has been exasperatingly vague about occasions when we will be able to meet, but in this she probably shows better sense than I. We have become spoiled by the relative anonymity of Budapest, where we have felt free to wander along Vaci Street looking in shop windows, or to linger in coffee houses over café au lait, or to watch the promenade of fashions while we have lunch in the open air at Wampetics in the City Park.

There can be no such freedom in our town, where my every move is watched in case it may have political significance, and where Estelle, too, is well known, being something of a favorite on account of her amateur acting career. Once, before she left for Budapest, I observed her walking down our main street: children called to her, men doffed their hats. You would have thought she was a celebrity. As such, I am sure that she has been much sought after by the young men, but I can see no signs that she has shown favor to any one of them. She says she would rather die than marry and settle down in a small provincial town, and intimates that she has been saving herself for something more glamorous than our home-grown product.

But I cannot keep away from her, however ill-advised it may be for us to be seen in the same places. People are not stupid and will sooner or later put two and two together, she tells me. I am driven. I want to possess her. I am driven to possess her in the most perverse ways. I think of Lothar and shudder at the thought of Nichole having to endure for a lifetime the touch of that debauched man. I know his foul imaginings, for I am becoming such a creature. My thoughts return again and again to Estelle's 'death' and to the frenzy of roses tearing at her body. Stacia also recurs in my thoughts, if you can call them thoughts. These are glimpses of scenes, as clear as if they were present, which are suddenly withdrawn from consciousness. They are eruptions of foul emotions, as if one might vomit from one's mind. More often, they are dreams such as one has in the depths of the night and forgets on waking, except for a haunting, pervasive residue too complex to call emotion, too formless to name as memory, and so strangely alien that it could be another's, borrowed, experience. I have a growing sense of presence within me. If I could have put it down to the syphilitic parasite curled within the compartments of my brain, stirring and hatching according to its own season, I would feel a sense of relief. But I know it is I who is waking.

Colonel Rado is arriving on the same train as Estelle. It took a bit of cajoling of Estelle and juggling of Rado to bring it off – far more effort, probably, than the fleeting glimpse of her warrants. As a mark of respect, I will personally be on hand at the station to meet the colonel. It is the kind of gesture which means a lot to him. I have decided to keep this fact from Estelle so as to surprise her: She enjoys these unexpected encounters, because they give her a chance to put her acting abilities to work in real-life situations.

Rado had more or less invited himself for a couple

of days of hunting when the deer season opened. This seems to be a pretext of some kind, since he has excellent hunting available to him on his own vast estates which are more convenient to Budapest. He makes a great show of friendship with me, although he does not strike me as a man who has much value for attachments beyond a superficial military camaraderie, which I expect he would prefer to call simply 'loyalty,' a word he finds much use for. I would have thought, if he had some matter he wanted to discuss with me (and he is a man who is never without some purpose in mind), that we could have more easily sat down over a glass of wine in town. But no, the colonel insisted, almost to the point of being impolite, that he wanted to engage me in my natural habitat. He is unmarried, which disappointed Elizabeth, since she is starved for company.

AFTERNOON

The station was a fiasco. But thank God I went. At least now I know what I am dealing with.

Unlike the inbound train, which is subject to all sorts of delays, the train from Budapest is almost always punctual. Therefore I arrived at the station exactly at the expected time of arrival so that I would not have to linger on the platform making awkward conversation with the Theissens. (There is a limit to the amount of playacting a fellow can be expected to go along with; also, who can tell what new and outlandish intrigues Estelle has told her parents she is now involved in, which I might be expected to know about?)

Colonel Rado would be traveling in the first-class compartment at the front of the train, and I had bought Estelle a second-class ticket, so I positioned myself, with a polite but brisk touch to the brow of my hat in the direction of Mrs Theissen, about one third of the way along the platform. Sure enough, the train came puffing around the bend and eased to a stop with the first-class carriage on my right and the second on my left. Almost before the train had come to a stop, the door swung open and Colonel Rado sprang down. He is an agile little man who is constantly on the alert, and he was looking left and right along the platform even though he had spied me immediately the carriage drew up.

'Jolly decent of you to come yourself,' he said gruffly, shaking my hand with an iron grip.

'Not at all. So glad you could come all this way for some sport.' I motioned Jacob to enter the carriage for the colonel's luggage but he held up his hand.

'Brought my own bearer,' he explained. 'Hope that's all right with you? I think your chap will get along with him splendidly. He doesn't know the terrain, of course, but he has this terrific nose for deer.'

'Absolutely,' I concurred somewhat distractedly, since I was peering over Rado's shoulder for a glimpse of Estelle.

'He's in third.'

'Right. Then why don't we make out way down there so Jacob can give him a hand?'

'Splendid. He's carrying the new Mauser. I thought you might be interested.'

'The repeater?' I asked doubtfully and saw Jacob look away in disgust.

We were moving along beside the two second-class carriages. Most of the passengers had already descended, and porters were closing the doors once again. Estelle was nowhere to be seen. The Theissens were before us, craning their necks to see into the crowd of people still milling about the third-class carriages.

'I hope you don't object?' Rado was asking. He had turned his commanding gaze upon me, forcing me to attend to him.

'No, not really.'

'Good,' he said, as if I had just passed a test. 'Some holdouts don't think a repeater's sporting.'

'Whatever it takes to carry the hill,' I said. It was a phrase I'd heard George use.

'Good show!' Rado clapped me on the back, so that I could not easily turn to see Estelle. His bonhomie seems slightly out of character, since he is usually reserved and correct. 'We'll make a cavalryman of you yet!' he declared.

Now I saw Estelle stepping down from the carriage into her mother's arms. Why had she traveled third class when I had expressly given her a second-class ticket?

Arpad, the colonel's bearer, was a massive, swarthy man with a fantastic mustache who stood apart from the crowd. He looked uncomfortable in civilian clothes and slouched with an unpracticed air. I should think he is a sergeant from Rado's regiment. I can't be sure of this, but when we came up to him I thought Arpad shook his head as if in reply to an unspoken question from Rado; but it's possible I was mistaken, because the movement was almost imperceptible, and anyway, I was distracted by other things.

Fortunately, Rado immediately busied himself in giving the servants most particular instructions for the disposition of his baggage, so that I was free to saunter a few steps to improve my view of Estelle. She stood on the emptying platform with her parents, looking into the carriage. Her eyes sparkled, and there was a heightened, emotional color to her cheeks. My Dresden shepherdess! I cannot tell why these moments, when I can view her while she is unconscious of my presence, are so precious to me. It did not last long. A hand held her valise at the doorway, and Theissen stepped forward and swung it to the ground. I thought they were waiting for further luggage, but instead a young man stepped down. He was the same fellow who had traveled with Estelle when she had first arrived in Budapest. It was the first time I had actually seen him clearly from the side, and then face on as he turned to shake Theissen's hand. He was a handsome devil with a confident bearing. Seeing him previously only from the back I had guessed that he was a clerk or some such; now he seemed more substantial – a professional of some kind, in the making.

Estelle was making introductions. She did so in a fashion which suggested that her parents had been previously acquainted with this young man but had not seen him for many years. She was reminding them of something, and I saw Theissen's pointing gesture to the man as if to say, 'I remember now: You're the one who . . .' The boy who had been to school with Estelle, what a coincidence that they should find themselves traveling home on the same train! Indeed.

Rado, cradling his new Mauser in its leather sleeve like a baby, giving orders to Jacob and Arpad, must have felt my absence from the proceedings and turned to me inquiringly. He misses nothing. But by now there was nothing to see: the parents and sister of a young man come to welcome him home, perhaps. Nothing to pique his interest. They were already on their way down the platform, walking away from us, with Mrs Theissen having taken Estelle by the arm, no doubt deep in conversation about what fashionable ladies were wearing in Budapest, sharing gossip, extracting confidences about the private life of the du Barry family. I was tempted to try out Rado's repeating Mauser there and then.

SEPTEMBER 20, 1887

I can scarcely move. My whole body aches from tramping up and down mountains with Rado all day. He has kept me busy every moment of his stay, and so I have had no opportunity for a casual visit to the Theissens' shop or to intercept Estelle on one of her evening walks by the river. Instead of talking to her, I have replayed endless conversations in my head as I have trudged up hills and stepped along narrow mountain paths. This is the contemplative aspect of the silence of hunting.

These imaginary arguments always come to the same sticking point: Estelle, with all signs of sincerity which an accomplished actress can muster, tearfully denies that she is having an affair with the young man from the train. She kneels before me in supplication, in a gesture of humble truthfulness. Or, she kneels before me in supplication: While her body appeals by gesture for forgiveness, she continues to deny that she has deceived me. There are endless permutations of this scene; together they make up an entire spectrum, from the forthright crimson of truth to the midnight magenta of the most cynical, Sicilian duplicity.

Truth? Lies? I shall never know without employing a system of spies. Gradually, as I have listened to her protestations in my mind (which borrow the rhythm of my footfalls on the forest path), I have discovered that at the center of my initial bluster and outraged masculinity lies a surprising indifference, as if this were not the center at all, as if the nodal point lies somewhere else entirely. It is clear to me now that the issue of Estelle's fidelity is fleeting – I would like to say, it is an issue which is ephemeral and human. This is not the point of possession which I realize now has always lurked, like an anarchist at the edges of a crowd, in the back of my mind.

These were my thoughts during the long treks of the last two days. I was almost going to write that we went everywhere, but now it strikes me that our journeys, however meandering and directionless they may have appeared at the time, remained within an arc which stretched from the northeast to southeast of town and stayed always on the east bank of the river. This was Rado's doing. From time to time he stopped for a terse exchange with Arpad during which they seemed to be discussing their position relative to some specific landmark. I was not included in their deliberations. Jacob, who was doing his best to find us deer, was becoming increasingly exasperated and eventually walked along with his head bowed, hardly bothering to look for tracks or check the thickets.

Not that there was any shortage of deer. We came upon a fine buck on the morning of the first day, but inexplicably Arpad had not thought to chamber a round in the rifle he handed to the colonel, and the sound of the bolt going home alerted the beast to be off. On another occasion, Rado missed an easy shot. This can happen even to experienced hunters, but was puzzling nevertheless, since on two other occasions he showed himself to be a crack shot. One occurred in the ravine where I had come so close to the doe earlier in the month. They seemed particularly interested in this piece of ground – excited, even. Rado discussed the topography with Arpad as if he were reconnoitering a battlefield. They were talking about lines of fire when Rado suddenly asked for the Mauser, and before our astonished eyes squeezed off five shots with amazing rapidity, completely severing several young saplings which were growing on the valley floor. Needless to say, after this disturbance, it was pointless to follow through with our plan to drive deer toward guns stationed at the valley's mouth, as I had done before.

'Didn't you say Count Aponyi's land begins on the other side?' he asked me, pointing to the mountaintop above us.

I told him it did, although I have no recollection of having told him anything of the kind, and asked myself whom he could have asked for that information. Now I think he must have consulted detailed maps of the area before he left Budapest.

He wanted to hunt in the direction which would have led us close to the boundary with Aponyi's property. I told him the count and I were not on very neighborly terms on account of the railway, and that we were careful therefore not to risk encroaching on each other's land.

'Where does this trail lead, then?' Rado demanded of Jacob.

'It goes around the mountain, Colonel,' Jacob said.

'All the way around?'

'All the way to Count Aponyi's valley.'

'Think we might find some game in that direction?' Rado asked Arpad, who grinned and nodded his head as if the answer to his question was obvious.

The second occasion happened at the end of the day, as we were making our descent along the path which led back to the road and our horses, when Colonel Rado abruptly dropped a deer at a considerable distance. None of us had even seen the animal, and I congratulated him. Most hunters would have been delighted with the kill, since it occurred at that point where the outer reaches of skill shade off into sheer luck, but Rado took it in a matter-of-fact manner, as if it had been a minor distraction from the main business of the day.

This has been his last night, since he is to catch the train tomorrow morning. I had Brod bring the brandy and cigars to the billiard room. It is a bit down at heel, but I thought Rado would be entertained by the trophies and the collection of ancient weapons which some ancestor had arrayed on the walls. It was a veritable profusion of barbarism, with lances, spears, and pikes standing in parallel order, or crossed with ancient helmets arranged in the angles; on one wall, a sunburst had been composed of swords and daggers which radiated in exact geometric progression from a mask. It was one of those situations in which one sees, as if for the first time, something viewed casually at an early age and never really regarded again until one invites a stranger into the room. Colonel Rado showed a meticulous interest in each item.

'No, I don't think it's a mask, old chap,' he said, scrutinizing the wizened face at which all the points converged. He chuckled. 'You know what? I believe this was some fellow's face, by God!'

I came closer to peer over his shoulder. 'Well, I'll be damned,' I muttered.

'Looks like a souvenir from Borneo. One of your relatives must have brought it back.'

'I don't think so. My family hasn't traveled much. Something of a family tradition.'

'Must be a war trophy, then. Come to think of it, the chap does have an oriental look about him. Don't you think?'

'I suppose, now you point it out.'

'Probably a Turk your great-grandfather dispatched.'

He turned to the collection of swords. 'Do you mind?' he asked, taking one down. He turned it over in his hands as a Chinese mandarin might a precious jade. 'This fellow fought along-side Napoleon against the Hapsburgs. The blade was forged in Regensburg.' He hefted it to feel the balance. 'Marvelous piece of work.'

'You look like you wouldn't mind trying it out.'

'Do you fence?' Rado asked.

'No,' I said quickly.

Reluctantly, he returned the sword to its place and sipped at his brandy while he turned his attention to the more primitive implements hanging on the walls. He seemed to have an encyclopedic knowledge of weapons and greeted each one like an old friend.

Rado was examining one of a pair of muskets with fanciful, ivory-inlaid stocks, but my attention was drawn to a Turkish dagger which, to my consternation, I did not remember noticing before. It hung in an inconspicuous corner, and was itself one of the least prepossessing of the weapons, since it was housed in a dull leather sheath without embossing or decoration. I grasped the handle and found that it fitted exactly to my hand; the knife came from the sheath in a smooth, workmanlike manner. The blade was in the shape of a huge, curved thorn, four inches wide at its base tapering to a point eight inches from the handle. If an object may possess an inherent cruelty, then this dagger had that quality. I felt a wave of excitement run through me which left me dizzy for a moment. The knife was strangely familiar, as if I had found it in a dream and it had magically been given substance for this encounter.

I suppose I must have let the conversation lapse, or in my preoccupation had failed to hear a question the colonel had asked me, for I became aware too late that he was looking at me curiously.

'That's a vicious piece of work,' he said approvingly.

'But quite limited.'

'I'd have thought it could take care of most business.'

'You see, the blade is too thick to risk a stab in the chest, because it's likely to be deflected by the ribs, and it's not long enough to feel confident about an upward thrust to the heart from below the ribs.'

'And so what is the prognosis, Doctor?'

'It's the weapon of an assassin. It's made for someone who approaches his victim from behind to cut his throat.'

'Laszlo, you are a devil of a fellow!' he said, clapping me on the back heartily. I suppose it was his highest commendation. He was chuckling, and his eyes were twinkling, but I knew that his mind was always on duty, that he never relaxed his watchfulness. 'Could you use it, do you think?' It was a casual question, apparently, still in the mood of playful exploration. 'Could you come up behind a warm human being, a person with all their life in front of them, loved by their family . . . and cut their throat?'

I looked at the dagger fitted to my hand and knew my answer. 'I don't know,' I lied.

'Good.' He seemed pleased. 'It's the only answer a decent man can give. Murderous fools with no ideals or sense of purpose answer yes – not that I'd for a moment considered you in that category.'

'I would think you'd be more concerned whether I'd view life as too sacred to sacrifice for any principle.'

'To be frank, I find you refreshingly unsentimental.' He was gauging me, sizing me up for some specific task he had in mind. 'I'm of the opinion one never knows what one is capable of until the moment comes,' he said, and I knew that he also lied.

MORNING, SEPTEMBER 21, 1887

It has been a miserable autumn day. Low clouds have been trapped in the valley, and we have been stuck with a slow, misty drizzle all morning and most of the afternoon.

I saw Rado onto the train after breakfast. With Arpad standing rigidly to attention holding the umbrella, we shook hands, and at the last moment, Rado leaned toward me and said, 'Hungary will have her King,' as if this was one of those elaborate greetings which country folk trade back and forth.

I waited impatiently for the wave of the flag and the shrill peel of the station master's whistle, standing back from the carriage so that we would not have the embarrassment of making forced conversation. Rado is constitutionally incapable of anything trite, which makes it a strain to be in his company at such times. At last the signal came, and the engine let out a blast of pent-up steam and slowly pulled away from the station. As the train receded into the distance, in the relative quiet of the platform, I breathed a long sigh of relief. Rado's scrutiny has been a trial. He demands one's constant attention. Under these circumstances, it seemed inadvisable to slip away for a chance meeting with Estelle.

The weather made me doubtful that she would later venture out for her walk beside the river. I was sorely tempted to pay a visit to her parents' shop, even though I knew that such a lapse would eventually bring attention to our connection. In a moment of weakness, feeling somehow that I had earned the right to be foolish because I had sacrificed three days in playing the dutiful host to Colonel Rado, I dismissed Jacob at the station, telling him that I needed exercise and would walk home. He stared skeptically into the drizzle which was falling onto the gleaming rails between the platforms and nodded his head somewhat wearily, indicating that he intended to humor me in this further example of my spreading eccentricity.

Each step on the road into town brought home to

me how ill-advised my decision had been. What had appeared to be no more than a heavy mist turned out to be an insinuating, soaking rain which soon drenched me to the bone so that my clothes clung to me in a most unbecoming fashion. Moreover, the road was muddy, and since I had set out for our journey to the station in the carriage, I was not dressed for such rough going. Instead of deterring me, these conditions only made me more stubborn, and I pulled my hat down firmly, tilted my head against the wind, and plodded on. By the time I arrived at the Theissens' shop I looked like a bedraggled scarecrow. In this state, I did not glance inside to see who might be there or hesitate once I had opened the door, but strode directly into the small space.

As if the bell which hung on the door had put him under a spell, the young man whom I had seen with Estelle at the railway station sat frozen, with his mouth hanging open and a forkful of strudel halfway to his lips. I was as surprised as he, but I am glad to say more quick witted, and at least I had the presence of mind to ignore him. I turned my back on him in order to peer into the back of the shop, but no one was visible, and no one answered the bell's call. Behind me I heard hasty gulps as the strudel was disposed of.

I turned back to the man and regarded him at my leisure. His face was stuffed with pastry and he appeared to be in some distress.

'Is there anyone here?' I demanded of him sternly.

He struggled to answer but was utterly helpless, in spite of one agonized attempt to swallow the mush which choked his mouth. I allowed myself the luxury of waiting in aristocratic dispassion for him to complete the humbling, piecemeal process of swallowing his food. His face gradually cleared, and the alarming, apoplectic flush receded. He was not without refinement, and had the straight blond hair and somewhat empty good looks which are typical of Saxons.

'I'm afraid not,' he said, adding 'Count' in a delayed and

utterly feeble attempt to undo the confession his eyes had already made, that he had recognized me when I entered the shop not simply in the role of seigneur but as Estelle's protector.

Had Estelle pointed me out to him at the railway station in Budapest? Is it possible that her betrayal had come so early in our relationship? As I stared at him, I found myself asking such questions. But they arose in me with a sense of objective curiosity; I posed them in something of the same spirit with which I had previously mulled over various diagnoses in the case of a patient who was gravely ill: with concern, but with emotions distanced by the fact that my feelings were for someone who was a stranger to me.

I had forgotten myself. I had been staring at the young man for such a prolonged time that I believe I had forced him to the verge of blurting out some clumsy confession, and I turned on my heel and left before he could relieve himself of the weight upon his conscience. In fact, I was almost grateful to him, for by the provocation of his presence he had made clear how things stood, not only in relation to the game Estelle was playing, but in relation to my own feelings.

I had arrived at the shop as a supplicant, as one in need; I left with a new sense of mastery of the situation. The rain and my wet clothes no longer bothered me; indeed, I didn't even notice that as I ascended the castle hill the sun was making an attempt to break through. I had forgotten my appearance, and when Elizabeth saw me she scolded me roundly and insisted on making me a hot toddy despite my protests that I didn't want one. The alcohol imparts a dullness to sensation which I dislike – I can feel it as I write these words – but I hadn't the heart to refuse her. I had Brod remove my wet clothes, otherwise Elizabeth would have done it herself. She craves physical contact in a way which evokes from me something close to pity.

NIGHT

In the late afternoon the skies began to clear so that I could plausibly leave the castle for some rough shooting. I took a small-bore shotgun and walked down the hillside through the orchards, crossing the road several times where it wound back and forth up to the castle. It occurs to me now that I was singularly directed for a man apparently out to bag some pigeon or a rabbit or two, and perhaps I should not have taken a route which pointed in a straight line to my goal.

I entered the wood where I had previously tethered my horse when I had been to meet Estelle beside the river walk. Immediately I set up some birds and wondered whether I should shoot them so that I would not arouse suspicion by returning empty-handed, but decided that the noise would spoil my meeting with Estelle. How differently everything would have turned out if I had followed my first impulse!

The sudden flutter of the birds told me that I was overeager and advancing too quickly, and so I made myself stand still beside the trunk of an ancient oak. I was impatient, afraid that dusk would fall, and that at this very moment Estelle was on her way back toward the bridge. When all was silent again I made my way through the wood in a direction which paralleled the river. In this way I planned to move past the end of the avenue and approach it from the narrow path which wandered through the tangle of thickets growing beside the river. I stopped periodically at the fringe of the wood and saw no one on the avenue. I was bitterly disappointed, but it was possible that Estelle was waiting with her back against one of the trees, and so I went on.

In the meadow, the cows were waiting to be called to the barn to be milked. The tinkling of the bells about their necks sounded from the mist which hung chest-high above the grass, and their dark shapes came up, mysterious and obscure, as I moved among them. I crossed the narrow open strip quickly, unable to prevent the squeaking noise of my feet on the soggy turf, and climbed the wall on the other side. I crouched in its shadow and listened. At first, all was silent except for the ghostly tinkling of the bells and the dull, rhythmic grind of a cow chewing on its cud nearby.

Then, to my surprise, I heard whispers coming from the thicket where the path meandered beside the river. Evidently, whoever was there had heard some sound of my approach and had stopped their conversation to listen further. These silences require patience. The quarry is never sure of what they have heard, otherwise they would have taken off, and it is necessary simply to wait them out and allow their natural confidence to return. After a few moments these two seemed satisfied that they were alone, and began to talk normally.

It was then that I recognized Estelle's voice. I couldn't make out the actual words she spoke, but I heard the familiar cadence and I knew from the tone of her voice – a flirtatious, teasing lilt – what the gist of her conversation would be. Next came the lower timbre of a man's voice in reply, soothing or cajoling. I could tell that Estelle didn't want to do what he was urging, because her tone became more abrupt and her phrases shorter. I wanted very much to steal closer so I could hear what they said, but I was afraid of the noise I might make if I moved. I would have found the ignominy of discovery unendurable. Now the man was using a wheedling tone to coax her, interspersed with sallies to make her laugh. I recognized the ploy well enough. It was my own customary response; I imagined her reticent smile and the dimple which appeared on her cheek, which I had always taken as a sign of encouragement. She played us as though we were seals performing at the circus, favoring us with a smile or a caress when our actions met with her approval, just as one might toss a herring! Were we men so predictable, so interchangeable?

I knew they could not linger much longer in the

thicket, for with the falling dusk Estelle would have to return home. Sure enough, I next heard her sending him on his way, with a reluctance and a tenderness which infuriated me. He passed close by me, walking backwards to catch a last glimpse of her, and entangling himself in a blackberry bush. I was concerned that he would see me where I crouched as he tried to extricate himself, but he was soon on his way. He was the young fellow from the train station and the Theissens' shop, there could be no doubt.

He was gone, and I was alone with Estelle at last. She was humming to herself in a wistful sort of way. I crept closer so that I could see her through the leaves. She had one hand on a branch and tilted her head one way and then the other as she considered something she held in her other hand, a flower perhaps which he had brought for her. Was she at that moment turning over her options in her mind, thinking whether to have one, or the other, or both?

Estelle lingered in the small clearing where they had had their tryst. I suppose her purpose was to give her young man a lead so that they would not be seen together emerging from the avenue at the bridge. I waited, thinking I might take her as she edged by the blackberry bush in which he had become entangled, but as she let more and more time pass, the urge to stalk her more actively, to go to the very edge of the huntsman's art, possessed me.

When she moved, I used the sound of her motion to mask mine as I crept closer to her between the tangle of bushes and vines. When she stopped, I stopped. She resumed humming her song, and I used the opportunity to move to a spot where I could hide myself behind thick foliage only three meters from her.

Estelle stood on the other side of the clearing; it was little more than a bulge in the path where it had deviated away from the river in order to avoid a muddy spot where drainage was poor. She wore a blue cloak with the hood thrown back on her shoulders, and I remember thinking the shade somewhat presumptuous, since it was the sky blue which the Florentine masters had used to color the robe of the Virgin. In her hand she held a gaudy paper flower of the kind Gypsies sell at fairs. The tune ended abruptly and I heard her sigh. And then she seemed to catch her breath. I am sure she could not have heard me, because I had not moved. Yet I am certain that she sensed a human presence nearby, because she became alert and turned her head quickly in a direction away from me as if seeking confirmation. Perhaps a bird had been struggling in the undergrowth farther downriver. My attention was too tightly fixed on Estelle to notice other sounds.

She seemed fearful. While she crouched to peer through the bushes, I emerged behind her, soundless on the packed earth. I could have tapped her on the shoulder, but instead I preferred to wait in delicious anticipation for her to turn and find me there, where before there had been no one. She turned slowly, backtracking, and would have bumped into me if I hadn't taken a pace back.

'You!' she exclaimed, in a mixture of horror and bewilderment.

She looked as if she would faint from the shock of the surprise, and I took her by the waist as her knees weakened. She sagged in my arms, and I held her to me. We stayed like this for a long moment, her head upon my chest, breathing in unison. I do not know when she recovered her wits, but I suspect that it was several seconds before she stirred against me and at last lifted her head. How that head must have whirred, preparing different fictions to feed me!

'I thought . . .' she began, pointing feebly in the direction of the undergrowth away from where I had approached her.

'What, my love?' I murmured.

'I thought there was someone. I thought someone might see us here.'

'Someone following you? Where?'

I let her turn in my arms. She positioned herself so naturally, of her own free will, with her back resting against my chest so that I could look over her shoulder. I breathed in the rich fragrance of her hair. Together we stared into those dark, misty shadows. With my left hand I made as if to caress her, from the tip of her chin down the soft, creamy skin of her throat.

'No,' she breathed, although she could have had no inkling of my purpose.

I pressed forward until I felt the curve of her buttocks against me, and using this as a fulcrum I arched her backward bit by bit, while I held her chin and turned her face aside. At the last moment, she made as if to shake me off, but the cruel thorn of the Turkish dagger pierced her throat. I thrust and pulled, and the blood spurted from her in a great fountain, and I felt a surge of exultation, an ecstasy which I can compare only to the expression on the faces of saints at their moment of martyrdom.

Then, suddenly, she was a dead weight and would have toppled into the mud if I had not caught her and slowly lowered her to the ground where it was dry. I stooped to kiss Estelle farewell, without sensation in my lips. I was emptied and numb. The moment had passed too quickly. I felt cheated. Already, the blood was forming into glistening clots, and signs of life as usual were reforming about me: crows cawing at the edge of the wood, the muffled sound of cow bells, the gurgle of the river, the gradual fading of color as dusk fell, the surreptitious movement of the animal which had attracted Estelle's attention as it went about its business in the undergrowth. It had been too short. The event was like a rock hurled into the river: a violent splash, and then the water closes over it. Life flows on.

She had been wearing a brooch which I had bought for her in Budapest, and I unclasped it from her blouse to keep as a memento. I have it before me now, an enameled butterfly in the Japanese style. Strangely, I miss her, in a numbed, partial way. I am dazed by what has just happened. My brain has not fully woken to what I have done.

12

EARLY MORNING, SEPTEMBER 22, 1887

What have I done! It is unnatural that the world should go on as before. Brod woke me as usual by drawing back the curtains of my bedroom. I sat immobilized on the side of the bed, praying that what I remembered would turn out to have been a dream. He held out my dressing gown, and I inserted my arms into the sleeves like an automaton. Yet everything proceeded according to the normal routine. My shaving water steamed in the chill air; the towel placed about my face was luxuriously warm; Brod lathered my chin in silence and scraped at my beard with those short, dexterous stabs I had learned to accept without anxiety. Everything appeared disconcertingly ordinary.

Brod shaves me with the most intent, murderous concentration. As he stooped and turned to catch each obscure corner of my jaw, I stared at him fixedly until my eyes could no longer sustain those oblique, uncomfortable angles; but I could find no evidence of a change in his impassive face, any awareness that the man who sat docile beneath the crisp edge of his razor had been transformed. At last I closed my eyes and immediately fell prey to the most hideous guilt. Alone with my soul, I experienced the full horror of what I had done. I had killed Estelle! If Brod had dispatched me at that moment, I would have thought justice served.

At breakfast, Trudi brought me my customary eggs and rolls. As always, she glanced up at me at the bottom of her curtsy, a quick look like a bird stealing a crumb of bread from one's hand. I watched her out of the corner of my eye, but her glance was no longer or more furtive than usual.

I have no appetite and can eat nothing. Elizabeth took her breakfast in her room, and I am grateful, because I cannot face her goodness. I cannot bear the thought of her looking at me.

I am loathsome. My shame is bottomless. I wish I could find a bottom, some resting point however debased, but I am falling, falling. If there is anything that I can do to begin to atone for this act, I will do it. Inwardly, I cringe in dread, expecting divine retribution to crush me. I imagine this as a meteor, even now hurtling through some remote corner of space at superhuman speed, which will meet me at its appointed time and place, crashing through the roof and obliterating me. I welcome it. I deserve no less. But God is subtle. His hand is invisible. My time will come.

And Estelle, that sweet girl, so full of gaiety, gone. At my hand.

MORNING

It seems I must put in an appearance at the scene of the crime. Suddenly, the grand question of God's retribution is moot. I am ashamed to acknowledge how desperately I want to escape arrest. I feel wretchedly reduced by the human concerns of a common criminal: how to evade the verdict.

A deputation of the more substantial citizens of the town, deferential but insistent, requested an audience at the castle. I gather my presence at the scene is requested both to show due respect to the departed and to parade the face of law, order, and continuity on this occasion of social breakdown. They have not needed me previously, when a Gypsy has been killed by one of his fellows in a knife fight or a drunkard felled; but there is something different about Estelle's death which I had not anticipated. I had not realized how widely she was known, or for how many people in the town she embodied undefined yearnings to escape our provincial circle and join the modern world.

I have thanked the good burghers and told them I will come directly. Meanwhile, while I wait for Jacob to bring round my horse, I chastise myself with the thought that I am a dog returning to the spot to lap up his own vomit. If I am so abject, why do I not consider suicide with more sincerity? Would it not make the most sense to obliterate this worthless existence?

There is mention of an Inspector Kraus who is in charge of the investigation. According to the deputation, he has asked if I would oblige him. Apparently he believes I may be of some help. Of course, this could be a trap. But I am certain there were no witnesses. The whole business took place in thick undergrowth, shielded from casual eyes, and it was quick and practically soundless. On my way home, so self-possessed and calculating was I, that I killed a rabbit in order to account for the blood on my clothes. I cannot recognize that person as myself.

AFTERNOON

Inspector Kraus is a little man, like a ferret or a weasel, or some such animal which sniffs about until it gets hold of a scent and then charges tenaciously after his prey, even if the trail should lead down the deepest rabbit hole. He is intent and overly alert, constantly sampling the wind in a slightly puzzled, inquiring way. He has a large nose with dark, close-together eyes which seem to sight along the bridge as one might down the barrel of a rifle. It is a nose for sniffing out clues, a nose for poking into things. His size, I think, is a bother to him. Perhaps because of it he does not get enough respect. Kraus is constantly springing up on his toes to talk to you at your own level, in his earnestness approaching rather closer to one's face than one might like.

At the root of his unusual manner is a blithe disregard for social distinctions; he insists on equality, on talking man to man without intervening layers of protocol. Somehow he manages to avoid impertinence. Actually, I find it quite a refreshing change from the hypocritical fawning I am accustomed to receiving from public officials. But he is odd. I think his manner is natural and not put on, and it is probably this absence of calculation, this lack of self-awareness, which enables him to avoid giving offense; rather it rebounds on himself, for he is a humorless, humorous figure. Kraus is one of those people who are unaware that they walk naked through life, who is innocent of the social clothes the rest of us use to hide our true natures.

I rode down the hill and tethered my horse in the usual spot just within the wood. The rain had held off during the night, but the clouds had gathered and threatened further rain. As I made my way across the meadow I saw a constable patrolling at the edge of the thicket which bordered the path, and he directed me so that I would approach the scene of the crime by way of the avenue.

It was in the shadows of the clearing that I caught my first sight of Inspector Kraus. He was pacing restlessly, like a confined animal. The body had been removed, but the place where it had lain was marked off by powdered chalk. I thought it looked like the remains of a children's game.

'Count!' he declared the instant he caught sight of me, as if he wished to resume a conversation we had broken off at breakfast. I proffered my hand, which he shook absentmindedly. 'This is a dastardly piece of work,' he went on. 'We must get to the bottom of it quickly.'

'I couldn't agree more. She was a fine girl, a credit to her family. And to the town.'

'You knew her?'

'In a manner of speaking.'

'How so?'

I was beginning to feel hurried by the staccato pace

of his questioning and wished to slow him down. 'I had tried to be helpful in a domestic matter. At the request of her parents, I had arranged for an introduction to a family who had need of a governess for two young children.'

'Where was this?'

'In Budapest.'

'Yes, yes, I know in Budapest,' he said impatiently. 'But where in Budapest, Count?'

'Monsieur is a diplomat. He was recalled unexpectedly to France, and the family has returned with him.'

'But the girl told her parents that she was coming home only for a visit.'

'Ah,' I said with as much ambiguity and suggestion as one can inject into a single syllable. 'Only for a visit?'

His nostrils twitched with excitement. 'A second clue!' he declared. He was subjecting this new piece of intelligence to a fierce inward concentration, but from the way in which he held his head tilted, nose to the air, eyes flicking back and forth, he could as well have been sniffing the breeze for fresh spoor. 'Very strange. Very strange,' he said as if to himself. 'You see, Count, her mother found the return half of a third-class railway ticket to Budapest on the girl's bureau.'

'Indicating that she intended to return, even though there was no longer a position for her to return to.'

'Precisely!'

'Suggesting?'

'Come, Count, the deduction must be obvious!'

'You're ahead of me, I'm afraid.'

'Suggesting, of course, that she was returning to *someone* in Budapest.'

'You mean – '

'We are men of the world, are we not?'

'Yes, but – '

'In my line of work one comes upon this kind of thing all the time. Regrettable, yes. But one must deal with things as they are, not the way in which they ought to be.'

'You're insinuating that she was involved in some way?'

'That she had a lover? Yes.'

'But she was murdered here. How can the situation in Budapest be relevant?'

'It's not.'

'You seem very confident about that.'

'When you've seen as many of these cases as I have, you begin to understand the principles which underlie homicide. It is, after all, a sickness like any other. You were once a doctor, I believe?'

'Indeed.'

'Then you will understand. Murder is a disease of the body politic. It is therefore subject to the same scientific laws which govern the kinds of diseases you are familiar with. It's exactly the same. Here – ' He pointed to the muddy ground beside the path where wrinkled clots almost blended into the black earth. 'Clue number one,' he said with some satisfaction.

'I think I see what you mean,' I began. 'The idea is that one might speculate – '

'Speculate be damned! Proof! These are facts which tell us as much about the crime as the rash tells us about measles.'

'One might conclude,' I resumed, summoning all my patience, because in every way the interview was going extraordinarily well. 'From the appearance of these blood clots – that is, from their depth of color, their texture, and the onset of decomposition – that the murder was committed somewhere between four and seven o'clock.'

I thought I had done quite well, but Inspector Kraus was staring at them with an incredulous expression.

'Let's say, an hour or so on either side of sunset,' I offered. I was afraid to overplay my hand, but the idea that the good inspector was hinting at some kind of collaboration seemed an opportunity too good to miss, 'I'm sorry. I don't think I can be any more precise than that,' I added modestly.

'I was referring to the footprints,' Kraus said.

With a queasy feeling, I looked again. There were indeed

two incomplete impressions, but they could not possibly be mine. They were small and narrow – obviously those of a woman, or possibly a slight man.

'Most likely made by the victim herself, wouldn't you say?' I suggested.

'Impossible.'

I felt irritation at his doctrinaire, schoolmasterly manner getting the better of me. 'Well, as scientists we would do well to remember – '

'I took the liberty of trying the deceased's footwear against the imprints.' He waved toward a corner of the clearing where one of Estelle's winter boots lay crumpled on its side. The forlorn sight of the soft leather which one of Estelle's pretty feet had once filled evoked in me a pang of grief, and I had to turn from him so that he would not see the tears which threatened to well up in my eyes.

'You see, Count, this is a science. Did you know that there are detectives who have published monographs on foot impressions? Yes, there is a whole taxonomy.'

'I had no idea.' I wondered how much snooping Kraus had already done and looked hurriedly around in case there were other prints, ones which could incriminate me. 'Shouldn't we be looking for others?' I asked, hoping he would grant me the opportunity to obliterate any clues that remained.

He nodded and I saw him smile for the first time, a sheepish little grin, as if any such expression of levity would have been out of place. 'I was in the process of conducting a search at the very moment you arrived.'

'Do we have some sense of the direction from which the murderer approached?' I asked as I skirted the clearing, close to the edge where I had clasped Estelle at that last moment. I cringed in recollection, and experienced a superstitious fear so intense that the hair on the back of my neck stood up. But another part of me noted that the ground was firm here, at the point where I had taken Estelle, and would leave no imprints.

'It would be foolish to assume anything at this point,' Kraus said.

I was circling the clearing at my leisure, peering here and there into the undergrowth for any details I may have forgotten, and I noticed that the inspector kept pace with me so that he always remained on the opposite side of the clearing. Without much difficulty, I had soon positioned myself so that when we began the search I could naturally assign myself the sector of undergrowth from which I had made my approach. I tried to remember the state of the ground at the spot where I had lurked while Estelle and her young man had made their good-byes: The earth was not soggy; it had been soft and untrafficked, and could well retain incriminating footprints.

'You mean, you don't have any hypothesis about how the murderer killed the girl?'

'Too early for that.'

'Or how he made his escape?'

'He?'

'I assume it was a man. I think that much is obvious.'

'How so?'

I was about to describe the nature of Estelle's wounds, but stopped myself in time. 'This.' I gestured toward the blood spattered on the ground. 'Would I be correct in surmising that the victim died from a knife wound?'

'You would.'

'From the pattern of blood, I would think the blow was most likely a thrust to the throat?'

'Correct. But why should the assassin be a man?'

'He'd have had to have the strength to control the girl while he cut her throat.'

'Assuming he delivered the blow from behind, assuming he held her while he killed her.'

'That's why I think these footprints are incidental. I think you should be looking for a man. A powerful man.'

'But have you noticed, Count, how the corner of this footprint comes on top of this blood clot here? See, how it squashes the end of the clot into the mud? So this person walked here after the blood was spilled.'

I stooped, hardly daring to believe my eyes. Sure enough, the little man was right. A foot had trodden on the blood, and from the rounded shape of the clot at the edge of the print, the foot had stepped upon it while it was still wet and fresh, although I did not volunteer this intelligence to Kraus. Had there, then, been a witness? If there was a witness, we would hunt that person together, with Kraus in the role of gun dog.

The inspector seemed quite pleased with my performance, as if I were one of his more promising students. 'Very good, Count,' he said, rubbing his hands excitedly. I think he does have the instinct of the hunter. 'I wonder if I could prevail upon you to examine the body?' he asked, popping the question like a nervous suitor.

I had not thought of this eventuality and was shocked speechless at the thought of seeing Estelle again. I wanted to remember her as she had been at the last moment of her life. But if I wanted atonement what penance could have been a more fitting beginning?

'Is that asking too much?' Kraus asked, seeing my hesitation.

'No. No, not at all. But what about Dr Czernin? He is the town doctor. He probably would be of more use to you.'

Inspector Kraus paused delicately, his head to one side, from which I gathered that he had already appraised himself of Czernin's intellectual limitations. How quickly he has taken the measure of our town!

'But you are a man of modern science, Count. You studied in Paris. Still, I must not impose on you.'

'I was merely wondering if I still have the expertise to be of use to you. It's been many years since I performed an autopsy.'

'I wouldn't ask you to do that,' he interjected hurriedly. 'Besides, the family won't allow it. What I had in mind was simply an examination of the external aspects of the body.'

'But how could that be of help?' I asked.

'Of course it will. It must. We have to gather all the evidence we possibly can. Only then will we be able to arrive by a process of deduction at the conclusion which will solve this case.'

Kraus is a very intense man, with all the unreasoning tenacity of a zealot, and I saw that there was no way in which I would be able to evade this task if I also wanted to be included as a searcher after footprints.

'Should we start here?' I suggested. 'I could look in the quadrant from the path over to that tree.'

'Do you know what you'll be looking for?'

'Prints like these, of course.'

'I thought you said they were incidental.'

'I think you will find that they are, but I'm a scientist, and I'm prepared to wait on the evidence.'

My reply seemed to bolster my credibility with him, and that is a good thing, because the more I see of Kraus the more formidable he appears, and therefore the more important it is for me to remain close to him. He has knowledge and intelligence, but that is not what worries me. Rather, he reminds me of a dog I once had; the animal was hopeless at picking up a scent. He would dash back and forth in an excited, haphazard manner, with no real pattern or consistency, but eventually he would blunder onto a spoor, and then his energy became focused in the most determined, dogged manner until the prey was killed. I must remain close to Kraus so that he does not approach even to the vicinity of the truth.

To my relief, he agreed to my proposal for the search, and he set off quickly, eyes to the ground, his head jerking from one fixation to another, in the wrong direction. It was not difficult for me to retrace my steps from yesterday evening. To my horror, I soon found clear footprints I had left while crouching in the undergrowth. There was no real need to obliterate them now that I could place fresh prints behind them so that they would appear to have been made during my search. I wondered about the field I had crossed from the wood, but concluded that the turf would be unlikely to retain secrets discernible to anyone but an Indian tracker.

I was just congratulating myself on removing the evidence of my presence when I heard Kraus calling excitedly. I parted the stems of a crowd of willow saplings and slipped into the dark undergrowth growing close to the river.

'Careful!' he cried out almost immediately.

I tried not to be put out by his impertinent tone, and reminded myself that I must regard him as an equal in this quest, since otherwise I was likely to make a dangerous underestimation of my adversary.

'Where are you?' I called. I was surprised that he had seen me immediately and that I could not spot him even when he had revealed his approximate location by the sound of his voice.

'Go along the path,' Kraus called again.

I struggled through thick weeds and skirted a bramble thicket to head in the direction of the river. The path narrowed again past the clearing, and after a few yards I found it followed a bend in the river and branched. I took the path which led away from the river toward the pasture, which was choked off with branches growing away from the thickness of vegetation toward the light. Overhead, birch and hazel almost met to form a tunnel.

Without regard for personal comfort or sense of dignity, or even for such a practical matter as the condition of his trousers, Kraus was kneeling in the mud examining another imprint with the aid of a magnifying glass.

'Step only in my footprints, if you would, Count,' he said without looking up.

I suppose the courtesy of addressing me directly would have been a bothersome distraction. After a minute of forbearance, in case he had forgotten me, I cleared my throat.

'Yes, yes. Just one moment,' he said somewhat peevishly.

Finally, Kraus sat back on his haunches and stared into the middle distance with an expression at once intent and vacant. For my part, it seemed instantly obvious that the print he had been examining was the same as those at the murder scene. Putting this together with the sounds I and Estelle had heard coming from the general area where I now stood, it appeared that I had been foolishly overconfident in attributing them to the movements of a small animal. Moreover, when I crouched slightly, I found that I had quite a good view of the part of the clearing where I had held Estelle for the last time.

'Was there anything special that you were able to see with the benefit of your magnifying glass?' I asked, managing to keep an edge of sarcasm from my voice. Perhaps I should have offered him the use of the microscope which has remained in its box in the library for these last twenty years!

'According to the monograph I've been reading, an investigator can sometimes detect traces of substances – soot, for example, or mud from another region – which are carried in the angle where the sole meets the heel and deposited as minute particles in footprints.' He sounded disappointed.

'I see,' I said charitably.

'She waited here,' he said.

'Estelle?'

'No, the murderess.'

'You keep insisting it was a woman.' I didn't know how to get him off this track and onto the far more plausible possibility of the tall, strong Saxon with whom she had traveled from Budapest. 'I suppose she could have been an accomplice,' I said by way of compromise.

'Or a man with small feet. I will grant you that.'

Elizabeth and I sit at opposite ends of the oak dining table for our meals. I don't know how we came to this lonely placement, but it has always been so. I rather think that Brod, who as butler has a hand in so many of the small, telling details of our domestic arrangements, set the precedent. For Brod, my brother, George, has never entirely left us, and my tenure as count is only provisional, so that in ways that are hard to detect and which would seem petty to argue with when one does notice them, he does his best to keep Elizabeth and myself apart. It is an act of loyalty to the memory of a master he deeply admired.

We are served venison pie, and I can hardly think of a worse meal to eat before viewing a corpse. The rank flavor of the game, which normally I would savor, disgusted me. The substance of the flesh in my mouth felt unnatural, and the hint of corruption and decay on my tongue was almost more than I could bear. Nevertheless, I wanted to ensure that nothing seemed out of the ordinary.

Elizabeth, too, I noticed was picking at her meal, making it appear through a show of activity with knife and fork that she was eating, when I observed very little food, in fact, pass her lips.

'I must examine the body of the girl who was murdered,' I said.

Elizabeth appeared not to have heard me. Over the years, we have fallen into a habit of silence. It is not easy to make conversation, the two of us at opposite ends of the table; Brod waits silently in attendance, ready to extinguish any beginnings of conversation by appearing suddenly at Elizabeth's elbow, stooping with a whispered question, or by noisily clearing dishes.

'An Inspector Kraus is on the case. Funny little chap. Looks like a ferret or something. Sharp as a tack, though. Asked me if I'd help him out. I said, "I'm a bit rusty." It's been twenty years. Still, I thought I should do what I could, give it a shot.'

Here Elizabeth put down her knife and fork with a clatter that was quite unlike her.

'Laszlo, I don't think this is a suitable topic of conversation when we're eating lunch.' She flashed a small, tight smile to show she meant it in the best possible way.

'I'm so sorry!' I blurted out. 'I wasn't thinking.' But I

was interested in how sensitive she seemed to be to the matter of bloodshed.

'It doesn't matter. I've finished anyway. Thank you, Brod, you can take that.'

'I have, too. We'll have coffee in the drawing room.'

The door from the dining room is behind Elizabeth's seat, and when she rose I got up, too, and walked toward her end of the table. She delayed to reposition a piece of silver which wasn't centered to her satisfaction. Normally Brod would have lifted the shawl which was draped upon the back of her chair and placed it around her shoulders. It is something of a ritual and holds some proprietary significance for him. But Brod had his hands full with the plates he had cleared from Elizabeth's end of the table, and he was forced to watch helplessly from the sideboard as I lifted the precious shawl and gently laid it upon Elizabeth's shoulders. At any time during the twenty years of our marriage she would have welcomed such a gesture and found a way for our fingers to come into contact as she made a minor adjustment to the shawl. But today she flinched when I touched her. Involuntarily, she turned to me with a startled and fearful expression before hurrying from the room.

EVENING

At the home of the Theissens, Inspector Kraus was uneasy. This had nothing to do with one's usual discomfiture in dealing with the family of the deceased, since Kraus is entirely tactless and appears oblivious to the feelings of others as he makes for his goal. I think he is a person who needs to be in constant motion, and in the home of a dead person everything moves at a slow, decorous pace.

I shook Theissen's hand. He was intensely grateful that I had come, and seemed not to appreciate that I was there as doctor, not as the count. Mrs Theissen is caught uneasily between a somewhat calculating awareness of the social opportunities afforded by the drama into which she had been thrust, and a genuine grief which she had no idea what to do with.

After some perfunctory expressions of condolences, Kraus more or less headed for the stairs.

'You were so generous to our dear Estelle, Count,' Mrs Theissen said through bleary eyes.

'I did very little, really,' I replied with a gesture of resignation.

I felt truly saddened by their loss. No doubt I should have felt ashamed, or else sly and deceitful, when I murmured bland condolences to the grieving mother of the woman I had just killed. As I lingered for a moment with Mrs Theissen's moist hand between my own, I should have felt like a damned hypocrite – but I did not.

Kraus was waiting impatiently, one foot on the bottom stair, his hand on the banister. I felt a flare of irritation at him for his all-too-brisk courtesies. With a lack of circumspection which now amazes me, I fervently condemned him for his lack of kindness toward the Theissen family!

Theissen could not bring himself to utter any further words, but his wife said, 'She's upstairs, in her room, Count,' and quickly placed her handkerchief to her lips, like a stopper to a bottle, to prevent the escape of further harsh realities from issuing from her mouth.

'Don't worry, we'll find our own way,' Kraus said on his way up the stairs.

'This won't take long,' I reassured them, slipping easily into the role of doctor.

A peasant woman sat on a chair in the room. I think she had been employed in laying out the deceased, and she showed no inclination to leave as we went about our business. She sat with her legs comfortably crossed and watched us with frank interest while she knitted all the while, and the continuous click of her needles provided a commonplace backdrop to the scene and helped to keep me sane.

There are those who, in describing the appearance of a corpse, state that the person seems merely to be sleeping. This is nonsense. The body lay on its back, covered to the chin with a sheet. There was no expression on the face. Even in sleep, Estelle possessed some implicit animation; I have watched her by candlelight and seen the slow evolution of dream emotions play across her face like the changing formations of cloud across the moon. And there was always the expectation that at any moment her eyes would slowly open, and that puzzled and then increasingly mischievous gaze would light upon me. Memories of Estelle – her excitement on her first boat trip – flooded me, and I felt tears come to my eyes; a sob of utter despair rose in my throat and threatened to betray me. I stifled it, and it emerged as a strange, vocal cough.

'What man could have wasted this precious life?' I asked myself in despair. I think this was the moment when I first felt the lick of fear, like a flame which would feed upon its own intensity, at the thought that there lay within me a stranger who would lay claim to my soul.

I struggled to master my grief by deflecting my thoughts to the work I must do, finding ways to engage reason as a bulwark to a flood of inchoate emotion which would sweep me away. Instinctively – the instinctive, tender gesture of a lover – I traced with my fingertips the curl of her silken hair across her brow.

'What are you feeling for?' asked Kraus, peering over my shoulder, greedy for knowledge.

'Possible fractures of the skull,' I growled to disguise the catch in my voice and to discourage him from asking anything more until I had had a chance to master myself.

To my outrage, he had picked up one of her hands. He had his magnifying glass out and was peering through it at the clefts beneath her fingernails. This action was a sacrilege to me, and it would not have taken much further instigation for me to have killed him there and then.

'Hmm,' he said. 'No signs of a struggle.'

It seems the height of hypocrisy, that I, the girl's murderer, should be willing to maim a man over a lapse of taste in handling her body, and yet I never felt more sincere, more justified. The murderer was nowhere to be found. As I bent over her face to examine the wound, I knew with certainty that the speck of exultation which I had felt in piercing her throat could never be redeemed, that its price could never be justified. He was not to be seen, the murderer, however much the bereaved lover longed to confront him. He could not be seen, any more than one can glimpse the back of one's head in the mirror, however quickly one turns. He killed her on an impulse not much more compelling than a whim – a wanton, frivolous act I no longer understood. What a humanizing, what a truly civilizing emotion grief is – and how tragic and useless, for it must inevitably come too late!

I turned to Kraus and told him, 'The laceration goes from left to right. It also curves around the neck. From these two facts I conclude that the murderer was right-handed and stood behind her. Since the wound is angled obliquely upward, I think it's safe to say that the person who cut her throat was considerably taller than the deceased.'

When I left Inspector Kraus at the Theissens' house he was on the way to the station to return to Kolozsvar. He must file a preliminary report, but I was not able to learn much from him as to its contents, and I thought it best not to push the Saxon on him as a suspect. I am confident he will arrive at that conclusion by and by, and it is far more convincing if he comes around to that point of view without any advocacy from me.

I returned to the river. None of the constables Kraus had stationed earlier were visible from the bridge, and I concluded that he had gathered all the facts he was going to from the scene of the crime. I tethered my horse in the wood, as I had on earlier occasions, and made my way across the pasture to the avenue. At the end, I followed the path that wound along the riverbank and soon found myself in the familiar clearing. I stayed still to listen for five minutes until I felt certain that there was no one about. There was no further information to be gleaned from that place, and I wanted to see if it was possible to learn the route the small-footed witness had taken to arrive at her vantage point. She could not have come from the direction of the town along the avenue, because in that case all three of us would have spotted her yesterday evening.

I took the left-hand fork away from the river and passed the spot at which our witness would have crouched in the undergrowth. The path was evidently little used, but the earth was packed hard enough to leave no traces of the route my quarry had taken. As I continued, the track became increasingly overgrown until it joined another path which led around the edge of the pasture. I was back on my own land now and on familiar territory, since I had often walked these paths as a boy. This one led to a large plantation of pine which my grandfather had established, and through it, across another meadow, it joined the road which led up to the castle.

In the plantation, I looked for signs that a horse had been tethered, since the paths by the meadow and beside the river were too narrow to allow a rider passage, and I quickly found some balls of fresh manure. The rider had tethered her mount to a sapling growing up in a gap in the pine trees, since there were some clumps of grass for the horse to pull on during the wait. But the gap also provided a patch of ground bare of the resilient pine needles, and I soon found what I was looking for: a clear imprint where the rider had dismounted, and come down hard with her full weight on one foot.

The match with the previous footprints was obvious. Jacob has small feet, and for several moments I struggled to make that possibility plausible, without success. There can be little doubt that Elizabeth is my small-footed witness. I find her revulsion from me today more compelling than any footprints. She had come after me when I had left the castle yesterday afternoon, but she had already known where to go, since she had not followed me to the river. Instead, she had taken this detour which would put her, almost undetected, at her vantage point. It spoke to some degree of planning, to a knowledge of my movements over several weeks. With these troubling thoughts in mind, I returned to the castle.

MORNING, SEPTEMBER 23, 1887

Last night, Brod brought word from Elizabeth that she was indisposed and would not join me for dinner. This morning I ate alone again, but then she rarely comes down for breakfast these days. I was most anxious to see her. Elizabeth is far from inscrutable. She is honest through and through and has the greatest difficulty from keeping her feelings from appearing on her face. All I needed was one brief moment, a short exchange of pleasantries, any pretext by which I could get her to look me in the eye, and I would know immediately from her expression what she intended for me.

I loitered in the hall for the longest time, reading a newspaper, ready to waylay her as soon as she made her appearance for the day. I intended the encounter to be casual and seemingly accidental, but there is a limit to how long one can lounge in such drafty and ill-lit circumstances without giving oneself away. Three times I ventured through the door to assay the weather. I considered going directly to her room and smothering her there, but that course of action was never really a serious consideration.

I had retreated to a more comfortable position in the drawing room when I heard Elizabeth's footsteps on the stairs. I sauntered toward the hall, but she was moving quickly, almost running for the front door, and was through it before I had a chance to do anything more than wish her good morning. I followed her outside and down the steps, but at the same moment (she must have been watching from upstairs and had timed her exit accordingly) Jacob arrived with the carriage. Elizabeth jumped in and immediately bade him be off. I could have ordered him to wait, but it is foolish now to make a move which is in any way out of the ordinary. I must not draw attention. I must not force her hand. Jacob cracked the whip, and they were gone.

I have no doubt that she has gone to turn me in. I feel almost resigned. Justice will be done. Things will be as they ought to be; order will be maintained: There is some faint, altruistic satisfaction in that thought. She has prayed over her dilemma, probably without sleeping a wink all night, and has reached a decision of unassailable moral soundness. I have made no attempt to sway her, because I know such an enterprise is futile. Besides, what arguments can I possibly employ, other than some species of begging? I shall retain my dignity, at least. I thought that while she struggled with her soul there was a faint chance that I might escape justice. I could flee, but I have no stomach for it. I am not afraid for myself. Mainly I dread the crushing shame which will come to the family name once my guilt is known.

I am resigned: Let fate play itself out. But I cannot bear the thought of allowing that man any semblance of triumph. Guilty I may be, but I shall not let myself become ridiculous. I have sent a groom to saddle my horse. I will go to Kraus and surrender myself. It is better that way, and he shall not have the satisfaction of arresting me at the castle.

AFTERNOON

I went to the police station, where Kraus has set up his headquarters for the investigation. But I saw no sign of the carriage. Inside, a sergeant sitting behind a desk came smartly to attention as I entered. When I told him my business, he crossed the hallway to a door on the other side and knocked loudly upon it. No voice called to him to enter; instead, after a pause, Kraus opened the door a few inches and peered into the corridor. Then, seeing me waiting for him, he emerged, closing the door behind him, but not before I had had a chance to see into the room and had caught a glimpse of the young Saxon sitting in a chair. He was slumped forward, and his head hung in a despondent fashion.

'Ah, Count!' the inspector called to me.

I had a moment of decision as he came toward me, and changed my mind.

'Your observations were most telling,' he said. 'You'll be pleased to hear we've acted on them already.'

'How so?' I asked.

Kraus looked to left and right in a conspiratorial manner. 'We are close to an arrest,' he whispered, then surveyed me shrewdly to see what effect this news had had on me. 'You are not surprised?'

'I have the utmost faith in you, Inspector.'

'We were fortunate,' he added modestly. 'We learned from the girl's parents that she had returned from Budapest with a young man.'

'Hmm, hence the return half of the train ticket to Budapest?'

'Exactly!'

'And this person is your suspect?'

'His name is Preisich. Apparently they were sweethearts when they were in school. Acted in a play together. It never came to anything, much to Preisich's disappointment.'

'So, a jealous lover . . . would that be the motive?'

He looked at me candidly. 'It would surprise you, Count, the things people do for love. I'm talking about ordinary people, not debased individuals or hardened criminals.'

'Has he been placed near the scene of the crime?' I asked hopefully. Perhaps someone passing had seen him on the bridge or even climbing the steps up from the river walk.

'Not yet,' Kraus said. 'It's the kind of information people will come forward with later, once they know we're interested in his movements.'

'What does he say for himself?'

'That he visited her that morning at her parents' shop. He claims it was the last time he saw her alive.'

I rejoiced. So Preisich had decided to withhold from Kraus the fact that he had been with Estelle only minutes before she was killed. That lie would prove damning if anyone saw him in the vicinity. Why had he lied? Did he have a guilty conscience? He could equally well have pointed the finger at me – a risky strategy given my position, but one he could have made plausible if Estelle had told him much of the details of our arrangement. Fortunately I do not have to produce the du Barry family, but I must close the Budapest establishment quickly and get rid of Lucy.

'But we'll break him down,' Kraus said grimly. 'We'll find the inconsistencies in his story and we'll trip him up with them. We'll get a confession before we're done.'

'I have no doubt,' I said, nodding with approval. 'Do let me know, won't you, if I can be of any further assistance, in any way?'

'Count, I thank you. You've been inestimable.'

He stuck out a hand in his curt, graceless way, in a gesture of fellowship. I shook it with a feeling of relief.

If Elizabeth had not delivered me to the authorities, then she had delivered me to God. Accordingly, I rode to the church, and sure enough I found the carriage waiting outside with Jacob sitting in the driver's seat smoking his pipe. I retreated back the way I had come before he could catch sight of me.

Elizabeth would be inside, making her confession to Gregory. It was not difficult to imagine what she would tell him: everything. I have difficulty, though, imagining the reaction of my friend. I am discovering the many varieties of shame. There is the great, crushing shame one feels before God or the world at large. Then there is the private shame one feels before a friend who knows you and loves you, and who over the years has gained the right to expect you to behave according to the rules of friendship. That shame is burning, intense, and focused like the sting of a bee.

I feel unworthy that I care so much whether they will turn me in. If I am truly contrite, I should not be concerned about this. My moral intuitions are failing, but I trust Gregory and Elizabeth more than any other people to do the right thing. Gregory cares about eternity, not some petty secular notion of justice. He will see my action as a sin which endangers my soul. Will they then try to save me – Gregory, impossibly hampered by the vows of the confessional which prevent him from even speaking of the matter, and Elizabeth, impossibly constrained by her illusions about human nature? Surely she cannot sustain the alchemy by which she transmutes all base human motives into goodness. Is it possible that she can change her own disgust, betrayal, horror, anger – all mightily justified – into the spiritual essence necessary to redeem a sinner? Elizabeth is of the stuff from which saints are made. I cannot even aspire to deserve her.

That leaves Kraus. Is he, then, my nemesis? Is this little man with the inquisitive nose to be God's instrument? He is all that stands between me and utter license, for I fear I will do it again. The act I performed on Estelle has loosened the restraints binding appetites which should never have been allowed to see the light of day. After Stacia, until now, I have kept them in abeyance, caged, in darkness. Merely to consider them, to allow them a brief period of exercise in one's imagination is to risk obsession, possession. Such desires burgeon and grow strong in the sunlight of consciousness, until they demand their own space there and crowd out human feeling.

Did Estelle play me for a fool? What if she did? I never believed I had a right to her. Nor had I expected her to remain faithful to a man twice her age. After all, I had no intention of being faithful to her. Jealousy, spurned affection, the rage of the cheated lover – these are ephemeral, human motives. Motives? Excuses! All I sought was that glorious, cruel moment when I am God and beast and nothing in between.

13

SEPTEMBER 26, 1887

When I reached the East Station in Budapest, my impulse was to keep on going. All Europe lay open before me, and I thought of the vast expanse of a continent in which I could travel incognito, shaming no one but myself, until I was extinguished like a rabid dog. Perhaps that is what I should have done while I still had the chance. Now the scope for action has narrowed. I am being forced down a path whose end I cannot see.

The day began well. There is a crispness to the weather which I find welcome. Outside the station, the breath from the horses hangs in the air, and the temperature imparts a briskness to everyone's movements. Only rumors of typhoid in the city mar the sense of industry and bustle. To sooth the situation, the authorities have simultaneously both denied that there is an outbreak of the disease and insisted that it is confined to the poorest sections of the Elizabeth District.

I called on Wlassics, the estate agent, to tell him that I would no longer be needing the apartment.

'The lease is paid for a year,' he began.

'Well, there's nothing to be done about it,' I replied somewhat impatiently. 'My plans have changed, and I have no further use for the property.'

'I may be able to rent it. Sometimes there is a need for a short lease . . .'

'In which case, so much the better for you. Whatever you can get for it is yours.'

'Most generous, Count.'

He regarded me speculatively with his fishlike eyes while his fingers played unconsciously with a set of keys on a ring. The calculations proceeding in his head were all too visible. I had revealed weakness in showing generosity that was neither deserved nor expected, and now he was routing about in his brain to see if there could be other morsels in the situation which would be to his benefit. Did he consider, for a moment, the possibility that he might outright blackmail me? I stared him down, and the moment passed.

SEPTEMBER 28, 1887

I am restless to have the apartment emptied. The expense is unimportant. I took the first offer the furniture dealer gave me, much to his surprise, on condition that he cart away all the furnishings by the day after tomorrow. Then there will be no traces, and whatever clues there were will be dispersed far and wide, and not even Inspector Kraus will be able to sniff them out.

I confess to a spirit of melancholy as I sit alone in this place, infused with the spirit of Estelle. Could it have ended differently, without her death? I am afraid to answer, because I know the roots of my action stretch far back to the beginning of the relationship. Even in quiet moments of tenderness, my pulse would bound with the stealthy approach of an impulse I could not allow to come into focus, and I would turn away to put a safe distance between us. Was there an element in the shadows of my love which hovered over her, hoarding her for this one possibility?

I cannot accept that her murder was premeditated. Emotion pushes that thought aside. I feel instead a simple, sentimental missing of the girl, a regret for the passing of whom she was. It is forced. These feelings are not real. They are maudlin. An actor who would assume the role of the true Laszlo must express emotions such as these:

sadness as evanescent as the morning dew, self-hatred which leaves no scars, grief which can be laid aside as the circumstance demands. Once more I whirl about, trying to catch a glimpse of the other side of myself, but find only someone giving a passable performance of the bereaved lover.

EARLY MORNING, SEPTEMBER 29, 1887

I had forgotten Lucy, the maid. She is a saucy little thing.

'Will there be anything more, sir?' she asked coquettishly.

She is not shy in signaling her readiness to step into her mistress's shoes. I am tempted. The Minotaur who wears my human mask so plausibly, who stares out through my eyes, has the narrow focus of a hungry beast, one who will not be satisfied by flesh alone. He would have her.

'Thank you, no,' I replied in an abstracted way, so that she may believe that I do not notice her cherry lips and raven dark hair. 'That will be all,' I said to dismiss her. Yet my eyes followed her, and as she reached the door I added, 'I will call you if I need anything.'

Lucy noticed immediately that the remark was superfluous. This only encouraged her. She pivoted rather engagingly as she made her exit, casting me a measured, backward glance.

All she requires is a word or a gesture. It would be so easy – and so stupid. I am foolish enough to let my imagination insinuate itself bit by bit, until I am possessed by the most vivid sensation of my fingers entwined with her thick black hair, pulling back until her neck is taut, her tender throat exposed . . . Enough!

I have called her back and told her that she is to be discharged. I have given her six months' wages in compensation for the short notice (she is to leave tomorrow after the furniture), but still she pouts. Evidently she had other aspirations. I have also insisted that she return to her village, a remote place northeast of here where news of an investigation into Estelle's demise would be unlikely to reach. It is a pity I must let her go, but I must be realistic, otherwise I shall be arrested before the week is out.

SEPTEMBER 30, 1887

Shortly after I wrote the above entry, I heard a knock on the door, and a little while later Lucy appeared. Curtsying somewhat sulkily, she presented me with the salver on which lay a card. I picked it up in some puzzlement, since I had been confident until then that no one knew of my pied-à-terre. An icy chill ran through my body when I read the name: 'Tristan Rado, Colonel, 57th Hussars.' Hastily, I recalled Lucy.

'He is here?' I asked incredulously.

'No, sir. He just left the card.'

'No message?'

'He didn't say a single word.'

I ran to the window and looked down into the square, but nowhere could I see the trim figure of Colonel Rado.

'A smallish man, about fifty, dark hair combed straight back . . . is that the gentleman who left this?'

'No, sir, I wouldn't say he was a gentleman. An older person. With gray hair. Quite tall.'

It would be Rado's factotum, the impassive butler who hovered at the edges of the meetings of the Magyar League. I turned over Rado's card and found a terse message: 'Please come at 8:00 P.M. We must talk.'

After much internal debate, I decided I had no choice but to brazen it out. Colonel Rado knew of my apartment, and so in all probability he knew, too, of my arrangement with Estelle. But her death had not been a story to interest the Budapest papers, and I thought it unlikely that he was in a position to put two and two together. Besides, I told myself, it was only my overwrought emotions which gave me any reason to think the meeting had anything to do with her.

Though the evening was cold, I decided to walk to the colonel's home on the hill of Buda. I wanted time to collect my thoughts, and I wanted to see if I was being followed. My initial suspicions that I was under surveillance when I had first taken the apartment had evidently been correct, but this evening, however much I doubled back on myself or paused at shop windows to glance back along the sparsely peopled street behind me, I saw no one.

I arrived promptly at the time Rado had requested, though it felt more like a summons than an invitation. The butler took my coat, and as I teased off my gloves and tossed them into the hat he held I could see no sign in his expression that there was anything the slightest out of the ordinary. Rado, however, was in a state of high excitement. As I entered the study, he stood in the center of the room, interrupted in the middle of pacing from one side to the other.

'My dear fellow, come in, come in,' he said, and took my hand warmly. I was thrown off-balance by his effusiveness, although more than a little relieved, since it was evident that my domestic arrangements were not a matter which concerned him now. 'I'm drinking some mulled wine to keep out the cold. Won't you have some?'

It seemed rather an old-womanish drink for a colonel of cavalry to be imbibing, but I have the impression that Rado lives a spartan life and is given to denying himself common comforts. I accepted the offer of refreshment, and the butler left the room without waiting for instructions from his master.

'The matters we discussed move on apace,' he said mysteriously. Rado normally keeps himself on a tight leash, and I had never seen him in such a keen state before. He had resumed pacing and was rubbing his hands together as if this would help him to discharge an excess of nervous energy. 'Everything I hoped for, everything I had no power to control or plan for, is falling into place.'

'This had been the culmination of a long effort. I'm sure it must be extremely gratifying to you,' I said, thinking I was offering an innocuous comment.

Rado almost pounced on me. He seized my arm fiercely. 'Not me . . . us!' he whispered intently. There was a wild, fanatical gleam in his eyes as he stared into mine, but I dared not flinch from his gaze.

There came a knock on the door, and the butler entered with the wine. The distraction seemed to recall Rado to moderation. He released my arm and patted my shoulder in a conciliatory way.

'We're counting on you, old fellow,' he said in a more conversational tone. The door closed silently behind the departing butler. 'Absolutely counting on you.'

I sipped cautiously at the steaming brew, an insipid infusion of cloves and orange peel with the distant flavor of wine somewhere in its concoction.

'I'm at your service,' I said with the greatest misgiving. 'I hope you know you can count on me one hundred percent.'

This polite formula did not have the effect on Rado that I had expected. He took my words entirely at face value. 'Do you mean that?' he asked in a most serious way.

'Of course,' I said easily. I had decided to be brazen to the end.

'You must be certain of that.'

'You have my word as a gentleman.'

'Yes, of course.'

I wondered if he scoffed inwardly; it may have been a small sardonic smile that played at the corners of his mouth, but then again perhaps a grimace caused his lips to tighten under the stress of the moment.

'But why me?' I asked.

'Because you're the right man in the right place at the right time.'

I paused uneasily to consider the situation. Until now, the activities of the Magyar League had appeared futile but harmless, and there seemed little to be lost from going along with their conspiratorial games. But Rado himself was a different matter; he was not a person to play games, and five minutes alone with the man was enough to convince anyone that he was far from harmless.

As if to nudge me forward, he added, 'I chose you, also, because you can't refuse.' He smiled in a way which was peculiarly menacing. 'Forgive me. What I mean is that everything about you is too perfect for you to refuse this assignment.'

But he had spoken plainly enough the first time. 'Very well,' I answered. 'Now you might at least tell me what's going on.'

He composed what he was to say carefully, and I wondered how much he was holding back. 'To cut the cord which binds us to Austria, we Hungarians must have our own king. But the closest we have to Magyar royalty are the Hapsburgs themselves. Therefore, we have decided to offer the crown to Prince Rudolph.'

'We?'

'There are others who stand behind us. For now they must remain in the shadows. When the time is ripe, they will step forward into the light.'

'You're proposing treason!'

'Only within the context of a Hungary ruled by Austria.'

'But what makes you think the Crown Prince would be interested in being King of Hungary?'

'We have sounded him out. Necessarily, there is a good deal of circumspection on both sides – you know how diplomats talk to one another, like porcupines courting – but there is interest on the Prince's part, we have no doubt of that.'

'But his risk is enormous. I can't see what incentive he has to take it. In time, everything will come to him.'

'But how long must he wait? The Emperor could live another twenty years, perhaps more. Rudolph is no longer a young man. He's impatient. He has policies he wants to put into effect. We offer him a kingdom now.'

'I can't imagine what role I have to play in this grand scheme.'

'But your part is crucial,' he insisted, taking me by the arm again as if I might get away.

'I don't see it.'

'You are the linchpin of the whole enterprise!'

'I'm gratified you think so highly of me.' I must have looked at him as if he were a madman.

'The Prince cannot abandon Austria until he is assured of the support of the people who control things here in Budapest. Our men in the shadows cannot step forward until they are confident that the Prince will commit himself to Hungary. We have an impasse. Your castle is, as it were, a halfway point. If the Prince is willing to go that far, our men will declare themselves. Then, once the Prince is sure of their support, he will board the train for Budapest.'

'I see.'

'We require a secure location,' he added, jogging my memory of the reconnaissance which he and his bearer had disguised as a hunting trip.

'And I am simply to be the host?'

'Precisely.'

It did not seem much to ask after such a sinister buildup. I felt relieved that the part he had assigned me did not involve any real danger.

'I'd be glad to do my bit,' I told him.

Rado appeared to relax, as if he had reached the objective he had set himself. 'I knew you would,' he said. His bonhomie had returned. 'Sorry, by the way, to have to contact you at your pied-à-terre.'

'That's quite all right,' I said in as chilly a tone as I could muster short of outright rudeness.

'You see, there was no other way to reach you, and I'd just today received the news that the Prince has accepted an invitation which will take him into your neck of the woods next summer.'

'I understand. Let us not refer to the matter again.'

'But you understand, don't you old chap, that we had

to vet you? Otherwise, how could we be sure you were the man for the job?'

His apologetic tone rang false. Rado was aware that I knew he was not the kind of person who apologized for any action he deemed necessary to the success of his mission. He was making a point – or rather, an oblique threat – and I had no choice but to hear him out, and pray that his spies had not brought him news of Estelle's death.

'I haven't had an opportunity to set eyes on the young lady myself, but I'm told she's quite enchanting.'

'We are no longer acquainted,' I said, full of stiff, offended dignity.

'Ah.'

'The young lady has returned to her family.'

'Well, it does make one's life simpler. We're all for that, by the way. The quiet, simple life is the one best suited to the needs of a conspirator.'

'I'm pleased to hear it,' I said grimly. There was little I could do. Rado had me pinned like an insect under the magnifying glass. I told myself it could be far, far worse.

'For a while we were concerned about the young man.'

'Which young man?'

'Damn! Have there been more than one? We were only aware of Preisich. You do know about him, don't you? Civil servant of the tenth grade at the Finance Ministry? Quite promising, apparently. A strapping, blond Saxon lad. Quite a frequent visitor at the apartment while you were away.'

'What do you want of me?'

'I was most curious to see what you'd do with Preisich. I mean, you could hardly call the fellow out, now could you? Fight a duel with a civil servant grade ten? It simply wouldn't do. But then again, one couldn't simply let it go. I'm relieved you've sent the girl packing. I'm sure it was the right thing to do.'

'I'm glad you think so.'

Colonel Rado reached for the bell pull to summon the butler. 'The simple life,' he mused, sniffing at his glass of mulled wine. 'I advise you to cultivate the simple life.'

There were no cabs to be had on that part of Castle Hill, and so I walked down the winding street at a brisk pace, moving from the circle of light cast by one lamp through a zone of gloom and then into the next area of illumination. There were few pedestrians about, and I heard no footsteps behind me. To be sure that I was not being followed, I chose a point halfway between two lamps where the light was dimmest and ducked into a courtyard; I moved swiftly through an archway which led into a small kitchen garden and let myself out through a gate on the other side. Then I circled around to the other side of the Hill, away from Pest, and finally felt sufficiently secure to engage a cab.

I gave the driver the address of the apartment and tried to settle back in the seat and allow the interview with Rado to seep from my mind. No harm had been done, I reasoned; he did not know the girl was dead, and now that he believed he had me where he wanted me, there would be no reason for him to investigate my personal dealings further, so long as my life appeared quiet enough on the surface to meet his requirements. I had become his operative: All he cared about was that I not attract attention.

But his meddling in my private affairs rankled, and I could not let the matter go. The more I thought about his spies and his attempts to control my life, the more truculent and defiant I became. Finally, as we were crossing the bridge to Pest at a fair clip, I tapped on the window behind the cabby. Slowing the horses to a walk, he slid open the small pane and leaned down to hear my new instructions. I told him the name of an orpheum in the Leopold District and started to give him directions, but he nodded as if he already knew it well.

Why are these places always underground? The entrance to the Angel of Mercy was scarcely noticeable in daylight,

303

but at night striking blue lamps flanked the gap in the iron railings leading down to the basement level, where an enormous swarthy man greeted each patron at the threshold. With a courtesy which seemed exaggerated given the nature of the establishment, he drew back the curtain covering the door and ushered me inside.

I was immediately enveloped by the warm fug of the place. To breath in this rich, dank atmosphere of cigar smoke, sweat, eau de cologne, the uneasy hint of bad plumbing close by, is an act of acceptance; simply by allowing this nefarious essence to enter into oneself is to loosen one's tight, ill-fitting morality and to surrender to the Angel's louche tolerance. A dim red light suffused the arched space of the cellar and played tricks with the features of people's faces, so that one saw no more than an approximation of the other's appearance.

I ordered a booth from which I could view the door. The waiter suggested champagne, but I told him to bring me brandy. On the tiny circular stage, a Gypsy woman was singing in her own language accompanied by a man on the violin. It was a melancholy song, full of trembling, resonant descents to a lower timbre, with the violin soaring above at the beginning of each line and sinking down again to catch up with the woman's voice at the end. Three girls sat dispiritedly on a bench against the wall; another four were gathered around a bottle on a table and now made some attempt to hide their boredom as they looked in my direction, ready, on the slightest sign of interest on my part, to come to my booth. No one was dancing. It appeared to be a slow night.

The music left me out of sorts. I had come to escape sadness and regrets, to while away a couple of hours in idleness, and I was glad when the Gypsies ended their ballad. Without a pause, they abruptly launched into a raucous song which had the patrons clapping in time, and even roused the girls on the bench. Several couples emerged from booths to dance, although one or two of the men were already drunk and required help from their partners to retain their balance when they attempted overly ambitious turns.

My curious gaze must have rested too long on one of the girls at the table, for she took it as an invitation to join me. Her name was Leila, she told me as she boldly took a seat. She was dark with a dull, floury complexion and far older than she had appeared at a distance. She kept up a practiced patter while she quickly downed the outrageously expensive glass of champagne the waiter had automatically placed before her. When she had finished, I thanked her for her company. She appeared put out at first, I suppose because she felt I had invited her over to my booth in the first place, but then accepted the situation and sauntered back to the table with her friends. I saw her toss her head in my direction when she rejoined them, and afterwards they paid me no further attention.

I ordered another brandy and sipped it while a woman sang Magyar love songs. The mood of the place was beginning to work on me, and I felt relaxed and in the mood to enjoy myself. Rado be damned!

One of the girls on the bench had caught my eye. She sat apart from the other two, and no one seemed to talk to her. Perhaps it was this vulnerability which attracted me, in the same way that the hunting wolf will choose an animal which strays from the herd. I bought some dance tickets from the waiter and when the music started up again I walked over to her, presented her with a ticket, and asked if she would care to dance.

It was a waltz, more or less. She clung to me uncertainly and would not look at me. I tried to guide her in time with the music, but she waited for me to move first before she began her next step, so that we were always slightly out of phase. Even in that steamy cave her hands were cold. There was a high color to her cheeks, but otherwise she appeared pale and thin, so that I wondered whether she was in the early stages of consumption. I felt sorry for her, and this gave me a sense of security, that I would not do her harm.

It hardly seemed dangerous to talk. I was in the mood for conversation, and sometimes a stranger serves that need best. I invited her to join me, and the glass of champagne duly arrived almost as soon as we had taken our seats. She hardly touched it, even though it was a rule of the management that she consume a glass for every three songs. Her name was Rosa, she knew no one in Budapest, and she came from a village thirty miles from Szeged. I suspect she had run away from a brutal husband or father. She could have been no more than twenty, but she looked as if life had already exhausted her, and she showed a fatalistic lassitude, as if she had been beaten into permanent submission and now had come to obey anyone who exerted the slightest authority over her. For all that, there was a fleeting prettiness which came over her waiflike features whenever she was animated, and she would have been quite striking if fate had served her more kindly. She was grateful that anyone was paying her attention and tried to please me in a pathetic, bewildered, stumbling way, much like her dancing. My heart went out to her, this natural victim.

I felt protective of her, and this made me feel that it was safe to take the matter further. She was inordinately pleased when I asked her with some diffidence what would be her price for the night. She named some trifling sum with pride, her chin held high to indicate she would brook no bargaining. Someone had taught her the gesture, I would think, as an act of mercy, since everything about her advertised compliance.

'Do you live near here?' I inquired.

'Not far, sir. In the Elizabeth District.'

'Then shall we go?'

'But we can't go there,' she said.

'Why ever not?'

'Because I share the room and only have the bed from midnight till noon.' She looked at me strangely, as if she had not realized that I might be a foreigner and therefore ignorant of how people lived in this city.

'Of course,' I replied, in some confusion. 'That wouldn't do at all.'

'The Carlton Hotel is only around the corner,' she suggested hopefully. 'It's clean, too.'

She had a thin, threadbare coat to keep out the cold, with no hood. We did not have far to go, but the wind came around the corners viciously, and I put my arm around her shoulders and drew her to me. My pity was an affliction I knew would pass.

The Carlton Hotel was a suitably shabby institution, and I was pleased to find that the concierge was drunk almost to the point of incoherence. In that state, it was unlikely that he would have any recollection of me the next morning. I signed the police registration form as 'Herr Schmidt' from Vienna, not that he took the slightest bit of notice. At double the going price, he offered to sell me a bottle of brandy and two glasses; it seemed to be a popular part of the Carlton's service and one of the perquisites of his job. We had begun to walk toward the stairs when, as an afterthought, I turned and went back to accept his offer.

The room was drab but clean, as Rosa had promised. I lit the only gas lamp, but she came across the room and turned it down low. Without any preliminaries, or attempts to charm, she began to undress. I would have preferred some attempt at mystery, but Rosa seemed incapable of beguilement. Her slip was torn, her bodice was patched, and I turned my attention to the brandy so that I would not be provoked to compassion.

'Would you like some brandy?' I asked over my shoulder. 'It might warm you up a bit.'

'No,' she said in a small voice. I wondered if the man she had escaped from had been a drunkard. I wanted her to remain out of focus, a stranger, and yet one detail after another would touch me and restore her particularity.

When I went to pick up a glass, it slipped through my fingers and fell into the washbowl on the table, shattering into several pieces. My hand was trembling.

'I'm sorry,' I said, turning to her.

The breaking of the glass had not made a loud noise, but Rosa stood terrified and naked with her arms crossed on her chest as if she were making a sign to ward off evil.

'I'm sorry,' I said again. 'I think the cold has made my fingers clumsy.'

Slowly, she lowered her arms and I saw the outline of ribs beneath her small breasts.

'Really, there's no cause for alarm,' I told her gently.

Rosa stood exposed as if she didn't know what to do with herself.

'We can turn the light off, if you like,' I suggested. 'Would that make you feel better?'

'Yes.'

Turning sideways to me, she managed a timid smile that contained the suggestion of flirtation. She was thin, but her body had more curves than I had expected, and her hips and thighs were graceful and lithe.

'Would you let down your hair for me?' I asked.

'It'll cost you extra,' she said uncertainly. 'Only because it takes so long to pin it up again.'

'That seems fair.'

Her hair was dark brown with little luster, but when she had shaken it out, she seemed to grow more substantial and take on form. It framed her face becomingly and gave her an almost spiritual quality. She was uncomfortable with my gaze upon her.

'Can we turn it out now?' she asked.

I undressed quickly in the darkness and slipped into bed beside her. She lay on her back and made no movement in response to me. The only sign of her presence was the sound of her breathing. I extended my hand slowly and came into contact with her shoulder: She neither shrank from me nor returned my caress; she was entirely passive, as if it was the most natural thing for her to give herself over to my will. She started to say something at this point – I think she was going to ask me what she should do – but I stilled her with a finger to her lips.

Rosa put her arms about me, and I leaned down to press

my lips against the hard, thrilling pulse of her carotid. The steady beat worked on me, awakening me, aligning me, coaxing my true love to come forth. I had no further need for subterfuge or self-deception. For the first time in my life, I knew full well what I was doing, and I took pleasure in the anticipation of pleasure, in teasing myself and tempting myself forward, in reining back the rush of sensation and in spurring onward to the end. I had turned her and mounted her. I held her fast by her hair, and as my passion rose I pulled back until her neck was taut – too tight, too late, for her to cry out – and a moment before I burst forth I took from my mouth the shard of glass and opened her throat, and as the God soared in ecstasy, the beast bent down to suck at the spurting blood.

EVENING

This morning the furniture and all the furnishings were carted away and I dismissed Lucy. She does not want to return to her village after tasting what the city has to offer, but she will do as I advise. She will never know how close she came to following in Estelle's footsteps.

I spent some hours before the train left at the Rácz baths in the old Taban section of Buda. King Matthias built them over the hot springs four hundred years ago, and they have not changed since the time of the Turks. A plump, ambiguous youth with rolling hips hands out towels. He is forever looking back over his shoulder to see whose eyes follow him. The men sit like monks in the steam room, making desultory conversation, but really it is too hot to talk. It is profoundly cleansing to sweat. It is almost too hot to think, except that I feel one thought like a weight pressing upon my mind: I know now what I am.

I am filthy. I have led myself deeper and deeper into this perversion by seemingly innocent steps. I have paddled at the edge of the maelstrom, averting my eyes from the force which would suck me in, until it is too late and I am helpless in the grip of my repulsive passion. It is a trick well known to every drunkard, who will pick up a bottle of wine in order to study the label – a scholarly interest, no more, he assures himself – only to catch a whiff of the contents, an aroma so insidious that the will is hollowed out within his mind and replaced by a craving supported by a thousand memories, a hundred crooked reasons to succumb. I am like the pederast who tells himself it is an act of kindness, a friend's gesture, to place a hand upon a young lad's knee. Little by little, we nibble on our sumptuous bait. The passion is the hunter, the beast who would catch a man. I sweated in the steam almost to the point of unconsciousness. The epicene youth oiled me, then scraped the excess from my skin with a wooden spatula, flicking the scum aside with a deft motion of his wrist. After the steam, I gave myself over to the lean masseur who pummeled my muscles and stretched my limbs on the hard wooden bench. He manipulates the body as one might any other physical object, with an intensity of concentration which excludes any awareness of the person beneath his hands. I wonder if I shall eventually be executed by such a man.

OCTOBER 13, 1887

This afternoon Gregory came for afternoon tea as he always does on Thursdays. No one could talk about what each of us knew. How strange that we should converse about the weather with the exquisite china teacups from Sèvres between our fingers when beneath the surface of our words lurked an act so foul and bloody! It occurred to me in the middle of the conversation that Gregory and Elizabeth cannot even acknowledge to each other what they know I have done, since Gregory is out of role – friend, not priest.

I was humiliated to be the cause of this farce. They are decent, straightforward people, and I knew that this deceit must have pained them. Several times, in the midst of debates about the likely severity of the coming winter or how long one can expect apples to keep if they are in dry storage in the attic, I felt the urge to blurt out a confession. It was an episodic spasm which grew in intensity by steps to an almost overpowering climax, like the need to vomit when one feels spoiled food in one's stomach. And if I had, I believe that we would all have fallen tearfully to our knees to give thanks and pray for my forgiveness. Nothing could have pleased them more, and I would have done almost anything to please them.

'Did you know Dr Czernin is poorly?' Gregory asked me.

'Oh, no!' said Elizabeth too quickly, before I had a chance to answer.

'Nothing serious, I hope?'

'Well, that's the thing. We don't know. There's no one to make the diagnosis.'

'Surely, one of the doctors from Kolozsvar would come to see him?' Elizabeth suggested. 'Czernin has his limitations, but he's always been there for people.'

'A loyal soul,' Gregory said. 'He certainly doesn't look very well.'

'If it's a matter of money . . .' Elizabeth began hesitantly, turning to me for support. Extorting money from me for her good works was the closest she ever came to sin.

'I'm sure that's not it,' I said. The town still expects me to make extraordinary contributions whenever there is a crisis, but this was not the time to insist on that point. 'But if it is, we'll foot the bill, of course,' I replied.

'Gluck telegraphed that he'd come, but at the last moment he had to call it off because there were too many cases in Kolozsvar for him to leave to his assistant,' Gregory said. 'Then yesterday Herczeg did the same thing.'

'What's going on in Kolozsvar?' I asked.

'I haven't heard.'

'Influenza?'

'Let us pray not,' Elizabeth said.

A silence ensued. I had the feeling they were waiting for me.

'Then what is to be done for Czernin?' I asked.

Gregory stirred his tea contemplatively. Elizabeth was more transparent; her eyes were fixed on me with a hopeful, yearning look. By what contortions of the human spirit could she still find it in herself to love me? I felt humbled and close to tears of gratitude, and experienced again the childlike need to confess. I told myself the impulse was self-indulgent, and it passed.

'Somebody has to do something to help the old fellow,' I insisted. I seemed to be speaking to myself.

Elizabeth was unable to restrain herself. She came to my side and laid her hand upon my arm. I felt healed by the faint pressure of her fingers, and I fancied the warmth suffused my body in a glow. As if I had been a leper, hideous and deformed, I felt at that moment that it was the kindest thing that anyone had ever done for me.

'Oh, Laszlo,' she whispered, for she was close to tears herself and hardly able to speak. 'So much good remains in you.'

'No,' I groaned, protesting, lest a mirror of words show me my face.

'Yes! There's so much good you can do.'

'I can see Dr Czernin, but I'm so out of practice . . .'

'It'll come back,' Gregory said. He was quite pale. 'The ability to care for others. You've lost your way.'

'But you can find it again,' Elizabeth said. 'I know it lies within you.'

'With God's grace.'

14

OCTOBER 15, 1887

Dr Czernin is a stern-faced man with hair close cropped in the German manner and a flowing military mustache. He served for twenty years in Uncle Kalman's old regiment, which explains why he is in practice in our town. One hopes for kindness in his eyes. It is not that he is callous, but he lacks the necessary tenderness which sick and frightened people need – civilians, that is, for I suspect that he was more than adequate in tending injured cavalrymen. But each craftsman must have a feel for the tendencies and limits of his raw material: the carpenter for wood, the potter for clay, the doctor for flesh and blood. Dr Czernin will prod at a tender abdomen with thick, blunt fingers, discomforting the patient far more from the alarm at his insensitivity than from any pain he inflicts. For all that, he is a dogged man who many times has trudged on foot to visit a patient when the snow lay too deep for the horses. There is a general feeling in the town that he is 'our doctor', a sentiment which forgives much.

Czernin's house was in a run-down part of the town in a kind of no-man's-land between the Saxon and Wallach quarters. When I saw how modestly he lived, I thought that I should have sent word in advance to let him know I would visit, for I came upon him unprepared, and I was afraid I would embarrass him. Sickness is such a vulnerable, intimate time, and for a proud man like Czernin it is intrinsically humiliating. His flustered housekeeper showed me straight in to his bedroom without conferring with him first.

The drapes were drawn tight and a fire was banked in the fire-place so that the room was stuffy and hot. A single candle burned on a table by the bedside.

'No, Mary, no! Not tonight!' he cried, seeing my shadowy outline in the dim light and struggling to sit up.

'It waxes and wanes, as the sickness takes him,' the house-keeper whispered to me from the door. I thought she seemed afraid to venture into the room.

'How long has he been like this?' I asked her in a low voice, but the doctor intervened.

'I see you! I see you there. Come forward so that I can see you in the light. Stop your whispering. Come forward I say, and speak your piece!'

'Three days, Count,' the housekeeper murmured. She seemed anxious to quit the room, and I gave her leave to go.

'Who the devil are you, sir?' Dr Czernin demanded in his most peremptory tone.

'Don't you recognize me, Dr Czernin?' I asked. 'Surely you know who I am?'

I made as if to come closer to the candle's ring of light and approached his bed, but he flung up an arm in abject terror as if to fend me off.

'No, I beg of you!' he cried out.

'I mean you no harm,' I told him in a steady, even voice. 'I've come to examine you.'

'You've come to take me with you to Hell, you fiend!'

'They're not ready for you there yet,' I said.

He chewed this over for some moments, all the while scrutinizing me suspiciously. Eventually he seemed overcome by the uncertainty and the effort of supporting himself upright with his arms and let himself slump backwards into the pillows in an attitude of surrender. I came closer so that he could see my face more clearly in the light.

'I know you,' he said in a more normal voice, though slightly doubtful.

'Of course you do, old chap.'

I proffered my hand and he reached cautiously to take it. His hand shook in mine, from the disease I thought, rather than fear.

'Count,' Czernin said at last, much to my relief. 'You do me an honor in coming to my home.'

'It was the least I could do. I'm only sorry you don't have a more competent physician to attend you.'

'So you've taken to doctoring again? Well, these are hard times.'

'I don't think I'm going to make a living at it, since you are my only patient.'

'You know the diagnosis then?'

'Not yet.'

In fact, given the evident clouding of consciousness when I had first spoken to him, and seeing at first hand the mean circumstances in which he lived, I thought he might be a drunkard going through delirium tremens. But the fact that he had gained some semblance of lucidity, together with his obvious physical distress, indicated that the cause of his condition lay elsewhere.

He beckoned me closer, and then closer still, and I was forced to lean over him and wait within the miasma of his fetid breath while he summoned the energy to speak.

'Typhoid, dear God!' he whispered hoarsely.

I looked across the bed to the other side of the room where the door stood open, and wondered if the sound could carry to the housekeeper, who might be loitering there.

'Nonsense, my dear fellow. You're delirious. You don't know what you're saying.'

'I have the rash. The rose spots. Typhoid fever.'

He wrestled weakly with his nightgown in an attempt to bare his chest.

'Would you permit me?' I asked him.

I was going to have to examine him one way or another, and this seemed an opportunity to do so with his cooperation. He lay back exhausted on the pillows once more and seemed to lapse into a private world in which he muttered inchoate warnings to long-lost comrades. His nightgown was badly soiled, as was the bed where he lay. With some difficulty I coaxed him to turn one way and then the other, so that I could raise the sodden article to his armpits to expose his abdomen and chest.

His skin was burning hot to the touch, but to my relief I saw that there was no rash, rose-colored or otherwise. He was breathing with difficulty, and I thought I was faced with a case of pneumonia, until he took his next deep breath and I felt the edge of an enlarged spleen descend beneath the margin of the ribs onto my waiting fingertips.

Outside the sickroom, I gave instructions to the house-keeper to engage a nurse who would bathe the doctor. She would do this herself, she insisted, since she had assisted the doctor on many occasions. She will ensure that he has adequate fluids; I stressed this, since the fever appeared to have depleted him. On one of Czernin's own prescription papers I wrote an order for a camphor infusion to aid in clearing the air passages of the lungs.

I returned to the castle with a timid feeling of self-satisfaction. Perhaps after all I am not entirely without use in this world. And if I have been maneuvered into this position by Gregory and Elizabeth, so be it. I yield to their manipulations. It is a benign conspiracy. They have my moral salvation as their goal, and I must admit I am incapable of saving myself. I need to work. Idleness only gives my imagination opportunity. The humble work of a country doctor is my path back. Gregory could not have set a more apt penance. Accordingly, I have caused it to be known in the town that I will assume responsibility for Dr Czernin's practice while he is indisposed.

OCTOBER 20, 1887

Last night a man brought word to the castle that Dr Czernin was worse.

'I didn't want to bother you, Count,' Mary, his house-keeper said. In the space of a couple of days she has grown quite haggard tending to him.

'Not at all,' I told her. 'Clearly, you did the right thing.' When she brought me into the room to see Czernin, there were two girls there, one of about seventeen, the other perhaps nineteen, whom she introduced to me as her daughters. I noted that Mary took Czernin's hand unselfconsciously, and I surmised that they have lived together as man and wife for some time. I wondered if the younger girl, Helene, was his daughter. She remained outside the candles' pool of light, perhaps to hide her tearstained face from the man in the bed. The elder daughter, Theresa, bustled about the room tidying and straightening, but she showed little sign of affection toward the sick man.

I was concerned to see the deterioration in Czernin's condition. He was unresponsive to my voice and turned fitfully now and again, moaning incoherently. His breathing was shallow, but not labored as one would expect to see in the final stages of pneumonia, and when I felt his abdomen again, the enlarged spleen nudged my fingertips, and I began to wonder with growing alarm whether he might not have been correct in his diagnosis.

The housekeeper recognized that the end was near. Mary is a handsome woman with iron-gray hair and strong features who has cared for the good doctor for fifteen years. I had at first found her severe and withdrawn, but this was a mistake, for as the night progressed she revealed herself as a quiet, generous soul who has had to keep her natural feelings on a tight leash. She asked if she could join me at his bedside, and I agreed, since there is nothing further I can do for the patient other than to keep vigil. She sent her daughters off to bed and sat patiently beside him, holding his hand, and I thought he looked at peace.

We talked fitfully through the night, with long periods of silence in which we each were lost in our own thoughts.

She told me Czernin took her and her daughter in and gave her the position when she was widowed. She had been married to a sergeant of the regiment; he had been the doctor's orderly, she said by way of explanation of her present circumstances – she didn't have to tell me that the issue of class had been unbridgeable. The result is that she has no more claim to his estate than any other servant would have, and will be turned out of this house, her home, to live on a tiny pension. There is a nephew in Galicia, apparently, who has never set eyes on Czernin, but stands to inherit the house and furniture and the modest worldly goods the doctor has accumulated. She is a person with a natural dignity and told me all this without rancor or attempts to evoke my pity.

'He was a good man,' she said, her eyes welling up with tears for the first time.

'A great-hearted man,' I murmured, inadequately. The tears seemed so painful to her that I was afraid what would happen if they came in earnest. She shook her head and smiled in a grimace as she attempted to master herself.

We sat quietly for a long while. I pondered on Czernin's simple, unreflective life. I had tried to live the life of a country squire, spending my time hunting and meddling in the management of the estate to disguise my idleness. I had looked down on this man as little more than a journeyman, but in his clumsy, bearlike fashion he had served his fellow man, while I, with all the advantages of education and position, had ignored the familiar moral landmarks with the result that I had surrendered to the most rank indulgence. I studied his face in order to implant within my own heart the humility of service.

Close to dawn, Czernin began to talk more understandably. I do not know if he was more coherent, but it soon became clear to me that the subject matter of his rambling was of a personal nature and involved intimacies of his life with Mary. I excused myself and, groping my way through the narrow hallway, found the front door and stepped out into the cold morning air.

It was too early for the town to be astir. To the east, the first glimmer of light outlined the mountains. Frost glistened on the cobbles, and I stepped carefully, with no particular destination in mind, down the street toward the market square. Some carters waited there, huddled in blankets their wives or mothers might have made, passing the wait in quiet conversation while their horses nudged feed bags and tossed their heads to get to the last of the grain at the bottom. I felt profoundly grateful for the ordinariness of it all, as if my world had not flown apart but persisted in spite of my profound unworthiness.

I was sleepless but alert, and the fresh air was a life-giving elixir to me after the fetid closeness of the sickroom. I was renewed, rededicated. I knew I must serve. Henceforth exhaustion was to be my friend, the guardian against my imagination. The filth and stench which are the country doctor's lot were to be the prompts to my humility. The gratitude of simple folk was to be my only reward. It was a monkish existence I swore myself to, and if my sentiments included some elements of excess, then this was the nature of conversion.

When I returned to Czernin's house, Mary was standing in the dark hallway.

'He's gone,' she said.

A sob came from her and she seemed to stumble forward; I caught her in my arms without intending it so, and found myself holding her while she cried openly on my shoulder. Perhaps it was the lack of sleep, or perhaps we had made a connection of friendship through the hours of waiting that we had shared, but it seemed natural for me to hold her fast until her weeping subsided.

'I'm sorry,' she said, backing away from me and dabbing at her eyes as if that would expunge her grief. There were red blotches on her face. For some people the act of weeping is almost too wrenching to bear.

'I wish I could be of more comfort to you,' I stammered.

'No. You've been too good already.'

She had pulled back into herself, and there was a grim determination about her which made it difficult for me to speak. 'It's hard to be practical at such a time,' I began. 'I hope you won't be offended . . .'

'We can take care of our own needs.'

'I know you can. It wouldn't be charity – I assure you of that. I know you are a proud woman.'

'I'll take no charity,' she told me fiercely.

'But if a position were to become available at the castle, something suitable to your standing and abilities?'

'You're very kind, sir,' she said, her neck taut, her head turned away as she struggled not to soften into weakness.

NOVEMBER 17, 1887

My work – Czernin's practice – takes me everywhere. I travel by horse along country tracks to outlying districts, and I have visited corners of this town which I didn't even know existed. I had not been aware of the squalor in which some of our people live. These conditions make them easy prey to disease. Clearly, there is an outbreak of some enteric fever, although since the cases are scattered I think I am the only person aware of it at present. I have discovered in Czernin's notes that there were two other patients he treated with a similar march of symptoms. Both of them died in the week preceding his demise. Our community is small; it will not take much more of this before people wake up to the fact that a deadly disease is among us. So far, I have said nothing to the authorities, since we must avoid panic at all costs. People are rattled enough after Estelle's death, and the murderer still at large.

At first the people were reluctant to call me when someone in their family fell ill, as if it were not proper for the count to be engaged in this lowly occupation.

Then my visits became some thing of a novelty, and I began to be pestered by women who thought that a visit to their home could be construed as a personal call and so used to advance their social ambitions. Even as a medical student, I have never had much patience with the role of the society doctor who caters to the trivial complaints of bored ladies, even though that clientele is financially essential to a medical practice. Such considerations need not concern me now, and I refer them rather peremptorily to Herczeg in Kolozsvar.

Elizabeth will find a position for Mary at the castle. In the meantime, Mary has thrown herself into working with the sick. I do not think this is a good idea in her present state since she is already weakened by grief, but she insists, and will not listen to me when I attempt to outline the risk involved. Particularly troubling is the fact that she brings her younger daughter, Helene, with her on visits to the afflicted. Mary has become quite listless, even fatalistic, and I think is unable to exert much parental authority over the girls, each of whom in their different ways is spirited and willful.

'They must find their own way,' Mary said without emotion when I had remonstrated with her about Helene's presence in the sickroom of a new case. 'She would come. There was no stopping her.'

And indeed, Helene does bring a ray of sunlight with her into these gloomy settings. Her father's death (I assume this to be the case) has left her bewildered, and there are times when she appears close to tears. I am touched by her profound innocence: She knew her father to be a good man; therefore the loss is incomprehensible to her. She is helplessly good-natured. Even gnarled peasants respond to her, and their wives, thinking they are comforting Helene, squeeze her hand and smile consolingly, stretching their faces against the grain of their wrinkles, it seems, for the first time in decades.

I cannot ignore the fact that Helene is pretty, although I wish it made no difference to me. She has glinting eyes, which make people feel noticed, and a small, slightly turned-up nose, which gives her a playful expression. Grief does not come naturally to her nature; like many young people, she easily forgets her sadness when she is distracted. I have seen her break into laughter at something, and catching herself, glance sideways shame-facedly and withdraw into a trouble silence. Not that she is superficial in spirit, since I know she feels deeply.

Mary and her daughters have continued to live in Czernin's house; I don't think anyone is in any hurry to inform the heir of his uncle's death, so they may stay there undisturbed for the time being and live on the money Mary earns from the nursing work which comes her way. There is a lot to be done and she is in much demand – so much, in fact, that Helene often accompanies her. I have stabled the horse and now have Jacob ready the trap so that I can begin my rounds soon after dawn. It has become part of my routine to draw up outside the house; Mary and Helene are already waiting for me, and Helene recites the list of the patients we must see in order of urgency and proximity. I don't know what I would do without them. I have tried again, somewhat halfheartedly I admit, to dissuade Mary from bringing Helene. This is more to settle my conscience than from any real fear for Helene's safety, since she is given a helping role which seldom makes it necessary for her to touch a patient, and it is Mary who cleans them and who must deal with the infected bedclothes. Mainly I am apprehensive at the extent to which Helene's presence brightens my day.

'You are a godsend, Helene,' I told her yesterday when she returned from Czernin's office with a speculum I needed in order to examine the patient we were visiting.

'Please, sir, you don't realize what you're saying.'

She crossed herself hurriedly. I suppose, strictly speak-ing, that my compliment could have been taken as some mild form of blasphemy. But was this the reason that she blushed? I find myself looking for these small signs of interest, such as glances crossing, both of us beginning to say something at the same time and then both waiting for the other to speak, or hearing her use a phrase I had used the previous day. She is a mere girl!

Yesterday she did not appear at the door when I drew up in the trap. Mary mounted to the seat beside me and said that Helene was indisposed.

'It's nothing serious.'

'Are you sure?' My heart was pounding. There was a great risk of contracting the fever for anyone who lived under the same roof as an infected person. They were all in danger. And the prodromal symptoms could appear insignificant.

'Tomorrow she'll be right as rain,' Mary said without a trace of concern. 'Or the day after.'

'But how can you be so sure?'

'Believe me.' She gave me a knowing look. 'I'm sure. Tomorrow. You'll see.'

I had the most graphic image – unbidden and consuming in its immediacy, it thrust itself upon me – of a trickle of menstrual blood finding its slow, deliberate course between Helene's thighs.

For the rest of the day I was grateful that I was kept too busy to think. During the night I was called out to see a man in extremis, but I was already awake and in need of business to occupy me. An hour before dawn I crawled into my bed, my wanton mind drugged at last with fatigue, and numb enough to allow a fitful slumber.

DECEMBER 1, 1887

I am not sure when Theresa first appeared. She was there when Dr Czernin died, but although she was busier and in some sense more evident, it was her sister, Helene, whom I remember from that day. Theresa remained something of a blur in the dim light of Czernin's room. I fancy that she was one of a number of relatives grouped around the sickbed of an ailing grandmother in the Magyar section of the town. I took her in with the same glance that surveyed the assembled family before they trooped from the room to leave me to my work. I must have assumed that she was one of the older children or a cousin. Perhaps she was, or perhaps it was an early example of that strange facility she has for turning up at the bedside, sometimes of perfect strangers, who are about to depart this life.

Helene tells me that her sister is destined for a convent. Already she has a religious pallor, which sets off her deep, dark eyes and her black hair. Theresa is much darker than her younger sister, and she is short and almost muscular in build where Helene is slim. I expect this is a reflection of the fact that they are perhaps only half-sisters, although no one mentions this. They are different also in their temperaments: Helene is optimistic and outgoing, whereas Theresa tends toward gloom; she is shy and evasive, rarely looking one in the eye. When she is talking, Theresa has an odd mannerism of fluttering her eyes almost closed, and at such moments I am reminded of the ecstacy of her namesake saint.

The first time I actually noticed her was in the room of one of her neighbors, who was the next person with the sinister symptoms of the enteric fever. I thought she seemed familiar, but seeing her out of context, and in my fatigued state, I had to stare at her for a moment before I placed her. As she left the room she smiled at me with a shy, dipping look. Later, on my way back to the castle, I drew level with her short, somewhat stocky figure in cloak and hood trudging with an undaunted, bouncing walk through the driving rain. It was only with difficulty that I persuaded her to ride with me, and then she agreed to travel only as far as the market square, since she would not hear of me making a detour on her account. She is an eccentric, otherworldly girl, with few conversational resources. There is something slightly sanctimonious in Theresa's manner, but much can be forgiven for her youth. She is innocent and already a little mad.

DECEMBER 14, 1887

This morning both Mary and Helene climbed up to the narrow seat of the trap beside me. It is quite cold and there is a certain amount of huddling together for the sake of warmth. We are getting quite used to one another and comfortable in each other's company. In the midst of an epidemic in which many people will likely lose their lives, I have a twinge of guilt when I feel so jolly. I have to remind myself that I am on borrowed time; my life no longer fully belongs to me, and so whenever a moment of happiness comes my way I experience it as a gift.

This disease is no respecter of rank. I was called to the home of a wealthy Saxon family that has been influential in our town for almost as long as my own. The younger son was one of the first victims and therefore one of those who must have passed on his fatal infection to Dr Czernin. Now the father is not well, and a sister is ailing.

A community can bear sporadic, dispersed deaths; they inspire a sense of fatalism, for it becomes a matter of chance whether or not one is affected. But when the disease affects several people in the same household, it becomes clear that one person passes it on to another. Then the fear of contagion separates people and makes them mistrustful and afraid of each other.

The Hermanns lived in a Saxon farmstead which the town has gradually absorbed within its boundaries. The family long ago moved all their farming to extensive holdings farther down the valley and built on the pastures, so that the farmstead is now surrounded by dwellings. It is built in the old style, with a tall stone wall extending from the main house, so that it would have been a virtual fortress capable of withstanding attacks from bands of Turkish raiders.

There was some awkwardness in the greeting I received from the lady of the house, which I initially put down to the social ambiguity of my visit. Where previously I would have been received as an honored guest, I come now with a status only slightly above that of a tradesman. But when I entered the sickroom, the cause of the lady's embarrassment became clear. The walls were lined with family members and trusted retainers, and Hermann's three sisters sat composed on a settee. The room was strangely silent, as if the court were waiting the king's pleasure. Hermann is an argumentative, tiresome man who has not kept up with the times – not that it matters anymore. He looked deathly sick and had trouble keeping his eyes open.

Little of the day's gray light filtered through the narrow windows into the heavily paneled room, which is why it took me several moments to realize that the focal figure was not Hermann, but Gregory, who was in the middle of conducting a service. He had paused to allow the curiosity aroused by our arrival to subside and now resumed the prayer. Helene and Mary knelt instinctively along with the others, and I noticed Gregory's gaze rest on Helene and then move, questioning, to my face. With so many eyes upon me, I knelt, even though I knew myself to be an impostor.

'We must let the doctor do his work,' Gregory said finally, gathering his flock and ushering them through the door. Several people stopped to talk to me, so that I did not have a chance to speak to Gregory. When I looked for him, I saw that he had taken Mary aside. He had a protective hand on Helene's shoulder, and was talking earnestly to her mother. Involuntarily, he looked in my direction, and I felt a stab of hurt, as if my friend had cruelly misunderstood my motives. Of course, I knew he would not mention anything about me to Mary; he would find some other hazard with which to arouse her fears for her daughter, or some subterfuge which would induce her to withdraw Helene from my company.

When Gregory grasped my arm in passing and said, 'I'll be in the garden when you've finished with him,' I was unable to suppress a small sense of betrayal.

Hermann was incoherent and far gone, and I did what

I could for him, which was not very much. Perhaps my greatest service was to speak to his wife and eldest son to make sure that they understood the gravity of the situation and the need to make legal and financial arrangements before death should intervene.

'There is little hope, I'm afraid,' I told them.

It is hard to be practical at such times. They had already discerned the worst and, staggering under the loss of their son and brother, hardly listened to my advice. I left them sitting silent and dazed and made my way through the back door to the walled garden.

It was a practical space devoted to the raising of produce, with rows of bare earth comprising a now dormant vegetable plot and a small orchard. I saw Gregory standing beside an old pear tree which leaned across the grass path and twisted muscularly to maintain its posture. Overhead, gray clouds suggested it might soon snow. I thought he did not hear me approach, since for a minute he did not look up even when I came close to him, and I surmised that he was in the act of prayer, or engaged in a contemplative exercise from which he could not be interrupted.

As I waited for him to finish, it occurred to me that this was the first time we have been alone together since Estelle's death. Without consciously doing so, we have avoided each other's company unless we can be sure that Elizabeth or others will be present.

'I didn't expect to see you here,' I said.

'And I'm glad to see you here.'

'Isn't it rather early for them to be calling in the priest?' I asked him with a smile. 'It doesn't show much faith in my abilities.'

I was glad when he laughed. We adopted the casual, irreverent tone of men who in their daily work are accustomed to death.

'They're hedging their bets,' Gregory said. 'Our customers would prefer to live, but just in case, they're glad of any intervention which will ease their way in the afterlife.'

'This is a busy season for both of us.'

'I think you and I are the only people who know we have an epidemic on our hands.'

'I'm not sure yet.'

'I am. I see the results. So do the grave diggers. They're starting to talk.'

'I don't want to start a panic.'

'We have to let the people know so they can prepare themselves. There are all sorts of rumors flying around. Last Sunday the church was almost full.'

'It's Christmas. Everyone wants to make sure his soul's in good order so he can enjoy the holiday with a clear conscience.'

'That's good enough for me,' Gregory said quietly. He let me steep for a moment in my own thoughts. 'You should come, Laszlo.' He was in earnest and had taken my arm. 'We all have need of the strength only God can give us.'

I hesitated awkwardly. 'I'd like to come,' I said. I dearly wanted to go.

'No sin is too great for God to forgive.'

'I'll give it some thought.'

'Don't think about it. You already think too much. After a point, it doesn't help you. You must have faith.'

'It's too late.'

'No, please God!' He seized me about the shoulders in a fierce embrace as if to clutch my soul and hold it fast lest it be plucked from me. I felt his arms tight about me as if he were wrestling with the Devil himself.

'Confess!'

'No.'

'It's the road back. It's the only way.'

'I've gone too far.'

'Don't you see: that's not possible.'

'It's my burden. I have to find a way to bear it.'

'Share it with me.'

'No, I would never do that.'

'You must.'

'I can't.'

'God will hear you. God will forgive you.'

'I don't care about God,' I said. I thought he looked angry for the first time. 'It's you I care about.'

'I don't matter.' He was furious. 'I'm nothing!'

'Can you forgive me?'

'If you confess, yes. If you're truly repentant. Of course.'

'I mean you, not the priest; Gregory, my dearest friend, can you forgive me?'

But the man flinched. His eyes, so much more exact, more fickle than the heart they supposedly mirror, left my face. The movement was instantaneous, little more than a blink, but it was enough to bring together what each of us had half known. Only God can truly forgive what I have done.

DECEMBER 19, 1887

Before I began my rounds this morning I stopped by the police station to see Inspector Kraus. He has now taken lodgings in the town so that he can devote more time to the case, but I hear of no new developments. I found him in the small room off the hallway which he was taken for his office. He appears quite dispirited.

I knocked on the door and entered at the sound of his voice. Kraus sat at a desk crowded with papers, his head on his hand as he labored over a report. He didn't even look up.

'Yes?' he inquired wearily.

'I was passing – '

'Count!'

'And I thought I'd drop in to see how the investigation was going.'

'A thousand apologies!'

'None required, I assure you.'

'I am writing my weekly report to the Commissioner.'

'Any progress?'

He started to speak and then changed his mind and slumped back in his chair. He looked miserable. 'No, in a word.'

This was puzzling. 'But I thought you had the prime suspect within your grasp?'

'The man Preisich? He's ruled out.'

'An alibi, I expect.'

'No. Better than that. He's left-handed.'

'But surely – '

'Your own deduction, Count. The laceration went from left to right. The throat was cut from behind. There can be no other conclusion.'

'But perhaps, because of juxtapositions, by force of necessity, he used his right hand. One never knows, in the heat of the moment . . .'

'It's incontrovertible,' Kraus said morosely. Gone were his cocky assurance, his arrogant declarations of scientific principle. Even his own method seemed to be playing against him.

'Murderers always use their best hand,' he insisted. 'It's a criminological fact.'

'I'm sorry,' I said. 'Aren't there any other leads?'

'That's what the Commissioner keeps asking. Last week I told him I didn't have any. Now he's demanding that I find some.'

'That seems rather unfair.'

'I even suggested I go to Budapest. To see if I could find out something about her life there.'

'Perhaps the murderer was part of her life in Budapest,' I suggested dangerously, sensing that the best place to be in relation to this line of thinking was out in front where I could lead it astray.

'That's what I told the Commissioner.'

'But then you'd have to wonder why he followed her hundreds of miles out here, a strange town where he's more likely to be noticed, when he could just as well have killed her there, in Budapest.'

'That's what the Commissioner said.'

'Well, he does have a point, I suppose. But on the other hand, you can't be expected to solve every case that comes your way. There must be times when no culprit can be found and the case must be closed.'

'No!'

I was surprised by the vehemence of the man who only a second before had appeared slumped at his desk in a posture of defeat.

'I shall not give up! I shall never close the case until this contemptible coward is brought to justice.'

The insult hit me like a smack in the face, and I stiffened and drew myself up before I could get myself under control.

'You're right. It was a cowardly act to attack a defenseless woman from behind,' I managed to get out. 'We must do everything we can to bring the culprit to justice,' I muttered, trying to mean what I said, though I still smarted from words which had carried the sting of truth.

I felt obliged to sit down and commiserate with him for a few moments. I wished he would not confide in me, but before I could stop him, Kraus told me that he lives with his sister in Kolozsvar; she is a war widow who is in poor health and misses him sorely. Kraus is her only support and so cannot afford to marry. He has raised himself from humble origins to his present position, a lone meritocrat surrounded by bureaucrats. They have him under siege because he is chronically behind in his paperwork. He is a lonely man who feels himself at war with the times in which he lives.

I do not want to know these things, but he has got it into his head that I am a kindred spirit. I wish to keep the relation impersonal so that he can remain small and ridiculous. I would like him to be a caricature, or a diagram even. I do not fear him, but his fervor, his fanatic certainty about what is right, confuses me.

I was on my way back to the castle for lunch when Jacob intercepted me at the bottom of the hill with a message from Mary: There were two new cases, both members of the same family. Yesterday there were four new cases. The pattern of symptoms is unavoidable. It was pointless to delay any further, and I drove straightaway to see Mayor Theissen at his shop.

He had not yet opened, but I banged on the door, knowing that he would be busy supervising the baking, and that it would be a good time to talk before the place filled with customers. He came to the door himself and peered through the glass with an expression of annoyance before he recognized me and ushered me in with a flourish. I was shocked to see how much weight he had lost. He seemed quite shrunken from his ruddy, flourishing self.

He pressed some coffee on me. 'Would you honor me by tasting one of my sweet rolls, Count?' he asked with something like his old smirk of complicity, knowing that few could resist the offer.

I was indeed tempted, for their spicy fragrance filled the shop, and I had had little appetite for the stodgy breakfast which is our fare at the castle. He set before me a hot roll from the oven, the steam rising to tantalize the nose with hints of cinnamon. We sat at one of the small tables and he watched me bite into the moist, delicious confection with professional satisfaction.

'I wanted to make you aware of a sickness which is affecting people in the town.'

'I had heard rumors.'

'I was afraid of that. But I suppose it's inevitable, given the number of people affected.'

'Just how many people have been affected, Count?' His attitude of attention had changed from a gossipy interest to one of mild alarm.

'Twenty so far.'

'So far?'

'There will inevitably be more. It's clear that we're facing an epidemic.'

'But when people are affected, they don't necessarily . . .'

'Die? I'm afraid they do. In fact, quite often. In the last two weeks we've had five deaths. Six, if you count a child who might have died of appendicitis.'

Theissen seemed staggered. 'Six deaths?'

'It's not measles, you know,' I told him, more shortly than I had intended. When you live with a dangerous situation for days on end you develop callouses around your emotions.

'Then what is it?' he asked.

'Typhoid fever.'

'Typhoid!'

'Dr Czernin was one of the first casualties. You weren't aware of that?'

Theissen had turned pale. If the doctor, of all people, had fallen victim to the disease, he seemed to be thinking, how much more vulnerable were the rest of us ordinary mortals!

'Typhoid's contagious, isn't it?' Involuntarily, Theissen glanced at the cup I was in the act of lifting to my lips, and at the knife and plate on the table. I saw that part of his mind was already taken up with the question of how he should cleanse these contaminated articles.

'You must tell the people to boil their water.'

'And if we do that, we shall be safe?' he asked hopefully, trusting as a child.

'Not entirely. Clearly the water supply is contaminated. People live on top of each other, and waste has seeped into the wells. If they drink only water which has been boiled they will be safe from infection from that source. But the disease can also be spread by food, or unclean cooking utensils.'

'And by touch?'

'By intimate contact, certainly.'

'But by something casual – a handshake, for example?'

'We can't discount it.'

'At all costs, we must avoid a panic.'

'But the people must know what kind of a thing we face now, and the dangers involved.'

'Perhaps we can be judicious, Count, in the information we reveal. Too much, all at once . . .'

Theissen was thoughtful. Was he calculating how much damage such an epidemic could do to his business if people believed they could catch their death from eating one of his dainty pastries? But perhaps I do him a disservice.

'And so close to Christmas,' he said, wringing his hands.

'This is your department,' I told him. 'You must do as you think best.'

By the time I came to leave, we had agreed that he would convene a meeting in the Town Hall at noon tomorrow which would be open to all concerned citizens. The mayor had persuaded me that the best policy was to make a short statement emphasizing the positive, preventive steps people could take, such as boiling their drinking water, but I would not take questions from the audience; such a procedure raises more concerns than it can ever entirely satisfy and only inflames the general inclination toward exaggerated fears and rumor.

EVENING

While we were having lunch, a Gypsy boy riding bareback clattered into the courtyard on a huge black horse. He demanded that I be interrupted, and Brod, who is superstitious of these people, came somewhat embarrassed into the dining room as I was in the middle of my meat. He cleared his throat with unusual deliberation from his position slightly behind my chair.

I glanced around in some irritation, which Brod took as his cue to speak. 'A young man to see you, Count,' he intoned.

'Very well,' I replied, turning back to my lunch.

'Please tell him to wait,' Elizabeth said.

But Brod made no movement to go. No doubt he feared the evil eye if he was to return to the kitchen without me.

'He says the situation is very grave, Count,' he muttered apologetically.

'Oh, really!' Elizabeth said, throwing her napkin down on the table and quite startling me with this unusual show of vexation. 'This is too bad! The Count has been up half the night tending to these people . . . is he to have no peace in which to take nourishment and regain his strength?'

I was touched by her concern as much as by this rare flash of spirit on my behalf. If in Elizabeth's puritan view my welfare was worth defending, then she must see the possibility of rehabilitation, however distant that might be.

'Who knows?' I sighed. 'It could be someone's life. I'd better go. My lunch doesn't really weigh heavily in the greater scheme of things.'

I had meant the words honestly enough, and felt a gratifying warmth suffuse me from this experience of goodness. Elizabeth accepted them with a glowing look, but then she tends toward the sentimental view of life. Sometimes it is not until you actually hear yourself speak that you realize that you are only trying on the persona of the person you would like to be. In the mind's echo I heard the falseness of the words, their sanctimony, and despaired of who I am.

The Gypsy boy rode fast, clinging to the mane of the vast black beast to keep his balance on the corners as we sped down the hill to town. He was as fearless as only a twelve-year-old can be. I hardly dared keep up with him, though Sabbath was more than ready to dash pell-mell down the steep slope. The boy took us through the center of town, and the clatter of the horses' hooves on the cobbles rang down the narrow streets as a warning to those ahead to stand aside. Gaping, fearful faces followed our passage in a blur, and then suddenly we were in the open, in the market square, with people scurrying to the safety of the edges of the space and carters whipping up their teams to move their wagons from our way.

I called to the boy to slow the pace, telling him that ten minutes one way or the other would make no difference, thinking to myself that the sight of the count in headlong dash through the town would only inflame the sense of catastrophe which gripped the populace. Already women were gathering their children, and others were hurrying home.

Seeing the disturbance we were creating, I reined in my horse, but the damage was already done. The boy turned and came back for me, urging me on angrily, and would have slapped Sabbath's flank if I had not quickly sidestepped him out of the way. I compromised on a canter – the horses by this time were capable of little more – and we came at last to the outskirts of town and turned to follow the railway tracks to a shack where the boy halted. He dismounted by sliding in a fluid motion down the animal's side and ran straightaway inside to warn those there of my arrival.

It was so dark inside that at first I could hardly see. The smells of close living mingled with the tang of woodsmoke strong enough to make me cough. I knew there were people about me, and gradually my eyes became accustomed to the gloom. A woman, the mother I think, led me toward the bedroom where the child lay. She led me past men who sat silently in the kitchen and regarded me with fear and suspicion as I went by. The child, a boy of perhaps eight, lay in a crudely made bed of discarded boards, and I saw at once that he was slipping away. There was another person there, but in the dim light I could not be sure who she was until she spoke.

'Thank heaven you've come, Count,' she said, and I recognized the measured, precise tones of Theresa's voice.

'What are you doing here?' I asked in some puzzlement, since I could think of no setting that could be further from a convent than this uncivilized and ungodly place.

'I'm doing God's work,' she replied.

'But here, alone?'

I glanced through the doorway toward a man who sat whittling a stick with a knife which seemed inordinately large for such a simple pastime. Theresa smiled placidly.

I leaned forward in order to whisper to her unheard by the others. 'But they're practically savages!'

She seemed delighted. 'Isn't that the point?' she asked, gazing fervently into my eyes.

'Does your mother know where you are?' I asked, feeling a little foolish.

'I no longer answer to her,' she said briskly.

I was surprised to see that she moved among these wild people quite naturally, fetching water from a barrel in the kitchen where the sullen men paid no attention to her coming or going. Even the brute with the knife desisted from his whittling for a moment as she passed by so that no shavings would fall on her dress. But when Theresa tried to uncover the boy to tend to his lower half, the mother put her hand on the blanket and would not let her turn it down.

'Your child is very sick,' I told her. 'I must see him.'

She looked through the open doorway to her man who sat scowling at the kitchen table. He folded his knife and got up; he had to stoop to enter the tiny room. Without any comment he roughly drew the blanket down. The boy lay in a mess of bloody diarrhea. Around his skinny waist was a red cord which held in place a small leather pouch covering his navel.

'What have you been giving him?' I asked the parents.

'Herbs our people use,' the man said eventually. He stood defiant; it looked as though he was ready to fight.

'I will give you something else.'

'He will die anyway,' the father said.

I looked to see the mother's response to this, but she was tearless and resigned, as if dried up by misfortune and the hardness of their lives. In the background, in the other room, I felt the dark, piercing eyes of the boy who had led me here on that wild ride.

'He means they have told the child's fortune,' Theresa told me. I was surprised to see that Theresa also seemed accepting of this fate. 'His future has been told in the cards,' she said.

'Nonsense!' I declared. Even if they were right, it was for the wrong reasons. 'We can't be ruled by superstition,' I insisted. 'We must do everything we can.'

I reached toward the child to feel his abdomen, but the man snatched hold of my wrist and I thought he would strike me.

'No!' he declared fiercely.

'He thinks you're going to break the spell,' Theresa said.

'I'm not going to touch the amulet,' I told him. He was beginning to cause me pain. 'Really, I have no interest in the pouch one way or the other.'

He released my arm warily, but hovered close to my shoulder as I placed the flat of my hand on his child's abdomen and slowly palpated. He groaned weakly whenever I pressed at all firmly. There could be no doubt that his spleen was enlarged, and with a sinking feeling I acknowledged to myself that the tarot cards had told the truth.

Without more ado, Theresa began to clean the boy and to call for clean bedding. I rummaged through Czernin's bag and found a bottle of paregoric.

'This will help stop the runs,' I told them.

The father ignored me, but his wife took the little brown bottle and studied it with the same curious skepticism with which I had regarded the leather pouch.

'Give him a teaspoonful four times a day,' I told her, and she nodded to humor me. Later she would make up her mind on whether to employ my potion along with the others.

'Are you going to bleed him?' Theresa asked. 'They expect it.'

'No.' I thought she looked disappointed. 'He's got precious little blood in him as it is.'

'Dr Czernin bled almost everybody. These people don't think you've really done anything unless a vein's been opened and they see good red blood flow.'

'I don't believe in it,' I said quietly.

The woman had gathered together the soiled bed-clothes.

'You must burn those,' I told her. She turned an exhausted look toward me as if I were mad. For these poor people the thread-bare blankets were things of value. 'I know,' I said, feeling her silent reproach. 'But they're infected.'

This was a new procedure which I had not before insisted upon, but I believe we must be ruthless if we are to survive.

'What are they infected with?' Theresa wanted to know.

'If they can't be burned, then wash them in carbolic,' I said evasively, and busied myself again in Dr Czernin's capacious bag to avoid further inquiries.

DECEMBER 24, 1887

I have had another night with little sleep. Driving the trap down the hill to meet Mary and Helene, I believe I dozed off for a minute, and if it hadn't been for the horses being so familiar with the steep bends in the road, I think I would have come a cropper.

I waited outside Czernin's house longer than usual before Mary eventually emerged. She looked poorly, but something in her manner told me that I was not to comment on her appearance. As was customary, I reached down my hand to help her; usually this gesture is no more than a token of politeness, since she is a vigorous woman. But today Mary leaned heavily, and I more or less had to haul her up to the seat beside me.

'Is Helene not coming with us today?' I asked. I was disturbed by the effort it cost me to inject a casual tone into my question. Such are the ripples by which we sense the undertow to our lives.

I was waiting to jostle the reins to get the horse going, but Mary did not answer, and I turned to see her expression. She seemed on the point of exhaustion.

'Perhaps you should rest today?' I suggested. 'After all, it's Christmas Eve.'

'I'll be fine,' she said. 'Helene's not coming. She wanted to, but I told her it's too dangerous.'

'I'm sure you're right.'

'We should be going.'

'I had brought Christmas presents for you both. And for Theresa.'

'You shouldn't have. You're too kind.'

'Nonsense. You get too little as it is for all that you do.'

Elizabeth had bought tortoiseshell combs for the three ladies and wrapped them in colored paper, but for Helene I had substituted a brooch I had bought for Estelle. It was not of great value, I reasoned, and so there was no need for me to tell Elizabeth of the change. This is how it begins, in these small, hesitant footsteps on ground which seems firm.

'You're right,' I told Mary. 'It's far too dangerous for Helene. She belongs at home.'

And so we set off on our morning rounds. The weather was as bleak as my mood. As I rode through town with the dying woman beside me (what can it be which ails Mary but typhoid?), people turned aside at our approach; women crossed themselves and hurried on, turning when they were at a safe distance to see who was to be visited next by these angels of death.

At noon today the Town Hall was practically empty.

Most of the councilors sent their regrets. Theissen shook hands with his gloves on. I was too fatigued to be angry, but I did cut him off when he appeared about to compound his discourtesy by offering me an explanation. These times allow any irrational behavior to pass as commonplace. The populace has voted with its feet. The people have opted for superstition over science. Though who can blame them, for I have little to offer.

To the dozen or so assembled citizens I gave a lame description of the current situation. The word *typhoid* caused some consternation, and one man at this point got up and left the meeting. The effect is like igniting a trail of gunpowder; in an hour the word will be all over town. Our strategy has backfired entirely. Where Theissen and I had hoped to calm fears with an appeal to reason, we have given them a word stripped of all its practical, medical context, a word to conjure with.

In the afternoon, it began to snow. We will have a white Christmas after all. The world is in need of a clean white covering, a veil to the dreariness and misery of these times. But nothing can obliterate the sharp, rancid stench of typhoid. It haunts me. I cannot escape from it, even when I am alone in the castle library.

Mary vomited in the bedroom of a patient I had been called to see. The family was terrified that we had brought the disease to their home and couldn't get rid of us fast enough. If I had not been there, I think they would have beaten her and thrown her into the street. Hysteria is in the air. People are mistrustful and drawn into themselves. Any social contact is suspect. The fear of contagion feeds upon itself. I noticed many people have placed crosses on their doors along with the other Christmas decorations, and on one occasion I saw a head of garlic, the ancient specific for warding off evil, hanging among the painted pine cones and sugar-plums above the threshold.

Although there were more calls to make I took Mary home. She is a stoical soul who expects little from life, and she protested weakly all the way, even though it was clear she could hardly stand. When I came around to help her down from the trap she began to fall forward into my arms and so I carried her bodily into the house. Helene put her to bed.

I allowed myself to stay long enough only to see Helene open my present.

'But it's not Christmas yet,' she said with an impish smile. She is still part child, an aspect I would call charming were it not so poignant and affecting.

'But isn't there a tradition that you can open one gift on Christmas Eve?' I suggested.

'I don't know,' she said doubtfully.

She glanced toward the room in which Mary had fallen into a deep sleep. Theresa was absent – who knew where – on one of her excursions to bring spiritual comfort to the afflicted.

'Open it,' I urged her. 'Only you and I shall know.'

For a long moment she stared at the brooch in her hand, and then she laughed with pleasure. Impulsively, she thought to kiss me to show her thanks, as if I might be an indulgent uncle, but then thought better of it, and was thrown entirely into confusion.

'You must try it on,' I said.

The brooch was in the shape of a butterfly, with the decoration of its wings picked out in enamel in what I think may have been a Japanese design. I was about to come forward to help her pin it to her dress, but when she unfastened the clasp and I saw the sharp needle which comprised the catch I knew I had come close enough to the flame.

I am filled with noise, as if my emotions were two pieces of music clashing together. I feel a tender pity for the girl who may lose her mother so soon after her father's death, and I would ruthlessly plunder her body. A savage, rhythmic chant jars against the exquisite harmonies of the string quartet, and the result is a jangling cacophony which I can only drown out with work and more work, until I drop with fatigue.

DECEMBER 25, 1887

The church was filled this Christmas Day. The fear was palpable in the fervor of the responses, the crowd roaring back the words almost before Father Gregory's lone voice had come to an end. Many in the congregation held handkerchiefs to their mouths as if the contagion might enter there. Gregory spoke well, in clear and measured tones rather than his usual fire-and-brimstone style. He told us that as a community we must live together and help one another, that together we are stronger than each one of us could ever be alone. But the handkerchiefs, I noted, stayed over mouths, and people left with downcast eyes so that they did not have to greet their neighbor and shake his hand. It is a plague mentality we are living under.

Theissen waylaid me as I was handing Elizabeth into the carriage. His nervous stepping from one foot to the other, and anxious glances in Elizabeth's direction, indicate that he has a problem, and one of a delicate nature. I turned aside with him a short distance.

'Yes?' I asked. I was impatient to resume my work, but he insisted on delaying what he had to say until the person passing has moved well out of earshot.

'There is a difficulty with the funerals, Count.'

'I long ago stopped going to them, I'm afraid. I'd like to pay my last respects, but there are just too many of them.'

'The problem is, we don't have enough graves. The diggers prepare a certain number before the ground freezes, and we've used them all up.'

'All of them?'

'Except for one or two. The word is getting around you can't get a Christian burial in this town.'

I sighed with exasperation. 'Am I to take care of every aspect of the quick and the dead?' I demanded.

The mayor seemed quite crestfallen, and I was reminded to my shame that he had recently lost his only child.

'Look,' I said in a gentler tone. 'These are unusual times. We can only do so much.'

'There is loose talk,' he said evasively.

'What about?'

He seemed embarrassed to repeat the gossip to me. 'People are superstitious. In some parts of town, the old ways live on. Some folk would worry about what would happen to their immortal souls if their bodies weren't buried.'

'Oh, for goodness sake!'

'Count, you and I know it's nothing but superstition. But to other people, it's real. Their souls are in jeopardy. They can deal with the idea of a disease, but more than death itself, they fear becoming the living dead.'

'This is what to do,' I told him after I had thought through the alternatives. 'Issue an order closing the cemetery until further notice. This would be for health reasons. Use my name if you like. At the funeral services, the bodies can be lowered into the graves as usual; but when the family's left, take the coffins out. You must speak to Father Gregory about storing them in the crypt until the spring thaw.'

I am uneasy with the subterfuge. It leaves the truth too easily blundered into. And if the deceit is discovered before the epidemic has burned itself out and tempers cooled, we will be faced with a reaction from the people far more intense than the one we are now trying to avoid. We have decided to buy time. Perhaps, because it is Christmas, we feel Fortune will smile upon us. Preisich is one of those who have died in the last few days.

DECEMBER 27, 1887

Mary is unable to get out of her bed today, though I am sure she would if she could. She is struggling to remain conscious and lapses from time to time into a fitful sleep which does not satisfy. Helene and Theresa care for her, and I left some tincture of opium which will ease her discomfort and quiet her bowels.

Helene accompanied me to the door. 'I can come with you,' she said.

'On my rounds?' I asked, surprised.

'Why not? I did it before.'

'Your mother needs you now,' I told her.

'Theresa will care for her while I'm gone. Besides, I must get out now and then or I shall suffocate!'

'I would not have you exposed to danger.'

'I'm exposed just as much if I stay here. Isn't that so?'

I hadn't the heart to lie to her and nodded reluctantly.

'What difference does it make?' she asked in a challenging tone, seeking to engage me as I climbed into the trap. But I was already whipping up the horse to be off.

DECEMBER 29, 1887

This morning, at first light, there was a banging on my bedroom door. Jacob was there with a note. By now I am so used to this kind of interruption of my sleep that I rise like an automaton, pull on clothes, gather Czernin's bag, and hardly know what I am doing until I am sitting huddled in a blanket in the trap. But this time Jacob was not waking me to drive me to yet another case in extremis. I did not rise like an automaton, since I had been lying awake on my bed for several hours. And I knew that the note would be from Inspector Kraus summoning me to another murder scene.

I waited patiently, pretending to listen to the directions the constable was giving to the place where I knew Kraus was waiting for me. Jacob made as if to follow me to the trap, since he would usually drive me on these early calls, but I waved him away. The snow was still fresh from yesterday and the horse followed the ruts at a cautious pace down the hill. I was not afraid. I felt a pervasive calm, as if the tensions of a storm had spent themselves and left me with an exhaustion close to peace.

Yet as I drew near to the place, an area some distance

from the center of town where the houses thinned, I felt a slight, distant pricking in my stomach. A constable was posted to keep away curious bystanders, though there were none. The crime had been committed in a large open area bounded on three sides by houses and vegetable gardens and on the fourth by the railway line; children play there among the few trees and bushes, and it is crisscrossed by paths used by people who walk the railway line as a shortcut into town. There would be plenty of footprints in the snow for Inspector Kraus to study.

I followed one of the paths which wound among clumps of alder and an occasional pine and thickets of blackberry thorns grown almost as tall as a man. I found Kraus alone with the body. When I had first encountered him at the murder scene by the river he had paced back and forth like a caged ferret, restless to be in pursuit of the culprit. Now he stood with his head bowed, still as a monk in prayer. It had begun to snow again, and light, fluffy flakes floated down and settled on his black bowler. He did not hear me or was oblivious. The muffled world had fallen silent and time seemed suspended.

'Bastard!' Kraus said at last. It was more a cry of pain than an expression of anger.

I could think of nothing to say. He staggered toward me. If he had wanted to beat me or pummel my face, I would have let him without raising a hand to protect myself, but it was the comfort of human contact he had need of. He seized hold of my shoulders and shook me as if to wake me to his state of anguish and horror.

'Do you see it?' he demanded. I smelled the vomit on his breath.

I looked far off, over his shoulder. 'Yes,' I lied.

'How could anyone do something like that?'

'I don't know.'

'How?' he beseeched me. There was a catch in his voice, and I knew he was close to tears. 'I've never seen anything like it.'

'Surely . . .'

'Never! Never in twenty years.'

He was starting to regain his composure as the anger and outrage suffused him.

'Look, Count,' he urged me, as if he feared he might be hallucinating.

I did, while he watched my face to see if it would verify his vision. I saw the slash of blood set in snow like a brilliant scarlet gem, the curled fingers, the eyes appealing heavenward just like the saint.

'I tidied up her clothes before you arrived. For the sake of decency.' A small, hysterical guffaw, like a cough, escaped him. 'It wasn't the most professional thing to do, I admit, but I just couldn't leave her like that.' He waved in the general direction of the snow, the open heath. 'It was obvious he interfered with her – before, after, who knows? – but that isn't the point. That isn't what bothers me. It's the wound. He did it with his teeth. Can you imagine that? He mauled her like an animal. Imagine! How long does it take a man to tear out a woman's throat?'

I imagined, as he suggested, the stalk at dusk, knocking her to the ground like a lion. It didn't take long at all. In fact, it was all too brief.

'And you say a man did this?' I asked.

'A fiend, more like. She was to enter a convent this next year.'

'Yes, I knew her,' I said. 'Her name was Theresa. She helped me sometimes with the sick.'

JANUARY 1, 1888

There is talk of vampires. Even educated people are quite open in discussing the possibility. The common folk insist that the plague has been sent to punish the community for harboring this monster among us. Only if we can discover him, so this line of thinking goes, and deliver him in the traditional manner, will we be saved from this sickness.

Mary has died without awareness of what has befallen

her daughter. Helene has been taken in by the Theissens, but it has been made clear to me that if I go near her I will be turned over to Inspector Kraus. I have not been permitted to attend the funerals in order that I have no opportunity for contact with her.

Elizabeth and Gregory have taken complete control of my life. They have assigned Jacob to watch me night and day. He carries an immense cavalry pistol which belonged to my brother, and is under strict orders never to leave my side, whatever I may tell him to do. He believes his charge is to protect me from the vampire, and confides in an unguarded moment that he is to shoot me rather than to allow me to fall into his clutches and join the ranks of the undead. Thus has he become the guardian of my soul. This sounds like Gregory's doing.

At night I am locked in the tower. Sometimes this arrangement is presented as a measure for my own protection, but I think it wise of them to segregate me from other people so that I do not spread the contagion. I am the only one to visit the sick. There is no one left to nurse them, and that task falls to me, too. I am immersed in filth. At the end of the day I notice that there is ordure retained beneath my fingernails, but I tear the bread and dip it in the soup they bring me, uncaring as any peasant.

My fate is clear. I am imprisoned, more or less. I must serve the sick night and day until I, too, succumb to the disease. I submit gladly to the ordeal. If God means to take me, I have done my part by placing myself square in the path of his destiny.

15

MARCH 1, 1888

It seems that I shall live after all. Gregory does not know what to do with me. It is rather late to hand me over to the authorities – they would ask too many awkward questions. If I had been arrested earlier, when he had first known, surely Theresa would still be alive? But if I had been locked up, would those whom I have saved from this plague still be alive? These are the terrible questions one becomes enmeshed in once one attempts to discern the hand of God, for he does not leave tracks in the snow. Gregory is much wrapped up in such speculations, especially, if I still know him, in the question of his complicity in Theresa's death. I grieve for him, because I know he suffers deeply for my sin.

I try hard to grieve for him. So little matters now. Perhaps it is fatigue, or the constant closeness to death, which has inured me to life. I scarcely keep myself clean. With a straggly beard and my hair grown long and reaching to my shoulders, my fine clothes stained and turned almost to rags, and a wild, vacant gaze on my face as I prowl through town, I resemble one of those crazed Russian monks who wander the countryside calling on the populace to prepare for the afterlife.

Yesterday a peasant woman lunged at me. I thought Jacob, my bodyguard and soul keeper, would shoot her. He struggled to extricate the huge cavalry pistol from the leather pouch at his side, but it is too heavy to be handled quickly, and before he could do so it became clear that her intention was not to harm me. She fell on her knees and

349

grasping my hand gave thanks for her deliverance from the plague, from the vampire.

'God save you, my lord,' she said, and before I could withdraw it, had placed a reverent kiss upon my filthy fingers. 'Remember me in your prayers, I beg you.'

'Tell me your name,' I said, turning to her.

She averted her face from me, as if the light which shone from my eyes would be so strong as to blind her. If my touch can ward off evil, how much more dangerous is my gaze! 'Anna,' she replied, her head downcast.

'I will remember,' I said and walked on.

Seeing this, a man kneeled and crossed himself as I passed by. Others, though quite distant, doffed their hats. A child, tentative and ready at a moment to flee, touched the edge of my cloak, looking up at me with wondrous eyes. I preferred not to notice them, but it seemed my lack of attention to my material surroundings only increased their inclination to see in me a saintly presence who is responsible for their deliverance.

It is true there have been no deaths for a week. There have been no further visitations from the vampire, although there have been numerous sightings, all preposterous but exciting the imagination of the folk to even greater invention. Soon there will be little more for me to do, since a new doctor will arrive in two weeks. How much easier it is to engage the services of these fellows when they are not needed!

MARCH 7, 1888

The spring thaw is late this year. The ground is frozen still. Yet this morning the sun shone brightly and has given Jacob an excuse to root moodily in the formal garden outside the windows of the library, all the while keeping a surreptitious eye on me. Nature stirs. Spring cannot be far away, and it was in spring only a year ago that I resumed this journal.

I was in a kind of daze I am prone to these days, in which I stare vacantly at some detail — a flaw in a pane of glass, or a knot in the wood of a table, for example. It is not unpleasant; in fact, I find it quite restful.

Elizabeth knocked, although the library door stood open. I did not turn around. I have little curiosity. I said, 'Come in,' and her footsteps came to a stop on the other side of the long refectory table where I sat. I seemed to dream, and it was not until I heard her speak my name that I turned my head to regard her. We have both changed. I have become a disheveled figure who gives every indication that he has no use for the trappings of the material world. But Elizabeth is enlivened. Elizabeth retains her optimism in the face of human nature. Her eyes sparkle with purpose. My soul is to be redeemed, evidently.

Remembering myself, I started to rise. 'I'll fetch you a chair,' I offered.

'No,' she said with an uncertain gesture, and I saw that she carried some papers in her hand. She glanced outside to ensure that Jacob was in attendance.

'He could at least do something useful,' I said. 'Those roses need pruning.'

'During the last few months . . .'

It is so difficult for Elizabeth to lie. Deceit is unnatural to her. Even when she employs euphemisms it is as though she is stroking a cat the wrong way.

'Will we ever wake from this nightmare?' I asked her.

'I have come to you to discuss some items quite specifically.'

'Very well,' I sighed.

'While you have been absorbed in your duties as a doctor, I managed the practical matters of the estate as best I could.'

'That was very enterprising of you.'

'There was nothing else for it.'

'How do we stand?'

'I'll show you the accounts presently. We have a comfortable surplus.'

'You did well.'

'I had good advice.'

'You could get along just as well without me,' I said simply, as a statement of fact.

'There was some correspondence which I could not respond to and which has awaited your recovery. I have it here.'

She placed several letters on the table, and I had the irrational fear that they might be incriminating stories, written from a far-off land beyond the grave, from Stacia, Estelle, Rosa, or Theresa.

'On the advice of Father Gregory, I took the liberty of opening them,' she said apologetically. 'In case there were matters which had to be dealt with immediately.'

'You did the right thing.'

'Here they are, then,' she said.

I thought she would leave me to read them alone, as I was wont to do in this room in happier times. But Elizabeth waited for me to go through the small pile. With little interest, I read an account from an old friend from medical school of his life in the army. I perused a couple of reports from scientific societies I had not kept up with. Reluctantly I scanned the fawning letter from a distant cousin; I had made the mistake of informing him that since I had no issue he stood in line to inherit the estate, though the title will die with me. Ever since, he has pestered me with oblique suggestions that he should pay me a visit. At the bottom of the pile was an envelope in stylish blue addressed to me in a hand I did not recognize. This, I noted, was the article to which Elizabeth was most intent on seeing my reaction.

At first, the names failed to evoke any understanding. The French, which I have spoken since the time I was at my mother's knee, was like a foreign language to me. I read:

My dear Laszlo,

So many years have passed since we picnicked in the Bois de Boulogne! Lothar and I have talked of you often, wondering what has become of you and how you have fared in life's great lottery. I regret that I never had an opportunity to wish you farewell when you were so abruptly summoned home in the event of your brother's heroic sacrifice. My mother and father (now both with God, as I expect you know, and sorely missed by those of us on earth) asked after you many times, but alas I had no news to tell them.

We have been subject to life's triumphs and its disappointments, as, I am sure, have you. We have been blessed in Stephanie, our lovely daughter. She is seventeen years old (Goodness, can it really be that so many years have passed since we talked of poetry and music at my parents' soirees?), and already quite an accomplished young lady! Lothar has been seconded from the Finance Ministry to Budapest, and we are now comfortably settled on Andrassy Avenue, close to the Opera House. Budapest is not Paris, by any stretch of the imagination, but it has a warmth and charm which more than makes up for what it lacks in sophistication. I cannot tell you what a pleasant change it is from the stifling formalities of Vienna, which we have come to find so unutterably stuffy. And the backbiting and gossip! Let me simply say that after Vienna, Budapest at its most boorish seems wholesome and refreshing.

I am sure that you and your wife (forgive me if I presume) must come up to town from time to time. Should you care to call, we would be absolutely delighted to see you. We are at home on Tuesday afternoons, but in Budapest no one seems to pay any attention to that kind of thing, and it might be best simply to let us know a time which would be convenient to you.

> *With warm regards,*
> *Your cousin,*
> *Nichole.*

'Would you care to explain?' Elizabeth asked. After the Estelle affair, she has a right to be suspicious of innocent-appearing letters.

'It's nothing more than what it seems,' I answered.

There is an unspoken understanding between us that there shall be no acknowledgment, that not even the slightest allusion shall be made to my secret activities of the last year. This injunction plays some part in Elizabeth's moral economy which I cannot fathom, but I am bound to respect it. In so much my sensibilities have become coarsened, but for some reason I remain exquisitely attuned to the slightest distress I may cause her. Does that not imply some capacity to cherish her, if not love her? I wish I could have loved Elizabeth. But even as I write the words, I know them to be a lie. I am what I am.

'Nichole is a cousin on my mother's side,' I explained. 'When I was studying in Paris I often went to her parents' home. She married Lothar. He's an Austrian who was something at the embassy in Paris. Filthy rich. His family made uniforms for the army.'

'Only, you've never talked about them before.'

'But I've certainly mentioned them, I think.'

'Not as if they were great friends.'

'It's a long time ago.'

'And now, out of the blue . . .'

'You've read the letter. Lothar was sent to Budapest. They probably don't know anyone. It put them in mind of getting in touch.'

'Don't you think it's odd, after all this time? It's not as if we live at the end of the world. We're not beyond reach. If they'd wanted to find out how you were, they could have written any time they wanted.'

'I suppose.'

'Don't you think?'

'All right, it's a bit odd. But not really.'

'We should respond, though,' she suggested. There was a firmness of purpose which I have encountered in her before only around matters of religion.

'By all means.' I picked up a pen without thinking and found I was waiting for further instructions. I had not been aware of the extent to which Elizabeth now rules in our household.

'Don't you think it would be a good idea to go to Budapest?' she asked.

'Yes.' I shrugged, puzzled by the direction she seemed to be taking. 'But what for?'

'Because we need a change. A complete change.'

I wondered if this was part of some plot which she and Gregory had cooked up. Was I to be done away with in the anonymity of the city? Would she have me put on board a boat waiting at the Danube quays, give me my passport and a money belt, and tell me never to return to Hungary? In her position, I would have chosen one of those options. And so, I knew, would Gregory. But there was a pleading look in Elizabeth's eyes. It seems there is no atrocity I am capable of committing which can cause this woman to give up on me.

'We certainly can't go on as we have been,' I said. I meant this in reference to the physical arrangements of my house arrest, but she took my words as an acknowledgment of the need for moral change.

And so I have written a careful reply to Nichole: We shall be visiting Budapest in a week; would two o'clock on Wednesday be a good time to call, or failing that, Thursday?

We shall be staying at the Bristol, on the Danube Corso, an extravagance suggested by Elizabeth.

MARCH 13, 1888

The new doctor assumes his duties tomorrow, just as we leave for Budapest. Until that time, I continue to tend the sick, but increasingly I am hampered as I make my calls by people, many who have previously been known to me as sensible men and women, who insist on touching me or kissing my hand. Just as the evil which has befallen the town has been personified in the shape of the vampire, so the balancing force of good has been made to assume form in the person of myself. This frenzy of superstition reaches its height just at the time when the real danger is waning. No one feels safe unless he has performed the ritual of touching this holy person. The sight of a respectable citizen falling to his knees before me infuriates Gregory. I find it merely a nuisance. Left to its own devices, the epidemic will burn itself out; the only danger now remaining is the risk of contracting the infection from my fingers. I refuse to believe that God has a sense of humor, however wry. I do suspect Jacob of selling squares of cloth purportedly cut from my clothes.

I had been to the police station to see if Inspector Kraus was making any progress, but the sergeant told me that he has been transferred back to Kolozsvar for 'lack of results'. I was disappointed: Not that I missed him personally, but murder is a lonely business, and I felt the need to rehash Theresa's death with the only person in the world who is in a position to talk about it in a knowledgeable way.

I was on my way across the market square in front of the police station, with Jacob in attendance of course, when a woman stopped me. I have developed the patience of a cow for these episodes; I stand stock still as if I am being milked of my benignity, giving up my body to their tender touches, and wait until they are finished with me. I was in this attitude when I noticed a fellow lounging against one of the railings where horses are tethered. He was looking in my direction, and I thought there was something strangely familiar about him. He was a small man, dressed carelessly with a flashy, disreputable air about him and wearing a stovepipe hat. I took him for a huckster, or a salesman of patent medicines, or some such.

When he saw me looking at him he jerked his head, summoning me in the most impertinent way. It gave me pause, someone of his station attempting such familiarity with me, and I wondered at the depths to which I had let myself fall. I looked away. I was about to move on, and I happened to glance again in his direction. He had taken off his hat, as if to adjust the brim, and I could hardly believe my eyes.

'Wait here,' I told Jacob. 'I must have some words with that fellow over there.' The distance could not have been more than thirty yards, but it was farther than I have been separated from my minder in a month, and I was relieved when Jacob stayed where he was.

The fellow had turned his back on us and was staring into the depths of the horse trough as I approached, so that I did not get a chance to confirm my first impression until Colonel Rado turned to face me at the moment I came up to him.

'Change of plan,' he said tersely. There was no grin of complicity or invitation to admire his disguise. 'The date's been moved up.'

'The Crown Prince's visit,' I muttered stupidly. I hadn't thought about it in weeks.

'Of course,' he snapped. 'Pull yourself together, man.' He looked me up and down as if he were inspecting a soldier on parade and didn't like what he saw. A look of pain and distaste crossed his face. 'What in God's name has happened to you? You look like you've been through a nervous breakdown.'

'There's been an epidemic here.'

'Don't go funny on me, Laszlo,' he said, gripping my arm urgently. 'Because if you do . . .' Jacob must have moved, because I saw Rado glance over my shoulder, and his manner changed. 'Look, we're counting on you, old chap. Absolutely counting on you.'

'Don't worry, I won't let you down,' I said. A man with no future can promise anything.

'It's set for the second week of April,' Rado said hurriedly, and before I could say anything, he was gone.

AFTERNOON, MARCH 14, 1888

The Bristol is rather grand in a modern kind of way. The entrance lobby is large enough to serve as a main railway terminus. Elegant items of furniture are arranged tastefully here and there, and potted palms line the red carpet which leads to the grandiose staircase which no one uses. Everyone, of course, takes the elevator, which is manned by a youth in white gloves and a pillbox cap perched jauntily on the side of his head.

'I think we've let ourselves get dowdy,' Elizabeth said, throwing open the French windows of our room.

I joined her on the balcony. A cold wind blew and we shivered, Brod having taken our coats when we arrived. Instinctively we huddled together. Elizabeth swayed, as if blown by the wind, almost touching me, and I wondered what was going through her mind as she allowed herself to come into such closeness with a husband whom she knew had recently killed a girl. She turned to me a quick, shy smile, and on an impulse I placed my arm about her shoulders and felt her more than ready to mold her body to mine, safely, companionably side by side.

I believe she intends to save me by a species of seduction, if necessary to sacrifice her life for my sake, like a heroine who extinguishes a person on fire by throwing herself upon him and clutching him to her in a desperate, daring embrace. I am touched by her naïveté as much as by her love.

Below us barques lined the Danube quays and the river slid by brown and swollen with the melting snows. It hardly seemed to move save for an occasional eddy which broke its oily surface, and yet it seemed like a great animal, powerful and irresistible, tended by boat-beetles and stevedores who plied the quays like ants.

'We must get ready,' Elizabeth said.

'It's early yet,' I replied.

'It's after one o'clock. I must have Dorothy do my hair.'

'They'll consider us gauche if we arrive on time,' I called to her as she stepped back into the room, and I saw her hesitate, feeling herself to be on unfamiliar social ground.

I lingered on the balcony, savoring the half-pleasant coolness of the wind on those places on my neck and cheeks where the long straggling locks have been cut back and the beard shaved. I have been made over. The change gives me a feeling of compactness, of a return to the essential elements of myself. The lethargy has left me. I feel myself condensing, concentrating.

The expansive vista from the hotel balcony across the Danube to the hill of Buda and the mountains beyond fills me with a sense of promise, and yet I know that I can come alive only at the risk of advancing my inevitable arrest or murder. Now is the time to turn back, before the blood lust narrows my focus to the point that human sensibilities, considerations of mercy or decency, can no longer sway me.

EVENING

We have engaged a carriage for a week, and this we took the short distance up Andrassy Avenue to the address Nichole had given us. Brod traveled with us on this call, which would have seemed a bit odd to an outsider, but his presence is necessary, I suppose, in case I decide to make a bolt for it. So much for the passport and the money belt; clearly the plan calls for me to be rehabilitated, and Brod is along to ensure that I jump through the required hoops.

The von Picks live in a new apartment building which is indeed near the Opera as Nichole wrote. It is a desirable address, as I would have expected from someone of Lothar's means, but when we got there, the porter directed us to one of the apartments high up in the building and at the back, so that its windows looked down upon an inner courtyard. The maid who greeted us at the door was polite enough, but clearly she was a girl just up from the country and not yet versed in the ways of the city. Evidently, they had not brought their staff with them from Vienna, which struck me as strange. These signs suggested to me that Nichole and Lothar have come down in the world since we were last together.

The maid showed us to a sitting room where a middle-aged and a younger lady sat. Nichole rose at once to greet Elizabeth. Nothing shows the passage of time so objectively as coming face-to-face, two decades on, with the girl one once loved. Life had drained the sap from her. She had kept her slender shape but she had lost her color and luster. Her hair did not shine and was streaked from the temples with gray. The palate of her face was so muted that she seemed almost colorless. Her lips were thin and drawn tight in her smile of welcome, and in repose there were lines which dropped from each corner of her mouth, so that one was aware of effort expended, the necessity of fortitude, the need to struggle for simple things and to endure in the hope that the future would bring something better.

Only her eyes retained their lively attraction, and when she later turned them on me in a gesture I well recognized – her head tilted to one side, her chin slightly uplifted, a hand arrested by a sudden thought halfway to her lips, one finger extended – I remembered that old frisson she had been able to evoke in me at will, though she no longer had the animal power to make me feel it.

Nichole finished exchanging pleasantries with Elizabeth and turned to me. We stared at one another, our eyes moving anxiously across each other's face, searching for landmarks on which to fasten, some telling feature which would unlock the sense of familiarity. We were like sleepers waking from memory as if it were a dream, finally reconciling to the reality of the present.

'Why, you've hardly changed a bit,' I plunged in gallantly. There are protocols for all occasions; they must serve when the truth proves too insubstantial to be confined by words.

'But you've grown quite distinguished,' she said. 'The life of a country squire must suit you.'

'Well, it's a quiet existence. Some might find life in that drafty old castle a bit dull. The world can pass one by.'

'Nonsense. It was charming. And if it lacked some modern conveniences, that only contributed to its Gothic appeal. That kind of thing is so fashionable now. Some people go to great trouble, not to mention expense, to put up country houses which look like medieval piles. And here you are with the real thing!'

The young lady who stood behind her shoulder was growing restive at not being immediately introduced.

'Mama!' she whispered.

Nichole reached back instinctively to find her daughter and place an arm around her shoulder, bringing her both forward and protectively closer to her.

'And this is our treasure – Stephanie.'

Stephanie was most proper. 'I am so pleased to make your acquaintance, Countess,' she told Elizabeth. I thought I detected a touch of awe in her tone, as though she had not yet been exposed much to society and was still impressed with titles.

'Enchanté,' I told her, kissing her hand half-playfully in the gesture of a courtier. I was rewarded for my tease with a blush, a color which much becomes her, and the momentary disarray of her poise during which I had the illusion of staring directly into her private thoughts.

She is utterly, self-consciously graceful as only a seventeen-year-old can be, and holds her head, precariously it seems, upon her long stemlike neck. She reminds me of one of those maidens from the time of Louis XVI whose paintings hang in the Louvre, a *Young Lady with Mandolin* by Watteau, perhaps. The resemblance to Nichole at that age is uncanny. I was immediately transported back to that summer before my mother died when Nichole, she could have been no more than a couple of years younger than Stephanie is now, came to visit us.

I had lost the gist of the conversation. Elizabeth was discussing with the ladies the current passion for plaid – tartan shawls, tartan ribbons in the hair, tartan dresses, tam-o'-shanter hats – the style derives from Queen Victoria's love of the Scottish Highlands. Apparently the stuff is now the height of fashion. Stephanie was wearing a scarlet plaid bodice to her dress which Elizabeth much admired. I have never known her to be so talkative.

'The material is quite unobtainable in Budapest,' Nichole was saying.

They discussed drapers in Vienna and dressmakers on the Elizabeth Circle who could be counted upon to give one's clothes some flair.

'But we must introduce you to people,' Elizabeth told Stephanie. I was wondering whom she still knew in Budapest society, but she surprised me by naming several families of prominence. 'Before I married, I used to come here all the time for dances and assemblies,' she said. I had forgotten how well connected Elizabeth had been.

'Oh, would you?' Nichole asked.

'Of course.'

'I would be so grateful, for Stephanie's sake. If we could just start her off by effecting introductions to the right people.'

'We shall make some calls tomorrow. How about that?' Elizabeth asked Stephanie, patting her on the arm.

Nichole looked immensely relieved, as if she had accomplished in this short time her main purpose for our visit. 'After spending all our married life in Vienna,' she said, 'Lothar and I are acquainted with members of Hungarian society who are active in government affairs. But they return to Hungary only to hunt on their estates, and so spend little time in Budapest. And then one spends years cultivating friendships only to have politics spring us apart. I have dear friends to whom I can no longer speak because they are on the wrong side of some political divide.'

'We don't go in for politics much,' I said hopefully, trying to join the conversation.

'But who can avoid them these days?' Nichole asked.

The maid came in with a tray of tea things, but I thought I had heard a male voice question her briefly in the hallway before she entered. Nichole paid no attention and busied herself with ensuring that everyone received tea according to their taste, but I thought Stephanie's manner changed subtly, so that she became more formal and alert.

How like Lothar to wait a moment on the threshold to observe the gathering before making his entrance known.

'My dear fellow!' he exclaimed when I caught sight of him. Before I had a chance to introduce him to Elizabeth he had a hand on my shoulder and was pumping my hand. He was most gracious with her, allowing his eyes to linger on hers with an extra warmth which was close to seductive. He has lost nothing of his charm.

Lothar has gained weight, which gives his contours a more comfortable and rounded look, though he is not by any means stout. His hair has receded to the crown of his head and he wears it oiled and brushed flat back, so that in profile he resembles a dolphin: irrepressibly cheerful and sleek.

'What are you drinking?' he demanded.

'Tea,' I told him.

'Nonsense!' he said, making a face. 'How about some whiskey?'

'Bit early for me,' I called after him as he made his way through an arch to a sideboard in the dining room. He still had about him the old swagger, I noted.

'Come on, be a sport,' he said, waving a glass of amber fluid in my direction. 'It's the only part of this Scottish fad I can endure. Elizabeth, tell him it's all right to celebrate this reunion of old friends.'

Elizabeth, to my surprise, laughed aloud as if they

were already her friends, and I marveled again at Lothar's uncanny ability to discern how things stood between people.

'I'd be the last person to stand in the way,' she said gaily.

And Nichole, to show that she wore the pants in her household, too, added with just a touch of severity, 'Lothar, I do think that if you're not going to join us for tea, you should take your whiskey to the library. Besides, we have things to discuss.'

Elizabeth smiled her approval and gave me a small wave. Her diagnosis of my condition is that I am too absorbed in myself. I must be brought out. I am to engage socially. Is it her intention that Lothar be part of this program of rehabilitation? It is hard to imagine anyone less suited to the role, unless he has undergone a religious conversion, which by the look of him, guzzling whiskey while he winks slyly at me, I very much doubt. If we are to make a tour of the Underworld, or the outskirts of Hell, Lothar would be a capital companion, since he already knows his way around.

'Since we last talked, it's been downhill for me,' he confided immediately.

'I'm sorry to hear that,' I said, glancing involuntarily at his glass.

'No, not the booze,' he corrected me. 'Sins of the flesh. Horseflesh, to be precise.'

I must have looked confused, because I had assumed that if Lothar had run into difficulties in his life it would have been on account of his tastes in women.

'That, too,' he said. 'But it's gambling that's been my downfall.'

'Apart from the stock market, I didn't think of you as much of a plunger.'

'That was where it began – do you remember? – with the tip from Nichole's father. He lost his shirt, and I made a whole lot of money. And I didn't even need it. Occidental Traders,' he sighed nostalgically.

364

'You were very generous with your gains, I remember.'

'And you spent it all on Stacia!'

I glanced uneasily toward the door, swallowed, and did my best to smile boldly.

Lothar tapped a finger to his lips. 'Your secret's safe with me,' he said, with the most untrustworthy smirk upon his face. He reached out and gripped my knee familiarly, as if we had been parted no more than a couple of weeks (and indeed, it seemed so). 'But you know how I can't help ragging you, old man. You're so damnably earnest, you're an irresistible target!'

'I'm pleased I amuse you,' I said in a show of good humor.

'Oh, Lord! You haven't changed a bit!'

He found this very amusing, and while he laughed, I considered what a simple matter it would be, his head thrown back so conveniently, to sever his larynx from his trachea. Lothar must have felt my eyes upon him in this vulnerable state, for he stopped laughing and appraised my face in a rare moment of seriousness. Who knows what he was looking for – signs of wisdom which the passage of time may have brought to me? If he thought in such terms, it was only to the extent that wisdom might make it harder for him to manipulate me. Lothar looks at a face in the same businesslike way a locksmith approaches a keyhole.

'You heard about my old man?' he asked.

'I don't think I did. I've been a bit out of touch with things.'

'There was a scandal. It was all totally unfair, but Father took it quite badly. Price gouging on the uniforms, profiteering from our gallant soldiers, et cetera, et cetera – the usual things one has to put up with when you have a government contract. But one of our competitors managed to whisper in the ear of the minister. Then a story was planted in one of the Vienna newspapers. It was a put-up job, but there had to be a Commission of Inquiry. We managed to reach several members of the panel, and they were more than happy to accept money from us, but apparently we didn't pay them enough. Anyway, the contract was taken away and given to someone else. Our whole enterprise was geared to making military uniforms. It's not the kind of situation where you can turn around your factory and get your workers making something completely different. Father went bankrupt in short order. The shock killed him, I'd say.'

'I'm terribly sorry,' I muttered.

Lothar looked at me with curiosity. 'Yes,' he said, as if to verify what I had just said.

'It must have been totally devastating.'

'Well, it was tricky, I'll admit,' he said. 'Of course, I had stayed at arm's length from the business – in fact, I'd never had anything to do it. All the same, I noticed a certain chilliness about me in the circles I moved in. You know the sort of thing – one fellow nudging another fellow, looks in one's direction when one comes into a room. Not a comfortable situation. But I decided I was simply going to ride it out. Nichole had a far more difficult time of it: She was actually snubbed by people she'd talked to only the week before. But then women are so much nastier than we men, don't you think?'

'On the whole, I'm not sure I'd agree.'

'Ever the gentleman, Laszlo! But I have the scars to prove it. Then there was the financial side,' he went on before I had a chance to ask him what he meant. 'Fortunately, I had money of my own. Then I'd been able to spirit some funds out of the company just before it went bust.'

I opened my mouth to say something and then thought better of it. Lothar delighted in making me appear naive.

'I know,' he conceded with a wave of his hand. 'It's not entirely sporting to pull money out of a business and then declare bankruptcy. But legally, it's a gray area.'

'You seem to have landed on your feet, though. Nichole said in her letter that you were with the Finance Ministry.'

'More or less,' he said vaguely. 'I had to leave the diplomatic service. The whole direction of foreign policy changed. A hundred-and-eighty-degree turnaround. The French, who had previously been our friends, now became our enemies, and the Germans, only a few years after they defeated us at Sadowa, became our bosom friends. It wasn't the best of circumstances to be married to a French wife. Not an attribute likely to advance one's career unless one fancied a posting to Sarawak. There . . . what was I telling you about backing the wrong horse!'

I was rather shocked by his lack of loyalty to Nichole, but I should have remembered that such candor was part of his nature. He saw no reason to bother with deception, nor did he seem to suffer from his indiscretions, since he had discovered that people find it difficult to believe that a person is both truthful and amoral.

'But I've been talking my head off,' he said. 'And I haven't heard a word about you. How has life treated you? I want to hear about all the mischief you've been up to.'

'There really isn't much to tell,' I replied.

'Come now,' he said with a knowing look. 'You can't really expect me to believe that!'

MARCH 15, 1888

Elizabeth talked excitedly about her plans all the way back to the hotel. She is quite taken with Nichole and Stephanie, and this afternoon they accompanied her as she made her calls on aunts, cousins, and old school friends, so that they could become acquainted with Budapest society.

There is a confidence and forcefulness about Elizabeth which makes me realize how much she has suffered from the isolation of our life at the castle. I see now that she might have been a different person altogether.

'They're totally delightful,' Elizabeth said. 'At first I thought Nichole was a bit of a snob, but now I see that she's just anxious to give Stephanie a start.'

'Some people may find her vain, but she has a good heart,' I said, although in truth I was surprised that Elizabeth and Nichole had hit it off.

We were dining in the restaurant of the Bristol. I had thought that the place would be rather frightful and gaudy, the kind of place men bring young mistresses in order to impress them with the pomp and lines of attentive minions, but the atmosphere was hushed and decorous. We dined by candlelight at a table overlooking the Danube, the crisp white of the tablecloth and the glint of silverware contrasting with the dark gap of the river between its embankments. On the other side, the lights of Buda twinkled cheerfully.

'Stephanie needs to meet as many people as possible as soon as possible,' Elizabeth said decidedly. 'All she needs is an entrée, and she'll do the rest.'

'I can't see what the rush is all about,' I replied. 'She's rather young, surely, for Nichole to be already thinking of marrying her off?'

'The girl is almost eighteen years old. It's never too early for a mother to start looking for a husband.'

'What if she finds someone right off?'

'If they're not ready to marry, they'll have a long engagement. Look at the Crown Princess. When she and Rudolph became engaged she wasn't yet a woman. They had to postpone the marriage ceremony twice until she began her womanly functions. Not that that would pose a problem for Stephanie, I'm sure.'

As she talked about this relative or that who might be helpful to Stephanie, I wondered by what ruses and stratagems Elizabeth had brought about her union with my brother, George, in the interests of her dynastic ambitions.

'And are you and Lothar still the friends you used to be?' she asked.

'It's uncanny. I feel like I saw him only yesterday. We've picked up just where we left off.' The truth of this statement gave me some misgivings.

'Then wouldn't it be nice to see more of them?'

'By all means.'

'You won't mind that I've invited them to stay at the castle for a few weeks?'

I felt a shudder run through me at the thought of Stephanie coming to my lair.

'Do we know them well enough for that?' I protested. If I resisted this visit but found my objections overruled by Elizabeth, I could claim that I had tried sincerely to stave off the inevitable. It was a justification only a lawyer could take seriously.

'Well, you know them pretty well, don't you? Don't you think they're nice people?'

'Of course they are.'

'Besides, what better way for us to get to know each other?'

'I was just thinking, they're city folk. I'm not sure what we'd do with them for all that time. Don't you think they'd be bored?'

'Nichole didn't think so. She was most keen to come. She talked on and on about her visit when she was a girl.'

'So, it's a fait accompli. You might at least have asked me first.'

'I was put in a difficult position. Nichole was hinting around that they'd like to visit, and then in the carriage coming back from the last call she more or less asked me outright. What could I do? I felt I could hardly refuse, without being rude.'

'You should have told them we have typhoid. That would have put a damper on Nichole's enthusiasm.'

'The funny thing was that I did. She was asking how you spent your time, and I told her how you'd pitched in and saved the town from the epidemic. She must have forgotten. But by the time they arrive in April, that will all be well behind us.'

'April? Why do they have to come then?'

'Why not? It's springtime. The valley will be very pretty.'

'It's so soon. It seems like an odd time to me. The weather's so uncertain, for one thing.'

'It's the only time Lothar is going to be able to take time away from his work. I think Nichole was quite embarrassed that as a guest she was seeming to set the terms of the visit. Do those dates conflict with some arrangement you've made?'

'No. It's just . . .' I thought of Colonel Rado's madcap scheme. Something about the cold, humorless glint in his eyes made me reluctant to mention it to Elizabeth.

'We can have no secrets from one another, Laszlo,' she said, reaching forward to grip my hand in a most uncharacteristic gesture. I could do nothing but meet her gaze.

'There was a meeting . . .' I suggested feebly.

'The Magyar League?' Elizabeth asked.

I nodded. She let go of my hand and sat back in her chair. I was sorry for the look of pain which mention of the name brought to her face. Gregory would have confirmed that the meetings actually took place, but Elizabeth could be in no doubt that I had used them as a cover for my assignations with Estelle.

'I'm sure the von Picks will understand if you have a prior engagement,' she said. 'If you must go to Budapest, Brod can accompany you.'

MARCH 16, 1888

Brod relishes his task. He will not reveal his enjoyment: that is an essential part of the relish. Instead, he presents an impenetrable, professional mien which reminds me of the white-jacketed male attendants at the Salpêtrière. I do not think he knows why he must not let me out of his sight. It is clear from his manner, however, that he does not think, like Jacob, that he is here to protect me. It is sufficient to Brod that Elizabeth has given him this task. He is fiercely loyal to her. This job is of a different order from her instructions to clean the silver a certain way or to hire a new house maid: Elizabeth has given this to him as a personal undertaking. Occasionally I find his eyes upon me and catch him in a gloating look. 'You may be the master,' he seems to say. 'But I am the minder.'

By a process of trial and error, I have worked out that I can go anywhere in Budapest, as long as Brod accompanies me. His presence drains whatever pleasure I might have had in going about the city. This morning he sat primly in the seat beside the driver, turning from time to time as if to check what vehicles might be following behind us, as if to see that I hadn't jumped out as the carriage slowed at the last corner, but in reality to enjoy the proprietary pleasure of looking at his charge. I loll in my seat, indolently gazing at the bustle about me, affecting not to notice.

Of course, I have thought of giving him the slip, just to teach him a lesson. But such a petty triumph must be set beside the larger picture. For each moment that I demonstrate my docility I accumulate trust in some notional bank account which Brod tallies inside his head. I do not want to fritter this away in dribs and drabs – an hour's freedom here and there – but to spend it all in one splurge at the right, cataclysmic moment. I cannot, as Elizabeth hopes so fervently for me, go back; and I have no intention of living out my life as a prisoner. Perhaps Brod senses this. Twice he has seemed to doze, and I have ignored these opportunities. Once, more temptingly, he appeared absorbed by the contents of a shop window on Vaci Street. He stared in open-mouthed wonder at the radiating geometric display of razors, scissors, nail clippers, and strange-shaped knives of particular but undetermined utility. It would have been a simple matter to merge with the throng on that busy thoroughfare and disappear, but I suspected a trap. Instead, I admired the tiers of soaps and lotions in the adjacent store and, in the window's reflection, soon saw Brod glance quickly in my direction to see if I would take the bait.

Brod is not a man to be trifled with. Although he is ten

years my senior, he is lean and strong, and he suggests in his attitude of grim determination that he cares little for his own welfare. I have no doubt that he is armed. The massive cavalry pistol which Jacob lugged about with him is too unwieldy for the city. I should think that a blackjack is something more in Brod's line, or a stiletto: Something quiet by which he can dispatch me with the minimum of fuss.

Such were my thoughts this morning as I contemplated Brod's narrow back from my seat in the carriage. We crossed the bridge to Buda and wound slowly about the hill toward Rado's house. I saw no reason why guests should muddle the mission he had in mind. Indeed, their presence might well work to our benefit by providing a distraction to the castle servants and curious persons in the town. Nevertheless, I admit I felt somewhat uneasy at having to confess this slight change of plan to the colonel, and found myself rehearsing the arguments as we approached his house.

Brod insisted on accompanying me to the door and reached past me to lift the brass knocker and rap rather more forcefully than was necessary. It was immediately opened by the butler, who recognized me by name.

'The Colonel is not at home,' he announced.

'I see. Perhaps you will make sure that he receives my card and that he understands that I'm calling on a matter of some importance.'

'I'm afraid that's impossible, Count.'

'And why is that?'

'Colonel Rado is hunting in Africa. We don't expect him back before the summer.'

I was stunned. 'But when did he leave?' I asked.

'Over three months ago,' the man told me.

I was about to insist that I had spoken to him only three days ago, but thought better of it.

16

MARCH 29, 1888

I have done something immensely stupid. With only four days before they arrive for their visit, I have been tormented by images of Stephanie. I will kill her, I know it. I desire to take her in my perverted way more than I care about life itself.

It is love, we monsters tell ourselves. We love too ardently, too anciently, too honestly. Too bestially. Love is the last great lie. There is little one can say of a love so consuming, so desirous of becoming one with the beloved, that the lover tears open her neck in order to drink the gushing flow, thick and hot, down to the last quiver of her dying heart.

And what is one left with, once the truth is out? A monster's life is stark. There is one obsession; all other details of daily existence are construed by their relevance to it. Humanity washes so slowly from the fabric of our mind that we scarcely note its passing until it is almost gone. It is that last residuum which troubles us most. The soul does not leave peaceably while the body yet lives. Excesses mark the death throes of the human spirit: maudlin, pity, overwhelming eruptions of moral sensibility, foolhardy acts of heroism.

This is the extent of my stupidity: Late last night, at an hour when resolve is at its weakest, I wrote a confession to Inspector Kraus. At least I had the presence of mind to disguise my handwriting. I figured each letter awkwardly with my left hand, and in the end the letter looked as though it had been penned by a peasant.

This morning Jacob accompanied me into town in the trap. He is far less attentive to the task of watching me than Brod because he feels less animus. Consequently he was easily distracted by a passing acquaintance, and I used the moment to take the letter from inside my coat and add it to the others which I dropped into the collection box. I stood, stupefied by my behavior, barely noticing a woman with a baby in one arm who darted in to kiss the hem of my coat.

During the last few days I have considered the exquisite resolve it must take to discharge a pistol into one's brain. How does the suicide pull the trigger? By a forced effort to remain stupid long enough to do the right thing. I am appalled at the boldness with which I have betrayed myself. The betrayer is ashamed that I have made such a weak and irresolute attempt at suicide. Yet I feel relieved. I have placed myself in Kraus's hands. I am no longer master of my fate.

MORNING, MARCH 31, 1888

Kraus has returned from Kolozsvar. He requests an interview. I had thought I would have had more of a breathing space and did not expect him to act so quickly. But of course he would rush back if he thought he could catch the perpetrator of a crime he feels so passionately about. I have set my affairs in order. Elizabeth has already shown she can run the estate. As for this diary, I cannot bring myself to destroy it, although that is without doubt the sensible thing to do. I have found a resting place for it in the library where it will not be disturbed for many years — until, I suspect, the castle is left without a count and everything is dismantled and sold off. So be it.

AFTERNOON

Brod accompanied me to the police station. He has become quite officious, and I thought how glad I would feel to be rid of him, even if that meant exchanging him for an underpaid, slovenly prison jailer. I would welcome the lack of personal interest.

Inspector Kraus was brisk and clipped. A professional coolness has replaced the collegiality he had previously enjoyed with me. It did not escape my notice that as he closed the door behind me he indicated to the constable that he was to remain at his station outside the room. He has grown quite pale and appears to have lost weight. I hope that they have not demoted him for his lack of progress in the case; with his widowed sister to care for, I know that his finances are strained enough as it is.

Kraus was visibly nervous and avoided looking at me directly so that he did not have to suffer the embarrassment of meeting my eye. He is strikingly inept when it comes to small talk, and we went though the preliminary comments on the weather, inquiries as to each other's health, and so on, like bad actors reading from a script. I thought he might be trying to give me an opening in which to make a verbal confession. Perhaps he hoped that if he subjected me long enough to his excruciating conversation I would break down out of social necessity, just to change the topic. Oddly enough, I came close to blurting out the truth for this very reason, such is the deeply ingrained strength of good manners.

Instead, I regarded the confession as something of a challenge. It was like hunting with a single-shot musket: a handicap one assumes to make the chase more fair. If I give the forces of justice every chance to stop me, and they fail to do so, have I not fulfilled my side of the social contract? Wriggle as much as I may, I am able to gain precious little comfort from my lies.

All through these preliminaries, the letter had sat within view on the desk among other papers, and both of us had avoided looking at it. Several times, Kraus's fingers, fiddling with a pencil or balancing a piece of red sealing wax on its end, crept unconsciously toward it and drew back. He steeled himself finally, and in a show of nonchalance which was comically at odds with his native style, tossed it in my direction.

'What do you have to say about that?' he asked. I had to grant him, he managed a nice ambiguity between the tone of one colleague soliciting the opinion of another, and the stealthy pressure of a policeman confronting a culprit who stood just beyond his grasp.

'This, I take it, is the reason for your return?'

'Be so kind as to read it.'

'Certainly. Aloud?'

'As you wish.'

I read:

'I cannot stand what I have become. What I will do. Do not hope for a change of heart. I will go on and on killing innocent women until you arrest me. I am a rabid dog which must be shot. That is the only way. You must stop me. Why can't you catch me? You botched the first one-if you had only followed the footprints, they would have led you to me. If you'd done your job, the other two would still be alive! Why can't you catch me? Is my position so elevated that you cannot raise your eyes to see me? They think I am a saint, but I am the epitome of evil.'

It was disconcerting to read the letter in this new context. The words seemed to belong to someone else. I had labored over their physical formation, while the sense of what I had been setting down had flowed impulsively from another part of my mind. I had remembered it as a cry from the heart, pleading for Kraus to stop me, but in reading it aloud I felt more its taunting, derisive tone.

'Well?' he demanded. He looked at me directly for the

first time that morning, and I saw in his eyes the burning hatred he had been hiding from me.

'Most interesting,' I replied.

'Is that all you have to say?' he said disgustedly.

'Most decidedly not. But I wanted you to have first bash at it.'

'I am interested in what you have to say.'

'Very well. Let us start with the obvious: the physical characteristics. The handwriting is clumsy, as if the letter had been written by someone practically illiterate. I think that must be an attempt by the writer either to disguise his own hand or an attempt to mislead the reader as to his educational attainments. The use of 'epitome' gives him away, of course. It's hardly an everyday word, and argues that the letter was written by someone well read.'

'Agreed.'

'I take it we can also agree that the handwriting is that of a man?'

'I wouldn't argue with that.'

'I think we can also conclude – '

'Can we come to the confession itself?' Kraus interrupted with some irritation.

'I think you're jumping the gun when you refer to it as a confession.'

'Then what would you call it?' he exploded. 'A sniveling, self-pitying rag-bag of lies? A self-serving, logic-chopping apology? A justification? Are we now to feel sorry for the unfortunate, misguided fellow because we have not stopped him in time? Will this worm, this piece of filth, claim next that he labors under a delusion? Will he say he has brain fever? Are we now to believe that he is no more capable of controlling his actions than the epileptic who bites the ankle of the stranger who stoops to help him?' He shoved the piece of paper away from him in disgust. 'It reads like the suicide note of a hysterical woman!'

I hadn't realized Kraus was so close to the edge. In attacking his professional vanity, the letter had piqued him in a way I had never foreseen. All the same, he failed to provoke me, if that had been his intention.

'What I meant,' I resumed mildly, when Kraus had regained control of his emotions, but before he had a chance to formulate a suitable apology for his conduct, 'is that we shouldn't jump to the conclusion that this was written by the murderer himself. It could just as well have been written by someone with no knowledge what-soever of who killed the women – someone, for example, who wants to incriminate an innocent person. Alternatively, the writer could be someone who does know who killed them, and – '

'Yes, yes,' Kraus said. I noticed he was grinding his teeth. Clearly my pedantic method, really a caricature of his own, was putting him out of kilter.

'I think it's important, don't you, Inspector, to maintain our stance of scientific objectivity. Especially now, when we're so close to an arrest. Which means we must at all costs consider every possible hypothesis. Anything less would be mere . . . emotionalism.'

'Can we proceed to the substance of the letter?'

'Of course. First, I want you to know that I think it's entirely unfair to blame you for the deaths of the last victims.'

'But which victims?' he burst out plaintively. 'That's the point! Who is the third one?'

'True, we only know of two, Estelle and Theresa. But so many people have passed away in the last three months. We might not have noticed if one of them had died from unnatural causes.'

'Oh, God,' he groaned. I had assumed the thought would already have occurred to him. Part of him really did assume that the murders were his personal responsibility. I even felt a twinge of guilt for poking on that raw nerve.

I pressed on to the most dangerous part of the letter. 'Then there's the last part,' I said. 'It suggests some vague identification, wouldn't you say?'

'I would say so.' Kraus watched me unblinkingly.

'He indicates he's a person of status. That confirms our earlier conclusion that the writer is an educated man.'

'If, indeed, the writer is the murderer,' Kraus reminded me evenly.

He had regained control of the interview and was closing on me in the correct manner, with no sense of hurry. I felt my heart pounding at this critical juncture, and reminded myself that as the hunter approached, the deer's best protection was to remain motionless, to allow his coloring to hide him among his natural surroundings. Above all, I was not to bolt.

'Then there's the part about being a saint,' I said.

'Hmm.'

'Perhaps the most intriguing part of all.'

'"They think I am a saint, but I am the epitome of evil,"' he quoted.

'It could almost be myself!'

'Almost?'

'Except for the last part, "the epitome of evil."'

'Except for that,' he said quickly, with too much hunger.

I shrugged and considered. 'For goodness sake, it could be me!' I chuckled.

'Did you write the letter, Count?'

'No!'

I tossed the word off. How much meaning can one put into the sound of a single syllable? I heard the tolerance of a good sport, the confidence of an unbiased scientist, the ease of a man unburdened by a weighty conscience, the grace of a count.

It was the interview's turning point, like the breaking of a storm and the sudden release of tension from the atmosphere as the rain falls. I saw Kraus's shoulders relax and realized that he had never wanted it to be me.

'This . . . saint thing people attribute to me,' I spoke the word with obvious reluctance. 'For you and I, men of the modern world, it's ridiculous, of course.'

379

'I had to ask,' he said. 'I'm sure you can appreciate, from my position, I wouldn't be doing my duty . . .'

I waved away the clumsy explanation.

'As for saints,' I went on, with a depreciating smile, 'I'm sure there are more plausible examples of the genre than myself.'

'The writer seems given to a certain amount of exaggeration.'

'Exactly.'

'He could be any of a number of husbands or fathers idolized by his family.'

'Social standing, saintliness . . . these things are relative,' I suggested.

All Kraus needed was a little prompting and he was more than happy to search elsewhere for the culprit. Clearly he was uneasy. The matter was far from resolved. But I had got him to the point where his feelings of suspicion toward me were a source of discomfort to him. He is excessively sincere. I wondered if he would later feel ashamed for having, so he thought at the time, insulted me to my face. Already I was disappointed that Inspector Kraus, the criminologist, the man of reason, had allowed himself to be swayed by emotion in defiance of the facts. After all, whom else could the letter point to, if it did not point to me? The thought would eventually occur to Kraus if I gave it time to percolate through his mind. It was far better that it come from him.

This pause in our conversation was an opportune time to go, and yet I lingered, pensively tracing with my finger the design of the leather bossing at the edge of the desktop.

'Well,' I said, rousing myself and rising abruptly, 'I mustn't take up any more of your time.'

'Count, one moment.'

I turned, my hand on the doorknob. 'You have had the same thought as I?' I inquired.

He flashed a smile of complicity and fellowship, then ducked his head to hide it because it would seem unprofessional. He is a gun dog, eager to please; his thinking is as circumscribed by his rationality as a dog is by his dogginess.

'Do you have enemies, Count?'

I made a gesture of resignation. 'That is indeed the thought I had had.'

'That someone might be trying to frame you?'

'I'm afraid so.'

His face took on a look of intense focus and his eyes darted back and forth as he riffled though these new possibilities.

'Is there anyone in particular who might have it in for you?' he demanded.

I considered the matter. The moment was ripe with opportunity. 'No,' I replied, with the minutest hesitation. Kraus's nose all but twitched. 'No, really,' I said, shaking my head, 'no one comes to mind.'

APRIL 2, 1888

I am far more affected that I expected. They arrived today. They are here, within my home.

Elizabeth had the carriage brought out from the back of the stables yesterday, and it was clearly in need of refurbishment.

'It simply won't do!' she said, stamping her foot. This display of temper was most unlike her. I think she is anxious about our measuring up in the eyes of these city folk.

'How can you have let it deteriorate so?' she demanded of Jacob.

He was most put out. The condition of the carriage is really an indication of how reclusive we have become. It was my mother's custom to take a drive in it of an afternoon, but we rarely use it now, finding it too grand. Since his dressing down, Jacob has had a team of servants feverishly cleaning the brass and polishing the woodwork, and it looked magnificent, if a little dated, as it stood in the driveway waiting to take us to the station to meet the von Picks this afternoon. Sabbath, against my better counsel, had been pressed into harness to make a matching pair. He knows himself to be a saddle horse, believing hauling a carriage to be beneath him, and I was nervous he would misbehave.

This winter seems to drag on forever, with tantalizing hints of spring without any real thaw. The sun shone brightly as we drove to the station, but in the shade of the platform it was chilly, and we paced up and down its length to keep warm. The station master came to tell me that the train had been delayed.

'Why don't you wait in the carriage?' I suggested to Elizabeth. 'You can wrap up in one of the blankets, and when they arrive I'll send Brod to let you know.'

She smiled, always grateful when I show thoughtfulness, and had started to turn, when we both realized that if I sent Brod, I would be alone and unguarded. Did it matter for such a brief period of time? Elizabeth hesitated.

'I'll stay with you,' she said. We are both humiliated by the arrangement.

The train was not only late, but for the last two hours of the journey the heating had broken down. Lothar was in a vile mood and permitted himself an observation about Hungarian efficiency in front of the servants. Nichole put a brave face on the situation and greeted us with an animated cheeriness, as though she had become well practiced in rising above adversity. The chill had brought points of color to her cheeks and a sparkle to her eye so that she looked younger and less worn. From the beginning she has worked hard to be a good guest, making a display of affection toward Elizabeth and on the drive to the castle, describing a number of details from her stay more than twenty years previously.

Stephanie remained demure and remote with her hands thrust deep into a fur muff and a large tartan bonnet hiding much of her face in shadow. On the platform, she hung back so that she could look around her; she must think that such curiosity is unladylike, because when Elizabeth turned to her to comment on a cockerel in a wicker cage which Stephanie had stooped to peer into, she nodded dismissively. Myself she ignored completely after a cursory handshake. I am ashamed at the depth of my chagrin.

Nichole's reminiscences have dislodged some of my own. I can hear Stephanie's voice calling to her mother in French; it is so like the sound of the Nichole I loved that I am transported back to that prior visit. In the forefront is the yearning of that boyish, unhappy love; in the background is the dim awareness of my mother's impending death. She was also a prisoner in this castle, nostalgic for France, longing for the trappings of civilization we could not afford, surrounded by superstitious peasant folk whose language she never learned to speak. In the background of my memories is the dry hack of her cough. It was such a constant sound that for long periods of time I hardly noticed it. That is not true. With some effort, I acquired a callousness that let me shut out the sound which would otherwise have driven me mad. Once, I asked her in some irritation if she could not refrain from coughing at the dinner table, and my mother, eyes full of liquid from the effort of coughing, smiling with embarrassment, unable to get out the words of a reply while she tried to suppress another spasm, nodded meekly.

I heard it at night, when the whole castle was wrapped in silence, the muffled, private sound of my beloved mother dying one grain at a time. She carried a linen handkerchief fringed with lace from Rouen which Nichole and her mother had brought her as a gift. At dinner when she coughed, she turned aside, placing the handkerchief daintily before her mouth. Without it ever being discussed, by common consent, whoever was speaking at the time was obliged to continue talking regardless, as if nothing of any importance was happening. Then, when the spasm passed, my mother would make a point of joining the conversation with some brief comment, but just before she did so, before the handkerchief was tucked in its place in her left sleeve, she could not help glancing down to see if there was blood upon it, just as we could not help glancing at her face, as if it were a mirror which allowed us to see what she held in her hands beneath the table. And now, a generation on, here we are again.

Before they came, I had never felt more alive. I no longer bothered with excuses and extenuations. I walked confidently, with the inner swagger of a beast that has come into possession of himself. I was the Minotaur awaiting the maiden's arrival at the entrance to my cave, passing the time in lewd and bloody imaginings. That was anticipation. That was fantasy.

The reality of their presence has shown me that I am a diseased beast. I am arrested before my transformation is complete, before I have achieved full brutishness. I am stuck in this hybrid state and can go no further. The memories of my mother and of the young Nichole test me with their poignancy; their bittersweet sentiments insinuate themselves into my breast to cause alarming symptoms of pity and decency. If I do not master these feelings, they will lame me. Gingerly, I prod myself here and there as one might press upon one's abdomen, suspecting appendicitis: tentatively, with a mixture of curiosity and apprehension, alert to the first sensations of shame or tenderness. I am afraid to poke further into the matter in case I burst the abscess and am flooded with the toxin of fellow-feeling.

This, too, will pass. Even as I write, I know that no amount of sentimentality will stop me.

APRIL 5, 1888

The von Picks have settled in quite smoothly and adapted to our country pace of things. They do not seem bored, except for Stephanie, and I think she feels obliged to

384

demonstrate a certain amount of ennui since otherwise she might not appear entirely sophisticated. After lunch, Stephanie and Nichole went for a drive with Elizabeth and I was left alone with Lothar. Brod had found time to arrange for the billiard room's renovation, and so we took our cigars and coffee there.

'I say!' he said appreciatively when he saw the table. He stooped to read the brass plate of the maker on the side. 'I thought so: It's a Braithwaite. Can't beat the British when it comes to billiard tables.'

I had never paid much attention to it before. 'My grandfather had it shipped over,' I said. 'It was quite an undertaking, before the railway line was extended.'

Lothar rolled a ball so that it bounced off the opposite cushion and watched it critically as it rolled back to him. 'There you are,' he declared. 'Straight as a die.'

We had played in Paris once, and he is as expert as I remember him then. He prowled around the table, cue poised in his hands like a rifle, stooping with a singular intensity of eye and arm that contrasted with the delicate finesse with which he caused the ball to kiss the next so that it seemed to no more than topple into the pocket. And all the time he kept up his talk, as if that part of his mind was freed to run on of its own accord.

'Sooner or later . . .' He paused to prod the ball, and it hit the red and then the black for a cannon. 'You're going to have to level with me and let me in on what you do for fun around here.' He strode around to the other side and sighted along the cue.

'Country squire sorts of things. You know – hunting, fishing.'

With a smooth, deliberate movement of his elbow, Lothar sent the cue ball down the length of the table and watched with his head slightly on one side as it clicked against the red and impelled it cleanly into the corner pocket.

'One sees quite a lot of one's neighbors,' I went on, picking the ball out for him and replacing it on the spot.

'Indeed?' He studied his options, stooping to sight along the of the balls. There were no easy shots. 'Count Aponyi has a shooting estate somewhere around here, doesn't he?' he asked, cuing the ball toward the red again and nudging it so that it seemed to pause on the brink before dropping down.

'Well done!' I said.

'It only looked difficult because I didn't cue the ball hard enough.'

'Nonsense, you make it look so damnably easy. I feel like a bear when I play with you.'

I think he missed his next shot on purpose. 'You remember, then?' he asked.

'Of course. How can I forget such a one-sided game?'

'I'd have given you a return match, except that you left in such a hurry.' He put away the ball I had missed on. 'Under such mysterious circumstances.'

'I thought you knew.'

'About your brother?' He had to reach far across the table, and with an abrupt plunge of his elbow let loose a shot which startled all the balls on the table and sent them spinning and colliding in chaos. 'Oh, yes, I knew about that.' As an afterthought, it seemed, the black fell into a side pocket.

'I should have written. I'm sorry. The castle was in turmoil with George's death. So many responsibilities all at once. And then, when I finally got my feet back on the ground, you know how it is, I felt I'd been remiss. Left it too late to write.'

'It was rather difficult' – Lothar was firing off balls in short order, his phrases punctuated with the smack of balls hitting the backs of the pockets – 'after you left . . . Especially with the business . . . about Stacia.'

'Stacia?'

He stopped and regarded me closely. 'You didn't know?'

'Well, I heard she died. Of course.'

'Murdered, actually.'

386

'A couple of years after I left Paris, I ran into a colleague from the Salpêtrière at a scientific meeting. He mentioned it to me.'

'Mentioned it?'

'He didn't seem to know many of the details.'

'It was quite sticky for a while.'

'But you weren't involved personally, surely?'

'I was the prime suspect,' he said. A sardonic smile played on his lips, but his eyes were hard and assessed every nuance of my face. 'It was quite an experience, I can tell you. And not one I intend to repeat.'

I was becoming more and more uncomfortable with my pretense of ignorance. There was a line which separated what I could admit to knowing from what I must conceal at all cost, but the passage of time had eroded the landmarks of that boundary. 'But why you?' I asked lamely.

'Because you were not available, perhaps?' he suggested.

For a vertiginous moment I felt the earth spin beneath my feet. 'I don't see what I have to do with it,' I huffed.

Lothar had given up on our game and was fiddling the balls about on the table with the tip of his cue, absentmindedly setting up some kind of trick shot.

'We both met her on that one occasion,' I said.

'Correct. Rue de Londres. But wasn't she also your patient at the hospital? Didn't we also see her at the demonstration you took us to?'

'I came across her from time to time. Lots of people did.' I was beginning to feel ridiculous.

'Oh, come on, Laszlo – don't you remember? You were having an affair with her!'

'I wouldn't call it that.'

'We both were.'

The pain of this truth took me unawares, so fresh was it after all these years. 'You should have left her alone,' I said.

'And would Stacia still be alive today if I had? Is that what you're telling me?'

'Probably not. She had hundreds of men. How do I know?'

'The police thought you did, at least. At first, the mysterious Hungarian count that Stacia had boasted of seemed like a figment of her imagination. She was a mental patient, after all. So they focused their attention on me. Most uncomfortable, since I didn't have an alibi for the evening, other than Stacia herself. So I said I'd spent the evening with you. Then a very helpful chap came forward, a colleague of yours from the Salpêtrière, who identified you to the authorities. Things didn't look good for you then, especially since you were nowhere to be found. But I was grateful that you'd taken the heat off me, and I insisted adamantly that you'd spent the evening with me. Messy, though. I had to get the ambassador to vouch for me as a gentleman and a man of honor.'

He seemed to have adjusted the balls to his satisfaction, the red and the black sitting side by side in the middle at one end of the table.

'Aren't you forgetting something?' he asked, seemingly intent on lining up his shot.

He sent the cue ball flashing down the table, splitting the red and black with a crack and sending them thundering into opposite pockets.

'I thought you would have wanted to ask me if I killed Stacia,' he said.

'Why should I?' I managed to laugh as though his suggestion was preposterous. 'The idea never entered my mind.'

'But why didn't the idea enter your mind?' He seemed to find this line of conversation amusing.

'Because you're a gentleman.'

Lothar laughed outright. 'You know I'm no such thing.'

'Because I know you'd never do something like that.'

He shrugged, as if it were not an issue worth pressing. 'That isn't the reason,' he said quietly, with a secret smile. He glanced once, shrewdly, into my eyes.

Then he had moved the conversation on to other things. Lothar is as adept at sideways movement as an eel. Evasion is second nature to him, and within the space of a few minutes the matter seemed to have been buried.

Lothar will not turn me in, but he will exact a price for what he knows.

APRIL 6, 1888

This morning I found Elizabeth in her sitting room writing letters. I have rarely disturbed her there, and I knocked even though the door stood open.

'Do you have a moment?' I asked.

She bade me come in, and I closed the door behind me so that we could talk privately without the servants overhearing.

'I understand that Inspector Kraus, with your permission, has come to the castle to interview the staff?' I asked.

'I hope it's all right?'

'I suppose so.'

'You were out with Lothar when he arrived, and I didn't want to delay him. So I said he could go ahead.'

'I don't think it will do any harm.'

'We have nothing to hide,' Elizabeth said with a fervor which made me nervous.

Did she mean that no one in the castle has anything to fear from the questions the inspector might ask the servants? Or that in my own case the cards must be allowed to fall where they may?

This was not a matter which I wanted Lothar, with his uncanny nose for human aberration, to catch wind of, and so I was anxious to circumvent the inspector before he ran into our guests.

I caught up with Kraus in the library. He had Brod in a chair and was leaning over him in a way which seemed calculated to put pressure on the man. Certainly Brod looked uncomfortable. He is a tall, lanky man and sat unbending and staring straight ahead while the diminutive police officer stood behind him and muttered some last warning in his ear. It occurred to me that I had never before seen Brod in the sitting position, and it must have felt quite unnatural to him, sitting in my chair in my library.

'Please don't let me interrupt,' I said.

Brod would have stood up when he saw me in the room, but Kraus kept a hand on his shoulder.

'Count, you are most gracious. In fact, I was just finishing when you came in.'

'Have you seen everyone you wanted to interview?'

'I believe I have.' He seemed rather pleased with himself. 'That will be all,' he told Brod, who immediately got to his feet and made for the door. 'For now,' the Inspector added, and I thought Brod hesitated momentarily in midstride as if Kraus had jerked an invisible string.

'He's lying,' Kraus announced as soon as Brod had closed the door.

'How so?' I asked.

'Have you noticed how he follows you about everywhere? Constantly watches you?'

'Yes, I suppose he does.'

'But not just accompanying you as you'd expect a servant to do. From time to time I've watched him when you've gone about the town: He sneaks along behind you, almost out of sight. The fellow never takes his eyes off you. You seemed oblivious to the fact, Count, which is the reason I bring it up.'

I was disconcerted to learn that Kraus had taken to shadowing my movements, though I thought it best not to comment on this for now. 'Well, what do you make of it?' I asked, trying to get some fix on the direction in which his mind was tending.

'It's pathological, don't you think, as a doctor? It's pathological the way the man watches you, the intensity of his eyes. I'm surprised you can't feel it on the back of your head. I'm telling you, he gives me the willies.'

'But Jacob follows me about a good deal, too.'

'Yes, I talked to Jacob. He's a simple man. Very much of the old way of thinking. Intensely loyal, in his own way.' Kraus allowed himself a smirk. 'Jacob believes he's protecting you from the vampire.'

'I value Jacob's loyalty,' I said simply.

'Now Brod, he's a different type altogether. He's educated, up to a point.'

'But I don't think "epitome of evil" is really his style.'

'You'd be surprised what servants pick up. You think they're going about their business, you take them for granted, but all the time they're listening to every blessed thing you say. I know, I've interviewed hundreds of them. They know everything that's going on in a house. And they can mimic. You wouldn't want to know how accurate they can be.'

'What does Brod say he's about when he follows me?'

'Refused to answer.'

'That doesn't get us very far.'

'At first he refused to answer. But I used psychology on him. You saw some of it when you came in.'

'And what did you get from him?'

'He thinks you're unbalanced.'

'I see.'

'He thinks you should be locked up.'

I smiled weakly, indulgently. Kraus made a gesture of complicity.

'Remember mad King Ludwig of Bavaria?' he asked. 'How he had a personal physician and a hefty attendant follow him about all the time?'

'I didn't know about the attendant.'

'Well, that's what the problem was. He wasn't there when Ludwig decided to drown himself in the lake and take the doctor with him.'

'But what have I done which would make Brod think I'm mad?' I asked.

'But that's the point, don't you see? It's Brod who's mad. The man is crazed. Just look into his eyes some time. He's a classic case of paranoia. At least, I'd say so. But I'm not a doctor. On the other hand, sometimes when things are so close to you, it's hard to see them. You need someone who can be objective. That's where I come in.'

'And you think it's Brod who's killing these women?'

'First things first. It's the letter that's the key to the case. First we have to find the person who wrote the letter.'

'Brod?' I repeated in a tone in which incredulity and enlightenment were perfectly balanced.

APRIL 7, 1888

Stephanie is not in the least bit demure. She has merely been biding her time. And her coldness to me at the station – and her behavior subsequently in which she has behaved as if I were no more than a piece of furniture in the room – is a ploy the purpose of which is to make me work harder for her attention. I am ashamed to write that the little minx's maneuvers have not been entirely unsuccessful. Nor am I in the least bit vexed to be so manipulated. I rather enjoy her traps and tumble into them knowing full well that I could have avoided the predicament if I had wanted to.

This evening at dinner Stephanie was up to her tricks. We had invited Gregory and some of the local gentry to make something of an occasion of it, and Brod had prevailed on cook to pull out all the stops and spare no expense. Stephanie wore a dress of a pale yellow satin with a polonaise in tulle gathered in a bustle which was much admired by the other women. Nichole leads us to understand it is in the style of Worth of Paris. I know it set off her delicate features and fine coloring. In appearance Stephanie has an angelic delicacy, and yet I see hints now and then of a waywardness which goes beyond mere mischief.

We were talking about trips to Paris, how we all longed to go. Elizabeth was especially keen.

'You must miss it so,' she said, addressing Nichole.

'I do,' Nichole sighed, with a trace perhaps even of bitterness. 'But the demands of Lothar's position are such that I cannot spare the time. The entertaining, the functions we must attend, keep us in Budapest.'

'I should like to go to Paris,' Stephanie said brightly.

'I have cousins on my father's side who live there,' Nichole explained.

'I could stay with them this summer. There's no reason for me to stay in Budapest.'

'Perhaps next year, when you're a year older,' Lothar suggested.

'I'm six months older than Mary Kemendy, and she goes everywhere,' Stephanie said. Her eyes remained on her plate so that we could not see their provocative sparkle.

Most of us, however, were in the dark as to the significance of this name. We looked to one another for clarification.

'And who, pray, is Mary Kemendy?' I asked, the gallant host coming to the rescue in an awkward silence, though in truth I knew I was aiding her in some naughtiness.

'Just someone I went to school with,' Stephanie replied, bestowing on me the flash of a conspirator's smile.

It was left to Lothar or Nichole to dispose of the matter.

'A rather fast young lady,' Lothar said.

'Someone with whom we have absolutely nothing to do,' Nichole assured us.

It was an ill-mixed party which served only to bring home how little we have in common with the von Picks. We knew nothing of the plays they mentioned, and they knew nothing of the local politics which loom so large in country society. Even Gregory, usually so eager for new company and an engaging conversationalist with a wide range of interests, seemed bored, and left with the excuse that he had to say an early mass the next morning. Our neighbors left early, too, on account of the distance they must travel.

Lothar and I took our brandy and cigars in the billiard

room. I am uneasy now to be alone with him, fearing what bargain he will try to foist on me as the price of his silence about Stacia.

'Surely you can tell me now,' I said in a bantering tone.

'What?' Lothar looked a bit startled.

'Who Mary Kemendy is.'

'Mary is an exceedingly voluptuous young lady who has set her heart on becoming the Crown Prince's mistress. Maybe she is already. I've lost track.'

'She's a friend of Stephanie's? How interesting!'

'Not for Stephanie's mama. Nichole is intent on finding a good match for the girl, while Stephanie seems to be doing everything in her power to wreck her marriage prospects. Nothing serious, you understand. Nothing of substance. Just silliness. Minor indiscretions of no real importance. But in these matters appearances count. Nothing actually has to happen for someone's reputation to be ruined. So the slightest breath of scandal sends the mamas into tizzies.'

I couldn't help grinning at the spectacle of Lothar being placed in this position. 'Now you're on the other side of the fence,' I told him. 'The guardian of female virtue.'

I had thought that his cynicism ran so deep that nothing could offend him, but for a moment I thought he might strike me.

'She's my daughter, for God's sake!'

'I apologize,' I said immediately. 'It was not a joking matter.'

'The tricky thing is, Mary's still part of society. She goes with her mama to the same functions we do, and of course she and Stephanie know each other from school.'

'That would pose difficulties. Who knows what ideas she might put in Stephanie's head?'

'The really tricky part is that Mary also knows me.'

'Ah.'

'Not intimately.'

'Why not?' I felt I had him on the run and should get

everything I could from the opportunity. It was the kind of question Lothar would have delighted in posing to me.

'Not my type. Anyway, she was silly about Rudolph.'

'You were part of the royal entourage?' I was impressed that Lothar had made his way so high up the social ladder without being part of the old aristocracy.

'There are two groups around the Prince. There's the official, daytime crowd of stuffed shirts, and then there's the other circle who share his interests in good food, good wine, and fast horses.'

'And fast girls?'

'Physically, he's rather an unprepossessing fellow, but all he has to do is nod in a woman's direction and she's his for the night. They consider it an honor, or an act of patriotism, or God knows what. Afterwards he gives them a silver cigarette case with the royal crest engraved on it.'

'It doesn't sound very chivalrous.'

'That whole circle of cronies and hangers-on is a bad lot.'

'But you were part of it.'

'I was the center of it. I was Crony-in-Chief, Keeper of the Royal Bedchamber, and Wager-Maker Extraordinary.'

I found that difficult to square with the comfortable but decidedly modest circumstances in which they lived in Budapest. He must have seen the growing doubt reflected in my face.

'I was the center of it,' he insisted without rancor. 'And now I'm not. You're either in or you're out, and I'm broke, more or less. I mean, we can get by – we're not at poverty's door. We can pay the servants' wages and the dressmaker's bill. But relatively speaking, we're broke, and to stay in Rudolph's circle you have to have the funds to keep up.'

'But you had millions, didn't you?' I remembered the splendid carriage and equipage in Paris and wondered how much of Lothar's aura of wealth had been illusion.

'Oh, yes. Millions. Indeed I did.'

'You ran through the whole lot?'

'Pretty much. Not all on my own, though. I had a little help from my friends. I lent them money. It made me very popular. I was soon known as a devil of a fellow. Always ready to help a chap out in a pinch. I found a quick way to advance socially was to lose a bet to the right man. It was better than making a loan, because when you lend money the person has this uneasy thought at the back of his mind that someday you might become terribly vulgar and actually ask him for the money back. Soon I was losing bets to the Crown Prince on a regular basis. I was a good sport. Eventually, I simply ran out of money. And I've precious little to show for it. I never made much use of the influence my position gave me. You know how connections work – a word in the right quarters can move mountains. When I really needed that clout I didn't have it anymore.'

AFTERNOON, APRIL 9, 1888

They have been here a week and we are running out of things to show them. They are polite and attentive. I cannot help wondering, Why? For how long has Lothar cultivated an interest in winter crop feeds? How many new variations on the traditional dress of our peasants can Nichole point out before she loses her enthusiasm for this form of couture? Stephanie, at least, is true to her feelings and makes no pretense of her boredom. Jacob has found her an old fur rug and she curls up in the corner of the carriage, by turns dozing, sulking, and then, when I think she has withdrawn altogether from the party, I find her eyes upon me. Curled in her rug, she is as inscrutable as a cat. When I meet her gaze, she sighs and affects an expression of ennui with a saintly roll of her eyes.

On our excursion today we came across a Gypsy encampment beside the railway line just past the station.

Since the government has taken steps to discourage their nomadic form of life, we rarely see their wagons parked on the heath outside our town. As usual, these men did not appear to be engaged in earning any manner of livelihood, but instead sat on the steps of their wagons whittling a stick or working on a horse's bridle. Several of them seemed taller than was usual for these people, and walked about the encampment with the bandy legs of men who have spent a lifetime in the saddle.

'A pretty tough-looking bunch,' Lothar commented.

I was puzzled by the fact that there were no women in the encampment. Usually they would be much in evidence tending the cooking pots perched over the fires or drawing water, but perhaps they had gone into town to knock on doors with trinkets and wild herbs to sell.

Stephanie woke up at this point and struggled to free herself from the fur rug. She was all set to descend from the coach to pay them a visit.

'What are you doing?' Nichole demanded in some alarm.

'I'm going to have my fortune read,' Stephanie pronounced.

'You're doing nothing of the kind,' Lothar said.

'Does anyone have a piece of silver?' Stephanie asked, unperturbed.

I suppose in her mind the Gypsies are a free-spirited, romantic people who are given to dancing and fiddling, rather than a gang of rogues whose stock-in-trade is robbery, kidnap, and worse.

'I really don't think it's a very good idea,' I began to say.

'Now don't be such an old fuddy-duddy,' she insisted, and gave me once again a secret look, so that in my confusion I behaved with automatic good manners and before I knew what I was doing, I had jumped to the ground and was handing her down.

Elizabeth leaned over the side of the carriage toward me. 'Laszlo, do you think this wise?' she asked anxiously.

'We'll only be a minute,' I reassured her. 'Jacob will come with us.' He was more than ready, and swung his leather bag down before him. To Nichole and Lothar, I said, 'We'll just step into the camp. I'll be with her at all times.'

Lothar shrugged helplessly, but Nichole looked doubtful. 'You know what she's like,' he said. 'If we forbid it, it just makes it more exciting to her.'

Stephanie was waiting for me to lead her forward into this new adventure, shoulders squared and hands thrust determinedly into her muff. Her eyes upon me glowed.

'The smell alone will be enough to disillusion her,' I said, and Stephanie wrinkled her nose and smiled.

The Gypsies had shown no awareness of our carriage when we had first stopped but had continued unconcerned with their occupations. But when I and then Stephanie alighted, they became alert and I was aware that our approach was carefully watched. As we crossed some invisible boundary point, several of the largest ruffians stood up and ambled toward us. Seeing this, Jacob immediately thrust his hand into the bag to grasp the heavy cavalry pistol. I made a motion to him to desist from this foolishness.

'I'll handle this,' I said, to Stephanie as much as to Jacob, since it seemed that both of them were liable to precipitous action which would put us needlessly in danger.

Three men came and stood before us, arms folded across their chests, barring our way forward, while a fourth lingered to one side. I wondered where the dogs were, the half-wild curs who slink about just out of range of their masters' boots and who are a constant feature of Gypsy encampments. There were none.

'Good day,' I said and told them who I was. My rank meant nothing to them; in fact, their faces made no acknowledgment whatsoever. 'We mean you no harm,' I reassured them needlessly. They were large men with brutalized physiognomies who gave the appearance of utter callousness.

The ruffian in the middle gave way and motioned me through while the two on either side of him held their ground. I glanced back, but the fellow held up his hand to signal that Stephanie and Jacob were to stay put. He pointed me in the direction of one of the caravans where a man whom I took to be their leader sat on the steps whittling on a stick.

I took the opportunity to look about me as I walked toward him. I had been wrong about the odor: The rancid smell of squalor and neglect was absent. There were no bones left to whiten where they had been tossed, nor liquefying pools of sheep entrails, or haphazard spots of children's excrement. There were no children. And the cooking pots were not black but had been polished to a shine and were stacked with military precision.

I should have paid more attention to the small figure sitting on the steps, because it was not until I came up to him and he turned to face me that I recognized who he was.

'What are you doing here, you imbecile?' Colonel Rado hissed, on the verge of losing self-control.

'I'm with friends,' I said lamely, indicating the carriage some distance behind me. 'We happened to be passing.'

'Mother of God!' Rado hacked at the piece of wood he held in his hand and a large chunk flew off the end of what might have been an intricately carved swagger stick. 'Do you think we're a tourist attraction?'

I was recovering slowly from my initial surprise, and I felt decidedly put out by the way he was talking to me. 'I hadn't the slightest idea I'd find you here' – I gestured ironically – 'in these surroundings.'

'And why,' he persisted, his anger unabated, 'do you invite guests at a time like this?'

He glanced automatically to his left and right in case someone should overhear. Arpad waited in attendance, uneasy in the slouch his disguise required of him; parade ground rigidity would have felt more natural while his commanding officer vented his ire.

Colonel Rado went on with heavy deliberation, his voice trembling with the effort of suppressing his rage. 'What can have been in your mind to do such a thing? This is not a game. We are risking our lives to bring about one of the most momentous events in our nation's history.'

'I tried to tell you about that.'

'Indeed. I heard.'

'I think the appearance of a house party is a good disguise.'

'Well, I don't.'

'If you find these arrangements uncongenial, I suggest you seek accommodations for your guest elsewhere.'

I turned on my heel abruptly with the intention of leaving him to stew in his own juice.

'Halt!' he commanded, loud enough that Stephanie and Jacob could not have helped but hear.

Perhaps it was the tone of his voice or, more likely, an awareness that Arpad was moving up swiftly to cut off my withdrawal that made me change my mind. I paused and turned slowly to face him.

'You're in this up to your neck,' he said. He spoke calmly and precisely, with a menace which I found far more threatening than his open anger. 'Do not for a moment believe that you can opt out of this operation. If we fail, you will have been part of a treasonous conspiracy, and they'll execute you along with the rest of us. That alone should bring a focus to your mind sufficient to prevent you from screwing up even your modest assignment, Count. And if that is not sufficient, allow me to remind you that if I have anything less than your full cooperation, I will kill you. I didn't mention that? Ah. Well, it's standard practice in clandestine operations.'

He waited politely while I assimilated this information. There was no boast or bombast in his threat, and I had not the slightest doubt, as I looked into those small, beady eyes, that he would do as he said.

'If you fail me, Count, I will personally take your life.

Is that clear?' he asked, as one might inquire if one's directions to Andrassy Avenue had been understood.

'Perfectly,' I said.

'We will be in touch with you at a time and place of our choosing. Don't come here again. Don't try to communicate with me. Don't do anything out of the ordinary. Just go about your life normally. Do what you would normally do. Is that clear?'

'Yes,' I responded grudgingly.

Colonel Rado was no longer attentive to my presence. He was examining the end of his ruined stick and shaking his head in frustration. I had no cutting retort with which to retrieve my dignity, and the longer I stood speechless before him, the more angry and impotent I felt.

I turned and stalked off, holding my head high for the benefit of those watching out of earshot. Jacob had one hand stuffed deep inside his leather pouch while one of the cavalrymen-Gypsies held him at bay with a hand on his shoulder. He began to struggle as I approached, but I motioned him to desist. Stephanie stood apart behind him with her eyes bulging wide in an irresistible mixture of titillation and fear.

'You were wonderful,' she whispered breathlessly.

I put my arm about her shoulder to shepherd her to safety. Jacob served as the rear guard, defiantly refusing to turn his back on the enemy while he retraced his steps.

'I feel faint,' she said.

Indeed, she sagged against me so that I had to take her beneath her arm in order to support her. We took a few paces in this way, but she seemed to weaken more, and I wondered if she would be able to cover the few yards that remained on her feet.

'Would you permit me to carry you?' I suggested. 'It's easily done, I assure you. And you've had quite a shock to the system.'

'Perhaps if you . . .'

I adjusted my grip as her movement seemed to suggest. Beneath the folds of her coat, my hand pressed against her chest and she allowed herself to be drawn to me.

'I feel stronger now,' she said, and waved to reassure her parents in the carriage that they did not need to come to her.

We made our way toward them slowly, and my fingers stole by imperceptible adjustments to find their places over the gaps between the stays of her corset. Was it my imagination, or did my preternatural fingertips sense, beneath the fabric of her coat and the bodice of her dress, the thrust of her heart?

Lothar had stepped down from the carriage to give Stephanie his arm, and Jacob even put aside the leather pouch so that he would not be encumbered, but in the end she did not need our help and seemed to mount without difficulty. Nichole and Elizabeth fussed over her, but she would have none of it.

'It's only a shock to the system,' she insisted. 'I shall be perfectly all right. Really.'

'That blackguard shook his stick at you!' Lothar said to me when we were once again seated in the carriage. 'The damned cheek of it!'

'And shouted an insult.' Stephanie had quickly recovered her strength and was anxious that no detail of the encounter be overlooked. 'But you turned and faced him down immediately. Did you see? The Gypsy chief flashed a knife, but Laszlo absolutely faced him down.'

'"Flashed a knife"?' Nichole asked. 'Stephanie, wherever did you pick up such a phrase?'

'We saw it all,' Elizabeth said proudly.

'I thought you stood up to him extremely well,' Lothar said quietly, man to man, tapping me on the knee with his cane to emphasize the point. 'It's the kind of jam where social standing does one no good – can even work against one, in fact. These chaps are no respecters of rank.'

Until, too soon, the journey came to an end, Stephanie remained silent, wrapped again within the secure folds of her fur rug. But I felt her presence, like a warm glow, emanating from that dark corner of the carriage, and whenever I happened to glance in that direction, it was to find her unblinking, feline gaze resting on me; nor did her eyes shift at this moment of contact to evade mine, but sought them avidly.

The conversation flitted around us, for the sightseers' brush with the untamed fringe of society had stirred them. But though I joined in their talk from time to time, I was alone with Stephanie in an invisible, secret communion, and I surrendered myself to the sensual sway of the carriage and the delicious flights of fancy that her ardor evokes in me.

When we reached the castle, I was rudely shaken from this reverie. As we rolled around the gravel circle, I groaned inwardly at the sight of Inspector Kraus pacing before the front door. Evidently Brod had retaliated for his grilling in the library last week by refusing to allow Kraus to enter the castle unless his master or mistress is at home.

'There's that fellow who's always hanging around,' Lothar said. 'Who the devil is he, anyway?'

'Just someone from the town,' I replied.

'Behaves like someone who's owed some money,' Lothar said.

Nichole cut him a glance to show that she thought his jest was in poor taste, but in the ensuing awkward silence, it was difficult to let the matter go without at least some cursory explanation which would serve to dampen their curiosity.

Elizabeth and I both began to talk at once.

'He's a policeman,' she said.

'I'm giving him medical advice,' I said.

'You mean, like reconstructing the deceased's last moments from all the gory details?' Stephanie asked excitedly.

I took a deep breath. 'As a matter of fact, yes,' I confessed.

'But wouldn't you have to look at . . . it?' she asked and shuddered deliciously.

'Actually, I can't talk about the case,' I said with understated modesty. '*Sub judice*, that kind of thing.'

'I understand implicitly,' she said, as if, as far as she was concerned, that would be the end of the matter.

When she walked past the inspector to the castle door she gave no more than a curt nod in response to his raised hat, but I already knew her nature well enough to guess at the building pressure of her curiosity, and I knew that there would be some future price to pay for this present self-denial.

I was in the act of following closely on the ladies, but Lothar detained me by the carriage with a cane placed upon my arm.

'Is there something I ought to know?' he murmured.

'I don't think so. You mean the policeman? I'm just helping out. People get the strange notion in their head that because I'm the count I can help them with their business, whatever it is.'

He regarded me skeptically for a moment and then chuckled. 'You're up to something, you devil.'

Elizabeth guided our reluctant guests toward the drawing room and ordered tea while I shepherded Kraus in the opposite direction.

He seemed especially grim and haggard. This investigation is taking a terrible toll on the man's spirit.

'I want you to have complete access to my staff,' I told him, 'but there has to be a limit. They're not sophisticated people, you know. They're not used to this kind of thing. When you ask them a question, they think it's because they're under suspicion. Your interviews are starting to unnerve them. But then again, perhaps that's your intention.'

'I came to see you, Count.'

'This really isn't a very good time, Inspector. As you can see, I have guests I must attend to.'

'It's important. I wouldn't take your time if it wasn't important.'

I sighed impatiently, forbearingly. 'Very well.'

'It's a matter of some delicacy.'

There was something in his manner, persistent yet regretful, which sent a premonitory chill through my body. 'I see,' I said. And I thought, 'Not now. Not yet.'

When we entered the library, I closed the doors carefully behind us and gestured him to a seat.

'I prefer to stand,' he said with unusual formality. He stood stiffly upon his official dignity, and yet he looked utterly forlorn in his shabby coat, with his moist, defeated eyes which would not rise to meet my gaze.

I arranged myself comfortably in one of the thronelike chairs. I was most attentive: The magnanimous host who must leave his guests to fulfill his civic duty. 'What is it that concerns you?' I asked.

'It's a detail,' he said in some embarrassment. I had not thought that he would experience such an intense conflict between his official duty and some private loyalty he felt toward me. Did he then think of me as a patron, friend, or kindred soul within the lonely world he inhabited? Did those feelings slow his progress; did they clog his mind so that it could not flow into certain considerations? Is that what, unknown to him, has crippled his investigation all these months?

He seemed to have difficulty knowing how to proceed. 'One should never overlook the details,' I offered. 'Sometimes it's some insignificant thing which gives one the diagnosis. I should imagine it's the same in criminology.'

In answer, he dug a small object out of his pocket and more or less tossed it onto the library table before me.

'Tell me what you make of that,' he said.

I picked it up and examined it. It was an enameled Japanese brooch in the shape of a butterfly.

'Why, this is the brooch I gave to Helene for a Christmas present.'

'You recognize it?'

'Of course. Where did you get it?'

'Mayor Theissen brought it to me.'

405

'But whatever for?'

'He states that it previously belonged to his daughter, Estelle.'

'I hardly think so.'

'I can only tell you what he has told me.'

'Then the good Mayor must be mistaken.'

'He came to me only with the greatest reluctance. He is constrained by the respect and admiration that he feels for you, yet here is an ornament which belonged to a young woman who was murdered and is now given as a gift to another young woman by yourself.'

'It's hard to evade the conclusion, I know.'

'The Mayor is adamant that an innocent explanation will be forthcoming.'

'Yet clearly his duty lay in presenting you with the evidence. I have no qualms about Theissen's sincerity. None whatsoever.'

'Nor I.' Kraus waited expectantly.

'I find myself in some embarrassment. You know, of course, that the brooch is hardly unique? It didn't come from one of those precious Vaci Street establishments. I bought it in a market in Budapest. There were a hundred of them on the peddler's stall. I must plead guilty of giving Helene a gift which looks expensive but was not.'

'But the enameling is exquisite.'

'It appears so, but if you look here and here you will see the small flaws which are the mark of manufacture – which, however superior, can never match the careful application of the craftsman to his art.' Dismissively, I returned the piece to him, and continued on quickly so that he would be distracted from examining it further. 'It's not beyond the bounds of possibility, I suppose, that Estelle acquired one for herself from that same peddler. Or for that matter, that an admirer bought one for her. But that's speculation.' I paused expectantly, as if to give him a chance to voice an opinion, though with a briskness which implied that I had other business on my mind. 'There was something more tangible I wanted to discuss with you,' I went on.

I could tell that Kraus was unhappy to be leaving the question of the brooch so easily. He wanted to worry at it like a dog with a dead bat, sniffing at it and shaking it in his teeth until he had exhausted all possibility of doubt that life had left it.

'I trust I have your attention?' I asked, somewhat peremptorily, because the inspector had begun to turn the brooch over in his hands and with an intent, puzzled look to inspect it for the flaws of manufacture I had mentioned.

'Of course,' he said. 'Sorry.'

'On your advice, I've been paying more attention to Brod's behavior.'

'Yes?' he asked, instantly distracted and eager to chase off in an entirely new direction.

I had him now, but I took my time. I felt a show of reluctance was in order, to indicate that it was not easy to say what I was about to tell him. My fingers drummed on the tabletop in one last spasm of conflicted loyalty.

'And?' Kraus demanded impatiently.

'His behavior's been damned peculiar. I don't know what to make of it.'

'Tell me.'

'I'm not sure I want to make something of it. I'm not sure I like the way this business is heading.'

'I understand your loyalty to your servant, but I need hardly remind you – '

'Please!'

'I apologize. That was uncalled for.'

'The investigation's put a strain on all of us. And this superstitious nonsense about vampires hasn't helped matters. I would be much in your debt if you could hold off asking further questions at the castle until our guests leave. Is that too much to ask?'

I suppose it was, for he hesitated uncomfortably.

Perhaps he was closer to catching me than I realized. Or closer to catching someone.

'Perhaps,' I went on, 'you'll be better able to consider how to proceed once I tell you what Brod has been doing. Last night I couldn't sleep. I tried to read but couldn't concentrate, and so I put out my light and sat by the window of my room. The sky was clear and a quarter moon gave light. My mind wandered; I may have dozed for a while, but all of a sudden I became aware that a figure was walking across the gravel below me. He was walking stealthily, placing his feet carefully at each step so as to make as little noise as possible. It was difficult to make out who it was.'

'Brod?'

'I can't be sure.'

'Come, Count. You can't protect him forever.'

'It was someone of Brod's general build and size.'

'And how many people in the castle fit that description?'

'I followed him. That is, I caught up with him in town, for by the time I had dressed and got on the road, he was long gone. But I took a shortcut through the fields and along the pathway by the river. So I can't be absolutely sure it was the same man I had spied leaving the castle.'

'What time was this?'

'About two.'

'Who else could it have possibly been at that time of night?'

'But if we are to proceed scientifically, we must be scrupulous in separating observation from opinion.'

Kraus waved away such caviling. He was on the trail of his quarry. 'This is a time for common sense,' he said. 'Not dogma.'

I went on with the charade. 'Anyway, the fellow went quickly through the town as if he knew exactly where he was going, past the station, and along the railway tracks until he came to the heath. There was more cover there, and I was able to get closer to him. He headed straight to the place where Theresa's body was found.'

Kraus grew so restless that I was afraid he would want to arrest Brod there and then. But the point of my story was to arrange a far more convincing demonstration for him.

'When he reached the spot, he got down on his hands and knees. He seemed to be looking for something. I heard him muttering and cursing, so I think he didn't find what he'd come for. I wanted to get closer, but the noise of an animal startled him, and he took off, looking back over his shoulder all the time, so that I didn't think it prudent to follow him.'

'That's all?' he asked impatiently.

'I'm afraid so.'

I must have looked a bit put out. 'No, you've been extraordinary helpful,' he hastened to reassure me. His eyes darted about as he played out in his mind the various possibilities. 'We must search the area where the girl was murdered. Inch by inch.'

'I thought you'd already done that,' I said innocently.

'Of course we have!' he said, scarcely able to conceal his chagrin. If he found a clue there it might crack the case, but he would have to explain to the commissioner why he had missed it earlier. 'We'll redouble our efforts, that's all. If he's looking for something, there's something there to be found.'

'May I make a suggestion?' I asked mildly.

He gave a long-suffering sigh. He had no choice but to humor me. 'Yes,' he said.

'Why not let him find it?'

'What?' He looked fully annoyed, as if I had gone mad and had now become yet another factor weighing down the investigation.

'Whoever he is. Whatever he's lost. Why not let him find it? He knows what he's looking for; we don't. It might be something incriminating, but to our eyes it could appear entirely innocuous.'

He gave a tight, reluctant smile. 'Very ingenious,' he said without warmth, and I knew he deeply resented not having come up with the plan himself. 'You're suggesting we lie in wait for him?'

'Exactly. I could meet you at the spot at, say, midnight?'

'That should be early enough. I'll put some constables into position an hour or two earlier, just in case.'

'One other thing?'

'Yes?' he said somewhat peevishly, thoroughly off-balance now, and safely misdirected from the truth.

'He may be armed.'

'I think I know my job,' Kraus replied stiffly.

'I have every confidence.'

'Very well, then. Midnight.' He got up and started to make his way toward the door, but was stopped by a sudden thought. 'He wasn't carrying anything, though? You saw nothing in his hands?'

'No, nothing in his hands. That's not to say he didn't have a weapon concealed on him. He was wearing a bulky kind of coat. It could have held almost anything.'

'I was thinking of a lantern. Funny that he seemed to be looking for something, but he didn't bring a lantern with him.'

NIGHT

I came upon the ladies having tea in the drawing room. Stephanie was indisposed with a headache and remained in her room. Lothar was absent on one of his periodic disappearances: Apparently neither he nor anyone else felt it necessary to pass comment on this behavior, and we had come to accept an unexplained hiatus every couple of days.

'I believe Stephanie has the most awful crush on you, Laszlo,' Nichole said teasingly, though I thought her laughter rang hollow.

'Nonsense,' I replied gallantly. I was afraid to look at Elizabeth to see her reaction. I felt color rise to my cheeks most alarmingly.

'Well, I think you have to admit it's a bit more than simple family affection,' she persisted.

'Oh, I dare say it's all to do with new surroundings, the excitement of travel. She's a romantic, impressionable sort, and this must all seem very exotic to her.'

'Men are so crass.' Nichole seemed disappointed, and I wondered how much she lived through her daughter, reviving memories of her own infatuation, if such it was, almost thirty years before. 'But women know these things, don't they, Elizabeth?' she asked.

To my amazement, Elizabeth found the situation amusing and seemed to enjoy teasing me. Perhaps she finds my discomfiture reassuring. 'I think Nichole's right. Stephanie was eating you alive with her eyes all the way back from the Gypsy camp. But you were so preoccupied with what had happened that you paid no attention to her whatsoever. You must be considerate, Laszlo, and let her down gently so that her feelings are not hurt. You can't ignore her completely, as you have been doing, it simply isn't kind.'

What can possess her? Can she have so much confidence in my pair of bodyguards that she believes the most alluring prey can walk before me with impunity? Perhaps she does not know my tastes. Or thinks me rehabilitated. But she has been cruelly disabused of that illusion once already, and now cannot help but be the wiser. Elizabeth is lulled into a feeling of security by the very domesticity of our arrangements. She thinks: How can desire so monstrous exist within the family home, in a situation so immediately normal, within a realm where kindness and gentleness and concern for good manners prevails, when it concerns one who is so palpably and healthily alive and vital, so unmutilated, so uncorpselike, someone who is, as it were, our own flesh and blood?

Stephanie appeared at dinner recovered but pale. She

cast a reproachful look in my direction, as if I were to blame for some emotional pain she has suffered during the afternoon. There was something absolute and tyrannical in her expectation that I intercept every covert nuance of her mood and respond to her in kind. It was clear, also, that there was a piece of mischief of which she was preparing to deliver herself at the time of her choosing. She sat quite primly, her eyes uncharacteristically downcast, with a suppressed smile tugging at the corners of her pretty lips.

Brod was pouring wine during the fish course, and the hand which cupped the bottle lingered close to my face; the pale, veined skin reminded me of a plucked chicken. I wondered with an almost abstract curiosity what his fate would be tonight. Would he draw his hidden weapon to defend himself against the unknown assailants who leaped upon him without warning from the darkness – and so die resisting arrest?

'By the way,' Stephanie said during a lull in the conversation. 'Did you know that the policeman we saw today hasn't even caught the murderer?'

I waved to indicate Brod that he might withdraw.

'In fact, they say he isn't even close.'

'Stephanie,' her mother interrupted her, 'I do hope you're not going to regale us with backstairs gossip at the dinner table.'

'Unless it's awfully juicy and interesting,' Lothar put in and winked at her.

'I just wish she wouldn't talk to the servants,' Nichole said with measured calm, a tense smile hiding her displeasure. I silently urged her on to use the strength of character she needed to prevail.

'Most of the time they know more about what's really going on than we do,' Lothar observed.

'And it's not just one woman he's killed,' Stephanie continued. 'There's been two of them. One with her throat cut, and one so dreadfully mutilated that everyone believes a vampire did it.'

'Stephanie!' her mother exclaimed.

'Not everyone,' Elizabeth said. 'Just the peasants and uneducated people.'

'It sounds like you've got a local Jack the Ripper,' Lothar said with relish. He seemed to be addressing himself to me in particular.

'No, this is supernatural,' Stephanie insisted. 'Jack the Ripper is some squalid, demented little man in the slums of London. This is entirely different. These women were murdered by someone with superhuman powers.' She looked intently at each person in turn before giving herself up to a voluptuous shudder.

EARLY MORNING, APRIL 10, 1888

Brod is the night watcher and takes up a position beside the front door in an ancient wicker chair which contains him like a shell. My difficulty tonight lay not in getting past him and out the door, but in finding a method of waking him so that he would be sufficiently alert to follow me when I left the castle, for when I had crept silently down the stairs I found him cocooned in a blanket and snoring peacefully.

I made several small sounds at the far end of the hallway which might have roused him, to no avail. In the end I decided that there was nothing for it but to approach the problem boldly, and so I stepped over his outstretched legs, took the key in both my hands, and with the greatest care turned it slowly in the lock. It is a massive, medieval mechanism with a powerful spring, and it took all my strength to keep the bolt from jolting back. Withdrawing the key, I swung the door open only enough to step out into the cold night air. Brod slept on. The door squeaked as I swung it to, and I quickly inserted the key and turned it in the lock, making no attempt to hide the sound this time. The bolt sprang to with a grinding thud. In the silence of midnight, I was afraid the noise would waken others in the castle. There could be no doubt about Brod's state of alertness now, for the door rattled as he shook it helplessly.

I took off down the road with a gladness in my step from this newfound freedom. The half moon shone upon the landscape and illuminated my domain; I looked out over the sleeping town and for a moment I considered freeing myself even from those internal checks which counsel me to curb my savage nature, and lead me to practice stealth and deceit. But I kept to my plan. That time will come.

I walked quickly to put distance between Brod and myself. There was a risk that he would raise other servants from their beds, but to do so would be to admit that he had failed in his duty of watching over me. Besides, Brod is a solitary man who is loath to ask others for assistance. It was much more likely that he was at that moment rushing to the kitchen door with the key in his hand; then he would have to double back through the courtyard by the stables to reach the road to town, and only then would he catch sight of me, on the winding road below him, the moonlight picking up the white silk opera scarf I wore tossed jauntily over one shoulder.

As I anticipated, Brod ran, alone, down the road behind me. From time to time the faint click of his heals reassured me of his pursuit. By the time we reached the market square he had narrowed the distance between us considerably, but was quite winded and had trouble keeping up with me as I drew him through the town to the railway line on the other side. Following the line, I remained visible to my pursuer so that I was able to quicken the pace and increase the separation between us quite considerably. At last, I left the rails and turned onto the path that had been worn into the turf, and wound between bushes and copses of young trees. The wind carried to me the scent of tobacco smoke and soon I could make out the intermittent murmur of male voices.

'You're late,' Inspector Kraus hissed. He seemed much

on edge, and I hoped that events would not disappoint him, for clearly he had high hopes.

'Not a moment too soon,' I said, somewhat out of breath. 'He's coming this way. Your men must take cover immediately or you'll scare him off.'

Kraus signaled urgently to the constables, and they disappeared into the shadows of the night. I crouched beside Kraus behind a bush and waited. It seemed like a long time. The posture became uncomfortable on the knees, and my feet soon became numb, but we dared not move. Five minutes passed, but still there was no sign of Brod on the path which led into the clearing where Theresa had died. It was on such a night, I could not help reminiscing, that I had stalked her across the heath, through the patches of shadow, using the broken cover to close upon her until that moment when she seemed to sense that she was not alone.

I began to worry that Brod had lost sight of me; then, behind us, I heard the sound of someone breaking through undergrowth. He seemed to stop to take his bearings and then came on toward us at a run, and I was afraid he would bump into one of the constables before he had a chance to enter the clearing. But the vegetation deflected him, and he was forced to come to a stop again quite near, so that we could hear him panting and cursing under his breath. He was listening for me now, because he walked a few paces in one direction to see if he could detect me, and then a few paces in another. Since we dared not move to observe him, the sounds made a fair facsimile of a man searching the ground for something he had lost.

Eventually, he found the path, and to my relief chose the direction which brought him to the clearing we surrounded. Brod looked about himself in that eerie half-light of the young moon. He was gasping with exhaustion and almost stumbling. He seemed beside himself with frustration and several times struck his thigh as if to goad himself to greater efforts, or to punish himself for his negligence in losing me. He paced back and forth in fury and dereliction, shaking his head, muttering, and striking himself, and we felt ourselves witnesses to an uncomfortably intimate moment of a man alone with his conscience. To our right, a constable coughed. Brod was immediately still, scanning the undergrowth with intent, abrupt jerks of his head.

He must have thought he had found me at last. Bent double to use the low cover of the bushes surrounding the clearing, and halting after each step, he moved away from the place where the inspector and I hid in the direction of the thicket of the unfortunate constable. He reached into his coat, and I saw the moonlight glint on steel. So that was what he had in mind for me, the faithful family retainer!

I was startled out of my wits by a piercing blast from Kraus's police whistle. A constable rose immediately in front of Brod; then he caught sight of another to his left and turned uncertainly, emitting something like the snarl of a cornered animal. The constable who had coughed, no doubt to redeem himself, charged forward desperately, and although the rest of us began to converge on Brod, for several seconds the policeman faced him alone. Brod fell back, and seemed to glance over his shoulder the moment the constable jumped at him. He was distracted, or I am sure he would have killed the man.

With surprising agility and a skill I had never suspected he possessed, Brod sidestepped and thrust his weapon into the policeman's side. Almost as quickly, he turned and began to run, and because we had all converged on that corner of the clearing, it seemed that Brod would escape through a hole in the net we had cast for him. The constables gave chase, but they had positioned themselves at a disadvantage, and I heard them crashing through undergrowth as they yelled in confusion to one another, while Brod ran unhindered along the path which led toward the railway line. I made my way at an easier pace along the other side of the triangle, cutting the corner, and emerged at the tracks in time to see Inspector Kraus running like a terrier at the heels of the lumbering Brod.

Brod was tiring and must have known Kraus was quickly gaining on him from the clatter of the constables' heavy boots along the rails. He turned and slashed viciously at Kraus's face, but Kraus ducked under the blow, and his momentum carried him forward so that he tackled Brod about the waist and brought him down. They struggled in a confused heap, Brod using his superior weight and strength against the little man to turn him on his back, but I saw that Kraus had a fast hold on the arm which held the knife. Brod punished him with his free hand, landing blow after blow in an effort to bludgeon himself free, but Kraus's life depended on securing that hand with the knife, and he clung to it tenaciously until his policemen arrived.

Brod was safely manacled and lay facedown between the rails when I arrived. Kraus stood over him, and I gathered he was having some difficulty maintaining discipline. The constables' blood was up, and only with great difficulty had he prevented them from beating the prisoner. To these raw men, such savage justice would be a natural conclusion to the chase, especially since he had wounded one of their comrades. They milled around in an ugly, surly mood and contented themselves with occasional kicks and taunts. Brod's stoicism in this thoroughly confusing situation did him credit.

I made a point of staying out of Brod's line of vision and tried to talk out of earshot to minimize his awareness of the part I had played in his arrest. The wounded constable was brought up now, walking with only slight difficulty with an arm slung around the neck of one of his fellows. This gave me an excuse to withdraw from the group around Brod, who had now been dragged to his feet for the slow march back to the police station. When I had seen the blow struck, I was afraid the policeman had received a penetrating wound to the chest. The man was pale and shivering, and in the light of the lantern looked thoroughly scared when he saw the amount of blood which had soaked through his shirt and tunic. I examined him and found a nasty flesh wound but was able to reassure him that he was in no present danger.

Kraus tapped me on the shoulder impatiently. One of his eyes was beginning to swell and a line of dried blood ran down his chin from a cut lip, but he was jubilant.

'You've got quite a shiner,' I told him.

He grinned, evidently pleased with himself. His standing with the men was immeasurably increased, and he wore his wounds like campaign medals. 'It's nothing,' he said proudly.

'Let me take a look at it, though,' I insisted, but he brushed my hands away.

'Take a look at this instead, and give me your opinion.'

It was an object which was at once familiar and defied immediate recognition, being so far removed in time and context. I turned it over in my hands. The fine Czech steel had stayed pristine and stainless all the years that it had sat in its place between the rest of its family in their wooden case. How deeply Brod had mined my life for this weapon! The handle was of a piece with the blade, and a groove ran along it into which my fingers curled as if the grip had been precisely made for them. My hand grasped this perfect instrument and remembered.

'It's mine, of course,' I sighed.

'I assumed that,' Kraus said. 'But surely it has a specific purpose?'

'It exists for only one reason,' I said. 'It is the scalpel for forelimb amputation.'

17

AFTERNOON, APRIL 10, 1888

On the morning after Brod's capture everyone came down to breakfast oblivious to the night's events.

'I'm afraid I have some rather disturbing news for you,' I announced. Elizabeth turned quite pale, and I went quickly to the essence of the matter. 'Brod, our majordomo whom you all know, was arrested last night by the police.'

'Whatever for?' Elizabeth asked, almost crying out. 'How could the police arrest him without our being aware?'

'They caught him on the heath, by the railway on the other side of town.'

'Whatever was he doing there?' She seemed quite shocked, mindful perhaps that wherever Brod had been, there also was I.

'That, I think, is the question the police most want to answer.'

Stephanie made no attempt to curb her intense curiosity. 'Does it have to do with the murders?' she asked before I could think of a decent way to present Brod's predicament.

Lothar watched me carefully, while Nichole stared into her teacup with an expression of polite tolerance in the midst of this domestic crisis.

'It's not entirely clear,' I began.

Stephanie sighed impatiently, as someone too old now to have the juicier parts of the news withheld. 'He must be a suspect if the police arrested him.'

'But we know Brod would never do such a thing,'

Elizabeth said emphatically. She gave me a level look, fierce and determined. 'There must be some mistake, Laszlo. Did you tell the police that?'

'Frankly, I wouldn't be surprised by anything my servants did,' Nichole said. 'Murder included.'

'In fact, I've protested to the Inspector quite forcibly,' I told Elizabeth meekly. My words did nothing to mollify her. 'I give you my word that if Brod is innocent, no harm shall come to him,' I added, and she appeared to relent. Lothar, to my distress, seemed to intercept these coded messages. I cannot tell what he made of them, but he looked thoughtful and preoccupied throughout the rest of the meal. I went on, 'But the circumstances of his arrest mean that they must hold him for the time being.'

The realization came upon her that I might have struck again in spite of my guards. 'No one was hurt, please God?'

'Brod was armed,' I said with just a hint of accusation. Now it was my turn to confront her with a stern gaze. Did Brod carry a weapon on her instructions? Had she given him orders to kill me if . . .? I thought she flinched and looked away. I fiddled with a piece of toast to cover my sadness. I did not feel betrayed; loyalty would have been more than I had a right to expect. But at that moment I felt terribly lonely, as if the whole human race was ranged against me.

'Unfortunately, he wounded one of the policemen who was trying to arrest him,' I said.

'What with?' Lothar asked.

'He stabbed the constable with one of my scalpels, actually. He isn't badly hurt, thank God. All the same, they have to keep Brod in custody.'

'But I don't understand what they thought they were arresting Brod for in the first place,' Elizabeth persisted.

This was the tricky part. 'Brod had been under suspicion for some time, apparently. He was acting strangely, according to Inspector Kraus. The first I knew of this was last night, when they let me in on their plans to arrest him. They tend to think his behavior during the arrest confirms he was up to no good. After all, what was the man doing in that godforsaken spot at midnight armed with a knife?'

As I was on my way after breakfast, Lothar sidled up beside me. 'This vampire business interests me immensely,' he said.

'You don't believe that stuff any more than I do,' I protested.

'Oh, but I do.'

'Surely not?' I looked to see whether he was joking. It would be too much to say that he was serious – such an attitude does not become his suave, ironic manner – but he was as intent as I have ever seen him.

'I want to join you in your researches,' he said.

'It's nothing. It's superstition. Nothing more than that. There is no vampire.' I began to walk away. 'Look, I must talk to that Kraus fellow about Brod. It really is a bit much.'

'You are the vampire.'

I chuckled at the thought. When he put it that way, it really did sound rather silly. 'No, I'm the antidote. Haven't you seen them touch me?'

'You are the murderer.'

'Don't be ridiculous!'

'Take me with you!'

'Now this has gone quite far enough. A joke's a joke, but this is over the top.'

'Remember Stacia?'

'Yes, of course,' I said in some irritation. 'Just what is this supposed to prove?'

'You killed her, too. You killed them all the same way.'

'Really, Lothar. You should listen to yourself. It's all pretty batty, if you want my opinion.'

He placed himself squarely in front of me. 'I won't get in the way,' he whispered. There was an urgency in his voice and the huskiness of emotion spilling over. 'I could help.'

'No.' I tried to turn but he grabbed my arm and held me with a bruising grip.

'It must be dangerous as hell. My God!' He seemed overcome at the thought, whatever it was. 'I could help!' I tried to shake free. 'All right. All right. I'll just watch. I promise.'

I stopped struggling. His face was close to mine. 'Do you have any idea what a disgusting human being you are?'

'Absolutely.' He grinned widely, emanating his specious charm. 'We both are. That's why we're so lucky to have found each other.'

Nichole came into the drawing room. I wondered if it was possible for her to have heard any of our conversation. Lothar is totally indiscreet and takes no precautions. He let me go, at least.

'Take me with you,' he called after me as I excused myself and headed toward the door. 'At least have the decency to think it over.'

'Take you where?' I heard Nichole ask him.

MORNING, APRIL 11, 1888

Yesterday, Jacob accompanied me to the police station, but his heart is no longer in it. With Brod in the cells, it is no longer possible to watch me day and night, unless another servant is recruited. I can think of no one I would put my trust in for a job so sensitive, and neither, apparently, can Elizabeth. Perhaps the hazards of the arrangements she has made have come home to her with the narrow escape the constable suffered at Brod's hands.

Surveillance has spoiled the pleasure I had previously taken in exercising in the open air. How can one commune with nature under the constant sensation that one is being watched? As a consequence, I had rarely left the castle except on business or to hunt with Jacob in his more natural role of gamekeeper. But today after breakfast I announced that I was going for a walk. It was Brod's day to watch me, and I waited for Elizabeth to suggest that Jacob accompany me, but instead she made some remark about the weather and retired to her sitting room to answer her correspondence.

I am free, at last. But what can be more terrifying than a stroll beside the river? I am like an invalid who has been released from hospital after a long illness: Every small transaction looms as a source of anxiety because he has forgotten how to live in the world. Except in my case I am not so much afraid of what the world may do to me as what it may evoke in me, of how its sights and smells may stir me, of what it will drive me to. I have indulged only in the prisoner's vices of memory and imagination. Now there is no one to keep me in check. I had not realized how reassuring the presence of my guards has been.

I followed the path beside the river, through the avenue of chestnuts, to the point where it narrowed and became little more than a path. The ground was rutted and frozen still with the morning's frost, and my breath hung in the still, cold air. I was recalling Estelle, of course. One needs to be alone to be receptive to memory's magic, and it seemed that at each spot on which my eyes rested I remembered some detail of our time together. I do not know how I can feel such sadness that she is no longer here, but I miss her terribly. I even feel a kind of anticipatory melancholy for Stephanie, for all her provocative antics.

At the end of the path, I stooped to enter the clearing where Estelle died. I fancied that one part of the packed mud was darker than the rest and, removing a glove, I crouched to touch the bloodied earth with my fingertips. I should not have done so, for it caused a stirring and excitement that I could not suppress, and I lived again the encounter in which the true nature of my lust was revealed to me in such a frenzy of delight that I had been changed forever.

My eyes were closed as my spirit struggled to discern

some dim glow, the merest shadow of that blinding, suffusing light, when I was startled by the sound of a man's voice.

'A message for you, Count.'

The tone contained an odd mixture of courtesy and command, and looking into the low-cast winter sun, I could make out no more than an outline through the thicket of twigs and branches. Caught unawares in that secret place, I had a premonition of danger. I listened for sounds of others.

'Say who you are,' I demanded.

'I am known to you,' the man said. 'I'll come forward, and you'll see who I am.'

'Wait!'

'I'm a Gypsy, Count. I bring you a message and good luck.'

He did not wait for any further instructions from me but pushed his way through and when he had straightened up again I saw that it was Rado's man, Arpad.

'And how is the Colonel?' I asked. 'I trust he's not having too hard a time roughing it?'

'We are not using names, sir.'

'Are we in danger of being overheard?'

'No. There's no one else near.'

'Then I can't see the harm in it. Don't you think it's possible to overdo this cloak-and-dagger stuff?'

'These are the Colonel's rules,' he said with a finality which suggested they were akin to the laws of God.

'What is your message, then?'

'Everything goes ahead as planned. Your guest arrives on the night of the thirteenth, as arranged. You'll meet him at midnight in the ravine where we hunted for deer and guide him back to the castle.'

'Will he be alone?'

He seemed uncertain whether he could answer that question without explicit authorization. 'We'll be about. You won't see us. But we'll be there in case of trouble.'

'Is that something you're expecting, trouble?'

He shrugged. 'It's an operation. You plan for it.'

For so many months the plot had seemed merely a fantasy concocted by Rado's overwrought mind. I had never really expected it to come off. Now I began to appreciate the enormity of what I was engaged in. I was meddling in history. In two days I would come face-to-face with the heir to the throne.

'But everything's going all right, isn't it?' I asked.

'Yes,' Arpad said in a clipped manner which suggested he was becoming irritated by my need for reassurance. In his mind it was clear that each conspirator must be capable of sustaining himself. Each was an individual link in the chain. Each must be strong enough to hold. He turned to leave.

'That's all?' I asked. I started after him.

'Don't follow me,' he turned to warn me in a voice thick with threat. I was unmilitary, and he despised me; I could see it in the way his eyes surveyed the signs of anxiety in my face.

'It's just that I don't want to make a mistake,' I insisted. 'It's so little to go on.'

'You'll be contacted. That's all you need to know for now.'

I waited until I heard no further sound of him and then waited five minutes more before going on my way.

AFTERNOON

'We so enjoyed meeting your neighbors for dinner last week,' Nichole said at tea. She lied in a bright, conversational tone of voice, even though our two sets of guests had had little in common with each other. It had been a most lugubrious evening. 'I do hope we'll meet some of the other families from the area.'

Elizabeth, however, seemed quite pleased, and mentioned people whom we hadn't seen in years, fusty old country aristocrats who would have bored Nichole and

Lothar rigid. She still thinks Nichole is on the lookout for an eligible elder son as a husband for Stephanie.

'And isn't there a rather grand estate to the north of us?' Nichole inquired.

'Count Aponyi's place?' I suggested.

'Really?' Nichole said, as if hearing this for the first time, though I felt sure the name had cropped up in conversation before.

'Now there's a name to set your sights on,' Elizabeth told Stephanie.

'He must be all of seventy years old,' I said.

'But isn't there something to be said for older men?' Stephanie asked, putting her head on one side in the most coquettish way, and we all laughed at her playacting.

'There's certainly something to be said for marrying a husband with one foot in the grave,' Lothar said. 'Especially when he's one of the richest men in the Empire.'

'Is he?' Elizabeth asked. 'I had no idea. And here he was all these years, almost on our doorstep.'

'Well, I intend to marry for love,' Stephanie said. It was not so much the idea itself as the fervent way in which she spoke which shocked those of us in the older generation to an embarrassed silence. Perhaps Stephanie's plea for passion echoed in the hollow places of our own marriages.

'But matchmaking aside,' Nichole continued in a overly bright, nervous tone, 'wouldn't it be fun to meet the grand old man?' She glanced toward Lothar as if to recruit his support, and I wondered if this conversation had a specific objective and whether they had discussed beforehand the general outlines of the route they were to take.

'I've had some passing acquaintance with the Count,' Lothar said. 'He was part of the racing crowd.'

'That was before Lothar decided to make a career in the Finance Ministry,' Nichole put in.

'Then why don't you pay him a visit?' I suggested. 'I can have Jacob take you in the carriage.'

'Actually, it's been a while since we had any contact,' Lothar said.

'Perhaps it would be more appropriate if we went with you,' Nichole said carefully. 'Then it would be simply a social call between neighbors. And then, when the Count sees Lothar, it will appear serendipitous. You are on social terms, I hope?' she asked when I showed hesitation in taking up her plan.

'I'm afraid the Count and I aren't even on speaking terms.'

'Why, whatever for?' she asked with a painful, nervous laugh, as if I might be teasing her about a matter of crucial significance.

'He's never forgiven me for arranging to have the railway line pass through this valley rather than his. He thinks I was underhanded. I feel he's been rather a poor sport about the whole thing.'

For a moment Nichole looked stricken, as if some last hope had been dashed, but she recovered quickly, gathering herself and erecting again the facade of vivacious cheerfulness.

She glanced behind her to ensure that the servants had withdrawn. 'Shall we tell them?' she asked Lothar. It was evidently her trump card, but there was a desperate, bitter glint in her eyes, as if she played it not in triumph but to avoid ruin.

Their eyes rested on each other in a silent wrestling of wills. Lothar conceded at last with a humorless smile, for Nichole's question left him little choice about whether he could retain their secret. 'You tell, my dear,' he cooed.

'We have heard, from an impeccable source,' Nichole began with the air of a conspirator, 'that Count Aponyi is to have a very special guest at his estate this week.' She looked at each face in turn, as if she might feed on the suspense she was creating. 'Crown Prince Rudolph!'

I think we disappointed her. I managed a look of polite surprise, and Elizabeth did her best to mirror some portion of the excitement Nichole exuded.

'These are rather more exalted social heights than we're used to,' I said.

'Papa has met the Crown Prince on several occasions,' Stephanie said proudly.

'Indeed?' Elizabeth said. 'Lothar, I had no idea you lived such a glamorous life.'

'Used to,' he said modestly. Humility in Lothar is always suspect. 'Now I'm just another civil servant.'

'No, you're not!' Nichole burst out, the flash of temper breaking through her self-control.

'Temporarily just another civil servant,' he conceded.

'That's why connections – not just connections, but personal connections – with members of the Court are so important,' Nichole went on. 'All it would take is a word from the Crown Prince.'

'If I could just speak to him for a moment. He's really an awfully decent chap.'

'One word!'

'If he remembers who I am.'

'Nonsense. All he has to do is set eyes on you.' Nichole turned her most intriguing smile on me. If she could have employed telepathy at that moment she would have used her utmost power, and a flood of fond memories from years ago would have come riding on her gaze to confuse me. 'Laszlo, I do wish you'd make it up with old Count Aponyi. Couldn't you do this for old times' sake? It's silly that some stupid railway thing should stand in Lothar's way!'

EVENING

It is dusk, the time when reason's light is dimmed and dark desires stir, gather strength, and come to power. I am unchained. I am unguarded. The whole world's scope lies before me. If I relax my grip for only a moment the monstrous urge will swell and I will lose myself.

Stephanie finds occasions to be alone with me. They are

fragments of moments only, encounters which appear to arise by chance, but I recognize the signs. She is in search of adventure. She wants experience to grow herself into the kind of woman she craves to be: worldly, sophisticated, cynical, though she is too young to know how drying and deathly that last can be. Our fingers touch when I pass her things at table. She is entirely indiscreet in her glances. The women take pleasure in teasing me about her infatuation. They seem to think that since it is overt, naive, above all, observed, no harm can come of it.

For my part, I am incapable of moderation. I cannot encompass a simple, brief dalliance with the seventeen-year-old girl, though she touches me most tenderly and evokes all the gentleness that I remain capable of. She reminds me uncannily of Nichole; how strange it is that I can scarcely recognize the real Nichole. At the back of my mind I feel it would be dishonorable to bed the daughter of old friends who are guests in my home. Although such ungentlemanly behavior may seem petty in the greater scheme of things, it troubles me almost as much as the thought that were I to love Stephanie in my own way, I would consume her – life, body, all. I have retained a fine, discriminating sensibility for the small scruples of life, as I grope numbly at the general outlines of humanity.

I feel the urge to roam. I have no illusions on this score. It is a sure sign of the hunting instinct. My mind is slipping again. I allow myself to indulge in grotesque fantasies – I call them grotesque only out of convention, for to me they seem so precise, so fitting, so profoundly natural that at times I cannot imagine that others do not secretly abandon themselves to such thoughts.

At lunch, Stephanie's hand was positioned on the table easily within my reach. It lay abandoned, as it were, while she toyed with a vol au vent on her plate, the fingers making tiny sympathetic movements as its fellow struggled to manipulate the refractory pastry with a fork. Her hand was pale and perhaps a little cold, but the white damask tablecloth brought out the hint of pink at the knuckles and the fingertips, and there was such a soft succulence about the limb that I was seized with the notion of biting into the fleshy bulge of the thenar eminence, of sucking at it, biting deeper until my teeth encountered the grit of fascia and tendons and could go no farther. Is that grotesque? Perhaps it is, for those too squeamish to acknowledge their true natures. If we can be transported with delight by such a vegetarian pleasure as sinking one's teeth into the summer's first peach and feeling the sweet juices overflowing the lips and dripping off one's chin, how then can we frame the magnitude of pleasure that may flow from devouring a maiden's hand? I cannot believe I am alone.

After dinner, I shall announce, 'If you'll excuse me, I think I'll take a stroll into town and pay Gregory a visit.'

Lothar will make a joke about my taking out insurance on my soul. I would ask him to come, but I cannot count on him refusing the offer. He has become edgy during the last couple of days and watches my comings and goings closely.

Elizabeth will smile anxiously, since she is not yet used to my going outside the castle on my own. Yet she knows that I have committed myself in front of witnesses to a destination, and if it is her hope that I pick up the routine of my previous life, then I must begin in this way. It is a risk, but what could be more salutary than a chat with Gregory?

I am aware of the risks. Yet I really am going to visit Gregory. I know that in the past I have been sly with myself, but I am convinced that I can forestall this present 'attack', that this urge will pass without the necessity of satisfying it, if I catch it in its early stages. I cannot give in to it now. Rado, Lothar, even Kraus, are closing on me. It is a matter of simple expediency.

Afterwards, I promise myself, when Rado's business is finished and the von Picks have returned to Budapest, I will reward myself. But now, only for now, I must

430

exercise restraint. I wonder if it may be possible to trick myself into a permanent abstinence by this expedient.

EARLY MORNING, APRIL 12, 1888

The night was cold with a stiff wind, and I gathered my cloak tight about me as I walked down the winding road to town. Clouds obscured the moon except for brief intervals when it shed its pallid light upon the bare winter countryside. I crossed the bridge and was glad of the protection the first buildings afforded. Few people were about, and those I saw hurried about their business with their heads down, as if intent on returning to the safety of their homes as quickly as possible.

When I got to the rectory I was ready for a cup of hot chocolate to warm my hands and my stomach, but the housekeeper would not open the door.

'You know very well who it is, Mrs Hatvany. Be so kind as to let me in.'

'Begging your pardon, Count,' she said through the keyhole. 'I know your voice, but with the vampire and all, you can't be too careful.'

'If you recognize my voice, then I think you can rest assured that it's safe to let me in.'

'But they say vampires can mimic a person's voice so his own wife would think it was him. A thousand pardons, Count, but I can't know for sure it's you unless I was to set eyes on you.'

'But you won't see it's me unless you open the door.'

'Ah, but then it could be too late.'

I sighed in exasperation. 'Perhaps Father Gregory can sort this out?'

'He's not here. He's at the church for choir practice.'

As I approached the church I could see the dim light of candles from within. With both hands I turned the circular steel handle of the main door, and it opened noiselessly to admit me. Inside, I leaned against the door, and with the faint click of the latch found myself in total darkness, breathing in the church's musty dampness, and struggling to identify another, disturbing odor: the faint, sweet whiff of bodily decay. I groped forward, my hands outstretched before me, to find my bearings again. It seemed a long time before my fingers encountered the heavy curtain which screened the vestibule from the main body of the church, and I fumbled blindly for an opening in the material before I was able step into the aisle and the light.

At the far end of the church, a choir of about two dozen people ranged in stalls to one side of the altar were singing a hymn with gusto. Gregory stood before them listening with his head cocked to one side and his arms folded about his black cassock. As I entered he raised his hand in the middle of a line and the singing died abruptly away. I remained unmoving where I was, but no one seemed to notice me in the deep gloom at the back of the church.

Gregory was giving them instructions on the distribution of emphasis and sang the line in an exaggerated way to make his point, chopping the air with his right hand to mark the time. I had forgotten what a fine tenor voice he had; the sound of it carried rich and full to the place where I stood. He stopped at the end of the line and immediately lapsed into speech as if his singing voice was nothing to be cherished, as if it were of no account, a tool merely for the purpose of illustration.

I made my way silently to a pew at the back and found myself, as if by habit, kneeling. I clasped my hands and rested my forehead on them, but I could not pray. Gregory had stopped the choir again. The music was to surge at that point; they had not risen to it. He took the phrase and his voice soared with it in a gorgeous burst of sound. Then he abruptly cut it off again, as if he were telling them it was the music, not the man, that mattered.

He had not always been so modest. At St Sebastian's he had been proud of his voice, and rightly so. Humility did not come to Gregory naturally, and I wondered what it had cost him to reach this point.

I thought of my mother, who had first brought me to pray in this church, and her lonely exile from France. She had sought solace here, but the priest then had found some doctrinal objection to her French habits of worship and treated her with a cool, suspicious manner. She had made France a kind of religion, and I was her first and only convert. What high hopes she had had for me! I was to be an artist, a man of letters, a professor of science. And all this had been within my grasp.

Perhaps at this point I prayed. I know I shed tears and asked silently, ardently for forgiveness. I do not know how much time passed in this desolate, penitent state. I lost track of my surroundings. At one point, I was filled with such self-loathing that I decided to hang myself. But although the act might meet some standard of natural justice, it seemed a dishonorable way out, and an expedient which would only debase the family name.

I was awakened from this reverie by an angelic voice which, without my being aware of it, had gradually taken hold of my mind. I raised my head from my hands and squinted through the dim light to see where the sound came from. Gregory stood in an attitude of repose with his hands clasped behind his back, and all save one of the choir were sitting. That one person I recognized as Helene. I had not set eyes on her since the epidemic.

She sang 'Ave Maria' with her gaze fixed on some lofty, indefinite place. Her burnished hair caught the light of a nearby lamp, and it seemed that she was the only thing of substance in that place, all else subsiding into shadows and gloom. The pure, virginal sound held me in its spell. It was of such an intensity that it penetrated me. I could scarcely bear the poignancy of it.

Helene herself was transported, losing herself in the delicate, quivering notes which seemed drawn from her, giving herself over to the song to the Mother of God. I believe she sang to her own mother who had been taken in the plague: Sadness and longing suffused her words, and yet there was a transcendent hope in those notes which seemed to soar and hang, lingering in the air past all natural possibility.

I was moved beyond reason. I felt touched by her very spirit. Tears gathered at the corners of my eyes and, overflowing, burned my cheeks like acid. Within that emotion, at its very core, my lust stirred for her.

What perversion is this that would take what is rare and good, and debase this beauty, rend it, tear at it, maul this precious thing, this human life? What curse is this, that all that is evil in me is most drawn to what is lovely and pure in womanhood? Helene touched my heart and aroused my darkest impulses. I would consume her, destroy her. How is it possible that the mind can meld this sublime feeling with desire so rank? They are not separate; the one springs from the other. I am filled with admiration for her beauty of spirit; my heart goes out to her; she evokes in me the most tender desire to cherish her. Is this not something akin to love?

At the heart of this adoration, this exquisite access of gentle feeling, lies a ferocity without hate. I am lured, guided to my victim, by tenderness. Love is the foreplay which at once heightens desire and sanctifies my bloody lovemaking. Love is blind; it never learns of the savagery it leads me to. The lovelorn ache I felt for Helene at that moment is my true essence, the flame brought to its most intense blue focus. And then . . . I would possess her utterly.

I waited in the shadows of an alley near the church until I saw Helene pass on the street. She walked with three of her fellows for safety, and I fell in behind them, keeping a good distance so that I did not alarm them. They had not gone far before two of them said their good-nights and turned down a side street.

I dawdled to increase the distance between myself and Helene and the other woman. They stopped before a house which was evidently the home of Helene's friend and looked about them anxiously, for from this point Helene would have to proceed alone. They stood on the doorstep discussing this quandary and seemed uncertain what to do. I wondered if my presence was exacerbating the situation, and to allay their fears I took myself down a narrow street to the left and disappeared from their view.

Walking at a brisk pace now, I took two further turns and came close to the point at which the side street met the main thoroughfare when Helene passed by.

'Helene,' I called.

She started at the sound of my voice, but stopped and turned.

'Who are you?' she asked.

She sounded quite scared, and when I came toward her, she took a step backwards and glanced behind her up and down the street to see if there were other people about. But at that moment the moon came briefly from behind a cloud and shed enough light for her to make out my features.

'Goodness, Count, you scared me so!' She seemed confused and uncertain how to behave at coming upon me so unexpectedly. 'I didn't know it was you,' she said apologetically.

'You're not afraid of the vampire, surely?'

She laughed, relieved that I wasn't offended. 'You never know.'

'I'll walk with you and see you safely home,' I told her, motioning her to come with me along the side street.

She hesitated. 'But I live with the Theissens now,' she said.

'Yes, I know that. But first I need your help with something back here.'

She peered over my shoulder. 'It's awfully dark, Count. Don't you think it would be better to go this way? It's not far from here.'

I said, 'I thought I heard a noise as I was passing, as if someone was hurt.' I could tell that she wanted to believe me, but her fears had got the better of her. 'I know this sounds ridiculous, and it's just between ourselves – I hope I can count on you for that? – but all this vampire talk has even made me a little leery, and I'm not too keen to go into a pitch-dark stable without someone at the door, at least, ready to go for help if need be.'

'But why are you here at this time of night?' she asked, and then, as if the question might have been disrespectful, added, 'You just happened to be passing, I expect. I'm sorry, Count. It's not my place to ask. I don't know why I did.'

The last thing I wanted was for her to have an opportunity to think. I began to walk slowly back along the dark street, as if I must go about my business with or without her help. Our conversation had been conducted in little more than whispers, and as I walked I stepped on my toes so that the heels of my boots did not click on the cobbles. Those windows which faced us remained darkened.

Behind me, I heard a rustling sound as she ran lightly to catch up with me. I turned to her and gave her my arm and she clutched me tightly. In the darkness, her eyes glistened with fear and excitement.

'We must be very quiet,' I murmured close to her ear, and she nodded in agreement. She had stopped thinking.

It was little more than an alleyway we walked along. Houses backed onto it, with small vegetable gardens surrounded by walls and occasional stables and workshops, and the farther we proceeded from the main street, the darker it became.

'I thought you said it was just a little way?' Helene asked.

'It's not much farther,' I said.

I was conscious that I was not so much supporting her on my arm as pulling her with me. She was shivering.

'This is the one, here,' I told her as we came to a pair of stable doors. One of them hung open a few inches. 'There it is again,' I said.

'I didn't hear it.'

She was reluctant to let go of my arm. 'Look,' I said, 'it's probably just a stable hand who's had too much to drink. But all the same, I don't think it's a good idea for us both to go in.'

'Couldn't we get some help? There must be people in these houses.'

'You've done enough,' I said. 'It was unfair of me to ask you. Go on home.'

For a moment, I was afraid she would take up my offer. She hesitated and glanced guiltily at the welcome glow of the street from which we had come.

'But if you do stay, I'd be awfully grateful if you'd hold my cloak and hat. Would you mind?' I released the cloak from my shoulders and she held out her arm to receive it without thinking. 'You don't believe I would have brought you here if I thought there was any real danger, now do you?'

'No,' she replied obediently, with misgivings.

Inside the stable, I could see nothing. There were no sounds of animals. My foot made contact with a mound which turned out to be clean straw. Opposite the door through which I had entered was a smaller door which I cautiously opened and found that it let out onto a garden.

Outside, Helene hugged my cloak to her and stepped from one foot to the other. I beckoned to her.

'It's worse than I thought,' I murmured.

'I must go home now,' she said, close to panic.

'I know,' I said. 'Just bring in my cloak.' I stepped back into the stables.

'I've got to go,' she whispered into the darkness, in a turmoil of indecision, from the threshold.

I simulated a groan. 'Over here,' I called to her. 'Quick!'

Helene came haltingly toward the sound of my voice. I stepped noiselessly aside, and she passed so close, so closely before me, that I could hear her frightened little gasps for air and smell the orange and cloves of the potpourri she kept in her wardrobe.

I came from behind her. She struggled fiercely, in a threshing, random fashion as I took her to the ground. At one point she almost broke loose when her bonnet came off in my hand, but I caught her by the hair and in a moment had her fast again. I have never seen a woman more alive, so suffused with the desire to live. But she did not cry out. I mastered her and pinned her and bent her back like a sapling, so that I could enter her, member and teeth, and taste the thick, spurting blood at that ecstatic moment between life and death.

I came to myself to hear someone calling Helene's name. I thought I was dreaming. Then I heard it again, closer. It was someone who also did not want to wake the neighbors, someone who was unsure whether to be alarmed or reassured when he heard no response.

As best I could, I wiped the gore from me on her petticoats and replaced my cloak and hat. I could hear footsteps approaching now, and I made my way quickly to the door at the back. But something made me wait. The footsteps stopped outside the double doors to the stables, and I recognized Gregory's voice calling her name again.

Tentatively he opened the door which had been left ajar, and as he did so, I slipped out the back door. He must have opened the door wide enough to let light in, because at once he let out a gasp and I heard him cry out. I heard the rustle of the straw as he turned Helene over, and then I heard him sob. As I left, I heard Gregory's voice, now disciplined and severe, in the flat chant of the last rites.

My passion is not a sickness, but a way of life. It is not a tumor which has infiltrated my moral fiber, but the very substance of my being. I am not monstrous, but quintessentially human and evil. It is not what I am, but who I am. I am who I am.

MORNING, APRIL 12, 1888

Elizabeth was called from the breakfast table this morning. At first, she waved the maid away.

'Later,' she insisted. But the maid whispered something

in her ear which seemed to catch her attention. 'Very well,' she said, tight-lipped.

Like good guests, the von Picks pretended that nothing out of the ordinary had occurred, and came to my rescue with a spirited conversation concerning the most lively balls of the Vienna carnival season.

When Elizabeth returned she was entirely hysterical.

'You promised me,' she said, almost shouting, almost choking on her tears, 'that an innocent man will never be punished for these murders.'

'What has occurred?' I asked levelly.

'Another girl has been murdered!'

'I see.'

'No, I don't think you do see. Father Gregory had been arrested. The news is all over town. People are already saying that he's the vampire.'

'That's infamous!'

'You must do something!' There was fire in her eyes. 'Gregory is being held in prison like a common criminal. He is behind bars!' Her expression went beyond threat; it was vengeance she wanted.

'This shall not stand,' I declared. 'I shall go to Kraus at once. I will do whatever is in my power. I promise you.'

Nichole fluttered elegantly with her napkin, folding and smoothing. Stephanie was agog. Lothar sat back nonchalantly in his seat, a cynical smirk on his face. He understood.

AFTERNOON

Jacob drove me into town. He insisted on talking, though I was sick at heart and gave him no more than grunts for responses. There is, as he said, a new warmth to the air. Soon the ground will thaw, and before we know it spring will be upon us.

There was a crowd milling about in front of the police

station, and Jacob had to shoulder a way through for me. Inside, I walked straightway into Kraus's office. He came around his desk as if to console a bereaved relative.

'Do not blame yourself, Count. We were all fooled. Even the best of us.'

'This cannot be!'

'I know. I know. If only we had caught him sooner, how many lives might we have saved? But who would have suspected a priest? Especially one so loved and respected by his parishioners? He was beyond reproach.'

'He is not the murderer.'

'This is hard, I'm sure. He was your friend, I understand? We cannot see those so close to us. We make allowances, excuses. We find other explanations for things which don't fit.'

'I know beyond a shadow of doubt: Father Gregory did not kill those women.'

'Count, be reasonable. He was followed from the scene of the crime to his church. I personally arrested him there. We found him kneeling on the bare flagstones, praying aloud for forgiveness. We lifted him to his feet. He didn't even seem to notice. I think he temporarily lost his sanity. That happens sometimes. You know that. They seem normal most of the time, to most people. But stress them only so much and you see their madness. He was quite a sight, I'll tell you. Looked like a lunatic. His hands caked with blood. There was blood smeared on his face. His cassock was stiff with the stuff. No, there's no doubt about it, Count. Sorry. He did it all right.'

'I killed them.'

'No, Count. We have our man.'

'I tell you I killed them! And one in Budapest you don't even know about. I followed Helene from the church after choir practice. I lured her into the stables. I raped her. I tore into her throat with my teeth.'

'That's more or less what we think happened. Except no one mentions you being at the choir practice. You're not a member of the choir, are you, Count? Don't you think someone would have thought to mention that you were there if they'd seen you? It's not like your presence would have passed without notice.'

'What about the letter? I wrote it. You suspected me then, didn't you?'

'It was a process of elimination. My consideration of you as a suspect was in the way of an experiment, no more than that.'

'You were right the first time. Don't you remember? There was a word in the letter, an unusual word. Damn it, I can't remember what it was! It's on the tip of my tongue!'

'Epitome.'

'That's it! And then there was the other part. The part about being good, about being a saint.'

'That would refer to the writer being a priest, surely?'

'But I tell you Gregory is innocent! I am the man who should be behind bars!'

Kraus put his hand on my shoulder and looked solemnly into my eyes. He was clearly moved, and his own eyes seemed moist with emotion.

'Count,' he said, 'it has been my privilege to work alongside you on this case. It would be presumptuous of me to claim that our relationship was in any way personal in nature, but I hope I may be permitted to say that I am proud to call you "collaborator." We have had our ups and downs – I won't deny it – but nothing has shaken me in my profound respect for your intellect and for your integrity as a fellow man. I would expect nothing less than your behavior today, for what greater nobility of spirit is there than that a man is willing to sacrifice himself for his friend?'

I was dumbfounded. I had ridden to the police station, steeling myself to the expectation that I would surrender myself and never again see the light of day save through the bars of a prison cell. And this fool not only refused to accept my confession, he delivered himself of a speech of appreciation!

I realized that all this occurred while the door was wide open. When I looked behind me I saw that several police officers were gathered in the vicinity. They made no attempt to hide their interest in these proceedings, and some even nodded their heads in sympathy with the sentiments the inspector had expressed. At any moment, I thought the sergeant might call for three cheers, or that they would launch into a chorus of 'For He's a Jolly Good Fellow.'

'Can I see the father, at least?' I asked.

I descended the narrow stone steps which led to the jail behind the sergeant, the keys jangling on a steel ring in his hand. The light was dim and the ventilation poor. When we reached the cellar the stink was appalling, and I inspired in shallow breaths in a futile attempt to avoid the close, fetid smell of men's sweat, stale urine, fresh ordure. I do not know how anyone could have endured it for hours on end, let alone days.

At the bottom of the stairs, the jailer sat at a dilapidated desk. He was a stout man huddled in a greatcoat against the damp, chill air. On seeing me, he rose resentfully to attention. The sergeant handed him the keys.

'Visitor to see the priest,' he announced and wrinkling his nose in disgust turned back to the stairs.

The jailer looked me over appraisingly, as if anyone who stepped into his domain was fair game. He nodded his head, having come to some private determination.

'This way, if you please,' he said.

We passed an empty cell, and I looked through the open door at the maddening, whitewashed space four paces at the most is all it would allow – and saw the wooden slab suspended from the wall by a chain at either end which served as bed, and the tiny barred window too high in the wall to afford the unfortunate a glimpse of the world.

In the next cell, Brod had been alerted by the sound of the keys and pressed his face to the bars of the small opening in the cell door.

'Count, have you come to set me free?' he asked.

His expression was resolute and uncowed, but I detected a jeering tone in his question, which boded ill for the time when he would be released.

'Get back, you,' the jailer snarled. 'It's not you the gentleman's come to see.'

Brod stepped back from the door, but even in the feeble light of the cell his eyes bored into mine, accusing and hateful.

'Rest assured, Brod, that I shall do everything I can to sort this out quickly.'

'They say the policeman he stabbed is taken bad and won't be back to work for weeks,' the jailer said, moving on.

I called to Brod, 'We'll have you out of here in no time, don't worry.'

I waited for him to say something, and in the gloom I thought I saw Brod smile, a rictus sour and wry as is his nature.

With much clanking and heaving, the jailer unlocked Gregory's cell and swung open the heavy oaken door. Gregory sat on the edge of the wooden shelf, hands braced on his knees, head down in despair or exhaustion. Even if he had been sleeping he could not have been insensitive to the jailer's noise, and yet he made no acknowledgment of our presence, not even so much as a glance in my direction.

'Visitor for the vampire,' the jailer announced with all the solemnity of an English butler.

'Have some respect!' I snapped at him.

Still there was no movement from Gregory. His eyes were open. He stared fixedly at some point on the flagstones just in front of his feet.

'Go on,' the jailer told me.

But some inhibition made me hesitate at the threshold. I was afraid, perhaps, to enter that place of my just destiny, in case by tempting fate I should never get out again.

'It's me,' I said at last. 'Laszlo.'

At the sound of my name his head slowly came up and

he turned to me. I was shocked to see that Helene's blood was still smeared on his cheeks. The backs of his hands and nails were black with the stuff.

'Yes,' he said. There was an absentminded smile upon his face. I wondered if he really recognized me.

'You haven't even let him wash!' I shouted at the jailer.

He shrugged. 'This isn't a hotel,' he said truculently.

'Get him some water, so he can clean himself! And a towel – a clean one!' The man didn't move. 'This instant!' I yelled, beside myself with rage.

The jailer smiled obsequiously, but still did not move himself. It took me a moment to notice that he was rubbing his thumb and forefinger together in the sign for a bribe.

I stepped closer, so that my face was almost in his. 'Do you know who I am?' I asked.

He nodded. His eyes, so close to mine, were cold.

'If you want to keep your job, if you or any of your family wish to have any livelihood within a hundred miles of this town, you will, this instant, fetch some water for the father to wash himself in. And a clean towel. Hot water. Do I make myself clear?'

'Perfectly.' Still he did not move.

'Then do it!'

'Just as soon as I make myself clear.'

'What is this impudence!'

'Up there' – he pointed vertically with his finger – 'you are Count. Down here, I am Count.'

We waited, toe to toe, for the other to flinch.

'Give him some money, Laszlo,' Gregory said wearily, without looking up.

There was no smirk of triumph on the man's face as I reached into my pocket. It was, as he said, a matter of jurisdiction. He was merely collecting a toll, though that thought did not lessen the sting of my humiliation. As I was looking though the coins I held in my palm, he reached out and rooted with his thick, dirty fingers through the small pile to pick out for himself what he considered a fair remuneration.

'Give him more,' Gregory said, 'so that Brod and I can eat some decent food occasionally.'

Obediently I held out my hand to him again, like a trusting child, and considered how long I could endure being at the mercy of this coarse brute before my spirit broke. He left at last to get the water, whistling and jingling the coins in his hand.

'I can't tell you how terribly sorry I am that you're here.' Without thinking, I had stepped toward Gregory, into the cell. 'We both know . . .' I was concerned that in the next cell Brod would overhear our conversation and struggled to be circumspect. 'We both know you didn't do this thing.' He showed no sign of interest, or even of attention to what I was saying. 'We can sort it out. I don't want you to worry on that score. There's been a terrible mistake, and it will be put right.' I waited for him to say something. 'I do wish you'd look at me. It will be put right. I promise you. I promised Elizabeth. She's most concerned about you.'

Behind me, I heard the clump of the jailer's boots. He carried a white enamel bowl from which thin wisps of steam rose into the cold air, and over his arm hung a worn, gray towel. I stood aside while he set down the bowl on the bed beside my friend. Gregory turned slightly to glance at it, then shifted fully round and with a sigh of appreciation sank his hands into the warm water.

Delicate pink spirals rose from the points where his fingers touched one another and loosened the dead black crust. I watched fascinated as the spirals slowly spread and weakened until all that remained of them was the water's faint tinge. His hands clasped one another tentatively, as if they were unfamiliar to each other, and moved one over the other with the greatest care. The storm cloud which was loosed swirled silently and burgeoned in the darkening water.

'Would you excuse me?' Gregory asked politely. I

had not realized that all this time his gaze had been upon me.

'Yes, of course,' I stammered in some confusion, for I was hurt that our relationship had changed so much that he would not even wash his hands or face in front of me.

'Because we have so little privacy,' he explained, as if I were a stranger who had come to visit him.

There was no place in that cramped cellar where one could sit and wait, other than in one of the cells, and so I stood by the jailer's desk. He made no attempt to conceal his curiosity, but examined me with a frank, professional regard, as a farmer might look over an animal in a market pen on which he was considering making a bid. Perhaps it was my imagination, but I couldn't help feeling that he was evaluating me as a prospective prisoner.

The sense of being enclosed was translated into an unendurable itch to pace. I tried the short length of corridor up to Gregory's cell, but after only one turn up and down I felt that I would rather put up with the jailer's scrutiny than pass back and forth before Brod's murderous gaze.

Gregory made no attempt to call me back, so after fifteen minutes had passed, I ventured along the corridor to his cell. He was sitting in the same position, hands braced on his knees, except that his head was up. He turned to me immediately.

'That feels a lot better,' he said with satisfaction.

I couldn't help feeling that he was talking to someone else. That is, he looked at me, and seemed to address his remarks to me, but there was no sense of familiarity in his expression.

'They think I'm a vampire, you know,' he said in a conversational tone.

'Utter nonsense!'

'In fact, the truth is far worse, did they but know it.'

'And they will know it! I swear to you!'

'But will they believe you?'

I was at a loss to know what to tell him. Gregory looked

up to the small window high on the wall of the cell and I thought he smiled to himself.

'I could hear them this morning,' he said softly, almost to himself.

'Who?' I asked. I was beginning to fear that he had gone mad.

'The crowd. They were calling for the vampire. I rather think they want to burn me.'

'I believe the definitive treatment is to drive a stake through the heart,' I corrected him and was rewarded with a wry smile and a flash of contact with the old Gregory.

Encouraged, I came forward spontaneously to embrace him, but he held his hands up quickly so that I would not touch him.

'I saw her, remember,' he said.

'Yes, of course,' I replied, backing away.

'I didn't realize until practice was over that it was you at the back of the church.'

'Yes.'

'Why did you come?'

'To see you. I wanted you to help me. I wanted to stop . . . everything.'

'I see.'

'I really did. I was ready to confess. I came to the church to confess.'

'When I realized it was you, I set out after her.'

'I wish you would believe me.'

'It doesn't make any difference, does it?'

'I don't know. I hoped it would.'

'I caught sight of you, but you ducked down a side street. And then I took a wrong turn and lost you and had to go back and forth along three or four of the streets you might have taken.'

'I wish you'd found me. Can you believe that? I wish you'd caught up with me in time.'

'It's different in the flesh. It's not an abstract idea, sin.'

He looked at me once more, pityingly, searching my face, taking his farewell.

'I want you to know that I told Kraus what happened.'

'And?'

'He didn't believe me.'

'But you told him?' He chuckled to himself, shaking his head.

'And I'll tell him again,' I said. Gregory was laughing harder and harder. 'There must be corroborating evidence.'

'Ah, yes!' This set him laughing all the more, as if it was the greatest joke.

'I don't think this is funny,' I said, but he was no longer paying me any attention.

He was trying to say something, sputtering and guffawing so much that he could hardly get the words out. He subsided to draw breath. 'I am God's fool!' he cried.

'No, you must not believe that!'

It was hopeless. Gregory was doubled up on the wooden bed in a paroxysm of laughter and tears, his hands locked about the chain anchored to the wall.

When I arrived, the crowd before the police station had been a loose composition of idlers and gossips talking among themselves. When I came out onto the front steps, it had swollen considerably and seemed more compact and unified. As soon as I appeared before them there were scattered cries of 'We want Brod!' 'Release Brod!' and at the back I thought I heard someone call out 'Burn the priest!' The shouting died away quickly when it became clear that I wanted to speak.

'Good people,' I said. 'A terrible miscarriage of justice has occurred.'

To my surprise, this was greeted by cheers. Then the chants of 'Free Brod!' began again, and I saw how they had misconstrued my words.

Inspector Kraus appeared at my elbow. 'We're going to drop the charges against your servant, Count. You can tell them that.'

'But he stabbed one of your police officers,' I protested.

'It makes no difference now. We jumped him in the middle of the night. What was the fellow to do? Tell them, Count. It'll take their minds off Father Gregory.'

'Hear this!' I shouted, for the din was beginning to rise in volume. They quieted to a low grumble. 'We do not have the murderer yet.' Here and there came the sounds of muttered disagreement, but no one would oppose me publicly. 'It is my firm belief that neither Father Gregory – ' The protests came loud again, swelling in volume so that I could not be heard. I held my hand high to command silence. 'That neither Father Gregory nor Brod is guilty of murder.' That sowed some confusion in their minds and quieted them. 'Inspector Kraus has told me that all charges against Brod are to be dropped.' Here there came a massive cheer. 'And he is to be set free forthwith.' They cheered loudly and without restraint, even though there can have been precious few among them who had even a passing acquaintance with the man.

'Father Gregory will be vindicated. I have no doubt about that. In the meantime, let us all remember him in our prayers,' I said, but no one could hear, even if they had wanted to.

'If tempers don't cool in a day or two,' Kraus whispered to me, 'I'm going to have to transfer the father to Kolozsvar for his own safety.'

I nodded sadly. 'Reason will prevail,' I said.

I saw Jacob coming toward me through the crowd and was glad to see that the leather satchel in which he transported the massive cavalry pistol remained safely at his side and that he was using both hands to make way for himself.

'I'm going to walk,' I told him when he finally joined us on the steps. 'Take Brod in the trap.'

'Better to wait an hour,' Kraus suggested. 'It'll be quieter. Then bring it around the back.'

'I don't think Brod's the kind of man to make speechs,' I said.

'All the same,' the inspector insisted, 'it wouldn't take much to get this lot going.'

I was looking for an opportunity to leave quietly, and the inspector offered to show me out the side door. On our way across the hall he picked up from the desk sergeant a brown paper parcel tied in string.

'This is yours, I think,' he said, handing it to me.

As soon as I took the package in my hands I recognized the hard outlines of the scalpel inside the paper.

'Does it all fit together, Inspector, in your tidy, scientific mind?'

'It never does, entirely.'

'Where does this piece fit into the puzzle?' I said, holding the scalpel before him.

'If it doesn't fit, that goes to prove it's not part of the puzzle,' he said, but there was something shifty in his look, as if he couldn't entirely believe his own words.

Jacob was right: Spring was in the air. By the time I reached the bridge I was quite hot, and I stopped to take off my coat. I laid it over the parapet and had removed my hat to mop my brow when I heard a voice behind me.

'Bravo, Count,' said Colonel Rado.

He must have been sitting on the bank behind the other parapet and now hopped onto the stonework and sat with one leg over the other. He seemed entirely at ease in his Gypsy garb.

'A most politic speech,' he said. 'Pontius Pilate would have been proud. "Free Barabbas!"' He did not smile. 'But we mustn't let local politics distract us. The new regime will see that no harm comes to Father Gregory.'

'Are we still on for tomorrow night?'

'Very much so. There have been some developments since we last talked. Nothing major.'

'What kind of developments?'

'We've discovered there's been a slight leak in our organization.'

'I thought you said it was nothing major?'

'Don't worry. We've already plugged it. It's not something that's going to stop us.'

'But how can we be sure this thing is going to go off?'

'We don't. There's always been the risk of penetration. Or that the Prince would get cold feet at the last moment.'

'He's definitely going to show up?'

'No, not definitely. But you are. You remember the ravine we scouted in the autumn? Tomorrow night you're to be at the bottom of it at twelve, with a lantern.'

'I'll be a sitting duck!'

'It's a matter of trust, Count. You trust that His Royal Highness is a man of his word, surely?'

'Of course.'

'Then there's nothing to worry about. Anyway, the Prince's people insisted on setting the rendezvous up like this: maximum visibility on the Prince's side, maximum vulnerability on ours. One man who knows the terrain, with a lantern. They wouldn't have it any other way.'

'And afterwards?'

'The Prince will remain at the castle until he receives word that political adjustments in Budapest have been made to his satisfaction. Then he will take the train to Budapest to a hero's welcome. I don't believe there can be any further questions. As you go on your way, Count, I suggest that you do not look back. From now on, we will always be close by.'

Perhaps even yesterday I might have crossed over to Rado, shown him my brown paper parcel, and as he bent to examine it, thrust the entire package at his chest and stabbed him through the heart. I could have tumbled him over the parapet into the river and have done with him and his political machinations forever. But today I begin to perceive the dim outlines of my true destiny. I feel the tug of the river's current, the flow of events which has caught me up, and I will not swim against it.

EVENING

I shut myself in the library, though I knew that eventually Elizabeth would track me down. She will stop at nothing to bring about a just resolution. My life, my reputation no longer concern her.

When there came a quiet knock, and the door opened before I had a chance to give my permission for the person to enter, I assumed that it was Elizabeth. But it was Stephanie who slipped in, with a quick glance over her shoulder to make sure that no one had seen her.

'This is an unexpected pleasure,' I said, taken off guard. 'Might it not be better to leave the door open while you visit?'

'I'm not afraid to be alone with a man,' she replied, casually turning over one of the books on the table to see what I had been reading.

'I'm sure you're not. But a lady must guard her reputation.'

'Why? Are you a man who can't be trusted?'

I should have become stern with her at that point, given her a good talking-to on the necessity of proprieties, and sent her packing. But I didn't. I have no excuses. Instead of listening to the arguments which counseled me against allowing the situation to go forward, I attended to the quickening of the pulse, a tightening of respirations, an intriguing tingle in the pit of my stomach, and that voluptuous, falling, swooning sensation which comes over me at the moment I am about to succumb to temptation.

'As to whether I can be trusted, you shall have to make up your own mind. But in matters of decorum, I've learned that people are demanding of appearances while they care very little to inquire into the substance of what actually occurs.'

'I think I can trust you to be discreet.'

She was walking to the very brink. I could see that she was frightened and hardly the practiced seductress she would have me believe. I came around the table to her.

'You are a very lovely young woman,' I told her. She tried unsuccessfully to suppress her pleasure in the compliment, a smile compressing her lips and puckering her cheeks. She looked up at me shyly, vulnerably, and quickly looked away. 'But I'd be a cad to take advantage,' I said, taking her hand.

She contemplated me with a faint mocking expression in her eyes. I was confused by her alternative naïveté and the worldly regard by which she seemed to imply that I was the one who was innocent of the wiles of the heart. In this she reminded me of the young Nichole. But she did not flee me. I did not have to chase after her.

'But I want you to take advantage,' she said. 'And so it wouldn't be taking advantage at all.'

A man can remain alone in a room with an unmarried woman for only a few minutes before discovery inevitably ensues. Mamas and chaperons have an unerring awareness of their charges and come looking for them when they cannot safely place them. At any moment, Nichole or Elizabeth, or a maid one of them had sent to look for Stephanie, would come through the library door and spoil everything. But Stephanie seemed to have no sense of that urgency. Her head was averted, and I was aware of the rapid rise and fall of her bosom. She waited for me to kiss her. As I came close, she turned and tilted her face to me, her soft lips parted, her eyes half-veiled in languorous, sensual abandonment.

'Shall we meet tomorrow night?' I murmured in her ear.

'Tonight,' she whispered. Her eyes were closed still. She smiled blindly as if not wanting to wake from a dream.

'Tomorrow is safe,' I suggested gently.

Her eyes opened. I had disappointed her. Caution was not romantic. Without danger there could be no adventure.

'Tomorrow,' I insisted. 'That gives you time to change your mind.'

'I don't want to change my mind.'

She would have embraced me, but I moved toward the door.

'Tomorrow night,' I said, with my hand on the handle. 'At eleven. In the gazebo in the rose garden.'

'I may be late.'

She was leaning suggestively against the door so that I could not open it, testing the extent of her new power over a man.

'You must take the backstairs through the servants' quarters and go out the kitchen door. I'll make sure it's open for you.'

These details were deflating the moment. 'I'll go straight out there,' she said, indicating the library's French doors.

'No!' I said rather more abruptly than a lover should. 'No. Brod will be watching at the bottom of the main staircase. At night he guards the front door.'

'Then tell him not to.'

'He always has. Since the vampire scare he spends the whole night there. I think it would arouse suspicion if we were to change things now.'

'Since they've arrested Father Gregory, you can tell Brod he isn't needed.'

On the other side of the door, I heard someone crossing the hall.

'No one in this house believes for a minute Father Gregory is the murderer the police have been looking for,' I said.

She was troubled. Like a cloud in a clear blue sky, a small frown of uncertainty had appeared on her forehead. Love was meant to be simple and direct. If arrangements had to be made, if things were so complicated, was this a sign our love was flawed?

I took her hand.

'Humor me?' I pleaded.

I held her fingers to my lips, looking at her steadfastly all the while, and gradually her face cleared. The confidence flowed back, and at last I saw the sparkle return to her eyes.

'Tomorrow,' she whispered and was gone.

AFTERNOON, APRIL 13, 1888

I can scarcely write. The disaster which has befallen us, the horror of what I have witnessed, is more than my mind can encompass. Yet I know that there is no way of coming to terms with what has occurred, save by writing; for it is only in setting down my thoughts in the pages of this journal that I have been able to achieve any measure of objectivity, any sense of perspective on the events of my life. And now I need this more than at any other time, if I am to keep my sanity.

Breakfast was a strained affair, on account of Gregory's continued incarceration.

'Sometimes people aren't who they seem to be,' Lothar observed. 'In fact, in my experience, people most of the time aren't really who they seem to be.'

Elizabeth's eyes blazed. 'The very suggestion that Gregory should come under suspicion for these sordid crimes is an outrage!'

'It sounds as though the Inspector's got himself between a rock and a hard place: The rabble's after the father's blood, and the powers that be up on the hill here want him set free.'

'I think Constable Kraus's next posting will be far less congenial,' Elizabeth said. I had never heard her so harsh.

'To Herzegovina?' Lothar suggested. 'Or the island of Krk?'

it's not Kraus's fault' I ventured.

'Then whose fault is it?' Elizabeth demanded. It was the first time she had been able to look at me directly since Gregory was arrested. In her face I saw contempt and loathing.

'I think he's only doing his job,' I said. 'He has to go on the facts available to him now. I'm sure fresh evidence will turn up that will put Gregory in the clear.'

'In town they're saying you offered to take the father's place in prison until he was found innocent.' Lothar suggested casually.

'That's not quite true,' I said.

Elizabeth glared fixedly into her plate. She has come to hate me. She wishes me dead, I am certain of it.

'I was told,' Lothar drawled, 'that you'd actually confessed to the murders.' He paused, letting the statement dangle before me like a piece of bait. 'But the authorities wouldn't let you sacrifice yourself for your friend.'

'Yes,' I sighed. 'That's what I told the Inspector.'

'And he didn't believe you!' Elizabeth scoffed.

'No,' I replied evenly.

'I suppose you weren't very convincing?' she asked.

There was nothing I could say.

'Still, it was a grand gesture,' Lothar said. He was enjoying the irony of the situation so much that I was afraid he would wink at me.

To change the subject, I said, 'I've had a message from Kraus this morning. He's concerned about Gregory's safety and he's going to move him to Kolozsvar today.'

'Can I see him?' Elizabeth asked.

'I don't think that would be a good idea,' I told her. 'The town's in an ugly mood. There was another disturbance in front of the police station yesterday afternoon. It's brought all kinds of riffraff out onto the streets.'

'Can't I see him at the station? It might be the last time.'

'This is confidential, but he's not going from the station. There are too many bad elements who hang around there.

Kraus has arranged to have the train stop after the station, a short way out of town, and they'll put Gregory on it there. No one must know this, obviously.'

'Then perhaps you will see him and give him something from me – a breviary?'

The ladies rose from table; Lothar stood, stretched himself, and said he would have a cigar; a maid came and cleared the table save for the cup of cold coffee which I kept before me. I was alone with melancholy thoughts of taking my farewell from Gregory when the door opened and Stephanie rushed into the room.

'I was sure I'd left my purse beside my chair,' she said. 'But it's not here.'

I stepped forward to hold the door for her, thinking that she had come to tell me she had changed her mind.

'You are so noble!' she whispered to me as she passed. 'To sacrifice yourself for your friend!' She let herself look into my eyes for only an instant, but I saw she was moved almost to tears.

I was reading the newspaper in the drawing room when Lothar returned from a stroll in the sunshine. I was sitting on one side of the double sofa, and he plumped himself with a sigh on the other side and picked up a magazine, and we read back to back. I could hear that he was restless, and after a short time he turned on the sofa so that he could whisper almost in my ear.

'You know, don't you, that you owe it to Gregory to do it again?'

'I haven't the faintest idea what you're talking about.'

'Lucky for you I'm not Kraus.'

'How is that?'

'I would have believed you. I'd have clapped you in irons before you could say "Jack the Ripper."'

'At the time, I thought it was worth doing. It turned out, as you say, to be a futile gesture. But I was trying to do whatever I could to get Gregory out of that stinking place.'

'Do you want him to rot in the Kolozsvar jail?'

'Of course not.'

'Then all you have to do is kill another woman.'

'Don't be ridiculous.'

'It would instantly clear him.'

'No!'

'You're going to do it anyway.'

'You're mad! This is senseless!'

'You're going to do it anyway. Sooner or later, you're going to kill another woman. Why not do it now, when it'll do some good? Do it now and take me with you!'

The morning was one of those pristine days of spring when the simple beauty of nature mocks the ugliness of men's affairs. Jacob drove me to the police station with the top of the carriage down so that I could enjoy the mild sunshine, and as we wound through the orchards on our way down the hill, I fancied that the apple trees would soon bud. For once I was glad to see the heavy pouch at his side, for tempers were running high, and the town was fraught with suspicion, superstition, and hysteria. In my pocket I carried the breviary which Elizabeth had entrusted me to convey to Gregory, and I found my hand gripping it tightly as we crossed the bridge and approached the first houses of the town.

My intention had been to say my farewells at the police station; to give him the breviary, and to reassure him that the charges against him would not stand, that I would do everything in my power to force the truth out. But the mood of the crowd gathered before the police station convinced me that I should use all my influence to gain Gregory safe passage to the railway station. This was not the angry, volatile crowd of the previous day; they were quiet, truculent, determined, and I thought them far more dangerous.

I was immediately recognized, and the crowd opened to let the carriage pass. Instead, I dismounted so that I could move among them and be seen. Here and there were men and women whom I recognized by sight if not by name, but there were many peasants from outlying areas who had congregated to gape at the vampire and a sprinkling of flashily dressed troublemakers and ragged rogues who are always to be found on such occasions. At the edge of the crowd, arranged around the square like an impromptu grandstand, were several carriages of bourgeois families who had come to see history in the making, complete no doubt with the accoutrements for a picnic.

They fell silent as I passed. Many dropped to one knee and crossed themselves. I felt unseen hands pluck at the hem of my cloak and raise it to lips. They had need of simple opposites, and as the murderous, devil-inspired priest has become in their eyes the very essence of evil, so has my sanctity increased. It was a fragile polarity which threatened to collapse at any moment. I saw them strain their eyes as they tried to see the saint in the man, the man in the saint, who walked in their midst. My ordinary, flesh and blood humanity was a puzzle to them. Peasants reached out gnarled fingers without ever making contact with my person, as if I might be charged with a mystic quality akin to electricity.

It was clear that Gregory's removal to Kolozsvar was no secret. Roving bands patrolled about the building watching for attempts to spirit him away by a side entrance. I gained entrance past a row of constables who stood rather nervously guarding the front door and found Inspector Kraus striding back and forth in the hallway. He knew that his original plan to put Gregory on the train on the other side of the station would no longer work.

'I will guarantee his safe passage to the train,' I said.

'I guarantee his safe passage,' Kraus snapped. 'It's my professional duty to do so!'

'I realize that,' I said, trying to project a calming influence over this tense situation.

'I've already cabled Kolozsvar for reinforcements.'

'But I think a show of force by the police is going to exacerbate matters.'

no more than a mile to the station. Once we get men, we can handle that.'

'That would mean putting off the move until tomorrow?'

'If we wait for reinforcements.'

'I don't think we should wait,' I told him. 'There are troublemakers out there who are stirring up the crowd.'

He threw up his hands in exasperation. 'Then what is your plan, Count?'

'I believe Father Gregory will be safe so long as he's with me. I have a reputation here. They won't harm us.'

'We're going to transport him in the police carriage. It's closed. There's nothing more than a small window, and that's barred. They won't see you.'

'We'll go in my carriage.'

'They'll snatch him out of it.'

'Father Gregory will be manacled to me. His wrist to my wrist. I will be his guarantee of safe passage.'

'I don't know. It all depends on psychology. It's not part of procedure.'

'I don't believe the Police Department has a recognized procedure for dealing with a vampire.'

Kraus snorted. 'Don't tell me you give any credence to that nonsense?'

'Of course not. But we have to deal with the irrationality of crowds on their own terms. Jacob will drive. You will sit on one side, Father Gregory and I on the other. We'll move at no more than a brisk trot – we don't want to look like fugitives. We're not running from them. We'll leave from the front entrance of this building. We'll be in plain sight all the time, and as we pass through the crowd, I shall raise my hand so that everyone can see that the father and I are inseparably joined, that his fate is mine.'

I was afraid for Gregory's mental state, given the uncontrolled emotion he had surrendered himself to when I had last visited him in the cells, but he was composed and, although subdued, appeared to be more or less himself. I was glad to see him recovered, but found this new equanimity strange in the face of such danger, and hoped it was the strength he derived from his faith. Certainly he seemed pleased by the breviary Elizabeth had sent him and asked after her. Ominously, he asked me to remember him to her, to tell her that he was calm and reconciled to his fate.

'Utter nonsense!' I told him. 'You're going to Kolozsvar. I'm going to put you on the train myself.'

But he smiled mysteriously. 'Ah, yes,' he murmured, looking not quite fully at me in a way which I found disquieting.

'Kolozsvar will be safer,' I insisted. 'It'll give us some breathing space to prove your innocence.'

I did not know that handcuffs were so uncomfortable. The constable rather apologetically placed the steel band about my wrist and ratcheted it to the customary tightness. I thought my hand would be in danger of losing its circulation and was about to ask him to loosen it a notch when I reminded myself that Gregory could not expect the same treatment and that I must endure the same discomfort as he.

There were shouts from the crowd when we came out on the front steps.

'He is in league with Satan!'

'Anti-priest!'

I began to tell them that justice must be left to the authorities, but I saw I could not make myself heard, and instead I held up our manacled hands to show them. They fell silent at this sight. It must have confused them, good and evil joined in this way. We took advantage of their hesitation to climb into the carriage and settle ourselves without any sense of hurry or duress.

'Easy!' I directed Jacob. 'No more than a trot.'

But in his anxiety he whipped up the horses, and they in turn, hemmed in by the crush of people who were prevented from getting out of their way, began to rear in the traces. A disaster would have occurred had not a peasant in the crowd seized the bridle of one of the horses and settled it enough for its fellow on the other side to be brought under control.

But this also left them in control of the movements of the carriage. Jacob could tug on the reins and curse for all he was worth, but we could go nowhere except by leave of the men who held the horses' heads.

'To the station,' I told them, and to my relief the man who had first seized the bridle touched his cap respectfully and urged the horse he held forward at a walk.

In this way we traveled the mile to the station. It was a strange cavalcade, silent and grim as a funeral procession, with the walkers filling the streets on either side of the carriage right up to the doors of the houses we passed. But it seemed that the force moving the crowd to disorder had dissipated. Gregory would be allowed to travel to the station, on their terms. Nevertheless, it was a daunting experience to be swept along within this great river of people and to feel oneself entirely in their power.

Gregory seemed oblivious. He was enjoying the sunshine. With eyes closed, he had turned up his face to receive the warmth; there was even a faint smile on his lips.

I clasped his knee with my free hand. 'It's going to be all right,' I told him, and he nodded slowly without opening his eyes.

The train awaited us at the platform, and from time to time great puffs of steam rose above the roof of the station. A smaller crowd awaited us here, and when they saw the procession, several men ran to meet us. They were agitated and shouting, but they were few in number, and I expected that the sentiments of the larger mass would prevail.

Our vanguard brought us to a stop in the plaza before the station. We were close enough to see the carriages through the iron grill of the main gate and hear the locomotive's panting. People at the front of the crowd appeared to be arguing with the men who had joined them at the station. There was much shouting and excitement, but I could not make out what they were agitated about. Then I saw that the people at the front of the crowd were not arguing but reacting with cries of grief and anger to what the men from the station were telling them. The sound grew as the news passed through the mass of people.

'Bodies in the church . . . bodies stored in the crypt . . . bodies allowed to rot without a Christian burial . . . bodies used in fiendish practices . . . drained of blood . . . undead . . .'

'What is this?' Kraus asked. We could hardly hear him amid the hubbub.

'They've found the corpses of people who died in the plague,' Gregory said calmly. 'We couldn't bury them when the ground was hard. Evidently they've thawed.'

I stood up in order to explain the mistake to anyone who might have paid heed, but the noise made this impossible. The carriage was rocking so violently with the tumult of people crushed against it that I could hardly keep my feet and was forced to sit down again.

As I recovered my balance, I saw Jacob flailing with his whip right and left, not at the horses, but at the men holding them to set them free. He threw it down as useless, and I saw him swing around the leather pouch which hung behind his back so that he could reach for the pistol inside.

'No!' I cried over the din, but he did not hear me. I struggled to my feet and seized the wrist which was even then in the act of dragging the cumbersome weapon from the pouch. 'Do nothing,' I shouted in his ear. 'We are safe if we do not resist them. We are dead if we fight.'

He heeded me – thank God! – or there would have been a massacre.

Those at the outside of the crowd were fighting their way toward us, determined to inflict their rough justice on Gregory. Those people around the carriage had heard only a jumbled account of what had happened with the bodies and were in as much danger as ourselves from the carriage overturning in the melee, and these people pushed back against them. I saw one fellow shove another, and immediately blows were exchanged, the two combatants sinking beneath the sea of shoulders still pummeling one another.

I think we had still a small chance of making our way very slowly toward the station's gate, until one of the horses let out a whinny of alarm. The next moment its fellow attempted to bolt, thrusting and heaving into the crowd. I fell backwards as the carriage lurched forward. A woman let out a sickening shriek as if she were being crushed beneath our wheels.

It must have seemed that we were prepared to make our way over the bodies of the people in front of us. The mob was united now, and we were swallowed up in a storm of noise. I saw hands reaching out for Gregory; they came up short and plucked at the air beside him. When they found they could not reach him, they spat on him and taunted him with the most vile abuse. And yet for all their anger and hate, they feared him. He was a disciple of the Devil, and they hesitated, not knowing the full extent of his powers.

Two men had hold of Jacob's ankles and were trying to pull him down from the driver's seat. He turned to me as he slid sideways, clinging strongly to the seat's back. I think he wanted my permission to defend himself.

'Do not resist,' I shouted. 'They have no reason to harm you. Make no move to defend us. I forbid you.'

I don't think he heard me. There was a puzzled, regretful expression on his face as he let go of his anchor and disappeared from view.

They tore off the doors of the carriage next and took Kraus. Gregory sat composed throughout all this as if he were on a drive in the country. I raised our hands again to show we were chained together, but it made no difference. They didn't care about me. It was Gregory they wanted, at any price. They were in a frenzy. Several strong young fellows hauled us to our feet and threw us into the boiling mass of humanity. I felt one person fall beneath us, but we were held aloft. They tossed us, and we separated to the full extent of our arms and came together in the most painful, wrenching way.

I heard a cry go up. It was followed by a roar of approval, though I could not make out what they had decided to do. We were lowered to the ground and pinioned there on our backs, side by side. Several men had hold of each one of Gregory's limbs. I was afraid they would pull him apart. They were waiting for something. I heard the crowd elsewhere chanting in unison, urging others on to greater effort, and then there was a great yell of triumph as the task was accomplished.

When I turned my head, I found Gregory was looking at me.

'Be brave,' he said. He was smiling to give me courage. I wish I could have clasped his hand. 'Many saints have died in worse ways.'

'What do they mean to do?' I asked.

'Surely it's obvious.'

He closed his eyes, I thought, in prayer. The chanting which had begun to one side was now coming closer to us. The crowd parted save for those holding us to the ground, and I saw what they intended. They had pulled a wooden fence stake from the ground. One man now tore open Gregory's cassock, and another placed the point in the middle of his bared chest. I saw a man in railway worker's uniform hold aloft a sledgehammer, and the crowd took up the chant.

'Drive the stake! Drive the stake! Drive the stake!'

I looked to Gregory. He smiled recklessly. He stared about at those standing above us and laughed defiantly.

'There is no God!' he shouted, and those who heard turned to one another at this confirmation of the anti-priest, the Devilworshiper.

I was not prepared for the solid thump of the hammer hitting the stake. Gregory's eyes flew open in an intensity of pain which seemed to amaze him. They bulged from his head. The stake appeared to bounce on the spring of his ribs. He coughed, but he could not draw breath to cry out.

In spite of the strength of the blow, the stake had failed to break the skin. Another man crawled roughly across my chest to anchor the tip firmly against Gregory's chest for the next strike of the hammer. I was looking into his eyes as it fell and saw the agony of the impact. The stake had penetrated him about an inch, and blood welled up and mingled with the earth on its tip.

'Pray!' I pleaded with him. 'Pray for us!'

The thud came a third time, and the stake seemed to break through some layer of tissue which had impeded it.

I thought he would die then. I thought the stake would split him open. I prayed for him to die. But he turned with a bloody froth on his lips and tried to say something to me. His lips moved silently, and as he struggled to mouth the words, the light in his eyes was gradually extinguished.

The fourth blow planted the stake deep in his chest. Even after the next one, he still lived, for I felt the hand attached to mine clutch and strain though his eyes were closed. The next blow broke his spine. His back arched, and his limbs were possessed by a spasm of such power that the men who grasped him could scarcely hold him down. The seventh blow impaled him through and through and fixed him to the ground. But they were merciless and called like harpies for him to be pinned securely lest he rise again.

I had not registered a new sound: shouts of alarm from the far edge of the crowd. And there lurked beneath this noise something more, a relentless rhythm, sinister and mechanical, which I now know as the rattle of sabers in their scabbards. There came cries of raw fear, and then I heard the thud of hooves and savage yells as if a gang of Cossacks were descending on us.

The men about me were distracted and looked in the direction from which the noise came. I was aware that the mass of people which surrounded me was starting to shift slowly, like a massive rock which is beginning to roll. Then there was shoving as people closer to the approaching horsemen tried to move away and were prevented from making progress by the densely packed crowd.

All of a sudden, people were running in all directions, and I was no longer hemmed in. Feet rushed past, inches from my head, and I was afraid I would be trampled. Above me, I heard shrieks of the panicked mob. I struggled to my knees, much hampered by the manacles still binding me to Gregory. At that moment I saw a horseman in Gypsy garb among the crowd, flailing to his left and right, whacking the backs and shoulders of laggards with the flat of his saber, driving them away from the station. On the other side, I saw Arpad spurring a massive black stallion into a knot of men gathered about the carriage, and they fled in terror, some scurrying beneath the suspension to escape his ringing blows.

There was no one near me now. I brought myself to my feet but could move no farther because of the stake anchoring Gregory to the hard-packed ground. Behind, the crowd was scattering where it could; at other points people bunched and got in one another's way; here the panic was intense, and I saw a woman lose her footing and fall beneath the press of bodies.

In front and to my right, a lone horseman watched the proceedings. He cantered a short distance toward me now, and I saw it was Colonel Rado. But at that moment of recognition he clapped his heels to his horse's flanks and hastened toward me at a gallop. I looked around me for signs of danger, but I was alone. His speed of approach began to alarm me, especially since the horse's head has pointed directly at me. I tried to take a step aside, away from the line of his gallop, but was tethered. I remembered his threat to kill me if the plan should go awry and fear gripped me. My instinct was to flee madly, blindly, and I grasped Gregory's arm and heaved at it desperately, but the stake was hammered fast and I could not budge him.

I turned to see Rado rise in the stirrups and unsheathe

his saber in a single lithe motion. A pang of abject terror ran through me, and my bowels turned to liquid. I could scarcely contain myself. I saw him lean forward into the blow. I heard the sizzle as the saber cleaved the air, and all was black.

I thought I was dead. It was pitch black, and I was surrounded by silence. I moved my arm experimentally; it seemed heavy but did my bidding. My eyes were clamped so tightly shut that it seemed I needed to exert a huge effort to open them.

It was still morning. Perhaps only a few minutes had elapsed since I had lost consciousness. Of the horsemen there was no sign. I wondered how long a man could live once his head had been severed at the neck. I raised my hand to find that I was still attached to my body. Had Rado topped my head like a hard-boiled egg, and was my brain now lying exposed to the sun and air and dust? Gingerly, I touched the crown of my head but could feel no wound. I felt my face for some disfiguring cut, but my hand came back clean of blood.

An odd, dragging sensation on my left hand disturbed me until I reminded myself that I was still tethered to Gregory. I sat up, but then I saw that I had fallen several feet from his body. With a gathering suspicion of what Rado had done, I turned to look at my left hand. Attached by the manacle to my wrist was Gregory's forearm, severed at the elbow by Rado's saber.

I thrust it from me, but this very act of revulsion caused it to rebound back at me on its chain. I lay, face down in the dirt, with this obscene relic before me and sobbed for the suffering I had brought upon my friend. I even reached out and grasped the cold, pliable fingers in mine and felt the warmth of my hand imbue the dead flesh with the illusion of life.

I lay unmoving for a long time, until I had no further tears to shed. I came to myself feeling exhausted and finally emptied of all emotion. A noise close by had brought me back to the world, and I turned and sat up and found that it was Jacob. He was trying to dislodge the stake from Gregory's chest. I was glad to see that he was still alive and relatively unhurt except for some bruises where he had been beaten about the face.

He managed to get the stake loose from the ground, but whenever he pulled at it he succeeded only in lifting the body, and was loath to show disrespect to the dead by shaking it loose.

'Let me help you,' I said.

I think Jacob had not noticed me until now, and when I stood up and he saw the arm dangling at the end of its chain, he uttered an exclamation and crossed himself. When I came toward him, he stepped back.

'I want you to do it in one clean pull,' I told him. 'Can you do that?'

'Yes, sir,' he replied.

I think he was still afraid and approached carefully when I stopped over Gregory's body. I laid my weight across the chest.

'Do it now,' I said.

Jacob heaved with all his might, and I felt the wrenching and shaking of his effort as he strained to pull the rough wood up and out. It came loose all of a sudden, and I imagined I heard Gregory groan, but perhaps the sound came from my own chest.

We carried him to the carriage and laid him on the front seat. One of the horses had been killed by a hammer blow to the head, and Jacob grieved over that murder almost as much as he did over the death of the priest.

While Jacob went off in search of the other horse, I looked about me in a dazed fashion. The plaza in front of the station was empty, and there was not a soul in sight on the open ground where the crowd had massed, save for one figure coming slowly toward me. The ground was littered with misshapen hats and caps, and baskets which had been discarded in the stampede and then flattened by many feet. I saw a crutch lying on the ground and wondered in a dazed, idle way, my mind working without volition, how that person had managed to make his escape. There were no more corpses, thank God.

The man coming toward the carriage was Kraus. He was limping badly and carried in his arms a girl of three or four who had become separated from her mother. He had lost the keys to the handcuffs.

We made our way slowly through the deserted town. Kraus sat beside me with the girl on his lap and tried to coax her to talk. She was recovering quickly from her scare, and with various childish stratagems I would not have thought him capable of, he soon had her telling him proudly about her older sisters. Though the sun was warm, I pulled my cloak about me and huddled the limb, like a dead child, against my heart.

EVENING

I feel the tug of my destiny. It requires only that I release my grip, only that I allow myself to be taken by the current and swept toward the future which awaits me.

It is not easily done. The sticking point is not a lack of courage, if indeed courage bears any relevance to what I now do. I am not afraid. I am resigned to whatever awaits me in the ravine. Rather, I am reluctant simply to let myself go. I do not want to give up my free will, my struggle to be a man in the face of the beast within me. But that cost has grown beyond reckoning. I am like an awkward tool, turning in God's hand so that the outcomes of my actions jerk always away from the line He intends.

I will submit to Rado's plan, although I believe my struggle has subverted his. Who would have guessed that this stern commander would have risked his mission to disperse a lynch mob? What romantic notion could have possessed him that he would intervene to save one man when he was sworn to save a nation? A regiment of Alpine troops is even now setting up camp outside the town.

Neither Kraus, Theissen, or any of the civil authorities know anything about them. Kraus tells me their orders to entrain came last night, well before the authorities could have been aware of any serious disturbance. The Gypsies are gone.

I think it most likely that the plot is blown, but I have persuaded myself that that possibility should have no influence on my actions. I sent Jacob out at nightfall to reconnoiter the forest close to the ravine. He has not returned.

At dinner we heard in the distance the faint boom of the cavalry pistol discharging, followed, much more faintly, by the snap of a rifle shot.

I had not seen fit to discuss with those who sat around the table all the details of this morning's atrocity, but no doubt they have their sources of information among the servants. Consequently, everyone was on edge, though we affected a brittle casualness.

'What was that?' Lothar wondered.

'Just Jacob scaring off some poachers, I expect,' I said.

'But there were two shots,' said Stephanie, whose hearing is much more acute than that of the others.

'An echo,' I told her. 'One of the peculiarities of the valley.'

Brod bent so low when he stooped to serve me the leg of mutton that for several moments I could plainly hear his regular breathing. Since his spell in the jail he is remarkably solicitous of me. Whenever I happen to glance at him I find his eyes upon me. He is a patient man.

After dinner, Lothar wanted me to play billiards with him, but I was too restless. I compromised by smoking a cigar with him in the library.

'Damned unusual Gypsies,' he observed.

'I didn't have a chance to notice,' I said.

'You didn't see they had sabers?'

'I suppose they did.'

'Every one of them. Just like a company of cavalry.'

When I said nothing, he added, 'I'll bet they were the same lot we paid a visit to last week.'

I examined the tip of my cigar.

'I don't suppose you'd care to tell me what's going on?' he asked.

'We're going to do it,' I said.

'Do what?'

'You said you wanted to come with me . . . when I do what I do.'

'Oh, yes.'

'You haven't changed your mind, have you?'

'Absolutely not.'

'Then we'll go out tonight.'

'Why so soon?'

'Having second thoughts? It's not for everyone, you know.'

'No, not at all – count me in.'

'Do you know how dangerous it is?'

'That's part of the fun. Where's the excitement if it isn't a bit dangerous?'

'You accept that?'

'Yes.'

'You'll need to arm yourself.'

'I came unprepared. Perhaps you'd be kind enough to lend me a pistol for the occasion?'

'There'll be no guns. We can't afford the noise. I told you it was dangerous.'

'You're the expert. What would you suggest?'

'Choose one of the knives from the wall of the billiard room. Not too long. Something handy that won't encumber you.'

'I'll do whatever you say. Just tell me.'

'There are others involved.'

'I assumed there would be.'

'You'll have to negotiate Brod.'

'He's part of it? It doesn't surprise me, the peculiar way he looks at you all the time. Is he the lookout? Or does he . . . participate?'

'Nothing is said of these matters between us. He follows me. What he does afterwards is no concern of mine. But he will prevent you from leaving the house. Therefore you must wear my cloak and scarf. Come down the main staircase; he keeps watch next to the main door. Keep your back to him. Don't talk to him. Make no acknowledgment of him. Come directly here and go through those French windows into the garden. Meet me in the gazebo at eleven.'

Stephanie made her rounds in the drawing room to wish everyone good-night. Her eyes sparkled and there was color high on her cheekbones. She is excited and afraid. When she came to me, she mouthed, 'Tonight.'

NIGHT

Will Brod allow Lothar to go through these French windows? He is a patient man, but he means business. I had returned the scalpel to its place in the box, and now I see that its slot in the green baize is empty again.

Perhaps Brod will seize his chance in the darkened hallway. Perhaps he will stab the figure in the cloak and the white silk scarf who so confidently presents his back to his enemy. But Lothar is a resourceful man and would not let himself be easily killed. In the morning, it could be Brod whom the chambermaid finds facedown on the floor.

I rather think that Brod will bide his time, waiting for a more compromising situation where blame for the murder will not be laid to him. I think he will wait to see how the night plays itself out. Brod will let Lothar step through the French windows.

And in the gazebo, Lothar will discover that he has come to mutilate not someone else's daughter but his own. Stephanie will discover, instead of the mysterious nobleman who would show her the many-sided face of love, a rogue much closer to home. How far, I wonder, will the assignation proceed in that dark chamber before their speechless denouement?

My destiny forks. I hold out little hope that I shall find the Prince in that ravine, but if by some freak of chance all turns out well, I will have accomplished a mighty deed for Hungary. Redemption is too greedy a hope, I know. However, if I am instrumental in bringing independence to my country, I may claim to have made some small measure of atonement.

If this journal ends here, then I have walked into the trap which I believe awaits me. I am a loose end which must be snipped off. The conspiracy must be made never to have existed. I accept my death, but I cannot accept that I have never lived, and so I am leaving this book where it will gather dust among my grandfather's theological treatises. They have not been disturbed in two generations, and in all likelihood this journal, too, will lie unopened for another fifty years. One day, when I no longer matter, it will be found, and I shall live again in the imagination of my reader.

Yet over the next weeks and months, the reason for my death will trickle out, and my reputation as a patriot and a martyr to the cause of Hungarian freedom will join the memory of my father and brother. I am the last of my line. The name dies with me. Other, more illustrious names – Aponyi, Kossuth, Karolyi, Tisza, Andrassy – are known far beyond our borders. Such names are immortal. Yet I have cause to hope that in the hearts and minds of the people in this small corner of Hungary, the solemn dignity of Dracula will linger fondly until it fades quietly from living memory.